DEVASTATING CONSEQUENCES

FOR A LIMITED TIME.
Get your free copy of the Edited version of the *Devastating Consequences* soundtrack.
Or for the Extended (2) disc CD version, which features every song listed in the book, there is a minimal $5.00 fee. Maximize your reading experience by listening, along your journey into my life.
Email your requests to:
Devastatingconsequences@yahoo.com

Copyright © 2006 Daminika Darlene Cunningham
All rights reserved.
ISBN: 1-4196-4794-6

To order additional copies, please contact us.
BookSurge, LLC
www.booksurge.com
1-866-308-6235
orders@booksurge.com

DAMINIKA
DARLENE CUNNINGHAM

DEVASTATING CONSEQUENCES

Based On A True Story

2006

DEVASTATING CONSEQUENCES

03/24/05 - 1/17/06

Every action has a consequence............

Dedicated To My Parents:
Ethel Darlene Cunningham &
James Edward Cunningham

In Loving Memory Of:
Maurice Dominic Hunter

1

I remember warm summers. Running carefree through the high grass. On a steadfast mission to a private playground. My biggest worry was, who was going to be the rotten egg. All of our visits to the country were wonderful.

My dad's side of the family lives in Bedford, Va., also known as Body Camp. We have a big family there, and they all live in walking distance of each other. We even have a street named after us, Cunningham Street. I'm proud to have that as my last name.

Having a cookout down there was just a plus, on top of the treat of the trip. It's beautiful and secluded.

Those were just some of the good times …. It gets worse. I took a lot for granted back then. I haven't since.

All my trouble started when my parents said they were getting a divorce. How could our seemingly perfect family of five be falling apart right before my eyes? I thought they were in love. My name is Daminika, and I am 10 years old. I have one sister who is 11. Her name is Victoria. We call her Shaun, and a little brother who's 4. We call him A.J. He is my adopted cousin, but quickly became our brother. He came at what I would call the perfect time. My mom had just lost a baby and she was heartbroken. In our family we believe that everything happens for a reason.

I don't think I can handle this. What could be so wrong that it can't be fixed? For a while, all they did was talk by letter. My dad would send a letter upstairs to my mom by me. He started sleeping downstairs on one of the couches. They were so much in love. What changed?

This man that she met at Upward Bound College, and who fathered two of her children. He's so handsome with his charcoal-black mustache and goatee. She's not going to find anyone that looks much better. I'm not going to like whoever it is anyway.

Mom started dating other men and flaunting them in front of dad as if to say, "I don't love you and I don't care." I remember waking up to see another man asleep on the couch. I asked myself how could she be so disrespectful? I can imagine how my dad feels.

Shaun and I passed the time by riding our bikes and having tea parties. We would walk to the bottom of the hill to the store to get soda and cookies. Soda is cheaper than tea. As we drank our tea/soda, we would talk. Shaun hasn't started her period yet even though she is older than me. She asked what it felt like. I told her it really doesn't feel like anything when it comes out, but my stomach hurts a little. I was 9 years old when I went to the bathroom to pee and when I wiped, I saw blood. Confused and concerned, I told my mom about it. She was happy for some reason.

She called all my family members and said "Dee has a bunny visiting her."

It sounded strange. What did that mean? She sat me down and talked.

She said "It's called a period, and you will get one every month."

I said, every month? For the rest of my life?

She said, "Yes."

I thought to myself, *That's not fair, that's too often.*

Mom said pick wherever I want to go and we can go, whatever I wanted to do. She made me feel so special that day. We went out to eat and to get ice cream. She called me her little lady. I was growing up. It was around the same age that I started wearing a bra. I've been called a husky child, so I had the boobs to go with it. She made me wear a bra everyday. One day I was wearing a white shirt and when I put my bra on underneath, you could see through it, so I took the bra off.

Mom came home and said "Where is your bra?"

I said, you can see it through my shirt, so I took it off.

She said "That's OK; it's better to see that, than to see your nipples."

I cried. I didn't want anyone to see my bra. I didn't want anyone to know I wore one in the 5th grade. But I'm around smart kids all day long at school. I was in the third grade when they realized, I am really smart. I am above average. They moved me to a school designed for advanced children. I didn't want to go. I didn't want to leave all my friends, and my sister. I'm glad I only had to stay there for two years. It was mostly white people. I think there were only about four black people.

Now I'm off to middle school. Mom made sure we got into another school with mostly white people, even though it was all the way on the other side of town. She pulled some kind of strings. She tries to shield us from as much as she can. You could even call her overprotective. We can't do a lot of things the other kids do. We live in a house on a hill right across the street from the projects, but we couldn't play with those kids. We played with each other. That just made our family even tighter.

My mom is a lawyer. Well, I thought she was a lawyer. She is a paralegal, someone who does all the legwork for a lawyer but doesn't get that extra zero on the end of the paycheck. Evidently, it is still good money. My dad is head chef at a fancy restaurant. Everything is perfect, and I don't want that to change. Something like the Huxstables.

Family photo. L to R: Ethel, James, Victoria, and Daminika

Divorce is a serious thing with a lot of consequences for us. What would the holidays be like? We always had a large, live, Christmas tree and it was overflowing underneath, every Christmas morning. Our parents would watch us open the presents one by one before they crawled back in the bed. Not this year.

Usually we would set our alarm clocks for 6am, wake our parents up and go downstairs, but this year dad stayed in bed. It didn't feel right. Why didn't he want to participate? Is this the feeling I'm going to have from now on with us living in separate houses?

The years passed and things didn't get much better even though they decided to stay together. To be quite frank, my mom treated him like shit. She tried not to make us listen to him but no matter what their problems are, he is still my dad. I resent her a little for that.

We moved out of our house on the hill, in a bad neighborhood, to a nice house in a prestigious neighborhood. They call it Wilmont. We settled in and began our new school. The same school that my mom prevented us from going to, when we lived less than three blocks away because of its criminal history. Isn't it ironic that we were forced to go there even after moving out of the neighborhood?

I was placed in honors classes and met some of my closest and best friends. One in particular Latonya Bolden. We could talk for hours. She understands me and could relate. Kelly is another friend who became close very quickly. We have the same bus stop and we spent plenty of nights over at each other's house. She treats me like a sister and likewise, her mom treats me like a daughter. I love them all for that.

We have a park right down the street from our new house. Summertime came around and it is beautiful outside. The flowers have bloomed and the grass has grown. Daddy is out in the front yard cutting the grass. I saw him sweating and wiping his face. He looks like he has dropped a couple of pounds. Yeah, he's definitely losing weight. I'd think so with as much stress as he's under around here. He hardly ever eats. I went in the house to get him some ice water when I heard my mom say, "Look at him out there. He better bring his ass in the house before he passes out." I said to myself it's not that hot outside.

Father's Day is here and I want to do something special for my dad. We decided to go to the store and get his favorite things. My mom saw how much it meant to us so she agreed to drive us to the store. We picked up Mary Jane candies, flip-flops, Bojangles barbeque chicken, and a card signed by us all. He loved it. I could tell by the huge smile on his face. Something that had been lacking for so long.

DEVASTATING CONSEQUENCES

All in all, it turned out to be a good day. When we went to bed that night, I noticed that one of my favorite TV shows, *Showtime at the Apollo*, was on and I really wanted to watch it because one of the members of our church was supposed to be singing on there. I guess my dad heard my TV still on real late because he peeked his head in to say turn it off. I really wanted to see the end but after grumbling under my breath, I turned it off.

I was awakened a few hours later by the sound of yells and cries. I jumped out the bed and ran to see what was happening. As I opened my door I saw my mom in the hallway yelling, "He's having a seizure!" I looked in the bathroom and saw my dad on the floor, flopping around, hitting his head on the toilet and wall. One of us called 911. It could have been me for all I know. That part is a little hazy.

The ambulance crew arrived after a few minutes. One of them was in the bathroom with my dad, trying to prep him for the ride to the hospital. The other medic was filling out a chart with all of my dad's information. My mom was sitting on the daybed in the front room with her back turned, talking to the medic. She must have thought no one was around when I heard her say, "He has H.I.V." I walked away. I know what I just heard, but in my mind I'm trying to find anything else that it could possibly mean, besides what I know it means.

I threw on some clothes and shoes. We watched them put him on a stretcher and roll him out to the ambulance. I looked at the clock for the time and it had stopped. I felt a chill go through my body. We loaded up in the car and followed closely the whole way to the hospital. I knew I had to tell Shaun, but when and where? We waited and waited. Dad was finally put into ICU, where we could visit. He had tubes up his nose and wires going everywhere, he didn't look good, and he couldn't talk. We sat for a couple of hours before we went home to try to get some sleep.

Over the next couple of days we sat almost all day with dad, but with no dramatic change. Today is Wednesday, June 23, 1993. My aunt Ann came out to the hospital and asked if we wanted to go with her over to Grandma's to get some spaghetti she had fixed. Sounded good to both Shaun and me. We arrived and heated up a couple of bowls of spaghetti to take back with us.

Within a block away from the hospital a song came on the radio that to me could have stopped time. The song is "Lately," by Jodeci. This song described my parents' rocky relationship almost perfectly. I began to cry very hard. As we parked the car, the song was still playing and I begged my aunt to let me finish listening to the song before we got out. She did so willingly.

As soon as we reached the floor that my dad is on we saw the looks on everyone's faces. I was told promptly that my daddy had passed away just minutes before. I could have been here for him if only we would have come straight in. We put our things down and went in to see him. The first thing I noticed when I looked at him, was one single tear that had fallen from his eye. I went over and gave my daddy a kiss on the cheek. Everyone took it very hard. They even had to put smelling salts under our noses to calm us down. I took a tissue from the shelf and wiped my daddy's last tear. I vowed to never throw it away.

That night we spent the night over at Grandma's house with my pregnant aunt Ann. We stayed up late watching *Juice with Omar Epps*. I think that's one of Ann's favorite movies. She said he's her boo. We were eating, telling stories and just talking. In spite of the day's events, we had a lot of fun. Our family believes in a life for a death so when my aunt told me she is having a boy, it was only fitting.

The next morning we woke up to some of Grandma's delicious oatmeal. We had to get dressed to go shopping. The dresses Shaun and I picked, matched. We thought it would be cute. We haven't dressed alike in years.

Dressed like twins, Victoria at four years old

My mom used to dress us alike all the time when we where younger. People always thought we were twins.

DEVASTATING CONSEQUENCES

Dressed like my sister, Daminika at three years old

A few days later we went to get our hair done for the funeral while mom made the arrangements. The food, cards, and condolences over those few days were overwhelming, but appreciated.

The day came for the funeral. The wake would be an hour before. We rode in a limo to the church, where we walked two by two down the aisle to see the body. Dad looked great in his black suit with red tie and hankie. We put little mementos in the casket with him. My mom had us prepare a little presentation to share with the church about our dad. I wrote a poem, and Shaun sang a song. It took a lot for me to finish once I'd started, but I pulled through.

The turnout was tremendous. All those Cunninghams from Body Camp came. Family members that I'd never seen before in my life poured in. I even saw one lady that took a picture of my dad in the casket. I thought that was so rude and a little creepy. The service was long and very sad. The worse part was at the end when they closed the casket. I knew right then that it would be the last time I'd see him. It tore me apart. I think I cried the hardest at that very minute.

We proceeded on to the graveyard and all of us put a single red rose on the top of his casket before they put him in the ground. I made a mental note of where he was buried. Dinner was served at Jerusalem Baptist Church in the basement. This has been our church for years and they are always there for support in situations like this. We ate and mingled with family members and friends. All of us stayed with my grandma for the next few days. Mom had all our calls forwarded from our house to Grandma's. I received a call from one of my classmates. She asked why I hadn't called in a few days. I told her because my daddy died, and as I heard myself say the words, I knew for sure he wasn't coming back. I got so choked up that I couldn't finish my conversation. I hung up the phone and wiped my tears fast. I want to be strong for everybody else. I had often dreamed of my dad bursting through the door dripping wet with mud all over him saying, "Why did you bury me? I'm not dead." I'm sad to say, that never happened.

After things calmed down a little bit, we went back home. We built a shrine, for dad in his favorite chair, using the items we purchased for Father's Day. Just as we'd finished, a song came on, "I Want to Run to You," by Whitney Houston. I stared at the chair and thought of him standing there in the doorway, just watching, like he sometimes did. It broke my heart to realize, I'll never see that again. Listening to the song, I took time to think ... *If dad had AIDS, he could have given it to mom. No, God is not going to take my mom, too. He just can't.*

I remember a nightmare I had where both my parents died. I woke up with the worst knot in my stomach. It was horrible. Maybe God was trying to warn me or something. After a couple of days I approached my mom and asked her if she died, would she come back and see me?

She said "Do you think you can handle that? You won't be scared?"

I said no, I won't be scared.

Then she replied "I'll try my best."

I felt better for some reason. My mom and I are extremely close. She encourages me to always do my best. She helped me to achieve things I never thought were possible. For example, when I was in the third grade, only eight years old, she entered me into this contest. She said it was called an Oratorical Contest, at my school. She wrote a speech for me on Dr. Martin Luther King Jr., that I had to memorize within a couple of weeks. She is one of his biggest supporters. Their birthdays are only a week apart. She would help me learn the speech, and we read it over and over. I finally memorized it; that was the easy part. Having the courage to get up in front of a packed auditorium and recite it, that's the hard part.

The day came and my mom was right there with me, snapping pictures from the back row. I listened to kids get up there and do their speeches, most read from papers. Then it was my turn. No paper, no problem. I did great! There were three winners. My name was called last. I walked over to get my third-place trophy, but as I read it, I noticed it said first place. They called the winners' names backwards. I won first place! I can't believe it. My mom came up to hug and kiss me, she looks so proud. I know she is.

The months passed and I think my tragedy made Tonya and me closer, considering her dad died also. Since my dad passed away during the summer, we had time to mourn before going back to school. We also had time to get our story straight. We can't tell our friends the truth; they can't handle the truth. I can't handle the truth! Since it's the early 90's, AIDS is not something that's been talked about often. I would tell people that dad died from a tumor on his brain. That sounds good enough. I hate lying. I hate talking about it at all. We became close friends with a lot of the kids in the neighborhood, especially the ones that go to our church.

There was this one little girl that came over our house often. She was about 8 or 9. My sister had dated her brother briefly. We sat on the curb in front of our house. She began to tell us a story about her brother. She said when they are alone in the basement, he makes her take her clothes off, and then he would have sex with her. That's called incest. The details sounded disgusting. I couldn't believe that all the while he was acting normal, and he was raping his own sister. He told her she better not tell, nobody. Nobody would believe her. But I believed her. She told us not to tell, that it made her feel better just by talking about it. But I had to tell someone, I told my mama. She was disgusted and shocked. I asked her what we should do.

She said, "I can talk to her mama if you want me to."

I said no, she had begged us not to tell. We dropped it and just prayed for their family. This bit of information could tear a family apart. I'm not in the business of making people feel the way I've felt over the past couple of years. I hope she'll have the courage to confront him one day.

November 3, 1993 is mom and dad's wedding anniversary. I heard their song, "It's our Anniversary," by Toni Tone Tony. I talked to Shaun, and we agreed we had to do something special for mom. So we got Granddad to drive us to the flower shop, where we ordered one dozen roses with a card and balloon to be delivered to her at work. That evening, mom walked through the door with her flowers and just burst into tears.

She said it was the nicest thing ever, and she was not expecting anything like that. She said she has some great kids for us to think about her like that. She even bragged about it to some of her friends on the phone later. I'm glad she liked it.

Mom has been losing weight. She could have HIV. We didn't know for sure until she was admitted to the hospital for some type of bronchitis. Shaun and I snuck a peek at her chart. I ended up telling Shaun what I had heard mom say that night, months ago, about Dad having AIDS. She wanted to know the truth just as badly as I did. We read the words that we never wanted to read: HIV positive. God is going to rip her away from me at anytime now. What am I going to do? I can't live without her. It felt like somebody jerked my heart out and jumped on it repeatedly, then kicked it to the curb. The waiting officially began.

Unexpectedly, when my mom got out of the hospital, she did break the news to us that she is HIV positive. She said, "When I die, your aunt Kam will come here and live with you all."

We said, "Ugh, we don't want to stay with her."

She said, "You know y'all like going over there, spending the night."

I said, it's alright, but she is mean sometimes.

Mom said, "Well, she's the only one with no kids and single. I've thought about this hard, and I've made my mind up. Your aunt Kam already agreed. You know your grandma is up in age, and she already raised nine kids. I know she would love to have you, but I fear it's going to be too much on her."

I shook my head and walked away. I have a lot to think about. I went in my bedroom and shut the door behind me, then I laid in the bed, listened to music, and cried. At first it was thoughts about who will walk me down the aisle? Now it's time to start high school, and I don't even know if my mom will see me graduate. She stopped working, and people were noticing her dramatic weight loss. She got so sick that we ordered a hospital bed for her and put it in the living room. Hospice workers came on a daily basis. There is always a family member, by her bedside.

They wanted me to sit in the house every day with Mom because she is sick. I know she's sick. I'VE KNOWN FOR A LONG TIME!

DEVASTATING CONSEQUENCES

Every day since I've worried myself to death thinking, will this be the day? Do you know how it feels to wake up every morning and walk by her bedside, and pray that she still alive? I can't do it. I can't do it every day like this. I need a break; I need to go outside and chill with some of my friends, be a teenager. I love my mom and I care. I want to be here when she passes away, but when is that going to be? I'm going crazy just by waiting!

It took a while to master the halls at Patrick Henry High School. I got lost a couple of times. My favorite class, by far, would have to be English. Mrs. Nancy Rosenbaum is the teacher, who gave me that same kind of encouragement my mom gives me. We grew close. She even fixed me a custard pie for my birthday. Sounds nasty, but it was delicious.

On the way home from school that day I saw a guy that I thought was cute. I told my sister about it. She said "Ewe, that's Adrian! I used to have a class with him."

I said, I want you to talk to him for me, get his phone number. She did, and after some convincing, we were officially a couple. He played hard to get. That just made me want him more.

Thanksgiving came, and we made a big meal. All the immediate family members came over to our house for dinner. We are so grateful that Mom is here with us for another Thanksgiving. Everyone is praying that she will make it through Christmas.

A week later the hospice staff said that she had about 24 hours to live. Everyone came to the house and sat for hours. They called it a night around 1am after Mom made it through 24 hours. My family went home. I held her hand and said in my mind, *Please don't go, Mama! Don't leave me!*

She couldn't talk, but in my mind I heard her say, "You gotta let me go, baby. Just let me go."

I sat down. I knew what I had to do. I closed my eyes, and I said to myself, *I'm ready. Its okay, Mama, I can let go.* I opened my eyes and looked at my mama. She gasped and took her last breath. It felt like my heart stopped at the same time hers did. It didn't but the clock did. It sent chills through me. This is the second time the clock has stopped on the same night that a parent has died. I know it means something.

    Kam moved in and started driving my mom's car. She is a teacher for slow kids. We went to mom's funeral together. It was much harder than dad's funeral. I knew after this I had very little to live for. There were a lot of people there from Mom's job. Mrs. Rosenbaum was even there, along with friends from the neighborhood. I won't try to describe my feelings on that day, but from every day since, it has followed me.

    I wasn't expecting Kam to replace Mom. She couldn't touch her. And she didn't try. She's very bossy, and she yells all the time. Even though it had been rumored that Mom and Dad had matching burial plots, she was not buried next to him. I took flowers from the reef and put it on Dad's grave too.

    Grandma made us go to church every Sunday. I like going to church, but not every Sunday. We went to church with Mom, but not every Sunday. Sometimes I like to sleep in. Attending church meant getting up early enough to catch the Sunday school bus, because Kam wasn't going to drive us. She goes to another church, a holiness church. We are Baptist, which means we don't shout at our church. I haven't shouted before in my life. I guess I've never been that happy. Can you blame me?

2

Christmas came over the next couple of weeks, and it didn't feel like Christmas unless we followed tradition and get the biggest, fullest tree we could find. Kam said she wanted an artificial tree; she don't like the way real trees smell. Tough luck, bitch. We got our tree anyway with our own money, and we even decorated the outside of the house.

We later found out that our gifts were hidden over at my grandma's house, and one of my crackhead uncles stole some of our gifts and smoked it up. We were heartbroken. My mom's job had even helped purchase some of those gifts. Kam said, "I know you don't believe in Santa Claus, but just humor me," While she wraps up what is left of our gifts. She took Mom's octagon glass table in her room so she could sit in there and wrap gifts.

On Christmas morning when we opened our gifts, there was this one package that stood out. It is an electronic learning game. Grandma said it was something that Mom had bought for us before she died. I fell in love with it and vowed to keep it forever. We also got a package from our godmother, who lives in Atlanta. We got matching purses. The purses were cute, but they had a big duck head on them. I only used it once or twice and then threw it in the back of my closet. A while later, I started seeing a couple of people walking around with the same duck on their purses. Come to find out, it is a Dooney & Burke purse, a very expensive designer purse. All of a sudden I appreciated that purse a little bit more, I dusted it off and began to carry it all the time. If Kam did get us something for Christmas, it must have been small because it doesn't stand out in my mind.

We will start getting a check every month because my mom died. Plus with her salary we should be just fine financially, plus my brother gets a small child support check from his real father. Since he's not Mom's real child, he doesn't get a SSI check like us. I know we were getting at least $500 a piece. Kam was taking us out to dinner every night. She gave us $150 a piece, plus paid to have our hair done every two weeks, which didn't hurt my relationship with Adrian. He always told me I looked pretty. We grew very close. My first love. Not my first. My first love.

My first was a guy named Jason I had met through my cousins. He is so cute. He was a virgin, too, at least that's what he told me. It made our encounter that much more special. He came over my house while my parents were at work. We started to kiss and things escalated. After we both were undressed, it all started. *Ouch,* it did hurt like everybody said. After a few moments it felt alright, but what was all the hype about? People actually do this every day. I can take it or leave it. We used a condom but after I was late on my period, we both were scared. He talked to his aunt and she said as long as we used a condom and it didn't burst, then I'm not pregnant. That was our last conversation. That was a year ago. I haven't had sex since.

One example of how evil Kam is. She shows favoritism for the child with no backbone. Both Shaun and I wanted to go on a trip during the summer. Shaun wanted to go to Hampton, and I wanted to go to Florida with the church. She paid for Shaun to go and told me mine cost too much. Grandma paid for me to go because she didn't want me to feel left out. Kam sure didn't care.

Kam gave Shaun her very expensive camera to take with her, knowing she's careless. She lost it. I'm the one who should have had a camera. Disney World was beautiful. I promise you, we rode every ride. That is normally an all-day event, with all the long lines. We were with a young lady in a wheel chair, which meant we entered through the handicapped entrance with no wait. We jumped straight on the rides. That was definitely a perk. A once-in-a-lifetime kind of thing. It did feel magical like they say on TV. What they don't tell you on TV, though, is that it is 1000 degrees outside. No matter where you go, even in the shade, it is burning up. It was so hot that it started raining, which cooled things down for a minute. Then here came the steam, fog, and mugginess. It was so hot and humid that I don't want to go back, even if I could. Even so, I do appreciate the gift that my grandma gave me.

Time passed and that glass table of my mom's that Kam took into her room. She never brought it out. I had fallen in love with the table. It goes with an octagon shelf we have. My mom had left it to us. She called it her crystal shelf. She did have actual crystal figurines on it. I love it, and I took care of it after she died. I wiped it off with glass cleaner at least twice a year or whenever it started to look dirty. Kam sat her stuff on the table and it became dirty with all her wasted soda and food on it. It was filled with lots of three-liter drinks, all kinds. Then one day, *Smash!* It was broken. She had broken it. I guess one of those three-liter sodas was dropped and went through it. Of course she had A.J. take it outside to the curb. He is her live-in maid and flunky. She makes him do all her dirty work, which was just another thing for me to be pissed about. I clung to that crystal shelf even more. Nobody is going to break this!

Kam didn't like Adrian for some reason. She called him fat, ugly, and four eyes. *Fat?* How dare she? She is over 500 lbs. This fat, nasty woman who had to put a towel in the seat of the car because piss would squeeze out every time she sat down in the car. She has the nerve to talk about somebody.

She did, however, take kindly to my friend Kelly, who is also a healthy girl. Obese would be a more politically correct term. She'd let Kelly come over the house anytime. I love him, and he loves me. He lives right around the corner, within walking distance, and right across the street from my best friend Tonya. She can keep an eye on him even when I can't.

When he wanted to start having sex, I was hesitant. My mind was at ease once he started oral sex. Sex is so much better now. I think I'm addicted. He has so many different ideas. We listen to music like "Freak Me," by Silk. While his dad is at work, we have sex in the shower, in his sister's room, the basement, and some kind of room with a pool table in it. Memorable moments ...

Kam encouraged us to start hanging out with some of our cousins, girls close to our age. One in particular Rhonda. She is married with kids. We went to her apartment and had a lot of fun. I would invite Adrian over sometimes. We would drink and play cards. Kam said stay out as long as we want since we are with our family. So that's what we did.

It was hard for my brother growing up in a house full of women.

That's all he was around for years, so when he started to try on some of his aunt's shoes and hats. She made fun of him and called him gay instead of helping him. Teaching him instead of talking about him. If he is gay, I'm going to love him anyway. She called him stupid for messing up something she should have been doing anyway.

As the months went by things, things went downhill real bad. Instead of $150 a month, she was giving us $100. We have to buy our own clothes and shoes. Then it slowly dwindled to $75, $50, and finally, $0.

Kam's yelling and hollering got worse. Especially at my brother, he is her slave. *Do this! Do that!* Giving orders. She treats him like shit, and it's tearing me apart. She makes him do everything, including emptying her pot that she has in her room. She is too fat and lazy, to go ten steps, to the bathroom. No steps to climb. Every time we want to go somewhere, Shaun I fight over who will ask her, because she is so fucking mean. She has an evil look of disgust on her face, before we can even finish a sentence. Even if the answer was yes, she would holler it. It would be followed by, "Close my door!"

Not only does the car smell like shit and piss, but the house is starting to stink. There are shit stains on the towels in the car, we giggle about it sometimes. But it's not funny anymore. It's past funny. How am I supposed to invite friends over? My mom left Shaun and me both the car, but with the condition that it's in now, I don't know if I want it. Mom left us a lot of things, including a ring for both of us girls. My brother would have one of my daddy's rings when he turns 18, the same age we'll have to be before we get our rings. My mom has a will, where she divided certain things between her brothers and sisters. But we were left the bulk of everything, like the furniture, certain jewelry and clothes. She left us the house. It wasn't paid off but with what we bring in a month, that won't be a problem.

Meanwhile, Kam is buying herself three or four new dresses for church every time you turned around. She has hats to match every outfit, and don't forget the shoes. All that time in church, then she treats us like this at home! She doesn't lift a finger around the house, but expects it to stay clean. She doesn't make rules but wants all of them obeyed. I guess since we are fourteen and fifteen, we should know how a household works and just do it. She does treat one of her nephews like a son, she spoils him, buying him anything he wants right in front of A.J. I can imagine how he must feel. She stopped cooking dinner for us. I had to step in and cook for the family damn near every night. So not only did I have the stresses of school, and being a teenager, but to add to that, stress over what I'm going to cook for dinner. Wondering if I remembered to take food out, and finding the time to clean, and wash clothes. We didn't miss her cooking too much anyway. Kam would experiment with stuff like cabbage, broccoli, cheese, kilbasa sausage, and bacon. All mixed together. Not only did it stink up the house surprisenly even more than it already did, but the food tasted just like it looked. *Did she scrap this off the towel in the car? Or is this fresh?*

It was about then that I met my second best friend, Tiffany Washington. She is funny just like me. Well, I would describe myself as hilarious. We laugh all the time and that's how I learned to deal with things. The other way I deal with things is by listening to music, anything by Boyz II Men. They make me cry, but it feels good to let it out sometimes. Boyz II Men is my favorite singing group in the whole world. I have all of their tapes. I even have a big poster of them right above my bed. I kiss it from time to time. I even remember one of the last things we did as a family, while my parents were still living. We heard an advertisement on the radio, Boyz II Men was coming to town and if you wanted free tickets, be caller number 106. I said, Oh, my God! Mama you got to stop; let me call. It's a 1-800 number so it's free. Please stop. She drove a block further and stopped. I jumped out and ran to the pay phone to call. I was caller 84. I called back and the line was busy. I called once more and it was a recording that said we have our winner, please try again. I walked away with my head down. Damn, I didn't win. I really want to see Boyz II Men in concert. Jodeci, SWV, and MC Hammer was going to be there too.

Went I got back in the car, my mom said, "I'm sorry you didn't get it." Days passed and then mom came home and put a ticket on my bed. When I saw it, I screamed in delight. Oh my God, I can't believe I'm actually going to the concert!

She said, "We are going to the concert, all of us." That's was one of the best days of my life. It was a great concert, but an even better family moment. We even bought pictures of the singing groups. We didn't get home until after twelve, so we stayed home from school the next day. That was so much fun.

Kam doesn't like Tiffany for some reason, so she can't come over my house. Meanwhile, Tiffany started driving her dad's car, a little lima bean. We call it that because it is the same color as a lima bean. I ride to school with her sometimes, because the same car that my mom promised to both of us girls, Kam gave it solely to my sister. She liked Shaun because she didn't speak up even when something was wrong. I always do. My mouth got me in a whole lot of trouble over the years. People still think I'm the oldest because I'm bigger, and more outspoken. Shaun never did let me drive. She said Kam told her not to. I said, So what? She's not here. She would still say no. She knows what mama wanted, but she didn't care.

Kam bought herself a van. Good, because it was hilarious seeing her try to get in and out of that little car. It's like an elephant getting out of a clown car. Ha, Ha! Let me tell you how she is paying her car note with *our* money. Come to find out, that's most likely the only bill she was paying. She didn't pay the rent. She didn't want to live there anyway. We heard her say it plenty of times. That meant Grandma had to pick up the slack. She pays all our bills. She's been paying them for a while now. In her mind, she doesn't have a choice. She doesn't want her grandchildren out on the streets. It' sad how she is taking advantage of her own mother.

I would sit alone in my room a lot of nights and cry, listening to music, one song in particular, "Cry for You," by Jodeci. I have a crappy life. I would listen to the quiet storm on rainy nights with the window open. The smell of the rain made me feel the most at peace. It's sad that not much else could make me feel like this. Thank you, Lord, for everything. I don't take anything for granted anymore.

Another way of obtaining peace was talking on the phone to my boyfriend. We used to talk all night long until we fell asleep on the phone. Kam had bought us a separate phone line to share. She's so evil that she would she would set a time for the phone to be in her room. We would have to bring her the phone around 11pm, even on the weekends. That sucks. Sometimes I want to talk later than that. As a 15 year old, I am very smart. There is a box outside the side door. A small off-white box, which contains both phone jacks. I discovered that after I took a butter knife and unscrewed the screws. Now, which one is my phone line? I guess with the process of elimination I'll find out.

I did find out, one day when Kam was one the phone. She yelled, "Damn, what happened to the phone? Oh there it goes."

I plugged it back in. That same day Shaun had locked herself in her room with the phone. I banged on her door and told her I have to use the phone right quick. She acted like she didn't hear me. Just silence. When she did respond, she said, "Just wait your turn." Who knows when that's going to be? The phone jack was in her room, so she thought she had me. She didn't have to open her door. Or so she thought.

I went right outside and unplugged our phone jack. Then I sat down on the couch, looked at TV and waited. Videos were on, my favorite. I bobbed my head and danced as if I were really into the program. A few minutes later, Shaun came out of the room with her head down.

She had the phone in her hand and she said, "The phone is not working."

I said it does that sometimes, but I know how to fix it. She shrugged her shoulders and handed me the phone.

I said, now if I fix this phone, you have to let me use it real quick. I'm just trying to call Adrian so I can verify what time he wants me to come over.

She said okay. I fixed the phone and made my call.

After I finished Shaun said, "How are you going over Adrian's house? Kam is not going to let you."

I said, I'm not going to ask her. I'm going to sneak out after she goes to sleep. When I hear her snoring, I'm going to leave. She snores loud enough to wake the dead. Her door will be closed. I'll walk quietly by, and I'm out of here. I am scared, real scared, but I did it. I shut the screen door quietly and ran down the street. I got a few houses down before I stopped running. I'm a fat girl, I had to catch my breath.

This is a nice neighborhood, but I walked as fast as I could. Once

I got over to Adrian's, he rushed me in the house and into his bedroom. His dad is in his room, asleep. He turned the music on because he knows I like that. "Before I Let You Go," by Blackstreet played. That's our song. Adrian reminds me of one of the singers in that group, David Hollister. I think it's the facial hair that does it. I make Adrian take his glasses off before we have sex. He's just that much sexier. We kiss and start to remove clothing. Every touch feels divine. I think the sneaking around makes it even more exciting.

He has a waterbed so as we began to have sex, the waves were bouncing us up and down. This feels good and it's fun. I didn't like performing oral sex on him. It was my first time. He liked it and asked for it often. I gave it occasionally. At the end of the evening, or should I say morning, he walked me to the corner. There is a stop sign at the corner. We always stand there and kiss and say goodnight. Tired or not, I always walked home happy. That morning when I got home I had to sneak back in. This is my first time doing this. I hope her bedroom door is still closed. I hear her snoring, that's a good sign. I tiptoed pass the bathroom and peeked. Swew, her door is still shut. I tiptoed the rest of the way in my room and shut the door. I am safe, finally.

I love him; I want to be with him forever. I even met his mom. She is no longer with his dad. She loves me. But then again, who wouldn't. *Kam.* If she does love me, she sure does have a fucked up way of showing it. That's just it. She doesn't show love at all. It's like she doesn't know how. She didn't even cry at my mom's funeral. Not one tear. She sat there stone-faced at the end of the row. That is her sister. They even called her Susta/Sister. She never has a good thing to say about anything, especially dealing with me. Everything is negative.

She has a Jeckle and Hyde-type of personality. To her church members and fellow teachers, she is a saint that works with slow children. She even took in her sister's children after she died. I applaud her.

Oh please, it is nothing like that. Really, I think it is all about the money. That sure is what it's turned out to be. I hate her. I know I shouldn't say hate, but she is the only person in the world that I hate. That's how bad she treats us. She has never laid a hand on me nor my sister. It's mental abuse. The full name of my attacker is Kamaline Danita Moore.

DEVASTATING CONSEQUENCES

This is a short list of things I've never heard her say: Do your homework! What are your grades like? I'm proud of you. How was your day? What's wrong with you? I bought this just for you. Good job! Thank you, I appreciate that. I love you! Not even, I love your money! It really seems like the more miserable she becomes, the more miserable she treats us.

All of our birthdays came and went, with no present from Kam. She didn't even part her lips to say, "Happy Birthday." It made us feel like shit. Mom would never do anything like that.

Not this year, I'm not going to let my sister spend her 16th birthday crying in her room. There'd been enough tears already. So I threw her a Sweet Sixteen Party. Kam didn't have anything to do with it. She stayed in her room with the door shut. It was a warm day in August and we had the party outside in the front yard. There was music and dancing. Everybody was having a good time, then Kam sent A.J. outside to say turn the music down. Then he had to go back in there, trapped with her. We turned it down a little and kept on partying. Even people walking down the street stopped at our party. We had a great time. Now I was there for my sister when she needed me, but she's so timid. Who will be there for me? Although she's the oldest, I've always been there to fight her battles. I've always been the strongest. I have a reputation to protect.

I dreamed of being grown. I feel grown anyway. A lot of my childhood was taken away from me just by worrying about my parents and taking care of my family. I want to have a baby. I don't want to live here with her. We thought of ways we might be able to put Kam out. Once Shaun turns 18 she can take custody of me and my brother. We will live here, and kick her fat ass out. If I have a baby, I'll have something to call my own. Someone who will say, "I love you," constantly. That's what I need. Unconditional love. My grandma gives that, but she's tired. She's been giving unconditional love for over fifty years.

I talked to Adrian about my plans. He said, "Hell, No! I don't want kids right now."

That pissed me off, but I continued my after-school and late night visits over his house. We always use a condom so the only way I can get pregnant by him is if the condom bursts. *Or if it has a hole in it.* That's an idea. I tried that. I brought the condoms with me over his house and before we had sex, I pulled one out. He put in on, and we had sex. The next month my period came like clockwork. Shit, it didn't work. The next time I went over Adrian's; he had this ruler on his bed that could turn into an airplane and other retractable shapes. It has small hinges on it, that allows it to move freely. I thought it was neat. We laid down on the bed together, "Can't Help Myself," by Gerald Levert is playing in the background.

He started to get a little frisky. He rubbed that ruler up and down my leg. I told him to stop being silly. He said, "I'm serious. You want to see what it feels like?"

Playing stupid, I said, what?

He lifted it in the air. "Just a little bit," he replied. Then he turned off the lights and began to eat me. It felt good. I listened to the music and relaxed. He inserted the ruler into me. It felt good in a weird way. The more he moved it back and forth, the wetter I got. I felt it drip down the back of my thigh. Just then, he gave that hinged ruler a twist. I yelled in horror. He took it out.

That shit hurt. Oh, my gosh. What was you thinking?

He said, "I'm sorry," and stood up. When he turned the light on and looked at the ruler, it was covered with blood. I saw little pieces of meat hanging off of the hinges. So when I felt that wetness on my thigh, it was evidently blood.

I yelled, "Oh my God! What have you done? You fucked me all up. He looked like he was going to throw up. No sex that day.

Tonya tried to talk me out of trying to get pregnant. This is one thing she doesn't understand. She still has her mom, and I'm sure she tells her she loves her every day. My relationship with Adrian is a little rocky, but he loves me and if I get pregnant by him, he'll have to stay with me. I know he will.

I got so desperate that after we had sex one night, I took the condom out of the trashcan and put it in my pocket. When I got home I lay down on the bed with no panties on and dumped the contents inside of my vagina. It didn't work. I don't think I can have kids. That's all I have left. If I can't ever have kids, I'll be heartbroken. How much more of my heart can break? What if what Adrian did to me does scar me for life?

DEVASTATING CONSEQUENCES

We broke up after dating for a year, but I want him back. I can't stand to lose anything else. We continued having sex. That was good enough for the moment, but every time I was with him, I wanted him. I wanted him to be mine again. We talked on the phone often. I cried even more often. This is a really tough time for me. I don't have anyone to talk to about my feelings that understands. Tonya wants me to leave him alone. It's not that easy, I can't let go. It's hard to describe.

He got a new girlfriend. The Happy Valentine's Day balloon that he bought at school, that I saw him walking around with, he gave it to her. Oh hell no. He gave me all the signals that we were getting back together. At least that's what I thought. Maybe that's what I wanted to think. I confronted the girl. I asked her how long has this been going on. Before she could finish her sentence, I let her know, every time you kiss him, you are tasting my pussy, bitch! Yes, we are still fucking. I'm mad at her, even though she didn't do anything. But she is taking my love away, and I'm not going to let that happen. Or do I have a choice?

I confronted Adrian next. I said, what the fuck is this? You are always all up in my face like you want to be with me, but you don't.

He said, "No."

Before a tear ran down my face, I turned and walked away. Three years have passed since we started dating, and I am just now starting to get over him. Who knew it would take this long? That's because we continued to have sex. The song that helped me get through this period was "Have You Ever?" by Brandy. I probably should have gone into counseling after my parents died. We had an appointment one day for counseling. Grandma had set it up. We pulled up to the building, and Kam went in. I think they wanted to talk to all of us one by one. Kam didn't like that, so we drove away. Maybe she was scared of what we were going to say. Maybe if I had the counseling I needed, I would have a way to cope with things, but right now, that's just it. I can't cope.

I miss Adrian. Especially our sessions. Not weed sessions - sex sessions. He was really freaky. Like coming to my bedroom window and listening to this certain song. I wish I knew who sings it, because I'd play it for you. It's called, "Sex in the Rain," and then we had sex in the rain. Yeah, we had sex outside in the rain in my backyard. It was kind of in the middle of my backyard and my crazy neighbor's backyard. It was dark, but the stars were twinkling. Kam's bedroom window was about 25 ft. away, so we couldn't be too loud. I didn't have any panties on anyway so I hiked up my gown and we lay on a blanket and went to it. It was great. I looked up at the sky and rain kept falling in my eyes so I just closed them. This is such a beautiful moment. I got choked up, a tear fell from my eye. Not a sad tear, but a glad tear. He couldn't tell the difference though after all, we were soaking wet. He kept going. His knees were sliding a little from the water. He gained his footing and finished up. I went back in the house satisfied. See that's just one of the things I'm going to miss.

Speaking of weed sessions though. I don't smoke weed. I tried it one time fucking around with Adrian. He and his friend was smoking a blunt one day when I was over there. He asked me if I wanted to take a puff. I said no. He said, "Just a little bit won't hurt." I grabbed it out his hand and took a puff. It wasn't that bad, so I took two more puffs. I blew the smoke out and gave it back to him. They laughed at me because I choked a little. I didn't feel high. Next thing I know, I was in his kitchen fixing sandwiches for everybody. That sandwich was so damn good. I didn't know what it felt like to be high, so I didn't know that I was. It wore off fast.

3

I got a job so that I could have some extra money. After all, I do have to buy my own school supplies, personal items, and clothes. That's were I met one of my close friends, Kyna. She laughs at all my jokes and I love that. Paycheck after paycheck rolled in and it is lovely. All of a sudden, Kam says she wants a piece of the pie. Wait a minute! She gets over $1000 a month alone for Shaun and me. Plus, she's a teacher, and she wants some of *my* check! I looked at her like she was crazy. I gave her what I wanted. Over time, it dwindled to nothing. Just like she had done us. She didn't like that.

Meanwhile, at school, I was nominated to be on Homecoming Court. How exciting. I am so happy. Who knew I was this popular? I do have an effect on people, though. I think it's my smile. I've been complimented on it a couple of times.

I attended the Homecoming Court meeting. Seems there is a lot of work behind being on the court. The car that we'll be riding in during the parade will have to be a convertible. We need a date for each occasion, the dance, the parade, and the pep rally. We'll also need to have a different outfit for each occasion. Damn, that's a lot to take in, and a lot to do. How will I afford that? I had quit my job after about a year, because they tried to suspend me for two weeks. Just because I missed a day that I didn't even know I was supposed to work. I acted like I forgot to check the schedule. I knew I had to work, but that is not the point. If they suspend me for two weeks, I'll miss a full paycheck and that's going to hurt anyway it goes. So I said that's okay and walked out the door. I called Kam and told her I got off early so she could come pick me up. I sat outside on the air conditioner while she took her precious time coming to get me. She always did. I hate waiting. Even though we lived right around the corner, I know it took her a hot thirty minutes to get there. Bitch!

Kyna agreed to buy me a dress with her credit card. She knows what type of situation I'm in. I'm going to keep the tags on it, and she'll take it back after the dance. I got my hair done at a shop for a deal because Tiffany works there. Afterwards, I walked in the house with my dress. Fatty is sitting at the table. I didn't want to hear her mouth, so I lifted my dress high in the air and walked straight in my room. The only reason she is sitting at the table anyway, is because she is fixing chicken dinners for her church to sell. I don't know what was said but next thing I know, I heard someone banging on my bedroom door and shouting. It sounded like Maria, my other evil aunt. I don't like her almost as much as I don't like Kam. She acts just like her.

She said, "Come on out of there and bring that beeper with you."

I quickly turned the beeper on vibrate and threw it under my bed. I unlocked my door and opened it.

She said, "Kam tells me that you put this lock on your door, and she didn't tell you to."

I said, well, I didn't have a lock on my door like everybody else, so I put one on there. Shaun has a lock on both her doors. My door won't even shut without this sliding lock on here.

She said, "Well, we'll put a fix to that," and walked away.

I knew it wasn't over, but I hoped it was. She returned a few minutes later with a hammer. She ripped my lock off the door like some kind of mad woman. It left big holes in my door. I began to cry. My room is my sanctuary. It's where no problems in the world really matter.

She keeps hollering, "Where is that beeper they say you have? Why would you need a beeper? You don't have no job. What are you, some kind of drug dealer?"

I said no.

She said, "Well, where is it?"

I said, I lost it.

She said, "Well, let me help you find it. Get up."

When I got up, she tossed my little thin mattress up in the air. She knocked things off my table and pulled my dresser drawers out. She threw clothes everywhere.

Then she said, "That's okay, I'll just call it."

Sucker, the joke's on you. I turned the ringer off. I am scared, though, since it is right under the bed. If she were a professional, then she would have checked there first.

Maria came back in there with Kam's cordless phone up to her ear. I was standing right beside the bed so I heard the vibrating, I hoped she didn't. I guess she was listening for a ringing noise because she walked towards my closet and opened it.

She turned the phone off and said, "I see you got this new dress. How can you afford this?"

I said my friend, Kyna, bought this dress for me, so I can go to the Homecoming Dance.

She said, "So, did your Aunt Kam say you could go?"

I said, I didn't think I had to ask if it was something through the school. I didn't choose to do this, I was nominated.

She said, "Well, until you ask her, I'll just take this with me."

She walked toward the kitchen. I followed close behind. Maria told Kam what I had said about Kyna buying the dress. They didn't believe me. Kam said, "Whoever bought this dress better come back and get it because you are not going. You didn't ask me! You say somebody named Kenya bought you this dress. Well, call Kenya and tell her to come pick it up, otherwise Maria is going to take it back to her house. I'm sure she can fit it. Ha Ha Ha."

I jumped on the phone and called Kyna on her cell phone. I told her exactly what my aunts said. She was pissed. She said, "How they going to take something that's mine?"

She came over a few minutes later with an attitude. The dress is hanging on the front door. She had her receipt in her hand when she came in. She explained that she was just trying to do something nice for me but she doesn't want to get in the middle and since I can't go then she would take the dress back to the store. They said okay, but before she could leave out the door with the dress, they tried to hem her up on the beeper thing. They asked did she know that I had a beeper. She glanced at me confused, and then she said she didn't know anything about a beeper.

As soon as she left, they just kept picking on me. Fatty got up and walked towards her room. I walked towards mine, and then I heard Maria say, "My sister might not have the strength to get you, but I do." Right then she jumped in front of me and slapped me in my face. I pushed her. She said, "Oh no you didn't," and bum rushed me. She was swinging, and I was swinging back. I know she is pregnant, but I just want to kick her in the stomach. I guess she remembered she's pregnant a few minutes later because that's when she stopped.

I know somewhere in there I said, You are not my mama.

She replied, "I don't have to be." She walked away satisfied, I guess.

I'm pissed but I know I got some licks in too. Bitch. I can't believe that fat bitch had the nerve to call for backup. They just can't stand to see me with a smile on my face.

Chicken, potato salad, corn pudding, green beans, and all kinds of other fixings. I went to check the refrigerator, and it was all gone. Mr. Cook had loaded it up and took it to his house. Mr. Cook has been her close friend for years. I think she has a crush on him but he's not interested. Who would be? She only showers on Sundays. After the food smells had flooded the house and made my mouth water, she didn't leave us any. I'm hungry. That isn't surprising, though she is trifling like that. I'm sure she got her a piece or three somewhere back there with her in that stinky bedroom. There were times when she didn't go to the grocery store. There was no food in the house, and we had to eat over our friends' or family's house. When she did buy food, it was mostly hamburger meat. If we didn't thaw it and were hungry, we cooked it frozen. That means you don't get to pat the meat out. We call it 'loose meat sandwiches.' We'd put mayo on bread and dump on some of the crumbled meat. Add some salt and pepper and you've got one damn good sandwich. That got old after awhile. But when there is nothing else around to eat, it becomes very appetizing. As long as it was meat, I didn't mind much.

The dress was kept at Kyna's apartment. That's where I got dressed. Did they really think they were going to stop me? They don't know how much effort went into pulling this off. Oh yeah, I'm going! I got my dates together and everything else. They were purely friends, nothing else. Everything went smoothly, except it rained on our parade, literally. We couldn't ride out in convertibles. We just waved from the bleachers under umbrellas. It was still an honor just to be chosen. I knew I couldn't be crowned queen because that's for seniors only and I'm a junior.

The dress looked great on me, I hate that it has to go back. There was some ring around the collar, but Kyna told the people at the store that that's how it was when she bought it. It was a present for her mom, and it hadn't been worn before. She got her money back. She went in with an attitude and they didn't want to fuck with her. She is a white girl in a black girl's body anyway. I'm sure the cashier made casual conversation with her. That's okay though because that's my girl. Who am I going to talk to now?

That's right, I'm jumping right back in the dating scene. I need someone to fill this void in my heart. What else is there? I got addicted to that loving feeling. The feeling you can only get when you are in the arms of your significant other. I would say a man and a woman, but you got to have an open mind these days. I have to include everybody because after all, my brother could be gay. It's too early to tell, but he does walk with a twist and kind of rolls his words. He's definitely not as masculine as some of those other little boys his age. Playing football or any other sport for that matter. It's just not him. I kept a close eye on him; after all, I had to ... I had promised. Mom wrote me a note, and as long as I honor it's contents, she will come back and see me.

Actual note handwritten by my mother Ethel Darlene Cunningham.

DAMINIKA DARLENE CUNNINGHAM

Dee, Dee, Dee,

What can I say to you? Mommy can't always be around to tell you or make you behave. You're a very intelligent & strong-willed child. You will eventually find out that you don't know everything. Grow & learn. Remember everything I've told you; live by it. Help your little brother, teach him, don't yell at him. Support your sister & help her. Remember, I'm always there in spirit. Don't let no one take A.J. away, my last request, he's a part of us now. I love you.

Love,
Mommy

Ethel Darlene Cunningham at 34 years old.

"A. J!" Kam hollered. He would go running. If he didn't, she would sarcastically say, "What the hell took you so long?"

I knew he was hurting, and I wanted so bad to take that hurt away. But there is nothing that I can do to help him. I can't even help myself. If I call Child Protective Services, we all could be split up. She held that over our heads. I knew that made her feel powerful. Power is a relative term. My dad had the power to kill my mama and never served one day in jail. It is a crime. It should be prosecutable. So many things make sense to me now. I see why Mom didn't want to talk to him. I see why she disrespected him right in front of his face. What would you do if your husband told you that he has HIV? What he did was the ultimate betrayal. So to me, power is relative term. I'll let her think she has the power for now. Then when we kick her fat ass out, I'll love to see the expression on her face. We'll give her a thirty-day notice as soon as Shaun turns eighteen.

Prom came around and I made all the arrangements. I really want to go, another chance to look beautiful and feel special. I had another little part-time job. I saved my money up, and Tiffany and I went half on a stretch silver limo. There is a nice guy at church named Charlie. He told me months back that he would take me to the prom. I thought he was joking, but when I reminded him about it, he agreed. My dress was made by one of the teachers at school. We bought the material and picked out a style. My dress would be navy blue and silver to match the limo. Charlie would get a tuxedo to match my dress.

The dress was finished about two weeks later. I brought it home on a hanger with a clear trash bag over it. The bag was tied at the bottom because the dress is so long. I took it in the house while Kam was in her bedroom watching TV because I didn't want to have another run-in like before. Tiffany and I bought matching after-prom outfits. Mine is white and hers is blue. We even bought scarves to go around our necks that went great with the outfits. That morning I got my hair done and went home to start getting dressed. I waited until the last minute to put my dress on because I didn't want any stains.

The limo will be here in 20 minutes. I took the dress out the bag. Oh my God! The dress is wrinkled! I PANICKED! It looked balled up at the bottom because the bag had been tied. Shit. I went and plugged the iron in. Just then it was like God sent me an angel. My Aunt Eva walked into the room. She is my brother's birth mom. I pulled that noisy ironing board out, and put my dress on it. She asked, "What are you doing?"

I said, I have to hurry up and iron my dress. The limo will be here in 15 minutes. I picked up the iron and proceeded to put it on my, dress.

She yelled "NO!" She scared the shit out of me, but I stopped.

I said, what?

She said, "You can't just iron that dress like that. You'll burn a hole right through it or get a burn mark on it. You don't want that."

Damn right I don't want that, I thought to myself. My life would be over.

She said, "We have to get a towel to put over it."

I went and got one and she ironed my dress for me.

She turned around and said, "There."

It is beautiful again. She zipped me up in the back and watched me walk out the door to the limo; She followed close behind with tears in her eyes. This is a beautiful moment. I'm sorry my mom couldn't be here to witness it. I'm sure she's looking down on me though, making sure everything goes smoothly. I know somebody is because I just avoided a major catastrophe.

I was already on edge because my date, the little cutie who had volunteered to take me to the prom, hadn't been answering his phone. I had called him back to back for hours from home. After all my attempts to contact him, I gave up. I can't believe I'm being stood up for the prom.

Thirty minutes before the limo was due to arrive, he calls me. He said sorry for not being at home all day. He had a funeral to go to that was long. I said that's okay, just be dressed by the time we get over there. He was, but of course, Tiffany wasn't. She is late for everything, plus her parents wanted to take pictures. We don't have time for all that.

Tiffany's date is her cousin, and we have to go pick him up too. Now Charlie is sexy, but I didn't particularly like his plaits. He is skinner than the dudes I usually talk to. I like big guys. Anyway, we look good together. Fuck it - I look good by myself. We took pictures together, then danced to music, even though they played white music most of the time. I enjoyed myself. Charlie attends our rival school, Fleming. He wants to go to their after-prom, so we dropped him off, he gave me a big hug and a kiss on the cheek. That is sweet, but innocent.

We went to our own after-prom. Tiffany and I acted a fool. We were singing karaoke songs. Like, "She's a Brick House," by The Commodores. It was like we had practiced our dance moves ahead of time, they were in sync. It was hilarious. We had a good time that night, and I am proud because I pulled it off by myself. I paid for all my stuff from the shoes to the nails.

I went home late and satisfied. I still had to go to church the next day. Grandma don't give a damn what you do the night before as long as you come to church the next morning. I nodded on and off during the service. They played great songs though. One in particular got to me, "Somewhere Around the Throne of God." I hope this is almost over because I'm so sleepy. I came home and went straight to sleep.

As we approached the end of the school year, there was this project about your family that Mrs. Rosenbaum had given us to do. I put my heart and soul into that project. I had pictures and a speech with music to coincide with it for more effect, and I aced it. I am still failing honors English. I called Mrs. Rosenbaum at home. She had given me her phone number shortly after my mom died and said to call her if I needed anything.

I asked her, what I can do to pass your class? I'm willing to do anything!

She said, "Don't worry about it; you already passed."

I said, Thank you, and hung up. I thought to myself, *I know I wasn't passing. What did she do?* Anyway, about it Thank you, Jesus. Class of 1998, here I come.

Shaun didn't go to the prom. She really missed out. She graduated a couple of months later. Kam attended her graduation, surprisingly, because she usually only goes to work and to church. But since it has something to do with Shaun though, she made sure she showed up.

We went down to the country the next day to visit with our family. We stayed down there for a couple of days because it is the summer. Uncle John and Aunt Melinda treat us great. They have a big, pretty house with a Ping-Pong table in the basement. That will give my brother and Michael something to do. Michael is their son. He and my brother are the same age. Samantha is their daughter, and she is right around our age.

Since we all have licenses, they would give us the keys to the car and tell us to go to Lynchburg to the movies. They gave us all about $20 apiece. We had money to eat with and for snacks after we got in the movie. Most of the time, we would smuggle the snacks in with our purses. We would purchase them at the store before, because it was cheaper and you got more for your money. I'm a connoisseur like that.

You might say one or more of us is a connoisseur. You see Kam had saved up enough of our money to pay for herself some gastric bypass surgery. In short, she got her stomach stapled. She is so fat that the doctor couldn't do all of the surgery at one time, only half of it. She is only supposed to eat blended foods. I'm sure they didn't mean pizza. She threw everything in that blender. We went out to a buffet after she was back on solid foods. She is supposed to eat very small portions. She ate and ate until she could not eat anymore. Then she threw up in a glass, right there at the table, in front of us. She grabbed my drink glass and threw up in that too. After she was finished, with her eyes still watering from the gagging, she put tissues in those glasses, pushed them aside, and kept on eating.

How did she expect me to do the same, after what I had just witnessed? I'm glad she's back in Roanoke dealing with that. We have A.J. with us, so he has a break from her too. He didn't get many.

A.J. at seven years old

We are just trying to have some fun for the next few days. Aunt Melinda would always tell us, "If you are bad off where you are, you can always come stay with us." That was a nice gesture, but I don't want to live in Bedford. It's too much country scene for me.

It's nice to visit, but after awhile, it does get boring. We rent movies and watch them together. Just us three girls. One of my favorites is

Jason's Lyric. My all-time favorite is *Dead Presidents*. That was a *Jason's Lyric* summer. You have to watch it to understand. After the movies, we did get bored again. In the midst of our boredom, something exciting happened. Some guys came over to the house. We were in the basement playing Connect Four. My uncle introduced us. This one guy named Q stood out. He is so sexy. We will call him Q for reasons later revealed. I looked him up and down as he did the same. I then heard my uncle say, "He is your cousin."

Cousin? I recognized him from my dad's funeral. How far down the line is he? I don't know what he said, but it wasn't first or second. We chilled and played Ping-Pong. He talked smack, it just turned me on. I told him how long we'd be in town. They left later on that night. Shaun and I talked about how sexy Q is, and Samantha agreed. Sam said she has his number and we can call him. We called him and talked awhile. We talked about him coming over. It would have to be after our aunt and uncle are asleep. We made our plans and jumped in the shower, all three of us, one by one. We listened to music while freshening up.

Sam told us she is on her period. She doesn't think she is going to go through with the plans. How could she back out at the last minute? She was the main one pushing the idea. But she said we could get away with it. There is a spare bedroom that has a blow up mattress. We would lock ourselves in there one by one while the others stood watch.

Q came over looking and smelling nice. We were all in the bedroom at first, talking and laughing. We decided Shaun would go first. Sam and I left out and went back to her room to watch TV. I can't wait until it's my turn. I have been through quite a dry spell since the breakup. I'm on the rebound and I know it 's going to feel good, fuck it.

When they finished, I went in. We talked for a few minutes and then he went down. What a surprise. I definitely was not expecting that. It's been too long. I let him do his thing. He put on a condom and went to work. Damn, he is large and in charge and he is throwing my big ass all across the room. We started in the middle of the floor and ended up with my head touching the wall. He is one of those muscular types, muscles just popping out like pow, pow. I loved every minute of it. He went longer than Adrian ever did. By time he finished, I was sweating. I didn't give a damn what my hair looked like. For him to have just had sex with my sister, he was at attention with no problems and ready for number three. Sam told him she has cramps. He understood, he hugged us, and we smuggled him out. That was fun.

It was so much fun that the next day Sam says she is going to invite a guy over that she likes. We will get away with it just like we did the day before. She will be the only one in the room with him. She said even though she's on her period, they could do a lot of other stuff. She took a shower and put on a bathrobe. The only other thing she had under that bathrobe was some shorts. But then she got impatient. I knew it didn't sound like her parents were asleep, since the TV is still on. She said that they will sit in there and watch it until they go to sleep. She told the guy to come on over. She went in the bedroom with him, and locked the door. We watched TV in her room and waited. An hour passed, then Uncle John came out of his bedroom. Sam's door was cracked so he peeped his head in.

He said, "Where is Sam?" We looked at each other.

I said, maybe she is in the bathroom. He walked to the bathroom, but the door was open. He turned around and walked to the spare room's shut door.

"Why is this door shut? he replied. "Sam are you in there?"

He began to bang on the door. It was loud enough to wake up everybody in the house.

Melinda got up, even though she has to go to work early in the morning. She said, "What is all this noise?"

Sam opened the door. He saw what she has on. Her robe was opened just enough to see that she didn't have a shirt on under it. Next he saw the mattress on the floor, he opened the closet to see a young man quivering on the inside. The boy darted out the closet and ran out of the house. He smacked her right in the face, which busted her lip. Blood dripped on her bathrobe. She tried to tighten it up so her little boobs wouldn't fall out. She was crying and hollering.

Uncle John asked us if we knew anything about this. We said, "No!" Sorry Sam.

I felt kind of guilty, letting her take the fall for everything. After all, we did do the same thing yesterday. Oh, well. We'll count this as payback. Sam used to be a little tattletale. We had a clubhouse in my Grandma Cunningham's backyard. We were all in there chilling with a couple of little boys that liked my sister and me. I guess Sam was jealous because nobody liked her.

When Grandma came out to bring snacks, Sam quickly told, "The boys were in here pulling their pants down, mooning us." We laughed and Grandma said, "It ain't nobody out here doing nothing like that." She didn't believe her. That wasn't the point. She tried to get us in trouble. So serves her right.

The summer was over sooner than we expected. Kyna and I had a wild one. Tiffany didn't get out that often, but we had a ball when she did. We went clubbing and just enjoyed being single.

4

I am a senior this year. Since I can't have a baby, I made plans to go to college. With a SAT score of 1000, I got accepted to some nice schools. Hampton, NC A&T, and Fayetteville State. This year I can be crowned Homecoming Queen and I'm in it, to win it. There has been a tradition of every year, alternating races win. Black one year and white the next. If that tradition was more than a coincidence, than it means a black girl would win this year. I have a good chance of winning. I also was put in the yearbook as the funniest girl, (the class clown). In fact, people say they saw me more in the yearbook then anybody else. What an honor! I think I saw the book once, and not all the way through. I didn't have enough money to buy one. One of my other close friends, Monica, was chosen to be on the court with me. She is a beautiful girl and just as popular as me. I want to win, but as long as one of us wins, I'll be satisfied.

The school chose to do something different this year. We brought in one of our best pictures. They scanned them on the computer. People were able to see who they were voting for. That' a plus. As a senior, I have lots of privileges. I work in the hall office so I have a lot of power. I write late passes, and I also learned funny ways of being mean to people. The lady that works in the office with me, is mean to everyone that comes in. We laugh about it after they leave. She is sweet to me. I appreciate that. Every little bit counts.

One day while walking down the hall, I stopped to talk with friends in front of the computer lab. There is a guy inside the computer lab who is staring at me. I continued talking. When I turned back around, he was still looking at me. He is cute, in a big teddy bear-type of way, wearing a big black, down coat. The coat makes him look even bigger.

I went inside the computer lab mainly to ask him why he was staring at me and to give him my number. I approached him and said, excuse me, I noticed you looking at me. I think you're cute; here's my number. I wrote my number down for him, and he gave me his. When he started to talk though, he sounded gay. I looked confused. He laughed; he was just joking. He doesn't talk like that. He told me that he saw my picture on the computer. He said, "You were the prettiest girl on there. I voted for you. I told some of my friends to vote for you, too."

That's sweet. I smiled and walked away. I said, I'll call you. The activities of the week were overwhelming. We had the same tasks as the year before. At the pep rally when we walked out, I did notice him in the stands. I smiled and kept my head up, trying to concentrate on the fine dude already on my arm. What a privilege, his fine ass agreed to be my escort.

The night of the dance was nerve-racking, and I'm still upset that the parade has been rained out again this year. I'd practiced my Miss America wave for nothing. I want to be queen! I tried to get those thoughts out my head. If I don't win, I'm going to be pissed.

We marched out and the drum rolled. Here is our class of 1998 Homecoming Court! The crowd roared, and the queen is...Well, it wasn't Monica nor I. My eyes watered, I am crying in front of half the school, but still trying to look beautiful. It was very hard, and I didn't succeed. My makeup ran down my face. This just had to be the year that the tradition was voided. A white girl won. It felt like all my work was for nothing.

After things calmed down some, I called Maurice. That was the name on the paper. It is a beeper service. I put my number in, and he never called me back. I still saw him around sometimes at school but I didn't have a lot of time to talk. He called me about two weeks later. He asked why I never called him. I explained the story and he said he doesn't know what happened but my call didn't go through. It doesn't matter since we are talking now.

We went to the movies together on a double date with Tiffany and one of Maurice's cousins. We had a real nice time. I do not kiss on the first date and he was a gentleman about that. Tiffany and the cousin were tonguing each other down. She is such a slut. We stayed in touch and started going together a short time later. I know he's proud to be dating a senior, he's a freshman. Yet just one year younger than me. I met his mom, and she seems kind of cranky. I don't think we are going to get along.

He only came over to my house once, and I didn't want him to come then. Kam had someone to come in and take up the carpet in every room. She said, "The house stinks because of the carpet. The smell is in the carpet."

Newsflash - that is you! However, underneath the house in the dirt basement, there is water. The water is slowly evaporating, but it smells moldy.

The floor is very ugly now, stripped and bare. She's so stupid. She's tearing this house down, piece by piece. I told Maurice about who I call my evil stepmother. He feels sorry for me. That's the problem. A lot of people feel sorry for me but they are not doing shit about it. I don't need your pity! I need help! We need help! Help us, please!

When my mom died, it tore my grandma apart. I know it must really hurt to lose a child. She is doing a lot, but I think she can do more. When I go to her and tell her about the things that Kam is doing to us. I'd think she would confront her since that's her daughter, but she is scared of her. We all are. But that's no excuse. If mom knew what she is doing to us, she would turn over in her grave. She would have never left us with her if she knew she would treat us like this.

The news came that Grandma can not afford to keep us in this house any longer. Grandma used up all of her life savings taking care of two households. We lost the house before we could put her out. We have to move. I can't believe because that fat, nasty bitch did not pay the rent, now we have to move. That is just greed. A glutton. A glutton with food and money.

We got packed reluctantly. Kam said the crystal shelf is not going in her new house. She made it clear the new house would be hers. Something like, we'll be visitors.

I said, I really want that shelf.

She said, "I don't want to take no bugs to the new house."

I said, there are no bugs on this shelf, it's made of brass. I will spray it down if you want. You know it was Mom's and I really want to keep it. I began to cry.

She hollered, "I said No!"

That's not fair, that's not right. A.J. dragged the shelf out to the curb. The glass that goes in it was the next thing to go. He dropped one of the pieces of glass and it broke in two. I felt like that was my heart breaking. Everything that reminds us of our parents, she is making us throw away. She made us throw out their old album collection, records that Shaun and I had danced to as kids, with pom-poms. Our favorite album was one with a big 19 on the album cover. She didn't care. It's like she is heartless, so cold.

I don't know what else she can do to make me hate her more. She has done so much already. I wish she would die. I won't even attend the funeral. One day A.J. jokingly said that he could kill her. That made me know how much he really hates her. I'm going to kill her myself, I don't want him to do it. I need a silent killer. I hope they don't do an autopsy. Maybe they'll think she died because of all her weight.

I looked on the table in my bedroom and saw a small bottle of Spirit of Ammonia. We were given this bottle when my mom died. You are only supposed to sniff it to calm down, not to be consumed. I'll poison her. I can't poison her food because she keeps an eye on that like a hawk. Fat bitch. I'll put it in her drink, all those three liters in her room. I waited until she went somewhere. I went in her room and poured in the whole bottle into one of her drinks. I don't know what's going to happen. It does have actual ammonia in it.

Kam came home and went in her bedroom. She ate take-out food that she didn't bring us any of. She made A.J get her a big cup of ice. I whispered in A.J.'s ear, don't ask me any questions, just don't drink any soda from out of her room. I knew he would sneak some, sometimes. She didn't give us any.

He said okay, then I sat and waited to see what the effect would be. She could really die. Oh shit! She started coughing. The coughing turned to choking. All I could do was laugh! An evil laugh, and it felt good. I walked out in the hallway. I pretended to go to the bathroom. As I walked back past her bedroom. I saw her pouring more drink. The more she coughed, the more she drank. She couldn't smell that? I guess piss strongly imitates ammonia.

The coughing and choking continued for as long as I was awake. She was still alive the next day though. Damn. Attempt failed, but hilarious side effects. I bet it made her ribs hurt, as hard as she was coughing. Ha Ha. I guess she switched sodas, because there wasn't much coughing that day. She did stay in her room all day though. There were worse things that I could have done to her, but they were too messy. Like chopping her head off and feeding it to her. She'll eat anything. I guess everything happens for a reason. If she would have died, I probably would be in jail. I am thankful for even the small blessings.

We moved out, and I hate, leaving. "It's so hard to say goodbye to yesterday." from Boyz II Men, is a good song to play, at a moment like this. I'm leaving a lot behind. I hate saying goodbye to the neighborhood. One good thing is that we moved right around the corner from my new boyfriend, Maurice. This could have it's advantages.

We moved out of a four bedroom into a three bedroom. Kam said Shaun and I have to share a room and a closet. We fight all the time. This is not going to work. Shaun can be bitchy sometimes.

Wait a minute! A.J. has to walk through our room to get to his room. I think Kam just moved in here to fuck with us. We do have a screened in porch off of our bedroom, that's good because I smoke Black and Milds. Just open the door and you can get fresh air. But Shaun is always so cold, she doesn't want to leave the door open. You see, that's what I'm talking about. Kam did make us feel like visitors.

If we are not downstairs when dinner is ready, then we don't eat. And we can't cook anything. My brother ate fast because he knew there was more work for him to do for her. She would work him until time to go to bed. Fun is not a word he used often. I know she makes his nerves bad. She hollers; she's impatient and very intimidating. I guess she's mad because instead of losing weight with that surgery, she gained weight. Since she is miserable, she wants to make everyone else miserable. God is not going to let her be thin and happy because of the way she has and is treating us.

I started smoking Black & Milds more often, They give me a head rush, and I needed one. The screened in porch came in handy. I would go out at night and smoke one. It relaxed me right before bed.

We visited our family in the country again. We told them about the move, and again, they propositioned us to move in with them. I told them I'm trying to finish my last year up so I can go to college. Shaun goes to college locally.

This time, they let us drive around in a brown hoop. Out of the three of us girls, I whipped that hoop. The car just felt right as I was driving. I jokingly said to my uncle when we got back, I love this car. Can I have it? He laughed and walked away. The next week he called me, and asked if I was serious about the car.

I said, Yes!

He said, "Having a car is a big responsibility. But, if you think you can handle it, I'll bring you the car on Sunday."

I said, Yes, I can handle it. So he brought me the car and showed me how to put oil in it. He said I have to do it every week or so. I can't believe my uncle just gave me a car. I worked a little part-time job so I could get my plates. I would say insurance too, but I didn't get any.

It felt so good to have my own car. I could come and go as I pleased. So much freedom and independence. Now I wouldn't have to steal Shaun's car anymore.

I did drive the car a few times without her knowing about it, just to go around the corner to Maurice's house. Maurice and I even had sex in it once. Sucker. I don't know how we pulled that off either. The car is tiny. With two big people in it, it was ugly, but the job was done. We won't have sex in my car though. I don't know, I just don't want to.

I took full advantage of the services at the Teen Health Center at my school. I got a pap smear; they said I have a scab on cervix. The only way I could have a scab is because of Adrian. They scraped it off, and it hurt like shit. Evidently that's all that was stopping me from getting pregnant. Because I am pregnant. It wasn't meant for me to get pregnant by Adrian. I can't believe it. I'm glad I will graduate before I have the baby. So much for college. I'm scared to tell Maurice, but I know I have to. I won't tell my family until after I graduate.

The morning sickness is horrible. I throw up every time I brush my teeth. I take my vitamins every day like I'm supposed to. Then I told my sister she is going to be an aunt. She just cried. She always cries, so it didn't surprise me.

Maurice doesn't have a job, but we are in love. I don't believe in having an abortion. I can't kill my baby. I wouldn't be able to live with myself. That is like killing one of my family members. I know I can't go through with that.

More pregnancy symptoms arose. I can't stand to smell chicken cooking because of . It's the grease, it's nauseating. My hormones are all over the place and I hate everybody, especially Maurice's little brother. He's so annoying. He jumps around like a little monkey and says, "Hee hee, hee hee hee."

Maurice's best friend is Fat Rob, he lives right around the corner from him, so they spend a lot of time together. My friends had mixed emotions about the pregnancy. I didn't tell many people about it because I didn't want it to get back to my family. I did confide in a guy that I've known for years. I used to have a crush on him. I told him that I am pregnant, and that I'm not going to tell my family until after I graduate. He attends my aunt's church, and he told my family for me. I want to take the time to sarcastically say, Thank you to him.

My grandma confronted me about it. I hate lying to my grandma. She asked me, "Are you pregnant?"

I said, where did you get that from?

She told me who told her. I said, well, I don't know why he would tell you something like that. There, I didn't lie. She dropped it. Answering a question with a question has gotten me out of a pinch a couple of times. You figure out how much they know.

Tiffany goes with me over Maurice's house sometimes. She really likes Maurice's cousin. She likes anyone who pays her any attention at all. Even though she has had more sex partners than she can remember, she has never had a boyfriend. I feel sorry for her. She can be pretty when she dresses herself up, but she was called Biz Markie in high school. He is a real fat, butt ugly rapper with a huge nose, and she looks just like him. She's still my girl though, and she makes me look that much better when we go out. I call her my second best friend. Tonya and I are a little bit tighter.

Maurice went to every doctor's appointment with me, and even to Lamaze class. I had a sonogram but the doctor can't tell what sex the baby is. Usually that means it's a girl. I didn't get my hopes up, but I really want a girl. I will name her Octavia, after a little girl that I fell in love with years ago. Maybe not though, because while watching *The Simpson's,* I saw a name that I played with a little. If I have a little girl, I will name her Azavia. I guess she can have his last name. I don't know what I'll name him if it's a boy, because I don't want a boy. If I have a boy, I won't like him anyway.

It was hard to hide my pregnancy from my teachers. But I think they could tell. My face was getting fatter, and I was sleeping through my whole class. It's funny though. I think I can even hear when I'm asleep. I was asleep one day in English class. Mrs. Rosenbaum sarcastically called on me, to answer the question she had asked. I gave the correct answer, even though I was asleep.

She asked, "Do you learn by osmosis, or something?" I think I do. Even though I slept most of the time, I still managed to get straight A's in most of my classes. My friends wondered how. They heard me snoring; they knew I was asleep. When end of the year exams came around for some people, it was the difference between passing and failing. In two of my classes, I didn't even have to take an exam. I slept during that time period.

Graduation Day couldn't come soon enough. Class of '98. I can't wait until this is over. I will miss my friends immensely, but I know we have to go our separate ways.

I made those graduation tickets stretch like Kam's tight ass draws. You never have enough. I had so many family members that wanted to come, that we snuck people in through the back entrance. Kam didn't attend. I wasn't expecting her to. I didn't give her a ticket either. She didn't ask.

I call Maurice's mama, Nettie. She told me to. I didn't want to; it didn't feel right. I was brought up to say, yes ma'am and no sir, and to put Mrs. and Mr. in the front of an elder's name. I had gotten used to her. We began to get along. She has known about the pregnancy the whole time and she has done her best to support us. She paid to get my hair done as a graduation present. I look beautiful. I think I even have a glow. That motherly glow.

I walked across that stage with my head held high. I said to myself, I did it. The tears started falling. I wish my mama could see me now. The lights were bright in my face as the crowd cheered. I was handed my diploma and paused for a picture. It has been a long road and now it's over. That reminds me of a song I love, "End of the Road," by Boyz II Men.

Daminika Darlene Cunningham, Class of '98.

After the ceremony, Tiffany and I spent a week in the country. Like always, we had a ball. When I returned to Roanoke, I found out that Kam changed the locks. She is so dirty. Little did I know, that during that week that I was gone, Shaun had been staying with Grandma. She made herself comfortable in one of Grandma's empty bedrooms. Kam kicked her out. Kam kicked us both out. How can she just throw us out in the street like this?

A.J. opened the door for me. I went upstairs and got everything that I could think of. I'm pregnant so I can't pick up anything heavy. I took what I could. I was too tired to get everything. I would stay with my grandma too. I spent the night on the couch. The next morning my granddad told me I couldn't sleep on the couch anymore because I would wear out the springs in it. My granddad is rude like that. He's a little grouch that smokes cigars all day. Where am I going to live at? My Aunt Ann called over Grandma's and told me to come stay with her. She made me feel so wanted. She is the coolest out of all my aunts. She is married with children, and they live in a big house. I made myself at home.

I got a chance to go back to the house and gather some of my belongings. Kam had her own brother to put our stuff out on the curb, my uncle. I don't know what she could have said to convince him to do that. I picked up a floor model TV and put it in my trunk, all while pregnant because I didn't want to leave it behind. It belonged to my mom and dad, and it's not even broken.

Even though I made sure to grab all my Boyz II Men tapes, A.J. had the cover to one. He gave it to me, along with a note. I read what it said on the side of the tape cover. It said, "Why did you leave me?" My heart broke and then crumbled. I cried uncontrollably. I forgot all about my little brother, and he brought it to my attention. He is stuck there with her. I can't protect him from her anymore. I didn't mean for this to happen, but with regret I did leave him. Honestly, I have to get my life together before I can help anyone else, even my brother. God knows I would if I could.

My aunt didn't even consider him our brother even though he grew up with us his whole life, ever since eight months old. His dad abused him and his mother when he was a baby. He was thrown out of the house into the middle of the street, in a car seat. It broke both of his arms and legs. He is my miracle baby brother. It hurt real bad when she would say things like, "That is not her brother, it's her cousin." She just said it to be hurtful and hateful!

Ann and I talked about the fact that Kam is still getting a check for me even though I don't live there. Now that she kicked me out the house, I hope she don't think she's going to keep getting that. Ann went with me to Social Security. We took Kam's name off and put Ann's name on. I wonder did she see that coming? There are four more checks before I turn eighteen. They added up to a little over $2,000, so we bought some nice things for the baby.

DEVASTATING CONSEQUENCES

It ended up working out nice for the both of us. I needed somewhere to live and Ann needed a babysitter. I watch the kids while they both work. Most of the time they are asleep. It's an easy job. The downside is that I have a curfew of 11pm. I have to be back before they go work. No visitors allowed. You might say, they don't know what you do while they are at work. Well, they have a security system. They lock me in the house every time they leave. No one in or out. That sucks. I made the best of it though. They do have cable. Yes, videos. I could also talk on the phone so it wasn't that bad. It's a lot better than being homeless.

Ann threw me a surprise baby shower. It was a surprise, until one of my friends spilled the beans. I didn't think anyone was going to throw me one. I smiled just because they care. Ann said, "Since the baby's name is going to be Azavia, her nickname should be Zay-Zay."

I laughed and said, ewe I don't like that.

Shaun got me a small gift, but she made sure she let me know that she paid for most of the food. Ann bought the baby a beautiful comforter set with balloons on it. Not as many people showed up as I wanted. Shaun said she didn't have any of my close friends' phone numbers. Oh well, we still had a good time playing games and everything else.

Tiffany went with me over Maurice's one day. She wanted to see his cousin. She is sweating him. The cousin only cared about sex and that's exactly what they did. They went out to the backyard together. There is table propped up against the house. They did it doggy style, on that. You might ask, "How do I know?" Maurice saw them. He said he went in his mom's room for something and got an eyeful. From her window, you have a front row seat. He watched. He came downstairs laughing. He told me to come look.

I said, why would I want to see them having sex? I asked him, why do you want to see them having sex? It's not funny to me for you to look at my best friend having sex. That's not cool.

That whole situation pissed me off. If she knew he was watching, I'm sure she put on a show. Let me tell you what took the cake. A few days later, I pulled up over Maurice's house. Tiffany and Kyna are sitting on his front porch. *What the fuck? Why are they just chilling over his house without me? Did I miss something?* Evidently I did. So I walked up on the porch with a real confused look on my face. I said hey to Maurice and went straight to Tiffany, for a little sidebar.

I asked, what are you doing over here?

She said, "I'm here to see Maurice. We can be friends."

I said, Y'all were not friends before we started dating, and you are not welcome over here unless I'm over here. I knew Kyna was her ride so I didn't say much to her. Tiffany stood up, and even though I'm pregnant, I am prepared to knock her back down.

She walked down the steps. Before she got to the bottom, she said, "He wants me anyway."

I said, bitch, don't nobody want you. If somebody wanted you, you would have had a boyfriend by now. All of a sudden, Kyna started popping shit right along with Tiffany, saying stuff like, "She has a right to be over here." She is such a follower. She don't have anything to do with it, but she wants to put her two cents in.

I went in the house and grabbed the first thing I saw, a football helmet. I swung it at Tiffany and missed. She ran to the car. Kyna, meanwhile, was still talking shit right below the banister. I took my bedroom shoe off and smacked her in the face with it. She was shocked and just stood there. I took my other bedroom shoe off and smacked the other side of her face with it. She tried to come back up on the porch, I tried to get off the porch. Maurice stood in between us to break it up. Then she went to her car. She can't fuck with me anyway.

I can't believe my best friend wants my man. The father of my unborn child. She is real desperate. I should have known that a person with nothing wants everything. Not only that, but she turned my other good friend against me. Just because Maurice is nice to her, she construed that to be feelings.

Maurice said, "I don't see anything wrong with her coming over here."

I said, I bet you don't. You wouldn't mind another peep show either. I don't know why he would even want to look at someone else. Our sex life is wonderful; we do everything from sex on the fifty yard line to in an alley next to a bakery. We do have fun together. I feel like we are soul mates; we even look alike. That's what a lot of people say. I guess that's what you look for in a mate, is yourself.

Looking like brother and sister Daminika and Maurice

Maurice is going to be a good father. He said he would be there every step of the way. He didn't want our baby to grow up like he did, without a father around. It made me love him even more. He went with me when I got my first tattoo. A tattoo of my name, right over my left breast. I do have huge breasts, might as well compliment them. No man's name though, not until after marriage. I'm not going to be stuck with that after a tragic breakup.

Speaking of tragic breakups, I just knew my Aunt Ann and her husband were headed for Splits Ville. While she was out of town on church business, he invited another woman over to the house. She was chilling like she owned the place. Is he stupid? Did he think that I wasn't going to tell my aunt? He haven't been having female guests over without his wife. I told Shaun what I saw. Shaun said she had been seeing in the apartment complex where her boyfriend lives. She told me to ask Ann if they know anyone who lives over there. When Ann got back in town, I did ask her. She said she doesn't know anyone over there. I said, well your husband must because Shaun's been seeing him quite often. I reluctantly told her the rest.

It was hard being the bearer of bad news, but I hope he didn't think I was going to keep his secrets. We didn't share an unspoken bond. My aunt confronted him. I heard some of what happened, but not all. The next morning I saw about two dozen red roses and a card. I guess they worked it out. I can't believe she forgave him. How could she? Later she told me that he said he was helping a woman move. *More than once?* Whatever was said, she fell for it.

Everyone is so nice to me now that I'm pregnant. All my grandma wants to do is feed me. But instead of gaining weight, I am losing it, which is not necessarily bad for me. But for a big girl, I am blessed to not have any problems associated with being fat. Besides back pain. I don't have diabetes, or high blood pressure, or even high cholesterol. God doesn't put more on us than we can bear. I was prepared to bring the baby home, to Ann's house. But the opportunity arose for Shaun and me to get an apartment together. My Aunt Eva is moving and we can take over the lease at her old place. I've been over there before and it is infested with mice. I'm scared of mice and so is my sister. In times like these, I knew I couldn't be choosy. I broke the news to Ann that I would be leaving and they'd have to find a new babysitter. She understood. According to her husband, I had worn out my welcome anyway. He's just mad that I told on him. Fuck him.

Shaun and I put our money together for the first month's rent and gave it to the landlord. The very same day I received a call that we could have an apartment that's based on our income so that if my sister would lose employment, the rent would be damn near free. No mice. The only thing about it is that it is in the projects. The place is right around the corner from my grandma's house. This would really be a better deal for us. I discussed it with my sister and we decided to take the new place. I got in touch with the landlord and told him we want our money back. Since it was meant to be, he said, "Okay."

5

We moved into our new apartment. It is a three bedroom and it looks nice. Shaun got the biggest room since the other two would be for me and the baby. Nettie gave me her old queen-sized bed. She said it hurt her back anyway. She got a better quality bed, but it was smaller. It was hilarious to see her and her new boyfriend in that full-sized bed. She didn't seem to mind. Her boyfriend is real cool too. He can cook almost as good as me, so he cooks for the family.

It's my eighteenth birthday today and it feels good to have my own place. Shaun pays the rent and I buy the food. I get food stamps and we make it stretch the whole month. We partied a little for my birthday, but nothing too intense since the baby is due within two weeks or so. Maurice is acting like he doesn't want to be together anymore. I don't know what happened, but I'm not going to have this baby alone. I'll drive my car off a cliff first. I told him exactly that. He eventually came around. I seriously couldn't have handled it any other way.

He stayed over my house sometimes, mostly on the weekends. He is still in school. I picked him up from school one day and dropped him off over Fat Rob's house. As soon as we pulled up, I noticed an octagon shelf on the porch of their neighbor. I stared at it, I couldn't take my eyes off of it.

I asked Maurice to ask the man standing out there if he wanted the shelf. There is a big dog standing right beside him.

Maurice said, "I'm not asking that man nothing."

I said, forget it I'll do it myself.

I got out the car and walked into his yard. I asked him, do you want that stand on your porch? He looked right at me and said, "No, you can have it." I know this shelf looks exactly like my mom's shelf, but what are the chances that it's the same one? I looked at the shelf and it didn't have any of the glass pieces to it. I said to myself that's not a problem. I'll just get new glass for it.

It just so happened that my uncle is in town, and he has a van. I told the man that I'd be back the next day to pick it up. As we were loading the shelf in the back of the van, the man said, "Here is some glass for it." I looked at the glass. There is one piece that is broken. A shiver went through me, and I tried to fight back the tears. I knew it was my mama's shelf. It was meant for me to have. Evidently, nothing or no one could keep me from it! It was a like a dream, when we brought that shelf back where it belonged; it's home. I feel a sense of peace. "A Dream," by Mary J. Blige, played in the background. I'll take care of that shelf just like I had done before. I'll let people know, don't get near it.

My crystal shelf and my miracle.

I did get the ring that I was promised after I turned eighteen. I wear it every day. The day I took it off was the day that I went into the hospital. It was late, I was asleep and very uncomfortable. I sat up to try to relieve the pain. I stood up after that didn't work. I took one step and goosh. My water broke. It is all over the floor. My reaction was to follow through with another step. I stepped in it and slipped. Next thing I know, I fell on my ass, hard.

I woke Shaun up and she drove me to the hospital. The doctor said my water broke, but I'm not dilating. Maurice came to the hospital soon after. They gave me medicine to help me dilate. It didn't work. The baby is losing fluid, and I'm not dilating. The word came in that I would have to have a C-section. I cried. I had gone to Lamaze class for nothing. I was ready to push the baby out. It took away the whole birthing experience, as gruesome as it was. Maybe I wanted to experience that. Maurice was there with me the whole time. He held my hand. I was numb, but it still hurt.

The doctor said, "It's a boy - no, it's a girl - no." He stopped and I started to cry.

What is it? The doctor replied, "It's a girl." Are you sure?

"Yes, you have a healthy baby girl." She began to cry. They let Maurice hold her first. I told him to hold her down so I could kiss her. God just gave me everything I wanted. I had to wait until I could wiggle my toes, before I could hold her. Those first moments holding my little girl were priceless. I didn't want to give her back. I looked at her good. Nobody was going to switch my baby at birth. My baby was born on my mom and dad's wedding anniversary. That made it just a little more special. It is also my grandfather's birthday.

When I got back to my room I rested. I was exhausted. Labor will do that to you. Maurice was eating all the food that everyone brought. I can't eat yet. Just liquids. I haven't eaten anything in over 24 hours. They brought me chicken noodle soup, I started to eat it and it was actually good. I smiled ear to ear when I saw actual chicken in the soup. It felt like I was cheating. *Do they know this soup has actual chicken chunks in it?* Well, I'm not going to tell them. I just grinned, chewed, and swallowed. Suckers!

The nurses tried to convince me to breastfeed. No, thanks. I just don't feel right doing that. It resembles sex too much. I don't know, that's just me. Bottle feeding works just fine, for my baby and me. I did name her Azavia Breonna Hunter. We do call her Zay-Zay, just like Ann suggested.

Once I did go back to solid foods, it was well worth the wait. Nettie has a good friend that works at the hospital. She hooked me up. Whatever I wanted, I got, even if I wanted two cheeseburgers. I just wrote down a two. I had enough sodas and snacks to feed all my visitors as they poured in. My family from the country came to see us too, including Grandma. They snapped Polaroid's of the prettiest little women alive. Nettie already had a coming-home outfit prepared for the baby. She looks so beautiful.

Azavia Breonna Hunter

I brought the baby home, but I can't do much traveling up and down steps. I split the baby's stuff up and kept half upstairs and the rest downstairs. It is really hard for me. I'm in a lot of pain and still have to manage to take care of the baby. My incision stinks and I have to clean it often. Maurice spent more nights with me. I know you are supposed to wait six weeks before having sex. Even with a C-section, you have to wait six weeks. I don't understand why, since I don't have any pain down there. We did celebrate our one-year anniversary with sex. That was about a week and half after the baby's birth. She looks just like me but she has her dad's eyebrows, thick and bushy. My blood must have become thin after the surgery, because I am cold all the time. So I turned the heat up as high as it would go and put extra clothes on me and the baby. I also called the maintenance man to come fix the heat.

He said, "The heat feels fine to me."

I said, I'm sorry. I just had a baby. Maybe it's just me.

He laughed then left. I snuggled in next to her for warmth, and she started to cry. I gave her a bottle but she spat the milk back out. She cried for a long time, and I couldn't figure out why. I just changed her diaper. I called her dad to come and help me.

As soon as he walked in the door, he said, "The first thing you need to do is turn that damn heat down." He walked upstairs where he said it was even hotter. He saw her lying there, crying. He started taking her clothes off and said, "You have it too hot in here for this baby." She only had on a diaper, but she stopped crying. I didn't realize that I was the only one who was cold. Dad came to the rescue.

Azavia was christened in a beautiful white dress, with a matching bonnet. Her grandmother takes great pride in picking out her clothes. She looks just like me. My little mini me. It's like watching myself grow. Great-grandmas from both sides of the family were there, and even the godgrandparents. Of course, her one and only aunt and both uncles came. I received a certificate to commemorate the day.

Within weeks I also received notice that my fat aunt who had kicked me out the house while I was pregnant, had claimed me on her taxes. She opened a piece of my mail and got my social security number. Now this is only legal if I lived in her house at least half the year. She kicked me out right after graduation in the middle of June, two weeks too early. Plus you have to provide food and clothing. Both of those are marked off. I told the IRS exactly that. She will have to pay the money back. Serves her right. Shaun decided to move out, I worried about the financial strain. It just means the rent will be based on my income instead of hers. Since my income is zero, my rent should be close to it. I was hurt by her decision, but enjoyed the benefits of a bigger room. I got a king-sized bed to help me fill it. I love this damn bed. The only thing is that sheets to fit the bed are twenty-five dollars and up. I'll just get one sheet set for now. That means I have an extra bedroom. I decided to make that a TV room/smoke room.

Shaun will be living with her best friend. They fuss all time, but always make up. They were drawn to each other by sharing similar tragedies. Both moms are deceased. Both of their younger sisters have the same nickname, and both their nieces have the same nickname. What a coincidence! To boot, our brothers are the same age.

A lot of time passed, and Tiffany begged for my forgiveness. We talked off and on. I do want her to see the baby. She was going to be the godmother till she fucked up. We have been really tight since high school. She didn't sleep with Maurice, so I guess I can forgive her. We got together one day and decided we'd go over to the school and show my favorite teacher the baby. She drove to the school, and we went to Mrs. Rosenbaum's class. I showed her my little girl. She told me she looks beautiful. We caught up on things. I told her that my child's father still attends school here. I described him to her, but she doesn't know who I am talking about. We went to Maurice's class since it is right down the hall. I asked his teacher can I speak with him. He said, "Maurice did not come to class today. He most likely didn't come to school today."

Maurice didn't call me and tell me he wasn't coming to school today. Where could he be? I know he is not over that girl's house! What girl? The same girl I had conflicts with when I was in school. She tried to tell me bad stuff about Maurice so I wouldn't want him. All the while scheming on getting him herself. I found out where she lived from a friend. I told Tiffany to drive past there. I know it's probably a waste of time, but it will make me feel better. I have the worst knot in my stomach.

We pulled up and we saw Fat Rob's car. Wherever he is Maurice is not too far behind. I felt rage take over my whole body. I got out of that car real fast. I went to knock on the door. The girl looked out the window. I heard her say, "Oh, shit." That's right, oh shit. Open up this door! Maurice, bring your ass out here. I gather they were scared because nobody opened the door. I twisted the door knob, and it was unlocked, so I opened the door. Someone was standing right beside it and quickly closed and locked it. I hollered some more. Maurice opened the door, and I smacked him right in the face. He pushed me so hard that I flew across the porch. I broke a couple of flower pots. I got up and pushed him. I grabbed his shirt and ripped it off. He pushed me down again. I got a couple of licks in, then grabbed that broken flower pot. I knew I had to have a weapon against this big motherfucker. I sliced his chest a little with the pot.

That nasty, yellow, bitch, started talking shit. I threw down my weapon and went towards her. She ran.

I said, you was talking so much shit, let's fight.

She pulled out a little, old-timey pistol. She said, "Get off my property, or I'm going to shoot you." She waived the gun around. I didn't care. I was going for her anyway.

I heard Tiffany say, "Come on, it's not worth it. That crazy bitch really might shoot you. You got your baby in the car." That definitely calmed me down. I forgot that she was even in the car. I jumped in the car, and Tiffany started it. Maurice ran and jumped in the backseat. He better had left with me!

We fussed when we got home. He swore that he did not have sex with her; he just wanted somewhere to chill at. Fat Rob was over there with one of his girlfriends. I can't believe he betrayed my trust like that. I have never cheated on any of my boyfriends. Spending time with another girl behind my back is still cheating. He doesn't have any good reason to be over another girl's house. She definitely doesn't look better than me, and she is not even worth listing her name in my book. I listened to "Brokenhearted," by Brandy and Wanye'. I let it all out. I am not going to let that bitch have my man. He has responsibilities over here, and *here* is exactly where he is going to be. I caught a trespassing charge fucking around with that girl. I forgave him though and moved on. But in the back of my mind, I'm not going to forget it.

He played a song that touched me, "Looking for Love," by R. Kelly. He tells me he loves me just a little bit more. Time heals all wounds, and that's something we have plenty of, if nothing else.

We started playing cards with other couples. We go everywhere together. We started hanging out with two of my cousins from Bedford and their boyfriends. Shelly and Wanda date a set of cousins. They have the same last name. We make fun of their last name by calling them McNastys. They live up to the title, believe me. We had fun together, all of us. We grew tighter with time.

I started smoking weed on almost a daily basis. To cope with some of the stresses of being a new mom, and just to relax. I also smoke cigarettes now. I even smoked a little during my pregnancy. The doctor told me the worst thing that could happen is that the baby would be a little smaller. I said I didn't want a big-ass baby coming out of me anyway. When my taxes came back, I bought myself a newer model car with tinted windows, music, and rims. We are riding in style now.

We went to the lake with the other couples and even though after drinking some alcohol, certain members would be hostile, it usually turned out well. We had so many cookouts together, that I can't even throw a number out there. Even in the middle of the night, we'd have something on the grill. Then we'd have breakfast where everyone would bring different things. Always a bag of weed in the mix. You know how they say friendship is priceless? Well, the beautiful thing is, we are all family. And they are too.

Speaking of family, Shaun broke the news to me that she is pregnant. I took it hard, I didn't really want her to have kids. Just an overprotective sister kind of thing. And I really don't like who she is pregnant by, and I let him know it. His head is humongous, and that's a strong gene. Shaun moved in an apartment right across the sidewalk from me. At least now I can keep a closer eye on her. Her boyfriend is crazy.

Sisters, Victoria(Shaun) and Daminika(Dee)

Let me tell you a funny story. The car that my mom left to us, that Shaun kept for herself, well ... She was so greedy that she didn't even let me drive while Kam was not around. It's not like I was going to tell her. The car's motor blew up on Mother's Day, and then she depended on me for transportation. Ironic, isn't it? I can't make this shit up!

Fat Rob would come over our house often for Maurice. Because by this time, he had dropped out of school and moved in with me. I can honestly say I suggested it. He can't have a full-time job and go to school. Fat Rob did pluck my nerve sometimes, but most of the time we just joked around. The more he came around, the better he looked. He had his facial hair trimmed up just right. Maurice could never grow any. He looks like a fat John B almost. Light-skinned with cornrows. He always looked at me a certain way, I know he wants me. A woman can tell these things. Who could blame him? I lost a little weight since the baby, and I look sexy as hell.

Don't get me wrong, Maurice has been great to me over the years, and has been more than satisfying. We both agree that stay-at-home moms are just as important as working moms. He really doesn't want me to work. He paid my rent for me and gave me an allowance when he was working and I wasn't. He is crazy about me. He even asked to marry me at Christmas, but the ring broke during the fight and I knew that was a sign.

He has been gaining so much weight though, eating my home cooked meals. I like big, sexy dudes, but damn. The more his stomach grew, the more his dick shrank. It was becoming to be a problem for me. Not to mention his wake-the-dead snoring, just like Kam. They both have sleep apnea. He can fall asleep anywhere, and he refuses to do anything about it. He don't want to go to the doctor. He don't want to take his nightly breathing treatments. He don't want to work, and he don't want to admit that he can't and get on disability. I think one of the reasons for this is because he doesn't want people to judge him. Even so, it is all beginning to take a toll on me. I do love him dearly, but I love sex too.

One day, I propositioned Fat Rob. I whispered in his ear, I had a dream about you, and I wanted to know if I can kiss you and see what it feels like.

He smiled and looked around. Maurice is upstairs. He said, "Are you for real?"

I nodded yes.

He said, "We can't do it here, but we can set up a time. Just call me.

I did call and we hooked up near some abandoned train tracks. We kissed, and it was magical. He made me tingle all over. He is one of the sexiest men I have ever talked to. The facial hair gets me every time. I used to get mad when my daddy cut his beard and goatee off. He was so much more handsome with it.

We hooked up again and things went a little further. We fogged the windows up. We kissed and touched. We had sex. If that's what you want to call it. I humped a lot but didn't feel much. He said that he dreams about me all the time. I'm the only girl that has ever been constantly in his dreams. I took that as a compliment. So for all that, I should make his dick hard just by showing my breasts.

Well, we did a lot more than that, so it should have been ready for insertion. I still didn't feel much. I forgot he is half white. But I'll give him a chance to redeem himself. After all, he is sitting down behind the wheel of a car, but for right now, I'm going home to have sex with my man. He got me so turned on and worked up, then didn't come through. This was a big waste of my time. I had to lie to get away, but we met again.

This time we got out of the car. He ate me on the trunk of my car, then we did it doggy style. It felt better than it did the first time. I moaned to turn him on more. I guess I should have kept that to myself because bam, he nutted. I am trying to make something into something it's not. We are using condoms, but he knows I'm safe. After all, I am with his best friend, so we talk about not using a condom. I told him that Maurice has cum in me before on accident, and I didn't get pregnant. He's been doing it since. We think the scab might have grown back. I told him that I think I can't get pregnant.

I was prissing and primping in the mirror more often. I was gone even more. Maurice is starting to suspect something. He is questioning me way too much. When I get nervous I laugh, so he knew when I was lying. I just got out the shower and dried off. I asked him to pass me a pair of underwear. He passed me some black cotton panties, very comfortable. I pulled them on and dressed quickly. I left before he could say much else to me. I met Fat Rob at the same spot. I told him to bring the jeep this time, so I could see how it felt laying down. He pulled up, and we made out in the front seat. He made me just as horny every time.

He could do that. If it feels like I want it to feel, I'm going to let him cum inside me. We are not going to use a condom tonight.

He popped the hatch, and we crawled in back. Then he said, "What is that smell?"

I said, I don't know, I don't smell anything. What does it smell like?

He said, "It stinks."

I thought to myself, I know it's not me. I just got out the shower. We began to kiss and touch. He started pulling my shorts and underwear down. He got to my knees and stopped. I took them the rest of the way off. I looked at him then realized the reason that he had stopped. The smell was coming from me. It smelt terrible and began to stink up the entire back of the truck. I started putting my clothes back on and looked very embarrassed. We said we'd talk later, and he pulled off.

Why do I smell like this? I just got out the shower an hour ago. I sat there in my car, shaking my head for awhile, just thinking. I said the only link in between the shower and here was the panties that Maurice passed to me. That nasty bastard. I think he got those panties out of the dirty clothes. I'm sure the first time I wore them they got their proper use. The second time wearing them, sitting in a hot car, twitching around for an hour. It made more than perfect conditions for a stink fest. Ladies, know, you cannot wear black panties twice without a catastrophe. Or any panties, for that reason. Label yourself informed.

Even though I knew what Maurice had done, I couldn't confront him about it. That would be like admitting that I had pulled them down at some moment while I was gone. I am embarrassed as fuck, but I think it would be even worse if I called him to explain the reason why my pussy stunk. I won't make that call, I'll just drop it. That whole situation proved to be to my advantage because three weeks later, I was pregnant. As I might have said before, everything happens for a reason.

If the stinky panties would have never occurred, I would be pregnant by Fat Rob instead of Maurice. That was a close call. I guess I was wrong about the whole scab growing back theory. It would have ruined their friendship and rocked the community. I live in the projects, and everybody up here is NOSY! They know all your business *before* you know it, especially certain ones in particular, who will remain nameless. Well, we'll just call them the gummy family. None of them have any teeth.

What a coincidence - we are already living in a three bedroom apartment. Exactly what we need. Otherwise, I would have had to move. Thank you, Lord. I hate moving.

This year when I got my tax refund, I started selling weed. Of course, the gummies know that and even visited me once or twice. Maurice does most of the work. He knows people. My money backs the whole operation. Business is booming and we are moving a pound a week. Talking small time, that is big money for someone living in the projects. We are hood rich! I helped cut the weed up and bag it. There is so much weed everywhere. Some hiding in the cabinet for downstairs customers. The bulk is kept upstairs in a small metal suitcase. The pound fit perfectly inside. All the weed that I want to smoke, is right at my fingertips. I smoke because it makes me feel happy and relaxed. That's all I want, is to stay happy. I don't need hallucinogens. That doesn't make you happy; it makes you crazy. We smoke everyday, at least four times a day. And always more if we have company. They expect us to. We matched.

My two cousins are still head over heels about their set of cousins that they date. The reason we call them McNastys is because combined, they cheat, steal, and abuse. One of them has his looks going for him, at least. The other is alright, but just very dark skinned. They can be nice from time to time, but the main attraction is the sex. The way I've heard it, all of them have nice sized penises. That's why when one more of the cousins came around, I was curious. My relationship with Maurice is going downhill fast. He can't keep a steady job and even though he's helping me make the money, he tries to spend it like it's his. I don't give him a monetary allowance like he used to give me. I do give him a weed allowance though. It keeps him happy. The more we smoke the more we eat. That's okay for me because I'm eating for two. Maurice acts like he is too.

I don't want another baby, but I know I can't kill it. I want him to be around for the baby, but I really don't want him anymore. I always kick him out and make him go stay with his mom, when he doesn't have a job. It does encourage him to get a new one faster, but then he'll stop going. Since he had a check coming, he knew that would buy him some time. That started to get real old. Fat Rob is working at my dream job. I know if he can do it, I can do it too.

6

Rodney is the third of the cousin trio. He started coming over my house to buy weed. He came pretty often, and would buy a large amount. He stands about six foot seven, 315 lbs. You know I like me a big boy. He is light-skinned with hazel-green eyes. They drew me in. He wears his hair damn near bald. It looks like he is going bald. But that thought disappeared as soon as I saw how trimmed and shaped his beard is. That really turns me on. Check one for that; tall is check two; money should have been check one, but it is check three; and look at his feet. Oh, my, goodness. I shook my head and laughed. I may have hit the mother load on this one friends.

I told Maurice I don't want to be together anymore, more than once, but he does not want to let me go. I heard that Rodney works at a furniture store, unloading furniture. That takes muscles. What a turn on! He started coming to all of our cookouts and blaze sessions. He doesn't talk much, but he does laugh at my jokes. I think that's cute. I think he is cute.

My stomach got bigger and I took pictures to remember it, just like I had done with Zay-Zay. You can see Rodney in the background on this one. He has a big white hoop with bang in it. I get excited just seeing him pull up in it. You know the neighbors noticed. We always had a good time listening to music.

This pregnancy is just as tough as the first one with only one added symptom, incontinence. I started wearing maxi pads just to avoid embarrassing moments where I'll be choking on the blunt and urine squirts out. I'm having a boy, and he is kicking the hell out of my bladder. I probably should stop smoking, but that's not an option right now. I'm not drinking, I don't play around like that. I put a lot of thought into this baby's name just like my daughter's. The names must be unique, just like mine. I want something that in someway resembles my daughter's name.

In time, I came up with Tayon. We can call him Tay, not Tay Tay. That's too feminine. Zay and Tay, it has a ring to it.

I am slowly building up the courage to approach Rodney. I don't wait on opportunity to come knocking. I go ring the doorbell. Only one of my boyfriends has ever approached me. If I waited, he would have been the only one I had. I'm not happy! I feel sorry for him. We only stay together for convenience. I'm not in love with him anymore. I want bigger and better things, and he can't give them to me, or even help me get there.

I will always love each and every one of my boyfriends just a little bit. They each have a little chip of my heart. I know for a fact that it's the same way for each of them too. I'm not on bad terms with any of them. They all give me a hug upon our seeing each other, unless in front of a girlfriend. Adrian tries to be funny, in front of his supposed fiancé. I know you remember what we had. Oh, in case I didn't mention the fiancé, she is the same girl that I wanted to fight over Maurice. The one that pulled a gun out on me. Coincidence, I don't know. She just happened to find my first love and they got together. I guess that's her payback to me. You got me, but hold on to him. I had him once, since you'll been together and it could happen again.

Rodney started to flirt with me. Before I approached him, he approached me. He asked if I wanted to go out with him sometime. I said, you know I have a boyfriend.

He said, "Yeah, I know."

I laughed and blushed. Maurice walked in the kitchen and I wrapped up the conversation. I played it off. I said, Shelly, I'll tell you more about it later. I'll call you back. I hung up the phone and went upstairs. If I stay downstairs, he will definitely notice the huge cheesy smile that I have on my face. It made me feel good that the dude that I was checking out, was checking me out too. Most of the men I want I get anyway. More yes's than no's. I want LL Cool J, but he doesn't know where I live at yet.

I met up with Rodney about a week later. I can't believe I am going on a date 8 months pregnant! I spruced myself up as best as I could. My friend Kyna helped.

She said, "You look the best that a pregnant woman can look."

I sarcastically said, Thanks, Kyna, you always know exactly what to say.

We laughed. He picked me up, and we went up to the star. A humongous lit star, with an overlook of the city. It's beautiful up there at night. And it's nice to have a man with a car, he can drive me around. We smoked a blunt and talked. He threw out a name, and asked if I know her.

I said, yes, and I don't like her. Why, do you go with her?

He said, "No, that's just my close friend. We have been best friends for years. She cuts my hair."

I looked at his head and saw that she doesn't do a very good job. He told me he has a daughter who was born a week before mine. He's no longer with the baby's mother, but he does visit his child. He told me, "I want you, and I always get what I want!"

I believed him. We have so much in common. Because as a matter of fact. I always get what I want. We talked a while longer, and then he dropped me off. My no-kiss rule still applies. I am a lady.

The next time we talked, he had something bad to say about Maurice. He said that Maurice had cheated with a girl from another project complex. He took me over the girl's house. We had a long talk. She told me Maurice used to come over her house, but they never had sex. I believed her. I confronted Maurice about it. I told him everything I heard. He had cheated on me more than once. Even though supposedly he didn't sleep with either one of those females, he still chilled with them behind my back. Rodney started coming over more often. Maurice calls him his boy. If he only knew that his new friendship is a facade to steal his girl. I made Maurice get out because he is unemployed. Plus, I want Rodney to come over.

I invited him over, I wore my zebra striped pajamas, I do need to be comfortable. It's elastic only these days. We sat at the kitchen table and talked. I like him more and more with each visit. We held hands across the table, then he leaned in for a kiss. Short but sweet. I do want this man. We moved over to the couch. He touched around a little bit, but I let him know that I am not having sex with him while I'm pregnant. He wanted me to want it, by his actions. First of all, my stomach would be in the way and that's not sexy. He only has a little over a month to go, and then there's the six-week period. You know how I feel about that. It may be sooner ...

I started collecting zebras. They remind me of my mom. She had a black-and-white striped daybed that she loved. I found out that zebras are intelligent and strong. It made me love them even more. That describes me to a tee. I have to be strong, to have dealt with all the obstacles that life has thrown my way. I had to grow up real fast. I missed a lot of those life lessons, I had to learn them the hard way. I won't let my kids grow up like that. My mama treated us great and I want to follow in her footsteps. Even though Shaun looks the most like her, I act the most like her. I feel her presence watching over us. I love you, Mama. I want you to listen to "Mama," by Boyz II Men. It is a touching song.

The baby is due on my dad's birthday. Another coincidence, but since I was to have a C-section with this baby too, I could tell the doctor when I wanted to go. I picked the earliest date, which was two days before my dad's birthday. I want to get this over with. To tell you the truth, the sooner I'm healed, the sooner I can see what Rodney is working with. Over the years, I have grown impatient. I don't want to wait for anything. I was told not to eat or drink after midnight the morning of the surgery. But I was so thirsty after smoking a blunt, that I did drink a little bit of blue juice. It's my favorite.

I went into surgery with Maurice by my side once more. I am numb from the waist down so they can begin the incision. It hurt a little but not as much as what they call a little tug. I was with my sister when she gave birth to my nephew. I call him Smelly Bottoms. Smelly for short. He has more bowel movements, than any normal child.

Shaun had a C-section as well. Since her child's father chose not to show up, it was me standing beside her in the delivery room, looking over the divider. What I saw when I looked over there scarred me for life. I saw them pulling on her stomach with clamps and forceps. One was on each side, and they pulled, and stretched her like play dough. When it was my turn and they told me I had to have another C-section, I knew exactly what they were doing to me back there. I freaked out, I had a panic attack. Then I started hollering and squirming around. They told me to calm down.

I said, I feel sick.

The doctor said, "On a scale from one to ten. How sick do you feel?"

I said, I feel sick enough to throw up! It's coming up! I can't move my body. I'm strapped down. I had to turn my head. I threw up blue juice in a yellow boomerang-shaped dish. Maurice wiped my mouth. It's those little things, that made me stay with him this long. Different little things are tearing us apart. Pardon the pun.

The baby was born healthy, and beautiful. The prettiest little boy I've ever seen. I don't swear, but if I did, I would. This is the truth. Laughing broke out in the delivery room when the doctor said, "This little boy has the biggest penis that I have ever seen on a baby." Watch out for him in twenty years, ladies.

I am concerned a little, because the baby is so light-skinned. He looks just like Maurice, when he was a baby, and he has those eyebrows. Family and friends came to visit me at the hospital. Rodney brought Maurice and Zay- Zay out there the next day. He sat a little while. It was a little awkward.

I am counting down the hours until I can go outside and smoke a cigarette. I was wheeled downstairs two days later, and it felt good to smoke a cigarette. I needed one. I also need some weed. I won't be going home for another five days. I got Maurice to stuff some weed in a Black & Mild. With the fragrance of that over the weed, you won't be able to tell. I smoked it right on the smoking block and I am on cloud nine. I feel more at home now. I had friends to sit down there with me just to double check that you can't smell it. I went back in that hospital high every night since then. The only snafu is that now, I'm hungry. I already ate dinner, but now I'm starving. I buzzed the nurse and asked if they have some chips or something I could have? She said, "No chips, but there is something you can get. You can get soup and a sandwich, with a banana."

That's what I want then. It was delicious and I ordered it every night around eleven. Rodney did call me and even came to see me once I was up and walking. I met him in the parking lot, where we sat in his car. He played the same song that he played to initially woo me. "Seems Like You're Ready," by R. Kelly. He told me that he wants to take our friendship to a higher level. He said, "I want you, and I will do anything, to have you!"

This is something for me to contemplate. All I keep thinking about is how much of a scandal this is going to be. Is it worth it? Everyone will hate me. Do I think about their feelings or my own? I think it is really sweet of him to come see me, while I'm in the hospital. That does count for something. He could be doing anything else right now.

I brought Tayon Maurice Hunter home. As soon as I walked through the door, there was a neighbor there to see the baby. The rumor is that Rodney is my baby's father. Stupid, nosy, people. I didn't even meet him until I was eight months pregnant. They picked the wrong light-skinned person to compare him to. If anything, you'll know the only other possibility.

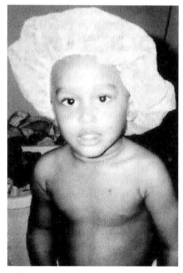

Lil' Maurice only one year old.

We continued to sell weed. The money is real lovely. I bought new outfits and got my hair done often. While on one of those trips to the hair salon, Maurice was at home, chilling with one of his new friends. When I pulled up in the parking lot, I saw two police cars. That's nothing new for the projects. It just means something interesting is going on, most likely a fight. I saw a lot of my friends and family sitting in chairs on the porch. I said to myself, this is a good time for me to be looking good, with all these people outside. I walked up the sidewalk like I was Miss America, waving and smiling at my friends.

DEVASTATING CONSEQUENCES

As I got closer to the front door, I heard my friend say, "Stop smiling. The police are over your house."

I said, what are they doing?

Just then a policeman came up to me and told me that there was a young man that they chased into my house. The young man is Maurice's new friend. He is sitting in the police car. They said he had almonds in his pocket bagged up and selling it like crack. You can get arrested for even having fake crack. He also said that since he ran in my house, that they had to search my whole house.

I wasn't there when Maurice first heard that they would search. Somehow he got to go upstairs away from the police. That's where we keep our weed. The policemen brought in drug dogs and searched the whole house. They found a scale, a dime bag of weed, and the suitcase that we keep the weed in. A certain policeman told me that from the scent coming from the suitcase, he is sure we had to have had a large amount of weed in it. They took everything they found and gave Maurice a ticket for the small amount of weed they found. The policeman told me he would not report the incident to the main office because I was so cooperative. I had to be because I know that there is a pound of weed in this house somewhere. I didn't say much of anything. I think my mouth is still open from shock.

Lastly he mentioned, "If I did tell the office, you would be kicked out."

That's the last thing I need, since I have a new baby.

I watched the police leave and gritted on the friend that was sitting in the police car. He mouthed, "I'm sorry." I shook my head. Maurice told me the whole story.

He said he was sitting outside smoking a blunt with a lot of our friends. The police came through the projects on foot. The friend jumped up and ran in the house. That's real suspicious in front of the police, genius. They searched him and wanted to search the house. Maurice said, "No."

The cop said if he has to get a search warrant, he would tear the house apart versus willingly allowing him to bring in the dogs and then he would be considerate of my valuables. Maurice agreed to the gentle search. He better since he knows I have fragile things in there. Somehow he got away and went upstairs and hid the weed.

Where could he have hidden it, that the policemen couldn't find it and the drug dogs couldn't smell it? I thought maybe since our bedroom window is open, with an air conditioner in it, that he put it outside the window on top of the air conditioner, but no. I wouldn't have thought about it. The easiest thing in the world to do. He threw it away. There was a big bag of smelly trash in the hallway, mostly stinky, raunchy, pampers. The pampers did stink, and I was going to tell Maurice to take it out, but I thought a little bit more could fit in the bag. One pound more. Just one more of those things that happen for a reason. It was my baby's ass that just saved mine.

I don't know what made Maurice think about that. He said because dogs can't smell weed through urine. Helpful tip. Feel free to use that one. I know the police are going to be watching us, so now I can't even make any money. I'm grateful because if Maurice would not have made that split-second decision, we'd both be in jail and homeless. All because some nappy-head dude decided to duck in my house. I could strangle him. I know one thing - somebody has my back, somebody is watching over me. Now I have a pound of weed and only one thing to do with it - Smoke it.

Maybe anyone else would have at least sold what they had left, but I am so paranoid now. I took it as sign or warning to get out of the game. So I did. It was fun while it lasted.

Less than a week later Shaun frantically called me. She slipped and fell while mopping her floor. I threw on some clothes and ran over and opened the door. She was lying on the floor hollering. Her bone was sticking out of her leg. I said, damn, you are going to have to go to the hospital.

She saw her bone protruding from her leg but hadn't called the ambulance yet. She called me first. I couldn't pick her up and she couldn't get up, so we called 911 and the ambulance came shortly. I picked up my grandma from around the corner and we went to the hospital. Shaun is delirious, just talking out the side of her head. She thought she was at work and kept asking for my credit card number. I laughed at her. My grandma said, "That's not funny." She rolled her eyes at me in the funny way that she does. I laughed at her too.

We had to leave while the doctor popped the bone back in place. She has to get a rod in her leg. I never heard of someone injuring their self so much just by mopping. I guess anything is possible. She ended up on crutches for her birthday and was very upset about that. You don't exactly look your best with two brown sticks under your arms.

There is this girl that I met at work earlier this year. She is married with kids. We sat beside each other often. When I told her that I was pregnant and showed my sonogram pictures, she seemed upset. She always changed the subject when I talked about my boyfriend. Well, she came over my house for the first time, to see the baby. That's what she claimed. She peeked at him and started talking to me more. She asked, did I have him naturally. I said, no, I had a C-section with this one too.

She said, "Yeah, I had a C-section with my last child." Then she unbuckled her shorts and pulled them down, along with her underwear. She showed me her pussy and said, "Here is my scar." I can't believe she just did that in my dining room, right next to my kitchen table. She must be gay or bi-sexual, because there is no other good reason for her to have showed me that. She even had on little red silky panties like she was planning to come over here.

That is not the first time a gay woman has been attracted to me. I was working with a girl at a department store. She was real cool, and she asked me to go with her out to dinner after work. I thought it would be fun. Since my sister picked me up from work every night, I invited her to go so I could have a ride home. The girl got pissed off about it. That's when I realized, I was on a date. She eventually admitted she was gay. I told her I could only be her friend. Maurice thinks it's funny that these women are throwing themselves on me. I don't have anything against gay people. I just don't swing that way. It is flattering, though.

I got my hair done and about two weeks later, I hooked up with Rodney. He got me a $100 hotel room. We met there in the middle of the day. The room is beautiful. We watched TV for a little bit, then started to kiss. We got right down to business. I have waited so long for this man. And is well worth the wait. His shoe size strongly resembles his dick size. He went down on me and it feels heavenly. I made him put on a condom and his dick went limp. He tried to get it hard again. We started having sex and even though I felt something, I knew it wasn't the three handfuls that I had peeped out earlier. My friends and I judge penises according to how many times you can stack your closed hand around one. If you can stack your hands on top of each other twice with some left over, than you have 2 1/2 handfuls. Which is good, but I'm ecstatic about the three I just ran across. Most men are 1 1/2 at least the ones I've come across. I don't even give Fat Rob a handful. It's more like a pinky.

Back to the story. Rodney did what he could, but I was not impressed. As we were leaving the room, he said, "Leave the keys."

I asked, why.

He said, "I won't be coming back."

I said, as much money as you paid for this room, and you're not going to sleep in it?

He replied, "No."

I shrugged my shoulders and walked away. I thought to myself, *Oh, well, it's not my money. I really don't feel well about the way things went.* When we met a couple days later at the park, he apologized about the way things had happened. Then he said, "It's all because I never had sex with a big girl before."

It hurt my feelings a little. Well, we don't have to have sex anymore, I replied.

He said, "No, no, I want us to have sex a second time, if you do."

I don't know what I want to do at this point. We continued to chill over Shelly's house. She mentioned taking a trip to Washington D.C., to see her brother. Rodney agreed to drive and I would ride along. Maurice knew nothing of this plan. He thought that we were riding on the bus. He wanted so bad to believe everything I said because he doesn't want to lose me. We left late like most black people. It is hot as hell outside and I decided to try a new, cheaper deodorant, trying to save a few pennies for the trip. I am paying the price for it now. My arms are rocking. I didn't want anything to ruin my moment with him. So much for that. I kept my arms down as much as possible. Time flew by and before you know it, we arrived.

We drove around and took in the sights. We rode through the projects. Compared to what their projects look like, I must live in a condo. The store in the neighborhood that we went to first took food stamps, but when I gave them to him, he looked at me like I was from the Ice age. He said, "Where are you from?"

I said, Roanoke, Va.

He said, "Oh, you'll still use these things? We have the card now."

I said, oh well, I can use cash for the sodas. I have to use cash for the deodorant anyway. I need to put some on as soon as possible. He said, "No, I can still take them though." I paid for my stuff and left. We rode around some more.

We got chicken from a place that Shelly bragged about. It was real good, and she needed a beer afterwards, so we went to another store. The next store we went to had more than a bulletproof glass. The whole store is *behind* glass. It has a small spin-around table that you put your money on, and the cashier will spin around whatever you want. I've never seen anything like that. I didn't think my two liter would fit, but it did. I guess they know what they are doing. Rodney brought liquor with him so I bought the mixer. Then we went looking for the room that he already reserved. He got the most expensive hotel room he could find. I'm impressed. He keeps throwing all this money around. I don't mind one bit. He knows I'm independent. I have my own money and car. And I have as much weed as I want to smoke. I can see why he's stepping up his game a little bit. After all, he is trying to steal me away from one of his so-called friends.

Shelly kept on saying, "You'll should have stayed closer to where I'm going to be." We have to drop her off at her brother's and we might not know the way back. We had to wing it, we got lost because of him, but we finally made our way back. Just as we pulled up, it started to rain. We ran in, trying not to get wet. I just didn't want my hair to mess up. How romantic, we'll have sex while it's raining. But that didn't happen because by time we finished smoking and drinking, we were starving. We decided to walk somewhere nearby to get something to eat since it stopped raining. We ordered our subs and I heard Rodney tell the cashier it would be together. I wasn't expecting him to pay for my food. It sure is nice though. I walked closer, and he asked, "Can you take care of this? I don't have any more money."

I paid for the food, confused, and we walked out. I thought to myself, *I can not believe that he went so broke paying for the room that he can not afford to eat while we are down here. That is so stupid. We could have stayed in a cheaper room for all that. It just shows me what kind of man he is.*

When we got back to the room, we ate and showered. Then he showed me what kind of man he really was.

I mean, he really put it down and around and every other way you can think off. Big improvement from last time. I'm impressed again. I want this man more and more each time we get together. The sex was hard and sweaty, just like I like it. I knew this was the last day of my period but I wanted sex anyway. He saw blood on the sheet. I said, he must have done it so hard that he brought my period on. He believed me and threw the sheet in a corner. Then we watched TV and a song came on called "Contagious," by Mr. Biggs and R. Kelly.

He said, "This song reminds me of you. You are contagious. I want you even though you belong to someone else and when I want something, I always, get it." It made me blush.

We slept together and he held me most of the night. He made me feel so wanted. He is just the right size everywhere. I can deal with the bald head. That next morning, we packed up our things and he cleaned out the fridge. There was like a mini bar in there with all kinds of liquor. I laughed because I knew that they would charge the card he used to reserve the room. He said, "I didn't use a card; I paid in cash."

Then we went to pick up Shelly and came back to Roanoke, but not before taking in a few more sights. We only stopped once for gas. Shelly and I went half on the gas because, of course, the loser doesn't have any more money. He did fill up for the ride down so I guess it's okay.

When we got back in town, Rodney had to drop me off at home. We agreed to let me off on the corner. Before he dropped me off though, we sat around the corner from the house talking and kissing. Then I walked in the house and went upstairs to put my stuff up.

Maurice went outside to talk to one his friends. I called Shelly to tell her about my night. I couldn't tell her in the car for obvious reasons. Next thing I know, Maurice swung the door open with a look of disgust on his face. I told her I have to go.

He said, "My friend told me that you were around the corner in the car kissing Rodney."

I said, oh, really? What else what I supposed to say? I got pissed off at the friend. He belongs to that nosy family that I spoke of earlier (The Gummies), so you know he had to run his mouth.

Maurice said, "I know you don't mess with that baldheaded motherfucker. He is a bitch. He's been chilling over here all this time, trying to be in up in your face? I called him my boy. I should fuck him up. No, I'm going to fuck him up."

I replied, we have to have a talk. I have never cheated on any of my boyfriends, but I told you I'm unhappy and you are not doing anything about it. You try to ignore the problem as if it's going to go away. We have used toys to try to enhance pleasure, but that's just not enough anymore.

He asked, "So what are you saying?"

I said, I don't know what I want to do. I don't want to hurt his feelings, and it's hard saying it's over after almost three years. I know he will have to go back to his mama's house for good, and he hates that.

With tears in his eyes, he asked, "Did you have sex with him?"

I looked at the hurt in his face, and I said, no. He can't handle the truth. It's written all over his face. Maurice slept downstairs on the couch. It wasn't uncommon. I made him go down there every time I was mad.

I debated if I should call and warn Rodney that he knows. For his safety, I did make the call. He didn't have much of a reaction. Then again, he doesn't talk much anyway. I have to force the conversation most of the time but I think he is slowly coming around. He better be scared because Maurice is a big dude. I've witnessed how strong he is, when he threw me across the porch like a lawn chair. Rodney let me know he has a gun and he will use it if he has to. I did relay the message to Maurice for his safety. I do still love him. I want my kids to have a father around and I don't want him doing anything stupid.

It was then that Maurice told me about Rodney. It seems they are taking turns telling on each other. He wants to make Rodney look bad, and Rodney wants to make him look bad. He told me about the girl that was supposed to only be Rodney's close friend. The girl that cuts his hair.

He said, "They are more than just friends."

They couldn't be.

Maurice said, "I have her number if you want it."

I said, why do you have her number? That's when it all came out that he used to mess with her too. So, someone has been sharing girls. He put it all out on the table. Fuck it, what could I say to him?

He said, "It's like Rodney is trying to be me. Everybody I talk to, he tries to talk to. Yeah, I know for a fact he messes with that girl. Call her; see for yourself."

7

If what Maurice says is true, than that means my relationship with Rodney is based on a lie that goes deeper than it might seem. This girl is a big girl, maybe a little bigger than me, and Rodney told me he had never had sex with a big girl before. That makes that a lie. Why would he lie to me about that? I stressed to him how much I hate liars. I am furious and I will not rest until I get to the bottom of this.

I went over Shelly's and called the girl. I wasn't about to call from my house so she could call back for Maurice or something. She answered and I told her all about me. We decided to set him up. He would be meeting me later that day anyway. She came to the park, where I said he would be. When he pulled up, I bet he wanted to pull off. We jumped out and approached his car. He turned the car off and got out.

She asked, "What is going on? Are you with her?"

He said, "It's none of your business. I told you I don't want to be with you anymore."

It looked like it hurt her feelings because she jumped back in the car and drove off. He said, "I told her I don't want to be with her, but it's like she doesn't understand."

That explained that, but what about the sex with a big girl lie?

He looked stupid when I came back with that one. He said, "I just didn't want to tell you that my dick wouldn't stay hard. I was nervous."

I don't know if that made me feel better or worse. Why couldn't I keep his dick hard?

I forgave him, but I went home with a lot to think about. He's lying already and we don't even go together. I am getting sicker and sicker. I'm in more pain after this baby, than I was with the first one. Maybe I'm doing too much, too fast. I told my doctor about my pain and he reluctantly gave me more pills. He said, he thinks I should be off the pills by now. He thinks I'm addicted.

I was offended by his comment. I don't need to be addicted to his damn pills. I'm addicted to weed, and that's all I need. I stopped going to church when I was eighteen. My grandma couldn't make me go anymore, so I stopped. I know I need prayer though after what my doctor said. He said, "If you have an abscess on your uterus, you are going to die."

Those are a strong choice of words, and if he said them to scare me, he succeeded. The pain is unbearable at times. I need help with even the little things. Maurice did get a job at a fast-food restaurant to help out and because he didn't want to hear my mouth. I am in so much pain that I don't even want to get out of the bed. I stopped eating because everything tastes so spicy. Maurice would bring all kinds of good food home from work. When I tried to eat it, my mouth was on fire. I drank a lot of water and ginger ale. I don't know why I feel so bad. I have been canceling doctors' appointments because I don't feel like getting out the bed.

The weeks turned into at least a month without me getting out of bed. The doctor said, since I still feel bad, I should take the test to see if I have an abscess. The way he talked was like he didn't believe that it was the problem, which made me feel better, thinking maybe it's just an infection. I took the test, but had to go home and wait on the results.

I received a call from one of the nurses within hours. She said, "You have an abscess on your uterus, and you need to come into the office as soon as possible."

I hung the phone up and saw my whole life flash before my eyes. I want to live to see my kids grow up. I don't want to die. The worst feeling is knowing you are going to die, but you don't know when. I am so scared. I told Maurice the news and quickly called my grandma. I could hear the concern and sadness in her voice.

I said, Grandma, I'm dying. Tears flooded my eyes. I haven't done all that I wanted to do. As we waited for my grandparents to pick us up, I told Maurice that whatever happens, never stop telling my children I love them. This could be the last time I see them.

When my grandparents pulled up, my grandma got out of the car and hugged me. She held me real tight, I knew she didn't want to let go. I didn't either, but we had to go. We got in the car and on the ride to the hospital, I looked out the window. Everything is so much more beautiful right before death. I treasured every glance, as if it were my last. If I die, it's going to tear my sister apart. She depends on me. I do have two children, and I want them to have a mother. It's been hard enough for me growing up without one. *Please, God, Help me!*

We arrived at the doctor's office and were called right back. The doctor apologized for accusing me of being addicted to pain pills. He also apologized about not giving me the test for an abscess sooner. I was hanging on to his every word. I would have to go right down for surgery now. They would try to drain the abscess. No extra cutting, just inserting some type of needle through the vagina, to drain it before it bursts. They put me in a wheelchair and rolled me through a long, connecting hallway to the hospital. I was put into a room where I changed clothes for surgery. Maurice was all to pieces. If he loses me, it will be just him and the kids. I know his mom will help, but to him, I'm the reason why he breathes. He loves me that much. I really need that kind of love right now. It makes me want to say, fuck everything, and just marry him! If I die today, that is something I can never say that I, experienced.

I had my whole wedding, already planned out! When I found the man that I could picture, sitting with me in the middle, of the ocean on a boat, at fifty years old. I would marry him, in a steepled church. The church would have, to have, one long aisle running down the middle. Flowers, everywhere! I would walk into a packed church. Wearing a pale silver, dress with matching heels and accessories. Especially, my crown. Not a tiara, a crown! My husband would stand there, up front, smiling as Boyz II Men played! Not a recording - I want them to actually, be there. There'd be doves and tears, released. Even a dedication, to my parents.

But now, it seems like I might be joining them, instead of enjoying myself. Enjoying my beautiful day. I was put to sleep and went in for surgery. I prayed, that I woke up. To see, all my family and friends again.

It's cold, as hell, in this recovery room. But that's a lot better than, waking up hot in hell! Hallelujah! I'm awake. I feel like my mama, is watching over me. And she's not, going to let anything bad, happen to me.

My doctor smiled at me and said, "We are out of the woods. We just have to go through the forest." I don't know what that is supposed to mean, but I hope it means I'm going to live. He said as long as I keep my appointments and take it easy, I should be just fine. Thank you, Lord! The taking it easy part is just that, easy. My housework has been suffering from it though. Maurice does more dirtying up, than cleaning up. Like most men!

Rodney was out of town during my whole ordeal. But, he did call. I think that is so sweet! When he got back in town, he came up to the hospital to see me every night. We would sit outside and smoke cigarettes and occasionally go for a ride. It made me feel good that he took time out of his busy schedule to sit with me. He made me another CD, this is number four. He always makes me a CD with songs, telling me how he feels. Maybe he is, the good man, that I've been looking for.

I told him that I have to stay in the hospital almost two weeks. It is the fourth of July weekend and instead of enjoying fireworks like I do every year. I'm trapped in here like an animal. Nobody even brought me a plate from a cookout. We went for a ride. But when we do, we can't go far because I have to be back for medicine at certain times.

Rodney took me to this deserted side street. We started kissing and fondling. I am horny as hell, and I don't think the doctor told me not to have sex. I don't remember him saying anything like that. I would remember something important like that. Plus it feels so good. Especially when he put his face in the place.

Okay, I'm going to do it, but if it hurts, I'll stop. I didn't hurt, I didn't stop. My ass was in the window on top of the steering wheel. A car came by with bright lights and saw a moon they'll never forget. He said, "Don't stop." I rode him until he came inside the condom. If I'm having sex, I'm going to be safe about it. I want to follow in my mom's footsteps, but not that close behind.

We listened to "Back at One," by Brian McKnight, and kissed. I think I am falling in love with this man. His charm can be overwhelming at times. He found me attractive, even when I was eight months pregnant. He is acting just as concerned as Maurice. I walked back in the hospital and just shook my head. I tried to fight back the tears. I hate for anyone to see me cry. I'm supposed to be so strong. I wipe other's tears, not my own. I am all fucked up. I don't know what I'm going to do. I'm confused, I don't know which one I want. *Do I throw away three years for someone who might not work out after three months?* He did tell me that, "I always get what I want." I wouldn't want to disappoint him. That's why I don't like making hard decisions. I know I have to but ... I have to weigh out the pros and cons. Maybe I can have both of them. I'm having both of them right now, and it's working out just fine for me. How come when you are in a relationship, everybody wants you? Then when you are single and looking, nobody wants you?

I went home and, remarkably, the house is clean, almost as clean as I could have made it. The closets are stuffed with crap, but at least it's out of the way. Maurice made me feel appreciated and loved. We had a nice night. All those nights of not eating paid off according to my waist line. I look and feel great with hardly any pain. We had a couple of good weeks together before the arguments started back. Maurice knows about Rodney so it got to the point where I would talk to him, on the phone right in front of Maurice.

Maurice is actually considering letting me have two boyfriends at one time, just so he won't have to lose me. Sometime or another he quit his job. That meant no money coming in. I'm so tired of this crap - he quits a job within 3 months. That is the longest he's ever been at one job.

The scale is slowly tipping towards the employed man with a car. I told Maurice to leave until he can get a job. Like always, he went to stay with his mom. It is Rodney's birthday weekend and I wanted the house to myself anyway. Maurice lost his key, so he can't get in unless I let him in, he has the kids.

I'm going to have sex with Rodney in my house for the first time. I might not because I'm on my period. He's counting on some when he comes over, but he might be disappointed. He came over, pissy drunk. I told him about my menstrual cycle before anything happened. He ignored me and went about his business. I learned that a drunk man will do almost anything. He did more than that. I thoroughly enjoyed the evening. It was then that I realized why the sex with him the first few times was not as good. His dick doesn't stay hard with a condom on. We laid together and slept through the night. He held me, and it was a beautiful moment.

When we woke the next morning, I went to freshen up for round two. He slept in his pants all night, but started to unfasten his belt when I came back in the room. I sat down beside him and we started to kiss.

All of a sudden, I saw my bedroom door swing open. Maurice and the kids are standing in my doorway. I jumped up and walked to the door to try to keep the two apart. I know it's about to be some shit. He called his cousin from downstairs to come and get the kids. I told him to calm down.

He asked, "What the fuck is he doing in my house, in my bed?"

Before I could answer, he grabbed Rodney by the feet and pulled him off the bed. He hit the ground hard. Rodney stood up, and they started to fight. Mostly Rodney was trying to hold Maurice back, even trying to push him in a corner. I think that was a bad idea because Maurice's arms were free. He kept punching Rodney in the face, first a right, then a left. I kept seeing his cheeks move up and down from the impact of the blows. I know they are about the same size, but Rodney is not putting up much of a fight. In fact, he is getting his ass whipped. Talk about the song "Contagious," I am actually living out the music video.

I yelled at Maurice to stop. I don't want him to fuck him up real bad. When Maurice looked at me I saw the fury in his eyes. It scared me real bad. I am scared of what he might do to me. I picked up one of the empty liquor bottles that I collect. I turned it upside down, and lifted it in the air. I will crack this mother fucker over his head if he tries that shit with me. I told him he has to go.

When he saw what I was holding, the fury in his eyes turned to hurt. He pushed Rodney down on the bed and walked towards me. I clinched the bottle even tighter and readied myself for the swing.

With watery eyes, he said, "I can't believe you would hurt me, over this motherfucker! He is a bitch! I'll even say it to his face." He turned to Rodney and called him a bitch and made reference to the song "Bia Bia," by Little John and the Eastside Boys.

I told him again to leave and to give me back my key. He said that he found his key over his mama's house. The only reason I didn't lock my bedroom door or the screen door is because I thought he had lost his key for good. It had been lost for months, and it was lost over his mama's house. He left the kids with me. According to him, that was the only reason he came over.

DEVASTATING CONSEQUENCES

Rodney didn't feel safe in the house so we left and went to a park. I wanted to access the damage to his face. You know he's light-skinned, so his face is kind of red, but he's not bleeding. Evidently he took those punches like a champ, but landing one would have impressed me. We agreed to go our separate ways for awhile. I need time to think.

How do I choose between these two men? Both were here for me when I was sick. Do I throw away three years for uncertainty? Rodney and I do have great sex, and I've been looking for that for a long time. I used to call Maurice my soul mate though. I can't picture him with me in that boat in the middle of the ocean. To be frank, he's too big. I think he may even be scared of water. We used to go to this boating dock and I wanted us to sit on the end, put our feet in the water, and talk. He could never make it more than halfway to the end, if that. I have so many good memories with this man and I have a problem letting go of people that I love. I hate change, and I try to avoid it. It will be a drastic change if I choose the other man. Think of all the people who won't like me anymore. Is it worth it?

We split up the days that we would have the kids. I went to take the kids to him on one of his days. One of his female cousins was there. I spoke, and she gritted on me. I guess she heard about the fight. She likes Rodney and is mad because I was supposed to be hooking her up with Rodney. Well, when she approached me about that, I couldn't say, no, he's mine. At that time, I was going with Maurice. I had to pretend like I was trying to hook them up, all the while informing him that if he ever had sex with her, his chances with me would be null and void.

She said she wants to fight me over him. *Why? Get over it.* I explained the whole thing and tried to get her to empathize with what type of situation I was in. She didn't care about what I said and still wanted to fight. I started to cry, not because I'm scared, but because that's how angry I am. I've fought a lot over the years and only lost once, and that was against a white boy. I fight dudes too, so what's one more fight? She does got me a little bit in size, but that might slow her down. How can she fight me over something that's mine? Rodney didn't give her one signal that he was interested.

Nettie said nobody can fight in her house. Maurice said, "Just leave it alone." I walked out the house, jumped in my car, and left. I am so pissed. It just makes me want him more though, just so she can't have him. On top of what's already going on, someone decided that he has a conscious. Fat Rob told Maurice that we had sex. What the fuck was he thinking about? Oh, my gosh, I could just strangle him! Maurice is still in love with me, and he still wants to be with me. He did call me a whore, though. I'll take that, but he drove me to that. In the back of my mind, I think he may have wanted Tiffany, and what about the other girl? None of my previous boyfriends cheated on me. It hurt deep. So in some ways, it was about getting even. Sleeping in a king-sized bed alone does feel good, but it gets lonely. I need to make a decision soon.

My birthday is coming up. I will be 21, and I'm going to have a party. I'll invite both men, and try to keep the peace. Shelly laughed at me and said, "You know they are going to fight."

It was scandalous, but I wanted to know how it would turn out. Rodney got locked up two days before my birthday. He was driving illegally and had a capiases out on him. He talked like he would be out on my birthday. He said he wouldn't miss it for the world. I think he is just trying to stop me from cancelling my birthday party. Which I am really considering doing. I bought a new outfit and my hair is already done. Why be all dressed up and nowhere to go, nothing to do? October 23, 2001, Happy Birthday to me! I am proud to be a Scorpio. Some say I'm on the cusp and that makes me a Libra, too. It's kind of weird reading two horoscopes. Even though both, usually describe me. I love two men, but it can't help with that.

I started off the morning crying. I miss Rodney. It's my birthday, and I can cry if I want to. I always wanted to say that. I'm going ahead with the party, and I hope he surprises me.

My sister paid for my second tattoo as a birthday present. I got my alias tattooed on my left thigh. *Queen Dee* or QD to you - get it, cutie? I like it. I forgot how much it hurts to get a tattoo, though. It hurt so bad that I couldn't cry. It was like it took my breath away; I could hardly breathe, much less cry.

I bought the biggest bottle of E&J that the liquor store had and a small, personal bottle. Then I made a sign that read DAMINIKA'S 21ST BIRTHDAY! I hung it right outside my front door. The party started around nine. Both my cousins showed up with their McNasty boyfriends, then there is Eva & Shaun. Some friends from the neighborhood stopped by. We were drinking, smoking, and having a good time. Maurice hasn't arrive yet. Everyone keeps asking me, where he is? My house is packed full of people., I don't even know some of them, but they brought weed, so it's okay. I am drunk as hell right now anyway, so not much really matters. I walked outside and down the sidewalk to talk to one of my friends. She had a blunt lit so I sat and talked to her a minute or two. Then I saw Maurice get out the car and walk in the house. My heart jumped, and I smiled. I need to get in there with my man.

I walked to the door and the screen was locked. They told me to wait until the song was set for my entrance. I waited until the signal was given. The song is "What if?" by Babyface. Maurice grabbed my arm and took me to the middle of the dance floor. We held each other and danced. The other couples joined us. I do wish Rodney was here, but this moment with Maurice feels so good. He mouthed the words to the song. It really made me think, not for long, though, because the alcohol and weed made me forget what I was even thinking about. A fast song came on and we all danced.

For a Tuesday night in the projects, we really have things jumping. Some of the coolest drug dealers from the neighborhood stopped by and rolled up. I asked them for some birthday cash, and they obliged. It made me feel good. This is turning out to be a good day after all!

Like always, as soon as everyone was having fun, a fight broke out in the corner. I looked in disbelief. Maurice had to break up a fight between my cousin Wanda and her boyfriend. I had a small wooden table at the bottom of the steps. That's broken, along with a brand-new tube of deodorant. There is deodorant and peg legs everywhere. Wanda was hollering profanities, and before we knew it, she spat on him. Maurice held him back. We took her outside and asked what is wrong. I tried to contain my laughter. She said, "We were both sitting on the couch, and I turned my head to say something to him, and he was staring at some girl's butt. I called his name over and over, and he was still staring. I smacked him in his face, and that's how we started fighting."

I said, where was I at? Okay, so the fight started at the couch and ended up at the bottom of the steps.

She said, "Yeah, he choked me out, all the way over there."

I laughed and shook my head, they always do this. I told her to chill out and enjoy the party.

We drank until the liquor was gone. I made barbeque meatballs so everyone had a full stomach before drinking. Some of us are prone to throwing up when drinking on an empty stomach. I'm one of them, and so is Wanda. We have to monitor her drinking because she throws up after her third beer. She gets carried away and we have to remind her, "Wanda, that is your second beer." We joke with her sometimes about being a little bit slow. I still don't think she got that joke.

I was warned that the police was coming. We tried to figure out who was the least fucked up to go outside and talk to the cop. I can't trust anyone else to act sober but me. I had police come in my house before, and it's not going to happen again. We'll keep his ass outside.

I stepped outside the door and closed the screen door behind me. I said, is there a problem, officer?

He said, "Yes, I got a complaint that your music is too loud. You are going to have to turn it down."

I said, no problem.

He read my sign and asked, "Is it your birthday?"

I nodded yes.

He replied, "Happy 21st Birthday. You have a good one."

I said, thank you and went in the house. Whew, I don't think I could have stood up straight any longer. We turned the music down a little and kept on partying. The party wrapped up around two and I was sloppy drunk by that time. When everyone left, I sat in a comfortable chair and closed my eyes. I can't move. I don't even think I can see. Oh, my eyes are still closed. I keep staring at the clock like the time is going to stop until I get up. I finally got up the energy to crawl upstairs. I took my clothes off and jumped in the bed, trying to keep all my liquor down. I have never been this drunk before.

I slept it off and I felt okay the next morning. I should say afternoon because I didn't roll out the bed until after twelve. Surprisingly, I did keep all my liquor down. Maurice called and asked if he could come over. I agreed. I know what he wants, and I'm going to give it to him, one last time before I start going with Rodney. We had sex downstairs on the floor. It was romantic but still not the quality that I get from Rodney.

DEVASTATING CONSEQUENCES

Maurice has been pressuring me to make a decision. He said, "You know I love you. I want you to be my wife. I want us to have a big happy family. That's what you always said you wanted."

I said, you never miss what you got until it's gone. I don't think you appreciated me enough when we were going together. Look how many times you cheated on me.

"I never had sex with any of those girls," he replied. I believe you, but it still hurts. They had your mind and your time.

He grabbed my face and looked in my eyes and said, "I'm sorry, I'm sorry for all the things I ever did to hurt you."

My eyes started watering and I thought about all the things I did to hurt him. I looked him in the eyes and said, I'm sorry for hurting you too, and I want you to know that no matter what, I will always love you. I'm going to always be in your life because we have two children together. You know we made some beautiful kids. He smiled. I don't want to see him hurt. That's what made my decision even harder. I wish he could read between the lines, because I don't want to say it.

I didn't say it either. I just left it alone, his ride came and he left. He's not stupid, he's in denial. I never wanted anyone to get hurt in all this, but that's not how life works. Those fairytale endings are few and far between.

Speaking of prince charming, I met the nicest, sexiest man. He works for the city; you know, cutting grass and keeping parks clean. He has the mustache and goatee that I was talking about. It gets me every time. I went over his house and we chilled. He doesn't smoke anything or drink. He doesn't really like that I do either. We don't really have a lot in common, and I told him that. He's not afraid to throw around a few compliments though, and he bought me a shirt for my birthday. We can definitely be friends.

The Friday after my birthday, I went to chill with the city worker. He's a fat boy, of course, but real sexy! In the back of my mind I wondered how much he was working with. We sat downstairs on the couch and watched TV. His aunt is upstairs watching TV, and I can hear it damn near over top of ours. I don't know how it came up, but next thing you know, his penis is sticking out of his pants. No pun intended. I was shocked. I hope my mouth is not open because that's just nasty. I wasn't expecting it to be so big! I touched it to see if I could pull off a sly handful test. I put my hand around it, and my hand did not even close. Fuck the handful test! This is width we are talking about, and I can see at least two handfuls with the naked eye. I looked at him in his eyes and said, Let's go upstairs!

He told me, "You have to go up the back way."

I looked confused. Back way?

"I'll go with you," he replied.

We went outside the backdoor and up some steps. It was something like what we had when we lived with the witch, a screened in porch. We went in his bedroom and laid together. I can't believe I ran across this kind of width. I smiled a lot while watching the movie. We kissed and started removing clothing. He said we have to be quiet because of his aunt in the next room. That made it even kinkier. It turned me on, and we started having sex, and it felt sooo good. I am the kind of girl that moans, and I have to keep them to myself. That is real hard, I tried gripping my lips together until they hurt, but he started going faster and I couldn't keep my peace.

We heard a noise in the hallway. His aunt is going to the bathroom. He slowed down, but stayed in it. I put a pillow over my face to stop me from hollering. He couldn't move a lot because the bed would make noise. He laid down beside me, and we waited. I don't know if she is taking the longest shit in history or what. I am tired of waiting, I'm falling asleep! I'm out of here. I put my clothes on and left out the same way I came in. Maybe we can try this again another time. I'll keep his number for future reference. It's funny though. I was worried about my breath because I smoke, but every time I see him, his breath stinks like garbage. I'll bring enough gum for both of us next time.

Rodney got out of jail the next day. I am, very happy to see him! We hugged and kissed outside before we came in the house. Some lady saw us and she commented, that it's good to see people so happy nowadays. We started officially dating the Monday after my birthday. You do the math.

Including Rodney, I had one hell of a full week. We have fun together even though he's just not that talkative. He doesn't enjoy every meal that I slave over like my ex, he's so damn picky. He doesn't do as much around the house either. I'm working on that. There is no perfect man, only perfect women to help mold them. Just kidding. I'm trying to mold him into husband material, I'm getting older now. Some of my closest friends are married, and I am a little jealous. Alright, a lot jealous, but I'm willing to wait my turn. I only want to marry once, and forever. I don't believe in divorce. So it has to be Mr. Right and until then, I'll settle for Mr. Right now.

Rodney treats me like the queen that I am, and he kisses that tattoo as if it's his name. He took me out and bought me a new TV for my birthday, to go in my bedroom. It impressed me that he is throwing around money like that. I've never had a man to buy me a TV before. Then I thought about it, and figured he probably went broke getting it, but it doesn't matter, it's mine. It did make me love him a little bit more, because I know he really has to care by trying to make up for the fact that he missed my birthday. The only reason I didn't already have a TV in my room was because Maurice took his TV back when he left, and the stereo. It did hurt not being able to listen to music as often as I wanted to, and having to go downstairs and watch TV without a remote was a pain. Now, we can, watch *Jeopardy* upstairs. We like to watch that together. It's nice to have a man smart enough to watch it! He just told me to pick which one I wanted, a stereo or a TV. It was nice to have an option. At the end of it all, he decided to show me, one more surprise! He got my alias tattooed, on his arm - a capital D with a crown sitting on top of it. Just to express to me, how much I really am his queen! Damn, I love him.

8

Rodney doesn't help with the kids at all, and it's like he makes it a point not to act like their dad. I guess trying to avoid another confrontation with their dad. Speaking of confrontations, Shelly brought a skinny, dark-skinned, short, ugly, girl over my house. She said, "This is Rodney's girlfriend and the mother of his child."

I laughed and looked her up and down. Is this some kind of joke? This bitch has on a Mickey Mouse overall bib outfit. Can someone spell tacky, and cornball? I looked at her in her face and with an attitude I said, I am Rodney's girlfriend.

The first thing out her mouth was, "That rat bastard." We talked for awhile and the more she talked, the more pissed off I got. I got the kids together so we could roll out. One last touch I have to comb out my wrap. I recently permed my hair and I made sure I combed it out in front of her so she could see how silky and long my hair is. The comb flowed through my hair with ease. I did a quick style by tucking some behind my ear.

Damn, I look good for a big girl; so what she's skinny? She's also ugly. She sure don't got nothing on me. She looks like a run-over bird. She rode in my car, and we made small talk. With hesitation in her voice she asked, "Is that Rodney's little boy?"

I said, hell, no, and then explained when I met him. She looked as if she believed me, but it don't matter no way. What was she going to do if it was? As long as she acts civilized, I won't have to backhand, her ass. We went over to Shelly's where the sting would go down. I would again lure him over, and then bam! He fell for it. He came over. As soon as Rodney walked through the door, she smacked him in the face.

He grabbed her wrists and held her. It didn't take much. Everybody fights over here so it ain't nothing new. They were screaming at each other, and he looked pissed. After they finished arguing, he sat down on the steps. He looked at me, and said, "I don't want to be with her. I'll tell that bitch to her face if you want me to."

I said, yeah, do that. She looked hurt after he said it, and soon left on foot. Rat bastard must be what she calls him at home because she used it more than a few times while visiting with us. I stood there with somewhat of a cocky swagger as I dragged on my cigarette. I saw her backpack purse flopping in the wind, and no, they are not in style anymore. I just shook my head. I was warned about the baby mama drama, but I just didn't believe it. *What have I gotten myself into?*

I asked him, how did you get away with not telling her where you live at, or your telephone number?

He replied, "That's my mom and dad's house, and they said they don't want her to know where we live at. She is crazy, and since we just moved, I just didn't tell her where. I block my number out when I call about my daughter."

I thought to myself, *Damn, he doesn't respect this girl at all. She doesn't demand much respect either. There is no way that I don't know where my baby's father lives.* I told him, she used to didn't know where you live or your phone number, I showed her both right before we came over here. He dropped his head and shook it. A lot was said, information overload. All I know is, he went home with me. I love his bald head, McNasty ass.

The thing about him is, he always makes it up in the bedroom, and sometimes that's good enough. Sometimes it's not, so don't get it twisted. I didn't let him get over that easy all the time. But I do admit, it was most of the time.

My cousins are no better. Wanda's man has two households that he alternates from bi-weekly. If both of them piss him off, he has a weekend house that he can frequent, too. They allow it. I call him The Game. He calls me The Gamette. He was hip to all my schemes back in the day before anybody else was. We compare notes. He acts like he is in competition with me. I give him his props. He taught me a lot, but the main thing is, you only get away with, what they allow you, to get away with. Secretly, we are so much alike that I know he wants to fuck me, but ... I won't go there for many reasons. One, he's Maurice's god brother. Two, he's my cousin's man. The most important reason is three: You can't handle all of this, and you won't get the opportunity to. Every time you look at me and say, "I can't stand you; you are not all that." I know what you are really saying. Take that Rodney! Just know that I can sleep with every one of your family members, if I want to. I just choose not to.

DEVASTATING CONSEQUENCES

Shelly has just as many problems with her man, with phone numbers leading to females getting cussed out on the phone. She may call him black and ugly, but he pulls his fair share.

One of the last things that Rodney's ex-girlfriend said is, "You can come over my house anytime and bring the kids. We can drink some beers or whatever." She showed me where she lived at while out riding. The next time I heard from her, she came over my house with a ring around her mouth. It was ashy and raw. I looked even though I tried not to. I know my face looks like something stinks. Ewe! She said she got it from Rodney, so you know what she was doing.

I said, what is it?

She said, "The doctor said, it's yeast, like one of his girls has a yeast infection."

Rodney said, "She didn't get it from me. Ain't nothing wrong with my dick. Have you seen anything? I didn't think so."

I let it go. Before recovering from one incident, I had another. This illiterate bitch had the nerve to write me a letter. Every word was misspelled. Pretty much it said she is fucking my man. Rodney tore it up. That didn't make it the end because I wrote her a real nasty letter back and politely left it on her porch. To sum it up, it said, Don't make me fuck you up, you liar.

I knew she was going to be angry, and I was going to park my car over Shelly's overnight. I don't know. I just have this bad feeling in the back of my mind. But, I decided to go on home. I got home late and I kept a close watch on my car until I couldn't keep my eyes open any longer. The second thought in the back of my head was that, that little bitch, don't have the nerve, to fuck with my car.

I went to sleep peacefully on that note. I woke the next morning and looked out the window. I don't see anything. Good! I got dressed to go over Shelly's house. When I walked to my car, my tag was hanging low in the back. I did a double take, there is grass hanging out of my gas tank. That nasty bitch, scratched BITCH on the trunk of my car.

I jumped in the car and started it up. Nothing, but hesitation. My car will not start! It finally turned over, and I whipped that thing like never before. I punched it over Shelly's and showed her what happened. She shook her head and said, "I hope she knows we are going to have to fuck her up for this one."

I agreed. We got the posse together. I don't need backup. It's just more fun with a lot of people there.

All together it was just three of us, we loaded up in my car. Once again, the car did not start. I tried again and again and the more I tried, the more pissed off I got. I heard my sister say, "Oh, she is going down. She scratched up the car and plus, now it won't start."

We switched cars and rode over to stake out the house. We parked in an alley in the back. Just then, a car pulled up around front. Even though it's the middle of the day, we jumped out of that car like camouflaged assassins. We ran down the hill and around the front of the house. I saw her standing on the front porch with a Bible in her hand. That's the only thing that saved her, because I was prepared to break that bitch's nose, over my car!

OK, she messed up my car in the middle of the night and then woke up early enough to go to church in the morning. I guess when you are on drugs, you really don't need that much sleep. She looks like a crackhead and her makeup job is hilarious. She is the same color as charcoal, but her makeup is the color of peanut butter. She didn't put any on her neck so just the middle of her face is brown.

Instead of trying to get in the house, she walked fast back to the car. I grabbed her and asked, why did you scratch up my car like that? She replied, "Why did you lie and say Rodney is not your baby's daddy?" I didn't lie! When we talked, I told you all about his dad. That's who both my kids are with right now. You acted like you believed me before. What changed your mind? Those same nosy neighbors have got some shit started again. That's another thing they are good for, getting shit started but not being able to finish it. They put all kinds of thoughts in this girl's head and what they did actually is hype her up for an ass whopping.

She jumped back in the car with her sister and her four kids. I blocked the door so she couldn't shut it. The sister decided to put her two cents in. See? That's why you should travel with backup. I had my sister for her ass, and I know Shelly can handle four little kids if she has to.

The sister was nice about things. That's the only thing that saved her. Pretty much she said that she would testify in court to what her sister admitted to. She wrote her number down, and I was satisfied for the time being. I pushed peanut butter face and walked away.

We went to take out charges on her. The magistrate said, "If you didn't see her do it, you can't take out any charges."

The criminal system is real fucked up. That's okay, I'll get my own justice. She doesn't have a car, but she does have a house. We put our heads together and came up with a plan. Within the next few days, we had a plan rehearsed and ready for enactment. All dressed in black, five of my closest friends and I got together around dusk. I assigned responsibilities and code names to each. No government names would be used on this mission. I have gloves for everyone because if we are going to do it, we are going to do it right.

#1 would knock on the door to make sure that no one is home. It's been said that she doesn't lock her back door so that will be the entry point. #2 would be armed with a knife to slash furniture and clothing, whatever is found. #3 will be armed with bleach to destroy curtains, carpets, etc. #4's job is to go through cabinets and the refrigerator and knock everything to the floor. #5 is the lookout, and then there's the boss. I will be armed with bleach also to finish whatever is missed. After we staked out the area for hours and waited for a neighbor to go in the house, the mission was a go. #1 already verified that no one is home. This time we are camouflaged assassins, we blend right in with the night. We ran in through the back door and went to work.

The adrenaline is pumping, and we went crazy. The more we bleached things, the more I realized that we are actually helping the place. The trashcan was already knocked over with stinky trash all over the floor. The smell is horrible, and it's dark. Damn it. I should have thought about flashlights. I don't want anyone to cut on a light. Do what you can, and let's go! We heard a small puppy barking upstairs. I started to feed it some bleach, but no, that's too evil. We didn't even go upstairs because we would need some light. We did what we came for, and we got the fuck out. We hightailed it out of there and met up over Shelly's house. I congratulated everyone for a job well done. We laughed at how disgusting her house was, and they agreed that the bleach probably helped. That meant I didn't do enough to hurt her.

I found out that something called dry gas would most likely help my car. They said it helped when someone put sugar in their tank. That made me feel a little better, because I can't function right without a car.

Over the next few days I came up with the perfect plan. I will call social services and tell them how nasty her house is. I will also inform them that she leaves her kids at home by themselves while destroying personal property. Let's see if she thinks that is funny. I thought about it hard. And before I made the call, I weighed out the pros and cons of doing so. If she loses custody of the kids, that means Rodney doesn't have to see her anymore. I told him I was going to get her back, he just doesn't know how.

I made the call and I gave my real name. I am not ashamed of the allegations that I am making. I want them to see how nasty her house is, and if she leaves the backdoor unlocked, you know she doesn't have anything.

More sooner than later, all four of her kids were taken away from her. They most likely validated my claims of her being a crackhead. They don't give notice that they are coming; they surprise you, no time for clean up. That nasty house that she is living in was taken away, right along with the kids. Section 8 was footing her bills - no kids, no house. She was forced to move back in with her mother. Ha, ha, ha. I just can't stop laughing. Serves her right, trying to mess up my stuff. I am prepared for retaliation though,. I kept my house even cleaner than usual.

Just like I expected, that same agency paid me a visit on a day when I was napping on the couch. Grumpy is not even the word to describe how I answered the door. I had to turn that around once I heard the man say, "Social Services."

I folded up my blanket and put my pillow away before I opened the door. Because of the delay, when I opened the door, he said, "Did you have to clean up?"

I said, no.

He looked around and saw my extensive zebra collection and the spotless Oriental rug on my floor. I'm sure he can tell I like nice things. He told me the reason for his visit. Before he could finish his sentence, I told him that I knew he was coming. I know who called you, and I gave him her name. He told me that it was alleged that I was outside, spanking a naked baby in the middle of winter. Even though the tears were already flowing from the notion that my kids might be taken away, I had to laugh at what he said. She couldn't come up with anything better than that. She'd been in my house before so she didn't dare use the dirty house card. That just proves how stupid she really is, because after weeks of thought, that's what she came up with.

The kids were visiting with their dad at the time, so the investigator said in order for him to close the case, he had to see them. We set up a date and he left. He didn't even go upstairs. He came back when he said and saw my daughter standing there looking just like me. My son was asleep in my arms. He looked at him, turned his heels, and left, just like that. I wouldn't have had it any other way. My children are why I breathe. I think that came across to him. Case closed, thank God.

I still pray, even though I don't go to church as much as I should. I'm waiting for my man to start going every Sunday with me. I didn't find that in Maurice, and Rodney is not to hip to the idea either. He says he'd be a hypocrite. We all have excuses for not doing what we should. My life has been getting worse the more I stay out of church. When all else fails, turn it over to God. I know God helped me out of so many situations that it's not funny.

I started going back to church at least once a month. I wanted to see if it would help me. I reluctantly parked my car, with the profanity on the back, in the church parking lot. The more the preacher talked, the more it seemed as if he were talking directly to me. It wasn't odd to see me cry at a service, especially with the help of a good song. Reverend Young would sing "Can't Give Up Now," by Mary Mary. I floated on his every word. He kind of reminds me of my dad. I always sit on the third pew from the back. My mom always sat there, it made me feel so close to her, knowing it was something she touched. My sister would join me on the Sundays that we happened to go at the same time.

I hate for people to see me cry, and I hold it back until I can't hold it anymore. I walked up to the front of the church and rededicated my life to Christ. It felt so good, just to let God know, that I am making a commitment for change. I prayed for the young lady that I was at odds with, that He would grant her peace. Peace enough to get over her vindictive ways because by this time, she had spray painted the wall outside my front door. She also had me arrested five times for assault and battery, and I had never laid a hand on her. She just kept going down to the magistrate and swearing out these warrants, and they picked me up on every one. They must have believed what I said because they never put the cuffs on me, but it was embarrassing walking through the projects with a police escort. I was fingerprinted and photographed like a common criminal. After about an hour each time, they would let me out on my own recognizance. It was aggravating, frustrating, and after the fifth time, it really got old.

One time I even had to call someone to pick up my kids because I was going to jail. She looked like a lying fool in court. She couldn't keep her facts straight, even with an iron. I sat on my side of the courtroom with crossed arms. They gave me a time for questions and comments. I lit into her and made her look even dumber. I laughed because I knew everyone could tell she was lying. The cases were dismissed. I told her I would pray for her, and I think it made her even madder. She says, she doesn't need my prayers, but I beg to differ.

Things calmed down a lot after that. Rodney professed his love for me everyday. It's like those run-ins with her, would make our relationship even stronger; it got better every time. I love this man, and he's in the running to be a husband. He used to say he would never get married. Now, he says maybe at thirty-five. I'm wearing him down, little by little. He knows most of my family, and I even introduced him to my grandma, and that's saying something. I warned him of her notorious questioning. It was rigorous, and you'd better be respectful with your answers. My grandma does not play.

As of yet, I have not met Rodney's mother. He says, that's a big thing and he's not ready for that yet. I'll be patient for now. Rodney and his parents received joint custody of his daughter with very limited visitations with the mom. They live in a very nice house in a nice neighborhood. Rodney signed up for Section 8 and was pushed to the top of the waiting list because it was marked as an emergency situation. He could pick a house or a nice apartment. He took me along with him on the hunt.

He said, "Your opinion matters to me. Do you like this house?"

It was a two-bedroom house on a dead-end street. Small, but not too small.

I said, I love it.

He said, "Then this is what I'm going to get."

It made me feel so important in his life, like I have a say in decisions. However, the landlord would still have to choose us over the other applicants. Soon after, Rodney received the good news and moved in. We christened the place as soon as he got his key. We made love on his bedroom floor.

His mom gave him a lot of her old stuff, just like Nettie had done with me. We make the best out of everything we have. I try not to bring the children over here with me, most of all because it pisses Maurice off.

Rodney has an aquarium full of beautiful fish. Some called Oscars, they are feisty little fish. I shouldn't even say small because it looks like they double in size every few days. I think he feeds them fish. We spent a couple of months in peace before his ex found out where he lives at. She broke the windshield on his car and flattened his tires. She just won't stop, and the police won't do anything because we didn't see her do anything. She so jealous that he is with me. Picture that a fat girl beating out a skinny girl. What are the odds?

The visitation with her daughter went from limited to nonexistent. With four less kids, she has a lot of time on her hands. She walks wherever she goes no matter the weather. She is no longer able to mess up my car because I don't have a car anymore. Let me catch you up. One night I was over Shelly's house, it was getting kind of late, but I told Rodney I would come over. We spend almost all of our free time together. I went to start my car and it wouldn't start. I tried over and over to no avail. Finally I went back in the house and asked Shelly, if I could borrow her car. She said she had to go to work in the morning, but she could drop me off. I didn't really want to get dropped off. I went to try my car one more time. Suddenly a strange blue spark came from under the hood. My car started straight up. Yes!

Shelly witnessed what happened and was outside to wave goodbye. I drove over Rodney's house and parked in his spot. He usually parks on the hill, and I park on the side, but since he's in my spot, I took his. He has his daughter tonight, and when I walked in, they were just sitting on his bed watching TV. I was there only a few minutes when we saw flashing lights outside the window, which is weird, considering he lives on a dead-end street. Next, we heard a very loud bang and looked out the window, we saw smoke. I thought my car was on fire.

Oh, shit! I jumped up and ran outside on the porch. There is another car halfway through my car. Rodney shook his head. I broke out into an uncontrollable cry. I can't believe this. My car is totaled! The car hit mine so hard that it knocked the tire off.

A policeman approached me and told me they were chasing a teenager in a stolen car. He said, "You guys are pretty lucky. If your car were not there, that other car would have gone straight through the house."

I just shook my head and told Rodney, I just saved you and your daughter's life. His bed is right in front of the window, and the house is at the bottom of a hill. The only thing that would have stopped that car would have been the house, and the car was pointed right at his bedroom.

I felt chills go through me and thought about the occurrences of the day, like that strange blue light that made my car start. If I would have been dropped off, I would still have my car, but not necessarily my health. The policeman also stated that since the car is stolen, I cannot go after his insurance company. I would have to sue the parents of this 15-year-old child. Suing the mother of a black juvenile that has to steal cars for a living - I pretty much just chalked that up as a loss.

Rodney told me he would help me, I can drive his car anytime I want. Which is something he does not have to do. Just like when he left me his car all those times when he went to jail. Those were the only times I ever interacted with his parents, mainly, his dad. He would bring me the keys to the car.

We watched the tow truck come and untangle the two cars. I already took what I could out my car, then I went in the house to lie down. This is all so overwhelming. Rodney didn't comfort me as much as I may have wanted, but what man does? I think he said, "I'm sorry," once. It's not that I think it's his fault, it's just if someone saved my life, I think I'd be a little more appreciative. We held each other the rest of the morning. I don't think I nodded off until 6am.

Things were rough after that with me depending on other people for transportation. I am so used to getting up and going, and now that I'm immobile. I feel like a trapped animal. My cousins come pick up me and the kids often, so it's not always that bad. Now the only car that Rodney's baby's mother can mess up is his, and she did. She threw a rock at the windshield and continued to flatten his tires. She is furious that we are still together and every time she sees us together, she does something else.

We chilled together one day until late into the night and then Rodney said he was going home. He hadn't stayed at his house for a couple of nights. I understood and kissed him good night. I didn't have my kids that night so when my cousin Wanda dropped by unexpectedly, I asked her to drop me off over his house.

We pulled up at his house and he is sitting out on the front porch, which did look a little odd for this time of night, but it is a beautiful July evening, so I rationalized it. I told him that I would come back out and join him but I have to go to the bathroom. I threw my purse on the bed and ran to the bathroom. I was just humming in the bathroom, excited to spend more time with my man. Just then, I heard someone say, "Rodney, Rodney." It was a female voice so I assumed it was his mom. I wiped off and pulled up my clothes while walking. Then I walked into his bedroom and saw his baby's mother standing beside his bed.

I said, what are you doing here?

She said, "Rodney invited me."

My eyebrows lifted even higher than they already were.

I said, oh, yeah.

I walked towards the front door. I shut, and locked it. Rodney is still outside somewhere. I want to get her version of the events.

She said, "He called me on his cell phone and left a message with my mom for me to come over. You can call her and ask her. Here is my phone number."

Rodney finally came to the door, banging and hollering. I pulled up the blinds so he could see me whip his bitch's ass. I don't know how she got by him. It doesn't matter though, she is here now. I noticed she was holding a bag. I said, so what's in your bag? I jerked it out of her hand. If it has some extra clothes in it, she is going down, and he is next! It has some E&J, my favorite liquor, and some orange juice. I should have taken it, but since my mind was eased a little bit, I gave it back to her. I said, so you thought you was going to sit over here, and drink and smoke with my man?

9

I opened the door for Rodney, who denied everything. I kind of believed him. Why would he want to be with someone who just busted his windshield? He loves that car.

I said, let me see your cell phone.

He said, "I lost it. I don't remember where I left it."

I said okay, and I shook my head a lot. A sign that, I was getting angrier by the minute. She took that as a warning and hauled ass out the back door. She saw there was no escape out the front and that might have been her smartest move. The only reason I didn't punch her in the face, is because she is good for taking out charges. Rodney and I argued and all kinds off thoughts went through my head.

He said, "The reason I was outside around back, is because I thought I saw the dog loose. It turned out to be a cat."

I think he was outside trying to catch her and stop her from coming over. She walks everywhere she goes, just like a crackhead. As black as she is, she probably blended in with the night.

We were arguing, but in between sentences when it was quiet, I heard some rustling outside the window. I heard it more than once, so I jumped up. I know she is not outside this window listening to my conversation! That infuriates me! I puffed my cigarette, and walked out the door very quietly. I walked to the side of the house and peeked. She must have heard me because I heard more movement. There is a light in the backyard which cast a shadow of her peeking back at me. Like a bat out of hell, I ran to the back of the house. I scared her.

I said, what is going on? She swung at me and missed. I said, oh, so you want to fight? I put my cigarette out, on that bitch's arm! In reaction, she swung and just grazed my face. I started punching her over and over. It flashed in my head that, I could kill this girl. *Stop! I'm losing control of myself! Get it together!*

I stopped punching her because I knew I could do real damage. I pictured her dying in the process and then we would have to hide the body, and all kinds of stuff. I bum rushed her, that knocked her down. She was hollering. Then I grabbed her hair and started yanking. I pulled that shit as hard as I could. She had a sew in before I started. While I was pulling, she grabbed the first thing she could reach, which was my nipple. She pinched and twisted it. I thought about dropping my whole body down on her head. That really might kill her. I finally got out of her grasp. That shit hurt! I pulled and yanked her hair even harder. So hard that I pulled out one of the braids underneath her sew in, not to mention all the tracks I had pulled out. My boob may hurt a little, but I know she's going to have a headache from hell.

Rodney finally realized what was going on outside and ran to separate us. She grabbed her stuff and ran! He said, "Just stop, for a minute. You are bleeding!"

He touched my face and pulled back a bloody hand. I said, she cut me! That dirty bitch cut me. He replied, "No, it looks more like a scratch."

I went in the house to look at my face. When I looked in the mirror, I saw a large, tear-shaped scratch on my face. The adrenaline went through me faster than a race horse. I am so pumped up right now, I could beat her ass again! I went back outside and saw her halfway across the football field next to his house. I ran as fast as I could, with all my might, to try to catch up to her. She saw me and took off running. The more I ran, the more tired I got. I made it to where she was standing and stopped. I'm out of breath and energy. But she kept running. She ran so fast that she was dropping stuff. I walked the rest of the way to see if she dropped anything of value. She didn't, so I walked back and Rodney was standing out there.

He stuck to his story and added, "All I want is you. I would never do anything to hurt you." I wanted so bad to believe him. We went to my house, and he begged to stay the night. Like a sucker, I did. The next morning, Rodney left to go to work. Shelly and some other friends stopped by. I went to the car to talk to them.

Shelly said, "You know Rodney's house burned down last night?"

My mouth dropped open, no way!

She shook her head yes.

I said, I got to call Rodney at work. I wonder if he knows.

Shelly said, "I thinks he already knows."

We jumped in her car and rode over to his house. The house is not totally burned down to the ground. The front of the house is intact with major smoke damage. I told my friends, that's okay, Rodney can come live with me.

You can see where the firemen used an axe to get through the front door. The fire originated in his daughter's room the detectives said. An accelerant was used. As soon as they said that, I thought about that bottle of liquor, that she had in that bag.

Rodney came shortly after we got there. He took it hard, but he was grateful for the things that the fire didn't touch. The fire was contained to one room because all three of the doors to the room were closed. Soot is everywhere. You have to be careful not to even touch the walls because of all the black stuff. Rodney's dad is talking with the detectives. He saw the scar on my face and asked what happened. He laughed and said, "You must have got her good, as much damage as she did here!" I still can't believe she had the nerve to do it.

The detectives gathered as much evidence as they could, including a lighter that was found in the backyard. We assisted by planting fake evidence. Her prescription glasses that she dropped while running the night before, we planted them in the front yard. Then we brought it to the attention of the detectives. She is going down this time!

We went downtown and took out warrants on her. I knew what apartment building she lives in, but not the apartment number. I made Rodney show me which apartment it was. We never had our day in court. Rumors are because she wouldn't answer the door for the police. Maybe, or we don't have the right apartment number. Rodney really seemed like he did all he could to bring her to justice. It's not my house, thank God. I hope she has better sense than to burn down a house with people in it. I prayed a little harder for her, as well as myself.

Rodney pretty much moved in with me. He only went home on occasions, mainly to oversee the construction project. He decided to rebuild and not to move. He said no matter where he moved, she would find him eventually.

I saw my life spiraling out of control. But the more I went to church, the better things got for me. I gave for giving's sake, and not just because I knew I would be blessed in return tenfold. It never fails; try it, and prove me wrong. I have given my last dollar because I knew I would get it back when I really needed it. I saw my loose change turn into something that will make your mouth drop.

After weeks of waiting and all the vigorous tests, that I aced, with God's help. I earned a position at my dream company. The same one that Fat Rob works at. This is a company that my mom used to work at. Making more money, than I ever have. It was like it was too good to be true. I won't start for a couple of months, October 21, two days before my birthday. The first 90 days are mandatory. Damn. I have a rule that I never work on my birthday. I will have to break that tradition this year because this is an opportunity of a lifetime! This is what I've been waiting for, for so long. My chest is still poked out with pride, more than I can ever put into words.

My grandma is one of the first people I told. She is very happy for me, but looks a little hesitant to believe that I'll keep this job for a while. My job history has been shaky at times. I was going through a transitional period, testing out jobs to see what I was good at. There was the proofreading job at the local paper. I did a fine job, but I think the supervisor smelled weed on me. They let me go with honors, and even gave me a pin to say no hard feelings. Fuck y'all! I loved that damn job. Now I have stepped up my game! From perfumes to body sprays. Blowing smoke from a cigarette on your clothes can cut down on the smell, too. Turning your face away from your clothing to blow out weed smoke is another tip. I won't give out all my tips for passing a standard drug test. Let's just say, Shelly gave me a tip and without going into a whole lot of detail, it involves a microwave. Now what I have to do is figure out which babysitter I want. Social service is going to pay for it.

I interviewed all the people that watched children from 3 pm - 11 pm. I picked this lady that sounded like she has the same principles as mine. It didn't hurt when she said she is from Bedford, like my family. I was hooked from there. Nettie said she would pick the kids up from over there when she gets off from work at eight thirty. She is overly protective of her grandkids, and I think some of her generosity was just being nosy. I'm thankful she is a good grandma though, so that takes care of that.

DEVASTATING CONSEQUENCES

I am however, concerned for the simple fact that I don't have a car. I am at this man's mercy. Rodney says he'll pick me up and drop me off. I stressed to him that I cannot miss a day for ninety days. He reassured me that I could count on him. He's good for getting pissed off and walking away. That might be one of my biggest pet peeves - for someone to walk away when I'm talking to them.

I nursed my face back to health. Slowly, but surely, with a cocoa butter stick. I rub it on my face two or three times a day. Usually not in public, because it makes your face, look really greasy. I wouldn't want anyone to make a fat joke. By implying, that I had been, eating chicken. People can be cruel sometimes, knowingly and unknowingly! I wished the scar would disappear before I started work. I was disappointed. I usually have such flawless skin. No bumps, no pimples, but now this. I call it my war wound.

I entered a training room to work, after not working in two years. I am the only black female with five black males; the rest are white. Our teacher is cool; he makes things easy to understand. I told everyone about my birthday coming up. I think Rodney is going to throw me a surprise party. There is this one fat black dude in my class that I would classify as my type. It's just that when he opened his mouth, it stayed open. He talks so much, he almost got the whole class in trouble. I do like him a little though. On my birthday, word came that Rodney would not be picking me up from work. It pissed me off a little, but I thought it might be part of his plan. The fat dude volunteered to take me home. I think that is so sweet! We broke for lunch and I went for subs with some white girls in my class. When we came back, I saw an envelope on my desk. I opened it, and started to cry! It's a birthday card signed by the whole class. So far, this is the only thing I received all day. I sucked it up, and said, thank you to the class.

The fat dude and I talked on the ride home. He told me he doesn't smoke weed anymore, but he sells it. I found that interesting. It was the next comment that left me totally disgusted. I asked him what kind of girls he likes.

He said, "White girls. All my children are mixed."

I'm not being racist, but I won't date a black dude that likes white girls. They are the ones that don't appreciate a sexy, caramel-deluxe woman like myself. He took me to the store, then dropped me off at home.

I don't even see Rodney's car when I got home, so that means no party. I walked up the sidewalk with my head and heart low. I opened the door and no one was home. I got in bed, rolled a blunt, and drank a beer. *Happy Birthday to me!* Then I heard his signature whistle, I jumped up and went downstairs to open the door.

He said, "My car is broke down. I will have to get it towed to the junkyard, to get it fixed." The next day, he got his car fixed, and while he was at the junkyard, he saw another car that he said I might like. He pulled up outside with the car. I looked out the window and fell in love with the car, a navy blue hoop. He said, "If you like the car, I will buy it for you. Go ahead and test-drive it."

I drove around the block a time or two. Everything works, I want it! I brought the car back and I told him I want it. The only reason he can afford it is because he got grant money for going to school. We picked the car up the next day. I love this man, he is so good to me! How many men buy a car for their girlfriends? He could have spent that four hundred on anything besides me.

To celebrate, we went to the park and smoked a blunt. It was that day, that I realized how long it really takes to smoke a blunt! We talked, and I agreed to pay him back for the car, but in installments. At least fifty dollars every two weeks. The clock was wrong in the car, and we lost track of time. We asked someone at the park, what time is it? To make a long story short, I am late for work! I panicked! I had to get Rodney to take the kids to the sitter. I punched it to work with tears in my eyes, and no one to blame but myself. What if I lose my job over this?

I told my teacher his car broke down. He said, "Have a backup plan; don't let it happen again." I didn't either. I passed the final test and put my ninety days in. My scar faded by the end of the training class, but not all my money problems. Money started to get tight, and I didn't pay Rodney some of the time. He grew tired of it and began to complain. It's all because Social Services said I make too much for them to help me anymore. I had to end up switching day cares. First of all, because it costs too much. Almost half, my paycheck. Second, the babysitter hit my son.

I spank my children, but it's totally different when someone else does it. I could have made her lose her license, but I didn't. I just laid her out on the phone because she tacked some huge fee onto the bill. I let her know I would not be paying it, and she can take me to court. I knew she wouldn't with the bit of information that I have on her.

She replied, "If you don't pay it, I'll turn it in to Social Services, and they won't give you any help you until you do."

I let her know, I am doing quite well with the money I make now. I don't plan to make any less. So if your fee does get paid, that will be saying a lot! I love this job, and I told my friends. I'm never leaving! They will have to fire me, and get a security guard to escort me out of the building. I won't go quietly.

People say if you get fired, you can't touch anything on your desk. They pack up a box for you to pick up at the front desk. I say, I'll be around to pack up my own box, when I'm ready to leave. Meaning, I plan on retiring from this company. I feel like my mama helped me get here. There are so many things that had to be just right, in order for this to happen. The only thing I don't like is how big the parking lot is. It feels like you have to walk a mile or two before you get in the building. Then the walk to your seat is another half a mile. I have to get me a fan to go on my desk, because by time I get in here, I have broken out into a sweat. If I didn't already feel at home, with the pictures of my family and my growing zebra collection. I did when I received my very own name plate!

Seeing my last name spelled out in white letters with a black background. It just made me feel how my mom must have felt when she got hers. I bonded with an older black lady who treated me like an extended child. She taught me the ropes and gave me the skinny on our supervisors. Speaking of skinny, I have the skinniest white lady for a supervisor. She looks just like the giraffe that she loves. I did grow to love her though, she has a heart of gold. We had our disagreements in the beginning, but she became attached to my personality, and I memorized her rules. I wanted to know what she expected so I could do it, without out her having to say anything to me. I don't take constructive criticism well, so I try my best to avoid it.

My other supervisor is a black man. He tries to show me he's cool by showing me how to get good radio stations at the desk. But he's married to a white woman, so he lost mad cool points right there. However he is smart and can help me out of any jam, so he's okay with me.

Right now, I am busy planning my vacation. We are going to the beach. I am so excited; I've never been to the beach before. The most I've ever seen is a lake. I can log onto the Internet to reserve our room. A room overlooking the ocean will be beautiful. Rodney agreed to go half on everything. A romantic getaway from the kids, with nothing but relaxation. That's just what we need.

The date is set, now I need a bathing suit. I also need to get my hair done. I can't wait. The days dragged on until my vacation started, but it's finally here. I got packed and double-checked things more than twice. I went over Rodney's to make sure he is packed. I asked, where are your bags?

He responded, "I'm not going."

I looked at him real confused, what? What are you talking about? What do you mean you are not going?

He said, "I didn't get my paycheck, so I'm not going."

I said, after I made all these reservations, you're not going? And some things are nonrefundable. So you would be responsible for that, not me! That's stupid. We can go, and you can just pay me back.

"I'm tired of borrowing money from you! I always have to get a loan!" was his response.

Well, now is not a good time for you to all of a sudden turn proud! I am ready to go! I'm ready to have a good time. I've been looking forward to this for a long time. You know I won't go by myself. I don't know where I'm going!

We argued back and forth like this for awhile until I wore him down. We decided to shorten the trip, but at least we are going. He got packed, and we left in the morning. The thing is, the license plates, on his car are expired, I wanted to switch them, for my tags but he couldn't get the screw loose on his car. The plan is he'll steal the stickers off somebody's tags along the way. We drove for hours before stopping for food and directions. I should have taken over driving from there, but I didn't. I guess I just wanted to eat. It doesn't make much difference anyway, because neither one of us have a license. Rodney is more of habitual offender, though.

DEVASTATING CONSEQUENCES

As we were driving, I noticed this sign that said Devil's Point. I always see these signs, and in the bottom of my stomach it was telling me, this is a sign. I said, no, and tried to ignore it. We drove no more than about two city blocks before a policeman came out of the cut. He just came from the other side off the highway, and on a humble, we met together at the same point in the road. He rode beside us for about another block.

Paranoid could not even describe us, or at least me. I hid the weed in my world-famous hiding spot. It hasn't failed me yet, right between the breasts. I've had to store a lit blunt there once so this ain't shit.

The cop trailed behind us. It's over. The lights went on! At least both of us have on our seat belts. I don't know what's going to happen. He approached the car, quoting the normal spiel. Rodney gave him everything he asked for, knowing it wasn't legal. I started praying, Lord, please don't let this ruin my vacation.

The wait was excruciating and drawn out. I thought, *What is the hold up? What's going on?* He finally came back to the car. He said, "Your license is suspended, sir, and unless she has a valid license, I will have to tow this car. You know as well as I do, I could have taken you to jail for driving, but I won't. Do you have a license, ma'am?"

Usually, when a cop asks you that, he takes your word for it. He wants my social and everything. I obliged, but prepared for the worse. I started to cry. Everything is crumbling right in front of my eyes. He came back after running me in and said exactly what I expected him to say. Then he added, "I've called the tow truck and he should be here in a few minutes. I'll sit here until he comes."

I just shook my head in total disgust. If only I would have paid attention to that sign. The tow truck driver pulled up and talked to the cop. Then the driver, came up to the car window and said, "Look here, you give me eighty-five dollars, and I'll take you out of this here policeman's radar, set you down, and you drive on your merry way."

I looked around nervously, but with a smile on my face, checking my back to make sure the policeman didn't overhear the plan. He was talking loud enough. *Damn, do you know how to whisper?* The hustler in me tried talking him down in price. He didn't budge. Oh well, split in two, that's not a big deal.

We hitched a ride for about ten miles, then pulled up in a gas station. We had to pay the driver before he unhooked us. He sat us down and before we could turn our heads straight, a policeman pulled up in the parking lot. I panicked. The tow man reassured us. It's not him.

The policeman got out and went in the store. We drove off and arrived at the beach an hour after scheduled. No big deal because when we arrived and walked into our oceanfront hotel room, our troubles temporarily faded away. Absolutely beautiful, the weather outside is warm but dreary. That doesn't take away one bit of this view. We took a lot of pictures. Then we went out to eat at this all-you-can-eat crab legs, shrimp, and steak place. I was determined to eat seafood while at the sea.

We let the food digest and had a couple of drinks. After we changed for the beach, I asked the front desk, does the beach ever close?

The response was no. That might be a stupid question for some, but I've never been to the ocean before. I know it was at least 1:00 am, when we went down to the beach.

I know about the dangers of swimming while drunk, but we did it anyway. I'm not going out that far anyway. I told Rodney to go in first, and then I walked out to him. The water is a little cold. I dipped my head under to get used to it. I didn't let the water get in my mouth, but from it just touching my lips, I can tell it's salty. Next, I wiggled my toes in the wet sand, and it feels great! I love it. Talk about romantic ... We hold each other and sway with the waves. It's fun to jump them. We both do it and laugh hysterically.

I love you, Rodney.

"Me too, babe," was his response. We played in the water, and since no one was around, we had sex in the water. Something else I told myself I wanted to do before leaving the beach. I forgot how sleepy swimming and sex can make you. The combination left me exhausted, so we returned to our room where we slept, with the ocean breeze blowing and the waves crashing upon the beach. I awoke to muffins, bagels, and orange juice. The view this morning is even more beautiful than the one last night. It's sunny and bright, and more people are out enjoying the day. Even though it's my vacation and I'm supposed to be totally relaxed. I know we are getting back on the road soon and I don't want to be pulled over again. Rodney never did steal a sticker. I am so paranoid about that. I'm driving from here on out.

We swam in the indoor pool and at the beach all before checking out. We really had a nice time, but now it's time to get showered and hit the road.

My stomach was in a knot the whole way down the highway. We took a back way that had less police. To make a long story short, we got home in one piece and ticket less. Phew! After we switched cars, I could relax more and enjoy the rest of my days off work. We stayed shacked up over his house for one more day and pretended to be still gone. I picked my kids up the next day and we got ready for school the following day. I returned to work a few days later with a lot of catch-up work to do.

There are so many rules around here. We have a telephone script to follow and if successful, the perfect score is a seven. I worked my ass off trying to get a seven. I did have an advantage though, sitting three desks away from the supervisor. I heard every time she was monitoring. I heard her working the tape recorder. Click, click. I made the phone calls at that time, seven calls. The rest of the time they are not much worse anyway. I just don't like saying, how are you doing? Because most of the time, I don't care.

My supervisor and I had a long talk about sounding happy on the phone. I asked, how do you sound happy on a day when you are not happy? From that moment on, even though she didn't want me to call it "faking it," that's exactly what I did. I smiled on every call, so my voice would sound like I'm smiling. I smiled, to the people in the elevator and the people in the hallways. I smile at everybody. I even say, how are you doing? Even when, I don't care. The least you could do, is smile back!

I had a co-worker ask me, "Are you this happy all the time?"

I said, not at home. Then I thought to myself, the marijuana helps a whole lot, too. I came to work every day high as a kite. Buzzed. I have fifteen minutes when I get here to read e-mails and check messages. I use those fifteen minutes to get it together enough to work.

I built a bond with another older lady with a funny last name. She sits right across from me and she laughs at all my jokes. My mother figure doesn't like her; she calls her fake and a suck-up. She says, "She sucks up to the supervisor and buys her stuff, just to get higher scores. She is what you might call a teacher's pet. Before you can blink, she'll rat you out behind your back."

This mother figure is in church and her husband is a preacher. She gossips more than the people who get paid big money to do it. I respect her, but it made me respect her less. I didn't even say ma'am when engaging in conversation with her. Which is highly uncommon, because I was brought up better, than that. Maybe it's because we spoke everyday. I don't know; I guess you give respect where it's due.

This woman brags about how much money she has. I'm not jealous. I'm proud of her, another black female who has made it. But sometimes her boasts were excessive. She does have a theory where it's *her* way or the highway. She's headed plenty of successful projects, she just wants to head them all. She put me in charge of things. I didn't want the added stress. It will kill my numbers. That's when she told me, "I get to sign off of the phone to do these things, and just put in an exception. An exception means they don't count that time against you." I was all aboard from there. Getting paid to do nothing.

I joined more committees, and I loved every minute of my free time. I talk a long time, and we stay a long time. Getting paid to do nothing but talk, I can get used to this. On the phones, you do more than talk. You have to listen. When you ask a question, you have to be ready for a response. You get those off-the-wall responses. If a customer curses at me, I have the power to disconnect that call. I have the power to say no to a refund if I want to. I have the power to give a refund if I see fit and how much I see fit. I do feel powerful! That's exactly how they want us to feel. It all depends on what kind of day I'm having, whether people get a refund or not. They discourage that, but I don't care. Luckily most of my days have been good ones. The people really love the smile in the voice. I've been complimented on it numerous times as well as the rapport I have with the customers.

I finally got my seven call. It was commemorated with a certificate and points. Daily Direct Points, they add up to buy an array of items. We traded points for doing great things. I gave when due, not like others who would fill out a whole page for a trade of the same. It lacked integrity, something I pride myself on.

My supervisor mentioned my culture. To quote her, "Culture is something that you are brought up with. I can't teach it to you. Your culture is unsurpassed." I thanked her for noticing. She mentioned, "Some of your fellow teammates lack it, and those are the ones who won't be staying long. You have to have it all, not just the numbers. Considering that, you are getting a raise."

An extra five hundred dollars a year won't hurt. As an incentive to making the numbers, there is a bonus. The bonus was rumored to pay at least an extra thousand on top of your paycheck. That program was cut down the same year I came. Now it's drastically less, and you have to work harder for it.

10

I bought a zebra throw blanket that made my desk look even better. Between the zebras and the radio, it kept me in touch with the outside world. It felt almost like home, anywhere but work. Don't get me wrong, I still love my job. It just gets monotonous after a while. You never know what to expect - that's what keeps me on my toes.

I am sleepy most days, and the glare from my computer is giving me the worst headaches. The headaches got so bad, that I had Rodney to drive me to the doctor. They tested me for glaucoma and other things. I thought to myself, *Yes! A prescription for weed*. I was wrong. They call it muscle spasms behind the eye. They gave me some medicine that took the pain away, but I am still squinting at work, so I started wearing sunglasses at work. Not too dark, cute butterfly ones. I am helping my eyes, yet being stylish all at the same time. I'm trying to memorize all their rules, I'm starting to get it down pat. There is a member of my team who is gay, I didn't know it at first. But off course, the gossiper filled me in. I don't have a problem with gay people and especially not him. He sits halfway across the floor but since I talk so loud, he heard a few of my conversations. He commented, "You are a natural. I can tell you are going to go far."

Our personalities go hand in hand. Not to categorize gays, but they are happy most of the time. Hence, the word gay, which makes them just fun, to be around. With my mother figure sitting right across from me, you'd think she could throw me a compliment once in awhile. She's good at accepting compliments though. I love her for who she is, but she does have her faults.

My cube mate and I work different schedules, so I sit alone most of the time. That doesn't bother me. I find it peaceful. You would think that means I don't have to talk over top of anyone. Wrong. There is this lady that sits all the way at the end, the last cubical in my aisle. She talks the loudest out of everyone in the building. She also brings a smile to my face every time I see her. She has this radiance, and perky is an understatement to describe her. She is happier than me. I've never seen her have a bad day. I can tell some of it is fake though, and that's what's so funny about it. I believe she is happy most of the time, but there are times when she doesn't want to be nice and does it anyway.

We are always having a food day to celebrate some made-up reason. Most times the food was good, especially store-prepared food. White people eat different foods than from black people. Three-bean salad is disgusting. I'm only picky about certain things. If the food looks good and smells good, then I'll eat it. If I can't smell it, or if it looks gross, I'll pass. If the person who made it looks like they don't bathe, then nine times out of ten, they don't wash their hands. You can put that right up there with my top five pet peeves.

I have hand sanitizer at my desk, along with a can of Lysol. If I think someone has sat at my desk, I clean everything. They could have been picking in their nose or anything. I don't even like when people touch my stuff. I labeled my stuff with my name, from the stapler to the tape dispenser. Lately, I had to put a label on my chair because people say sometimes they come up missing. I have the perfect chair for me and if anyone moves it, I'm going to be pissed!

I met what I thought was a friend on the smoking block. The more we talked, the more I knew I didn't like her. She thinks she is better than me because she takes her kids with her everywhere she goes. That's why her kids are bad and always in grown folks' business. She looked so stupid when she said she is taking her kids with her to Red Lobster for her birthday.

I said, where is your man?

She said, "I don't need a man. I spend time with my kids."

Maybe because her kids are a little bit older than mine, but what would I look like with a two and four year old at Red Lobster? Why throw my money away like that? Oh, I forgot, she lives with her mama and doesn't pay any bills! The funny thing is, she's perfectly content with that. I laugh to myself. *Can anyone spell loser?*

Strike two was when she judged me because I smoke weed every day, and she only smokes on the weekends. The way she looked at me when I said it was like I said I smoke crack. Disgust. I was disgusted by that. From that day on, I only talked with her at smoke break time. Casual conversation used to include gossip. But I don't tell her any of my business anymore.

Sometimes I would be late on purpose just to avoid talking to her. She approached me one day and asked me if she could borrow my zebra throw because she is cold. I agreed for the simple fact I am not cold at this moment. She returned it to me at the end of her shift. She started to approach me more frequently for it. Then it got to the point where she just kept it at her desk and didn't return it for weeks on end. I am pissed that I have to go over there and retrieve my blanket. That's rude to keep someone else's stuff. She needs to bring her own blanket if she is so damn cold.

On the way back to my desk, a supervisor stopped me and said, "You might not want to mess with that blanket."

My eyebrows moved into the intimidated position.

I said, this is my blanket!

She said, "I know. It's just that the girl that had it is out with the flu. You might want to wash it first."

I said, thank you for telling me.

I took it back to my desk and sprayed down both sides with Lysol and stuck it in my desk. I should charge her for my dry cleaning bill. When she returned, she inquired about the blanket. I said, I put it in the cleaners. Knowing full well it is still sitting in that drawer. It's none of her damn business. She violated the blanket rules. You borrow, you return. I ended up just washing the blanket myself by using some Woolite, and it turned out great. I let it air dry on my couch at home and I left it there for a while. I'll bring it back when I'm ready and even then, she better not ask for it!

Now I've been working a year now and the people at the Housing Authority have been asking questions about it. I can't hide it any longer. My rent will go from ninety dollars to over three hundred dollars, to live in the projects. *I can't do it, I can't see it. I got to go. If I'm going to pay that kind of money, I want a house!*

Nettie discouraged me from getting a house. She doesn't think I can handle it, and she doesn't think I can afford it. But when I want something, I'm going to try my best until I get it. I can't get Section 8 for three years because of my marijuana possession charge. I refuse to give up though. God blessed me with this job, and I went to Him for the answer about my house. It didn't take long before He pointed out to me this little black-and-white house on my route from work. I wrote down the number and called the first chance I got. Rodney went with me to look at the house.

The owner left the key on top of the light on the back porch. It has two big bedrooms, living and dining rooms, and even a screened-in back porch. A sunroom even, or whatever you want to call it. I love it! It's a secluded spot back off the street with a nice yard with a private alley entrance.

When we first pulled up and looked at the address, it was like God gave me a sign, 777. I asked Rodney, does that say 777 or 111. It looked like both. There are two signs. We looked at the neighbor's address and discovered it is 111.

I jumped on it and filled out all appropriate paperwork. About two days later, they called and said if I want the house, I can have it. I am so happy! I saved up enough for the deposit and first month's rent. Nine hundred is not easy to come by, but I have it ready. The catch is that they won't wait until my thirty days is up with my landlord. They won't hold the house. You know what that means? I have to move right now within two weeks instead of next month. My landlord understood and cut me a break. He better. I've been living here for five years.

We packed up everything that's going with us. Most of the items will be sitting at the curb because it's infested with roaches. We are not taking any bugs with us. We have bombs to put in the back of the moving truck. Smoke them out before arrival. We moved in and made ourselves at home. Only being able to unpack on weekends and late at night made it go by very slowly. I rushed to get everything exactly how I wanted it, so I could see the finished product. I finally found a zebra rug for my living room on Mother's Day. All the other ones I'd seen were black and off-white. I wanted one that is black and white. I saw it, and made a quick U-turn. I hustled the price down to what I had in my pocketbook, then I walked away a happy mother. Nobody's going to be walking on this with their shoes on.

I wasn't the only one happy though. I got my daughter a puppy for her birthday. She'd been begging for one, a little white one named Snow White, nicknamed Snowy. She is a beautiful dog. Your guess is as good as mine as to what she is. We'll call her mixed. She was so young when we found her, she couldn't even bark. We kept her in the house through the first winter months, trying to house-train her. It didn't work out too good. First of all, we didn't give her free run of the house because she sheds so bad and she's known to crap in the most unexpected places. She also chews on whatever she can get her mouth around and will tear up anything she can find, stuff I didn't even remember I had.

The kids love the dog, and she is quickly becoming an equal member of our family. Snowy was growing fast and it wasn't until she broke out of her first habitat that we put her outside. She stayed in an old playpen of my son's. She was in there almost three months before she learned to chew through it. She got out and shit all over my back porch.

Even though Snowy is my daughter's dog, I did most of the cleaning behind him and feeding him. The dog broke a loose one day when I had got off work early. I got home just in time to catch him. Yeah, I said him. I know it's a girl, but I always call her a boy. I told her not to be offended. Rodney doesn't like the dog because it's not a name-brand dog. I don't know the difference. All I know is some cost more than others. In my book, they all do the same thing - bark, crap, and eat. Dogs are more work than I thought. As a kid, you don't work this hard with a pet. You just see the fun times. I forgot all about that.

Even though I'm working on Rodney to make him start paying some of the bills, I made sure I could afford it without him. What do I look like, moving somewhere really expensive and counting on him to help out? Then he loses his job, and everything falls on me. I won't be caught with my pants down. So many people doubt me already. I want to prove them all wrong. Especially, that fat bitch Kam. I want to prove to her that, the best revenge is success. Grandma made sure the news spread about me having a house. Thank you, Grandma! I have always agreed with subtle bragging. I don't have to tell you, or show you! Word of mouth is something you can't put a price tag on. If you live in Roanoke, you most likely know or have met my grandma at some time in your life. She's just one of the people that I feel I should be paying to work for me - my boasting entourage!

Rodney's resume is almost as blotchy as Maurice's. He gets jobs and don't stay that long or calls in during the first week. I make good money and I need someone who is going to help me.

Another expression I live by is ... I can do bad by myself; I don't need no help! Love, doesn't pay my bills! That was just one of the problems with my ex. I hope I can expect more from Rodney. I'm not one to hold my tongue for very long. I made him feel the pinch and let him know he better step it up. I don't get child support because my kids' daddy is sorry, in that aspect. But he does watch the kids when I need him to. If I pursue child support, he will most likely be in jail and I don't want that. Take another father from his kids? No thanks. Rodney doesn't let his daughter come around us for some reason. Like he's scared of what his baby's mama might think. Do I smell a small amount of respect? The only thing he has ever done in front of me, to show respect for her, was to give her a ride home after one of our small confrontations. Even though it pissed me off a little, I understood.

It doesn't look like he likes it when I call her crackhead. Hey, I have to call them like I see them! I have little to no respect for those type of people. There's also a certain amount of pity, I feel sorry them. We all make choices and decisions, where we weigh out the pros and cons. Most of all, the consequences. That's number one in all of my decisions. The consequences. To all of those who don't like the term I use - crackhead - most likely that means that you smoke, and I'll say this: You can sugarcoat the name, but it still doesn't change what you are, or the people affected by your actions.

I've seen what crack can do to people. The look in their eyes is frightening. Households deteriorate, marriages crumble, trust is broken, and valuables sold. I remind Rodney almost daily, that I need to be able to trust him. He reassures me, "I love you, and I want this to work." He started doing more stuff around the house. He already takes out the trash. That is a stipulation he must meet because I don't take out trash, and I don't like it building up. I feel as if, since I am a lady, I don't have to touch trash. Women should never take out trash if they have a man, or carry anything heavy, for that matter. I laugh at those who do. Rodney knew what kind of person I was before getting into this relationship. He watched from the sideline for months. I don't hold back any of that. I expect the same from him that I expected from Maurice. No exceptions, just because he is light-skinned with pretty eyes. I usually don't like light-skinned people because of their cocky attitude. He reminds me so much of myself, that's what drew us together.

Those same factors that brought us together, are what cause most of our arguments. We are both stubborn as hell. He wants his way, and I want mine. I won most of the time and fed his ego to let him win a couple of times, but nothing major! I told him helping me with food is good for right now, but that's food stamps. He is not showing any initiative, I discouraged selling drugs. I'd been there and done that. I'm trying to do everything legal now, down to the license. Selling drugs is easy money, and money is money, and that's good enough sometimes, but I want more for him. He stays with me most of the time, but it feels good having the choice of making him go home.

Rodney discovered after time that he doesn't do well with animals. He's not at home long enough to take care of them. Approximately ten pets have died under his care, including, but not limited to, dogs, fish, and hamsters. I hinted that maybe he shouldn't waste anymore of his money. I love him, but not enough to move in his gerbils, hamsters, etc.

We had to invest in a better dog chain, because Snowy continued to break a loose. It's up to about seven times, I call her our miracle dog because she continues to come back unscathed. We don't live far from a busy intersection, and I've seen her duck and dodge between cars to respond to my call. I think there's a reason why we have this dog. We found her, and she keeps finding us! We might have saved her life, and she just might save ours! I don't know why she leaves, almost like she comes and goes as she pleases. We had to step up the way she is tied up. I bought something like a clothesline that connects to two trees. Since it runs through the air, it's less likely to tangle. That's the problem anyway. She would get so tangled and try to break free.

Dogs are so stupid. Why can't they just figure out if they go back the same way they came, the line would untangle? After I invested big money in this state-of-the-art leash, I came home from work one day, and he was gone. We looked and looked until it became hopeless. I started to cry. She has never been gone this long before! The children's faces turned from desperation to despair. Rodney said, "Maybe she's not coming back this time."

If looks could kill, he would have died at that moment. I shot him a look that made him quiver. Around here, we think and talk positive.

Even though raising Snowy was similar to having an extra child, something I cannot afford or need. I miss her presence. It hurt more than I thought it would. I became very attached to that dog, and that fueled my fire. Some may call it desperation or a waste of time to put news about her disappearance on the Internet, but I did and I called the local pound, too. I want to do all I can to get Snowy back.

The chances grew slimmer as the weeks passed by. Cookouts didn't seem the same with no dog around to throw the dropped meat to. But we carried on in spite of.

Family gatherings mean spade games, and I label myself a professional. I learned from the best, my mama. She taught me everything there is to know about spades on a cold, snowy day. In fact, I think it was during a blizzard, when we had nothing but time. Rodney doesn't like to lose, especially in our own house. A tie is okay, but we will play until we win at least once.

Another situation where I feed his ego. Don't get me wrong, I don't like to lose either, but he hates it more than me. The game was getting good when we were interrupted by the phone. Someone said, "I got your number off the Internet, and I think I have your dog."

I perked up, but was still very reluctant and doubtful. They described what the dog looks like, and the collar style. It sounds like her, but I don't know for sure. They told me where the dog was found. I think it is her! I got so happy. I shed tears of joy. I rushed to get my shoes, I gathered the kids and told my company that I would be back. They'll be okay until we come back from around the corner. Rodney told me not to get my hopes up. I tried not to, but that failed. My heart is beating so fast, the excitement and anticipation is building. We pulled up in the parking lot of the store that was designated. We failed to say what color car each other would be driving, so we circled the entire lot and then parked near the front. Another car did the same, then numerous people got out.

I looked, just waiting for Snowy to come running around that car. I opened my car door and got my daughter out of the back. I heard a lady say, "Is this your dog?"

DEVASTATING CONSEQUENCES

We looked at what was at the end of that leash. It is Snowy!

"Hello, Snowy; we missed you so much," replied Zay Zay, almost in harmony with me.

I am so happy to see her. Her tail wagged in joy. I took the leash out of the lady's hand and said, Thank you so much for returning our dog. We wished she would have made it home for Christmas. But now is better than never. We really appreciate it. You can just say thank you to someone, but I always like to let them know, that I appreciate it.

The lady responded, "You are welcome. We are glad that we could reunite you guys. You know, I have a doghouse she can have. Do you need one? You would have to follow us to our house to get it, but you are more than welcome to it. Otherwise, I will be throwing it out."

I said, that would be nice! We followed them to their home, in what I call the cut. There were a lot of twists and turns. These may be the nicest people in the world. They took my dog in, fed her, and looked for the owner. She said she could tell Snowy was a house dog because of how white she was. I feel so grateful to have my dog back. It really does feel like she is a member of this family. I don't have much money on me, but it feels like I should give them something. I pulled out my last five dollars and approached the mother of this nice family. I told her I don't have much, but at least I can pay for her food while she was here. She refused it firmly. I thanked her again and left with a smile on my face. There are still descent people left on the earth. I can tell Rodney is not what you would call happy. He had talked about getting a pit bull puppy in her place. He wanted me to treat that dog like I treated Snowy. He often mentioned how good I treat Snowy, including, but not limited to, me getting up in the middle of night for a forgotten evening feeding. Now that she's back, he knows his pit bull plans are off.

Everyone is entitled to an opinion, but it's the nonreactional moments that get me the most. Rodney didn't even pretend to be happy or happy for me. I resent that. Everyday I pretend, I give people the reaction that they want. I tell them what they want to hear. Like when someone at work shows me a picture of their child. I feel obligated to say something, like how nice, or, they look just like you. Some people will look at a picture and hand it straight back to you and leave you to give your own child a compliment. Try it out and see.

I very seldom call children cute or pretty unless they really stand out. My children are so beautiful. I have seen few that even compare to them. I know they could be models, but I don't have the money that it takes to make that money.

Some mothers go bankrupt trying to back their children. They move to big cities or commute. I'm not going anywhere without my sister. Add my brother and grandma, for that matter. I can't leave them behind, plus I'm to scared to leave. I'm scared of change. I'm just now getting street names memorized where I live, and I'm 23 years old. What if it takes twenty-three more years to memorize them out of town?

Before I do anything, I have to picture myself doing it. The places I could never picture myself living, are New York, Florida, California, or Texas because they are as follows too big, too hot, or too big and too hot. I like where I live for the simple fact that it's just right. Not too big, and not too small. There is always at least one black club jumping off. I still manage to get out to one every once in a while. Virginia is for lovers, I can see it. I'm in love, and I want to marry this man!

I'm looking for my soul mate, and even though I love Rodney more than anything. I don't feel him in my soul, mostly because I can't convince him to go to church with me. Whoever I marry, I don't want him to just attend church. I want him to get something out of it. That's something that you can't force. Maybe it's something that can be taught. I'm trying! I'm trying to mold him, I think it's working. He has his faults, and he knows how to push my buttons. We argue just like everybody else, and it usually ends with him walking away while I'm talking. He knows that pisses me off. The thing about it is that he always comes back, within 24 hours. He misses me, and he doesn't like to be alone.

I don't like to share my bed with anyone else but him. That includes my children. They want to sleep in my bed when Rodney is gone. No way; if I'm not happy, nobody's happy.

Sexually, Rodney does everything just right. It doesn't always last that long, but the quality is next to none! He has a very healthy sexual appetite, so we do it almost everyday. I'm trying my best to make sure I keep up. I don't want to give him any reason to stray.

I was surprised to hear that Rodney got a job out where I work. I don't know how that's going to work. I won't have any time away from

DEVASTATING CONSEQUENCES

him. We both realize that sometimes we need a day or two to miss each. Every once in a while won't hurt. It makes the love grow stronger, and the heart grow fonder. He pointed out the fact that he'd be working on second shift. Just the thought of the combined income made me smile. Finally I can get some help with these bills. Once he started training class and the money started rolling in, he did help me with the bills. He even gave me money for groceries. I can tell he is trying.

We hardly see each other at work. When we do, he doesn't act how I want him to act. I'm proud of him, and I brag to my friends about him. I let everyone know that's my man. I want to be lovey-dovey every once in a while. He doesn't. He never kisses me in front of co-workers. I don't know what's the problem. He usually doesn't have a problem with public affection. Lord knows, we did it in public enough times. He wants me to be awake when he gets off from work. That's around 1am. He wants me up and ready to smoke a blunt. But I have to go to work in the morning, and I need my sleep. Sometimes he understands, sometimes he doesn't.

Occasionally I set my alarm clock, so I can wake up and sit with him. I feel every minute of that the next day, when I'm nodding at my desk.

I don't think I could have stressed anymore to him, that the first ninety days are mandatory. He still missed a day. That's exactly what happened, and he was cool as a cucumber. I was panicked just from being late. I said, you are going to be fired! He made up some lie. I think he said he was in the hospital or something. I said to myself, I can't control whether he gets fired or not. That is his stupidity! I can't let that stress me out. As long as I still have my job, that's all that matters! I guess they bought it, because he was back in training the next day. Why didn't they fire him? Maybe they just say that to scare people into showing up every day for the first ninety days. Emergencies are excused, I assume. They don't double check. Whatever he does or doesn't do, I can't let him bring me down with him. I'm not leaving, I am good at what I do, and I take it very seriously! I really don't think he has what it takes, anyway. He doesn't even talk. I have to make him talk at home. I'm breaking through to him, though. He tells me more stuff now. We'll see how long he makes it here.

I smoke every day, in the morning before I go to work, on my lunch break, and before I go to bed. Not many people know that. Rodney does the same thing, and he goes to work with his eyes red and smelling just like weed. He is starting to make me look bad. I don't want his actions to reflect on me. I spray perfume, and I don't let the smoke get in my eyes. I blow it straight out the window, which can get very cold in the wintertime. I feel like I have to smoke on my lunch break, just to make it through the day. It gives me the ability to be happy when I'm not. I can laugh the day away, and no one is the wiser.

It's tax time, and I took the bulk of my money and bought a new car. A real good deal! How would you feel going from a 1981 to 1999 car? I know I look good in my champagne-colored car. I call it gold, and it rides like gold.

While riding around, we decided to stop at the liquor store. Rodney and I got out and walked to the door. All of sudden, I saw this girl riding by, waving at Rodney. She wasn't waving at me, because I don't know her. She is in his training class. I asked him, why the fuck is she so happy to see you?

He laughed and replied, "I guess because she's in my class. Stop tripping. Everybody knows I go with you. Come on now, she works in the same building with you. I'm not that stupid."

Don't make me fuck her up, Rodney. I swung open the door to the liquor store. He just shook his head. He knows I'm serious, though. My scar just recently healed from my last brawl. I'm glad it's gone, even though I proudly called it my war wound. I'm ready for World War II if I have to. I won't let the same thing happen twice.

When Rodney got his own desk, I made frequent visits, just to be seen. That girl sits right beside him because of assigned seats, but not for long though. She moved to third shift. One less thing for me to worry about. I want him to put up a picture of us. Or just of me. The one and only picture that he has up, is of his daughter. I finally convinced him to go take pictures with me, knowing full well about the picture-taking jinx.

What is the picture-taking jinx? There is a jinx, that says every time a dating couple take professional pictures, they breakup before the pictures even come back. My sister and I have been witnesses to this jinx.

I made the appointment for two weeks after Valentine's Day anyway. I guess they get busy around that season. For Valentine's Day, we went for a drive. We ended up in Christiansburg, in the middle of a snow storm. We got a hotel room with a red Jacuzzi bathtub, shaped like a heart. He got me a big gold teddy bear, two dozen roses, and dinner. I got the drinks. I also bought him some new tennis shoes. We had the most romantic evening, and we didn't check out until well after two the next afternoon.

We waited until the snow slowed down some. I don't like to drive in that kind of weather. I like to be snowed in, with everything I need, just like we were. A snowy wonderland / fairyland. We stopped for breakfast after inching our way back to Roanoke. A buffet, and it is delicious. We just plain enjoy each other's company!

I think I'm one of the only ones who can make Rodney laugh. It's a cute laugh. He laughs at stupid stuff and disrespectful stuff. This is one of the most memorable holidays by far. I love him, and he loves me. Sometimes I think he loves me more than I love him, just by his actions. It was when we got back that reality set in. He didn't go to work! He didn't call in, and a combination of the two is what got him fired - that and a whole lot of other things that he didn't wish to elaborate on. Mostly a lot of other things!

I just started shaking my head. A fool gets fired, but with the money we make, you'd be an even bigger fool to quit! I throw my hands up at him.

11

I just recently got my tooth pulled, which was making my ear hurt on the inside. The pain grew more and more excruciating! I am popping Aleve like nobody's business. I went to work regardless, I don't like to be sick on my off days! Most of my paid days off are not scheduled, like they prefer. I just call in whenever I'm too sleepy to show up.

I told my supervisor and some of my friends about my ear problem.

One lady mentioned, "You should not play around with your hearing."

That comment scared me, so I went to make a doctor's appointment after my last call. They can squeeze me in early this morning. I informed my supervisor that I am leaving. I don't ask. I told her that I would try to come back, if all they do is give me some medicine.

When I left she said, "I hope you feel better."

Thank you!

My family doctor took a look at me and said that I have an ear infection. He gave me a prescription for some eardrops and antibiotics. I drove to the pharmacy to drop off my prescriptions, then I went home. I don't see Rodney's car. I went in the house and laid across the bed. I turned the TV on and enjoyed a couple of videos. One video made me get up and dance. I shook what my mama gave me and dropped it like it's hot! Then I came to a complete halt. Something in my gut said Stop! Just stop! What if he is at home? Let's go see!

I grabbed my purse and my keys and walked out the door. Once in the car, I noticed, I am all out of cigarettes. I started up the car and began to drive. I thought to myself, *I'll get cigarettes later.* Later - that don't seem right. I need a cigarette now! It's almost like I don't have enough time to stop!

As I got closer to his house, a sad song came on the radio, "Never Gonna Let You Go," by, Faith Evans. A sad song, it was like a sign. I shook my head no. *I'll prove you wrong.*

I pulled up in front of his house. His car is here. Yes! I bet he's in there playing his game or something. I got out of the car and shut my door just enough to turn the light off. I didn't boop, boop, my car alarm like usual. I want to be quiet. I walked down the hill to the door. I reached for the doorbell, but instead grabbed the handle to the screen door. I opened it. That's funny. He usually locks this. I turned the doorknob and swung the door open. There is movement coming from the area of the couch. I looked in confusion, I saw the face of his baby's mother. It looks like they are wrestling or something. That's when I heard the moans. He is bouncing her up and down on his dick. They are having sex right in front of me. She looked up.

I heard her say, "Oh, shit!"
She finally saw me, he peeked from behind her.
He said, "What?"

He pushed her off of him. He jumped up, and ran to the door covering his penis. Most likely because, he is not wearing a condom. Remember, he can't keep his dick hard with a condom on! He struggled to put his clothes on, while she just stood there with a mid-drift shirt on and nothing else. Naked from the waist down. All of this happened within 70 seconds. Many of you are asking the same question. *What the hell did you do?* I'll tell you the same thing that I'll proudly tell anyone else. I WALKED AWAY! I turned on my heels and walked right back out that door. A million thoughts raced through my mind during those seventy seconds. Number one, murder! If I would have taken one more step inside that room, I would have killed both of them. I would not have been able to control myself. I would lose my job, my kids, and my freedom.

Rodney ran after me! I jumped in my car, locked all my doors, and threw that car in reverse. I backed my car all the way down that driveway. Something rare, because I was always too scared. That driveway is long and narrow. I am even more afraid of him though. Once he realizes I don't want to be with him anymore, he might try to hurt me! I am all to pieces, I can't stop crying long enough to drive. But I did say, Thank you, Jesus! Thank you for showing me that. Two million more thoughts raced through my mind. *Picture jinx*. Ha. That's not even funny. Next I thought about my safety. I made an abrupt stop at a hardware store.

I sucked it up, dried my face, and went inside. I asked the clerk for his sturdiest lock. He pointed out some samples. He said, "Now this one is what they use at hotels. It works just like this. You won't be able to burst in." It was his demonstration that made me cry. I looked around, watching my back. He would see my car if he rides past. I have to go. I paid for two locks and I left in a hurry. He has a key to my house, and I doubt he's going to give it back. Who's to say there's not a copy? I know the cashier could tell something was wrong. I couldn't hide it but so much. I am totally distraught. I drove fast to the house. If paranoia had not set in already, it definitely has now. I opened all the blinds and curtains, so I could see him coming from every angle. I rushed to get that lock up on the back door. It's the only door he has a key to. I did the best I could. I think you are supposed to use screws instead of nails. Oh, well! I'll reinforce it later. I want to show him I'm not playing. An hour or two passed before he graced me with his presence. I had time to call my supervisor and tell her, I will not be coming back in. I just had a life-altering event happen.

He pulled up and got out, smoking a cigarette, wearing a black hat that covered his eyes a little. He knocked on the door.

I asked, what do want?

He replied, "I want to get my stuff."

I didn't even notice the decline in items that he has here.

I said, come in and get your shit! Then you roll the fuck out! I was right beside him for every item he grabbed. I don't want any of his stuff here anyway. I am disgusted just to see his face!

I forced out the word, why?

He had the nerve to say, "You wasn't feeling me like that either!" My mouth dropped, my eyebrows arched, and I heard my heart break just a little bit more. *I wasn't feeling you like that either!* Oh! I loved you with all my heart, you stupid motherfucker! Just leave. Get your shit and get the fuck out of my house! And don't come back! In case it's not obvious, It's Over! It hurts to hear that aloud, the pain is overwhelming.

I watched him walk away and locked my new lock, along with the old one. I feel like I can't leave, or he'll use his key to get in here. Who knows how long this has been going on. I can't even work in peace, for the fear that he's cheating! I sat and cried for hours, too embarrassed to admit to anyone what just happened. Things like this are not supposed to happen! Not to the smart ones. Did I miss the signs? Were there any signs? The good and the bad times ran through my head. The main image that I just can't shake, is the image after the smoke cleared. When my eyes admitted to what they were really seeing. When I saw her face and the reaction on it.

That bitch was so into it, and the fact that he didn't use a condom just boggles my mind. He had unprotected sex with her and would have come home and did the same to me. After I bared my soul to this man! I told him my parents died of AIDS. After about two years, I finally told him! I don't trust many people with that secret. It's embarrassing and I don't like to be judged or pitied. I just need a little help copping sometimes.

Laughter has helped me through the toughest times in my life. I can't find anything to laugh at right now. I realized I would have to go back to work and pretend to be something that I'm not - happy!

Friday, February 27, 2004, not even two good weeks after Valentine's Day, and he has his dick in somebody else. That nasty bastard. I'll call in tomorrow, too, I have to. How do you hide a broken heart when it's written all over your face? I'll be questioned if I don't smile like usual. I've jumped from one relationship into the next for years. Now I don't have anyone. What will I do without that man? I count on him for the little things, and the big. Who will bring in my Christmas tree? Who will carry out the trash? I will if I have to. But that's the problem. I shouldn't have to. My sister called, and I answered the phone sniffles first. She heard the hesitation in my voice and quickly asked, "What's wrong?"

I responded, everything. The tears started again. I have to get this off my chest or I will explode!

With concern in her voice, she asked, "What? What is it?"

I said, you can't tell anybody. Gasp! I walked in on Rodney doing it to somebody else.

"What? Who was he doing it to?" was her reply.

His baby's mama. I let her in on a few of the details, and then we hung up.

She never did have a knack for saying something to lighten the mood. What could she say? You'll find somebody else. She might have said that, but I didn't want to hear that anyway. I would have probably blocked it out. In spite of everything, I don't know if I want anyone else.

I listened to "You Got It Bad," by Usher. I do have it bad, but I can't allow him to disrespect me like that. He doesn't give a damn about his life and evidentially he doesn't give a damn about mine! He don't know what that girl is doing or who she is doing it to.

The rest of the day was a blur, and I woke up the next morning feeling like shit. The first thing that popped in my mind was my situation. As if I didn't go to sleep on the same subject. I called in, and just dropped back down on the bed. I've learned that no matter how much my heart is broken, the world doesn't stop long enough for me to grieve. I stared at the ceiling and thought everything from loneliness to diseases. I have to go get tested! I can't believe he put me in this situation! I hate him, and love him all in the same breath. You can't just turn off your feelings for so one overnight.

I returned back to work on Tuesday as scheduled, to perform what will be my best performance ever! I tried to act normal, but that didn't work long. The first thing I saw when I got to my desk was a picture of him. To be specific, a picture of us at the beach. One of the few pictures that we have together. I flipped it over, then I jerked it out the frame. I replaced it with a solo picture of myself.

When I saw the face of the lady that urged me to leave early that day, I thanked her. It all came out after that. I made sure only the elite heard. Everyone sympathized with me and I fought back the tears. They even gave me a couple of stories to chew on. All were interesting and eventful, but my story took the cake. It got to the point where I to tell my supervisor, after looking for many ways around it. I had to let her know why I'm acting however I'm acting. I don't know how to act. I feel like an actor on stage that forgot his lines.

The look on her face was priceless! It touched me when she gave me these reassuring words, "Everything happens for a reason. Sometimes God points out the things that we would've never seen ourselves."

It let me know that she understood on another level. She can understand all the events, that had to take place, in order for me to get there at that exact moment. Five minutes later, and I would have missed it. Like if I had stopped to get that pack of cigarettes. Five minutes earlier, and nothing would have been started yet. Before I got too choked up, I stood up to walk away. She hugged me.

I whispered to her, I'm glad he doesn't work here anymore.

She asked, "What happened?"

I said, I guess he got fired.

I'll tell you this, the members of the James Gang was very supportive to me. It seems like everyone on the team has their problems. From baby daddy drama, to the mistress who works fifty feet from the wife. It did make me laugh a little. At least I'm not the only one with a fucked-up life.

They did talk my head off a little with their problems, though. I'm known as councilor to more than one of my friends. Anyone demanding answers today is in for a rude awakening. I didn't try hard to please my customers today, and they could tell. I heard everything from, "You must not be having a good day" to "Rough night?" But my customers never complain. I'm surprised so many of them noticed.

I told one of my customers, thank you, I needed that laugh! One sentence can turn a day around. To bad no one muttered the magical phrase to brighten my day. A smile was the best I could do and even then, my cheeks felt heavy.

I heard from Rodney about a week later. When you go from talking to someone every day to talking once a week, it can seem endless. Every hour felt like seven, which made the days drag by. The words that came out his mouth were, "I'm sorry, I didn't mean to hurt you. I know I did some fucked-up things, but you know I love you. I need to talk to you."

Talk then! "I want to see you. I miss you!" Well, you are not too grown for your wants to hurt you. You better be glad that I'm even talking to you. He came back with, "I have a surprise for you! When you are ready to see me, then you'll get it."

I tried not to sound intrigued, but I can't help it, I am. If he thinks cheap gifts will get him back in, he is sadly mistaken. We hung up, and I thought harder about what it could be.

The next day at work, my mother figure shared a story with me. She said, "My husband was unfaithful at one time. You know what I did? I took him back. You have to learn to forgive him. God says you need to forgive a person, not seven times, but up to seventy times seven."

Her words rang in my ears repeatedly. Maybe I can forgive him. It's gonna take a lot of time to get over this. I know it would make me feel a lot better, and it would make my job production better.

When I thought about things, I realized, he's making this harder than it has to be. It's different when the man you walk in on still wants to be with you. Usually that's the perfect time to break the news that it's over. I've pondered what's worse, a woman who knowingly accepts the cheating that she doesn't see, or a woman who sees the cheating and accepts it? I know deep down in my heart, that if I didn't see it, I might not have believed it. The answer that I've come up with is, once a cheater, always a cheater. If I forgive him. If I accept it, am I stupid? More questions than answers floated around in my head.

At the end of the day, I decided, I will see him. It will be restrictive and brief. I will make him feel like shit. I want answers, damn it! I contacted him to let him know about the scheduled meet time. He agreed to come over after the kids go to bed.

I heard the doorbell ring and quickly answered, wearing a coat. I opened the back door and closed it behind him. Then I sat down in a chair on the screened in back porch. It's enclosed, but it can still get very cold. I pointed to another chair for him to do the same. I puffed my blunt and listened to what he had to say.

Without saying a word, I just told him a lot. One is, he is not good enough to even come all the way in my house. Two is, he will not be hitting this blunt. Three is, he can talk whenever I'm ready, to listen. Not at anytime before that.

All the Mr. Tough Guy stuff melted when he said, "Will you marry me? I want you to be my wife! With every day that passes, I've come to realize I can't live without you."

The first thought that crossed my mind was, *God, why would You reveal his infidelity to me, if it's meant for me to marry him? You know how much I've been awaiting my dream wedding. I need You to tell me. I need You to show me. Give me a sign. I love him so much, and I just want to be happy.*

I turned to Rodney and said, why now? Why would I marry you after you cheated on me?

His reply, "Because you love me, and you can't see yourself with anyone else but me."

The problem is, I can see, and saw, you with somebody else. What were you thinking?

He said, "I wasn't thinking. I admit, I was stupid! I went home to check the mailbox. I realized that I got both my state and federal income tax checks. I was just about to leave and call you, to tell you to get off early. Then she showed up. She walked right in and closed the door behind her. That's why it was unlocked. You know I lock everything, down to the screen. She came in and just started taking her clothes off."

So you just couldn't resist. You couldn't tell her to put her clothes back on and get the hell out of your house. I can't even expect a man to be that strong. The ones that are should be commended. If everything really happened the way he said it did. I can understand a small bit. But I doubt his story is bulletproof. He got greedy. He thought he could have his cake and eat it, too. He thought he would get away with it and go on with life as normal.

He is not ready for it to be over! That's exactly why he is over here, begging. The one thing we are missing out of this marriage thing is the ring. I asked, if you are so serious about marrying me, where is the ring? He came back with, "I have it. Remember, I told you I have a surprise for you. Well, that's it. I didn't bring it with me. Because if I set the moment right and propose for the first and final time, and you say no, I'll be heartbroken. It would make me never want to do that again. If you tell me right now, that that's what you want to do, I'll go get it."

I said, how do I know you are for real, if I can't see the ring? What does the ring look like? What does the ring box look like? He replied, "It's a diamond. The box is blue, octagon-shaped."

Can I at least see the box?

He agreed to bring it upon our next meeting. He weaseled out another one of those.

Some might say he twisted my arm. I say that partly joking because there is a part of me that didn't need convincing. There is a small part of me that feels sorry for him. Sorry that she bamboozled or coerced him in any way, to stray. Dangling the goods, so to speak. In this case, however, dangling the nasties. I'm just hating, but really, if you dangle meat in front of a dog, he's going to bite. I do compare them to dogs now. I want to make sure he knows he is in the doghouse. When we met next, the arrangements were no different than before. We sat on the back porch, and he was prepared this time. He wore his coat. He started by saying, "Earlier, I was thinking about us. How much we have in common, and how it drew us together. Then later, it caused arguments. I thought about all the good times we had together. We fit so good together. I know I'll never find another you. I don't even want to try. You were on my mind the whole time. We were about to do it and then you walked in." No, no, you stop right there! First of all, it's a little bit too late to play the 'I'm innocent' card. I know what I saw! You cannot sit here and tell me different! You cannot alter or change my memory in any way! She was moaning, and you jumped up covering your penis, trying to hide the fact that you were not wearing a condom.

"I was wearing a condom," was the best thing he could come up with. I just shook my head in disgust.

Do you even have the ring box? Let's start there. I'll see if you know how to be honest. He pulled a blue octagon-shaped box out of his pocket. It made me cry, talk about a mixture of feelings! On one hand, we have a man who is baring his heart and soul, in the hopes of some sort of miracle. On the other hand, we have a devilish, sneaky, gross individual, who could cause history to repeat itself, by transmitting diseases. Am I to follow what God said about forgiveness and marry this otherwise magnificent man. Or should I take it as a warning and wait for the next man to propose?

Let's face it. I'm not getting any younger. I've put on some comfort pounds during this relationship, too. Part of me says, you better take the first thing you can get. The best way I can describe it, is to say, my heart says yes. But my mind is telling me, no!

He added, "I will do whatever it takes. Whatever you want me to do, for as long as it takes, to rebuild your trust. To prove that I used a condom, and that I don't have any diseases. I'll go get tested. I just want to make it right somehow! I can't live without you. Please!"

I don't know what to say. You chose to bring her back into our lives. You let her take me away from you. I hope it was worth it. You know how jealous I get! I can't even go to work because I think you are screwing around with her. Time heals all wounds. I just don't know how long it'll take to mend mine. If I even thought about giving you another try, it would take a long time to get things back to normal. That doesn't mean that I will. That means that I'll think about it. He left on that note. I closed the door and exhaled. I hadn't exhaled in years really! Ever since, I met him. I shook my head to the thought of, *How he has this hold over me?* A little more than love, something like devotion.

Damn, these feelings! They can take control of you and make you do things you'd otherwise never do. I still love him more than anything and I hate that. As much as I tried to hide it, I know he can tell. He knows me, and vice versa. I listened to more music than usual. Hoping for some kind of sign. A sign to make my decision for me. I hate making hard decisions. The more time passed, the more my heart took charge. To be quite blunt, I feel like a crackhead must feel without a fix. It actually feels like I can't live without him. I can't sleep. I don't eat, which made me knock off a couple of pounds. I don't mind that, but I did consult a doctor. My supervisor told me about a program they have through the job. They set you up with counselors, someone to tell your feelings to. I took her advice when it became unbearable. I ended up at my family doctor spilling my guts, for medication or advice. He reassured me. "You came to the right place."

I do appreciate his comforting words. He started me on an anti-depressant. Depressed, that's a good word to describe me. I need something to make me feel better. I'll get my hair done, micro braided. I'll spend the money that I was saving for our upcoming vacation. I'd say that's cancelled. The sitting time for micro braids is 10-14 hours. It's usually broken up into two days, but I can't sit that long. If I drive to North Carolina I can get it done in 4-5 hours. They have several people that work on your head at one time, to cut down on the sitting time.

I'm scared to go out of town by myself because I might get lost. I wouldn't know how to read a map, if my life depended on it. I'm smart in a lot of ways, but directions is not one of them. I tried to find someone willing and able to travel at any time. Plus the person needs to know where they are going.

It was just a coincidence that I ran into one of the girls from my childhood. In a sense, we grew up together. Our mothers were good friends. We caught up on old times, and I mentioned going out of town to get my braids done. She said, "One of my good friends just went down there to get her braids done. I went with her. Do you want me to ride with you? I can show you where it's at."

I smiled in somewhat disbelief. This is almost too perfect. We exchanged numbers, and she added, "We can go out together and everything. I don't have any friends to go out with."

I left and thought to myself, *I found a cool person to go clubbing with.* The next day I called and asked her if she was ready to go. She said, "Damn, I don't have a babysitter. I have to wait until my mama gets home from work. That will be in about two hours, okay?"

I agreed. What choice did I really have? She's my eyes through all of this! I showed up two hours later, blowing the horn. She came out to the car and told me to come in. She needs a few more minutes to finish getting dressed. Two steps before we entered the house, she whispered, "Don't tell my mama where we are going."

I looked very confused. We walked in, I spoke and made small talk with her mom. She asked her daughter, "Where are you off to?"

She replied, "We are going to the store."

Her mom replied, "Well, hurry back, because I'm tired. I want to lay down. I'm not playing around with these kids all night."

We left on that note. It's about time. Well at least we can hit the highway finally. When we got in the car, she mentioned, "I don't have any weed! I have to pick up some from my friend. I don't even want to go over there with what I have on. I know he's going to say something! He also doesn't like when people are around, when we are doing business. You will have to park up the street, I'll only be a minute."

I could say no, but that would mean a four-hour trip to and from smoking only my weed. I sacrificed more time, for weed. It paid off, about twenty-five minutes later. After they got through arguing about her outfit. To describe her and her outfit in one word - outspoken. I have never met another person in my life, who tries so hard to be different. In her attempts, she can sometimes be construed as scandalous and slutty.

I humored her though, and even respected her a little, since it was not unlike myself to be different. Outspoken, is a word I'd use to describe myself, as well. I felt maybe she was misunderstood. Then it hit me, what I failed to mention before. I talked and drove, while she rolled a blunt.

I said, you told your mama we were just going to the store. The travel time alone is four hours. That's not including the sitting time, which is a minimum of four hours. I think she'll know we went to more than just a store.

Her cold remark was, "She'll be okay."

I can't believe she just dumped her three kids off on her mama like that. With no concept of the possible return time. Now that's dirty! We drove and followed the signs there. I let her drive after awhile and monitored her speed. She has quite a lead foot, and no license to back it up. The last thing I need is to get pulled over with weed in the car. I failed to tell you about the outcome of her twenty-five minute transaction. I guess she bought enough weed to sell because she has about a half a pound in her purse. *Thank you for bringing that on the highway with us!*

We slowed up when we drove through town. She drove me to the same salon that her friend went. The salon name is as different as night and day, compared to what I told her it was. What is this? It was at that moment that I realized, *She doesn't know where she is going! She doesn't know what she is talking about!* I'm starting to think this was a just a ploy, for an adventure. I'm not up for adventures. I just want to get my hair done and get back.

It's sweet of her to sit and wait, while I get it done. I hope she doesn't think she is going to drive my car around without me during the process. She would be sadly mistaken! From there it was like the blind leading the blind trying to find the right place. We stopped and asked all kinds of people for directions. Nobody knew what we were talking about. We need to go ask some black people! We stumbled upon what looks like a black-owned store. They gave us directions - right around the corner! We finally found it. We pulled up, and I smiled!

Somehow everything that I went through, to get me here faded away. I got out the car and went inside. A nice African lady said, "We are closed! Yeah, we closed five minutes ago."

I quickly responded, No! You'll advertise 24 hours! I just drove from Roanoke to get my hair done! Come on, what's five minutes?

In denial, I walked towards the styling chair and sat down.

She said, "What did you want done?"

I whipped off my scarf, revealing my nappy head.

I replied, I want some micro braids!

She said, "Well, you are going to have to come back tomorrow. We open at seven. Only certain locations are open 24 hours, and you would have had to be in here a lot sooner than five minutes ago. That's a four or five hour job."

I felt deceived, conned in some way! I'd just traveled all this way for nothing! I threw a few more pleases in there, before I left. As soon as I walked out the door, the last worker's ride had arrived. They turned off the lights and locked the door. I just shook my head, then I put my scarf back on. Unbelievable! It's all her fault! She got us lost! This was one huge waste of gas. The drive did prove to be a little therapeutic though. I just won't think about the fact that, I still look ugly with my hair like this.

When we got back to Roanoke, she didn't even go straight home to her kids. I dropped her off somewhere else. Good riddance! She just boils my stomach. I pondered who I could get to travel with me during normal business hours. I know one thing - it won't be her.

Rodney knows the highways like the back of his hand. He was my last resort, but he agreed. Anything to be close to me! We went and arrived in record time. I got there when the shop first opened. They put me right in a chair. He went for breakfast. I let him drive since it was right across the parking lot. He has never driven my car before. I got it right before we broke up.

I ate the best way I could, in between holding my breath. I didn't know it would hurt so bad. He slept most of the time, just looking up to check the status. The sweet part is, he is here, patiently waiting, for my beauty transformation. There are four girls working on my head at one time. Pulling my head in four different directions.

It became tedious and tiresome. I took a break, at least every two hours, to smoke a cigarette. I told her, you take a break! We both need one! Four hours and four Aleves later, my hair is finally done. I woke Rodney up, and we left. We made good time in the salon, but we still have a two-hour drive home. If he felt used, he should. Because I just used him, to make me look more beautiful. For other men and to also make him jealous.

The time flew by and before you knew it, we are back at home. I dropped him off, exactly where I picked him up at. I won't step foot inside that place! We said our goodbyes outside. Very short and sweet. I came to the realization that, if I do it to somebody else, it will make me feel better. The sooner I fall in love with somebody else, the sooner I can get over him.

We can start with just sex though. I'll call the city worker and see what he's doing. The only reason we never clicked, is because he doesn't smoke. Not even cigarettes, and he barely drinks. I know he doesn't like the fact that I do. I'm not going to stop smoking for him, or nobody else. So like it, or lump it. We did get together for an incredible night of passion. I do feel vindicated. But it's sad that, as soon as we finished, I was thinking about Rodney.

12

To try and get my mind off things, I decided to get dressed up and go to the club. I called my friend that went out of town with me, and asked her did she want to go.

She said, "I always want to go out, but I never have anybody to go with. Yeah, I want to go!" I picked her up at party time. She wants to go to two clubs. The second one was already agreed upon. The first one is an old head club. Her dad works the door. They never have had a good relationship, but she is his daughter.

I said, you have to be older to get in there!

She said, "He'll let us in!"

We parked at the top of the hill and walked to the door together. Her dad told her she needs to change her shirt, she is showing too much. She didn't want to hear that. She talked shit the whole way back to the car. She hollered, "I don't want to come in there anyway!" Then she put her jacket on and said, "Come on, let's go in!"

We walked back down the hill to the club. Her father then checked my ID and said, "You are too young to come in."

I'm only one year younger than his daughter. That infuriated her, and she cursed up a storm. They argued back and forth. We walked back to the car again. This is getting real old! I wish I was, so we could get in the damn club. We went over one of her friend's house, to kill some time. About two hours passed, then we went to the club. We had a good time dancing and whatever. She knows there is this certain dude, that I'm looking for in the club. I think he's real cute. Since she doesn't know who he is, she can't help me look for him.

The night went on, and I saw my sister's best friend. She is with this light-skinned girl that my friend doesn't like. They grit on each other and start popping shit. Don't put me in the middle of that shit. They keep their distance in the club, and my friend goes back to dancing in the corner. I was in my own little world, when I saw the cutie I'd been looking for. I smiled at him, he smiled back and made his way towards the wall. Before I could bat my eye good, my friend came from out of nowhere. Shaking and popping her ass all over the dude I had come to see!

Oh, my gosh! She dropped it like it was hot and wiggled it all over him. I cannot believe her! Out of everybody in this club, she backs it up all over him. I stood in total disbelief. I hope my mouth is not open! Before I could turn away, I looked at his face. He was loving every minute of it. *No, thank you, I don't share.* I counted down every minute until it was finally over. The crowd filed out into the parking lot. That's where the shouting match started. It is between my friend and the light-skinned girl that is with my sister's best friend. They called each other every name in the book! My friend started taking her shoes off. They closed off the area, pulling a gate between them. I'm on the inside, along with my friend and her brother.

She continued to fuss with the girl, but nobody's fighting! Then I heard somebody say, "Stop talking and start fighting!" That's what I'm talking about. Be about it, don't talk about it. I'm tired of hearing them shouting. I want to see something, or I'm ready to go home!

They opened the gate to let the rest of the people go home. A person who really wanted to fight, would have darted out that gate, and jumped on the girl. She stood there, fiddling with the clasp, on her necklace. If she wanted to take that necklace off, it should have come off after the shoes. She's had nothing but time. She was still fooling with that necklace, long after everyone left out the gate. Almost like, she didn't want it to come off.

I asked her if she needed some help. She jerked away from me and kept staring at the girl. Her brother tried to help her, and she jerked away from him too. I called her name over and over! I said, come on, let's just go!

She continued to stare at the girl, with her hands still on her neck. Never blinking and never moving. Almost like she went crazy! Or is possessed! I told her again, come on, let's go. I'm leaving! When the girl finally walked away, she went chasing her up the hill. Her brother stepped in between the two. I walked down the hill to my car, about to leave her crazy ass! That's exactly what I did, too. With all her stuff still in my car, and all! I'm not going to be just standing around, while she pretends to fight. I don't have time for it. She is supposed to be so big, and bad! The next day I took her clothes to her. I told her I didn't know where she went. The truth is, I don't care where she went. Now I know why, she doesn't have any friends. I see why she doesnt' have nobody to go out with. I know I won't be going out with her anymore.

Less than two weeks later, I heard that she shot her dad. Most likely at the club! He is still living, and she went into hiding. Her mama moved from that house, too. I'm glad it wasn't me out with her that weekend! She has a bad temper! If her dad turned her away again, she probably got so mad that she went and got a gun. It's not that serious! I saw that light-skinned girl out one day, and she said, "I whipped your friend's ass! She was talking all that shit, but when I saw her by herself, I ran up on her and I fucked her up."

I just laughed. Rule number one, don't talk shit, if you can't fight! I know a couple of people like that! No luck on the club scene, and little luck on the dating scene. I entertained a few men with no prevail. Most of the men out here are losers. I continue to compare them to *him*. His charm and his statue.

A man that plays a little hard to get is somewhat cute to me. Within weeks, I was back with Rodney. With a lot of stipulations and big promises. We went together to be tested for disease. With positive results, we are negative! He promised never to do it again. He says, "You are all I need, sexually and everything else. I'll continue to use condoms with you, until you feel comfortable with me again. I want to rebuild your trust for me. I promise to go to church with you, every holiday and big event. As long as you tell me a couple of days in advance. I'll even move. Somewhere she won't know about. I'll even change my phone number. I've missed you and the kids! Tayon's whining and Zay Zay's worrisome ness. I want all that back. I want to do all that I can so that on September 10, 2005, we can get married.

Yes, I have already picked a date, that's to show you how serious I am! What's that, about a year and a half? You can plan your perfect wedding by then, right? I want you to be my wife, share my last name!" All that he said was all that he did. We agreed to take things slow and try to work on our relationship! Even though the news of his infidelity, spread like wildfire. Certain members of my family were impressed by his efforts. My uncle Wilbert for one. He actually saw the ring, he said, "It's a nice diamond ring. Rodney said, he's going to get his girl back. I told him go for it. Don't let your true love slip away, like I did. I saw him in church Sunday; that's good. He is really trying, Dee! Give him another chance."

Married and *diamond,* have a certain ring to them. Get it, diamond ring. Ha ha. Anyway, every time I hear those words it sends a chill down my back. In case you have the same symptoms, I want you to know you're not the only one. I have to admit it, it is the marriage part that put him over the top. I don't have anyone else right now, offering the same thing. Maurice does not count. I told him he needs to get his life together first. That doesn't stop him from proposing almost every time he sees me. He'll meekly say, "You going to be my wife? You ain't marrying nobody else!" I have to admit, I gave him, his turn while Rodney was gone. Nothing has changed! If I do marry Rodney, it's going to break Maurice's heart, though. Whoever I marry, Maurice is not going to approve.

Even though I have the nerve to write it, I don't have the courage to say it. There's no hope, for Maurice and me. For years, I've led him on with maybe's. Maybe this, maybe that. He thrives on it. He has to make a lot of changes to be back with me. He has it in his head that one day we'll be one big, happy family.

Don't get me wrong, the love is there! But not to the extent that he obviously wants. I have to admit though, I am somewhat jealous of the girls he talks to. I don't know what it is, no matter who she is - I don't like her, I grit on her hard. Let me clarify jealous: None of them look better than me. I just don't want them around my kids; don't play mama to my kids! I won't stand for it! That includes, but is not limited to, styling my daughter's hair, holding my children, or talking to them in front of me. Don't say goodbye to my children; just be glad that they're gone. For heaven's sake, do not put your hands on my children, to scold or correct them. You want to talk about somebody going postal. I think Maurice just picks some of these girls for the attention, my reaction. Anyway about it, I know he gets a kick out of it. I can't help myself! In a way, I don't want him to be with anyone else. I do want him to be happy, without me, though. So I'll try to learn to swallow it.

Rodney moved into a run-down duplex. It is smelly, and dank. Dead water bugs decorate the corners. It's not far enough off the street for me. His ex will find out where he lives, by just riding by on the bus. I let him know, I do have her phone number and I will be using it to check up on your whereabouts. He commented, "That's fine, because I'm not doing anything. Whatever it takes for you to trust me again. I don't care."

This place will have to do, for the time being. It's a start. He's showing real initiative, and I can really tell he's trying. As the months passed, he was actually keeping up the bargains he'd made. I am so proud of him! But if it's not one thing, then it's another. Things at home are starting to turn around. Things at work took a big swirl. My supervisor decided to take a position in another department. Even though she is feared, by some employees. For being the toughest. I'm one of the best employees, so I'm up for the challenge! It took a while to build the rapport that we have. The fact that, that's being snatched away, changed, and replaced. It's certainly not a comforting feeling. She knows some of my darkest secrets. She understands me, and I understand her. I know exactly what she expects. I do it, with words unspoken. I don't want to hear her mouth, and she doesn't want to hear mine. We have an understanding. *I don't want a new supervisor!*

That means, I'll have to get to know someone else. They'll have to get to know me. I don't feel like going through all of that. What if they don't like, or understand the funny, quirky, cunning person that I am? My customers love me! What if the new supervisor doesn't recognize that? I'm different, but in a good way! I take the script they give me, give it a new spin, and still say all of what they wanted me to say.

We had a going away party for my supervisor. I take that back. I think we had two. One onsite, and one offsite at a nice restaurant. Saying goodbye, is never easy for me! There were tears shed by all. I will miss the caring, sympathetic, tenderhearted soul, that makes her who she is. I don't like change, and I don't fancy this one. Team members became friends, became ex-team members. People came and went like the wind. I stand firm to my oath, through the good days and the bad. Every call is different, with just enough spice to keep me interested. I didn't know what kind of customer I'd get next. A pervert, or a cry baby.

I've even talked to millionaires and criminals. The line between the two is minimal at best. The millionaire has employees taking her trash out. Just to keep her business! The criminals are employees, some of the time. Embezzlers. There were two, stupid black girls in particular. Cousins, that would refund money to each other's account. They got caught and fired. What a waste of such a promising career.

I refuse to go out like that. I am on my toes every day, and I keep my illegal shit to a minimum. Even though they tell us not to act on emotion, I do anyway. If you piss me off, you get nothing. Smart-mouthing me does not help to get your fee refunded. Grandmas always tug on my heart strings. With their, "Oh, my word," and "I declare, I din messed up again." I always help them. A good sob story will get you half at least; if you make me cry, you're getting all of it. No matter if I have to go beg my supervisor for approval.

Since we started with two supervisors, we are now left with the male supervisor. He is cool to a certain extent. They all are. One of the things that bug me about him is that he won't admit when he's wrong. He'll change the story around before he goes down for something. He's trying his best to impress these white people. I guess he's just trying to get his piece of the pie. Sometimes you have to step on other's dessert to get to what you want. I respect that in a way. The ambition part, not the shiesty way it's achieved!

Rumor spread that we would be getting another tough supervisor. *Bitch*, was one of the words used to describe her. A real stickler for the rules. I've seen the woman of whom they speak. She speaks when she sees me, but I've seen some of her bad days. She doesn't smile often. I even heard that some of her teammates track her time of the month on a calendar to expect turbulence! If she's not a happy camper, on a dry day. I know how the wet ones can get. Maybe she's going through the change; she's old enough. Whatever it is, I don't want any part of it! She better control her emotions around me!

The final word came in, and she will be our new supervisor. She will be attending our next team meeting. She'll start the Monday after that. My close friends and I rolled our eyes to the upsetting news. We got through the first couple of weeks with the new supervisor OK. She does a lot of observing. Nosy is what I call it. I guess she took detailed notes, because at the next team meeting, she started by talking about integrity and fairness. She said, "It is not fair to your fellow teammates, when they have to take your calls. Especially when you are doing something you are not supposed to be doing. We pay you to be at your desk taking calls! I've been noticing people going to get breakfast on their business break! That time is allotted for business purposes, only! To catch up on e-mails and to check voice messages. I want you to know, that I did an audit! Oh, you didn't know I audit?"

My mouth dropped and my eyebrows arched. I quickly raised my hand to ask what she meant by that. Her response was, "That means, I have a total of how many minutes that each rep was not on the phone. Some people were off an extra hour or two in a week's time. Sixty or seventy minutes of unaccounted for time. From now on, you will need to be able to account for that time, or you will be written up. It can escalate all the way up to dismissal."

She used my name, but mispronounced it. I'll correct you now, and a few times thereafter. But get it right!

I'm sure almost everyone in that meeting was blown away by her reveal. I can tell it by the expressions on their faces. Also by the gasp, when she said the total time. She told us to approach her individually to address the issue.

Shortly after, I did. She said I'm one of the ones closer to two hours. I'm always off the phone doing something for the team! I thought about it though. I go to the bathroom at least twice a day. Five minutes apiece is ten minutes a day, sometimes longer. Multiply that by five days a week. That is damn near an hour right there.

She made all that fuss and most of the time off the phone, is for bathroom breaks. Stupid bitch! That's exactly what she came across as. A bitch, that doesn't even know what she is talking about! Threatening us with an audit! The stupid part came across when I announced to the team that it's just bathroom time.

I confronted her about it. I let her know, I shouldn't have to feel rushed when I go to the bathroom. I don't like cutting my pee short, just so I can run and get back on the phone.

She responded, "I don't want you to feel like that. Take your time using the bathroom. That's not the time I'm worried about. I know you are off the phone helping the team though. Just make sure you put in your exceptions. Then it won't count against you."

I left it at that. She still hasn't learned how to say my name though. But yet, her last name is a doozy, and she wants everyone to pronounce that right. She is a real piece of work.

Soon after we received word that one of our teammates' husband had been in a bad car accident. He was on a motorcycle that got hit by a car. The supervisor drove her to the hospital because she was so distraught. The funny thing is, that just moments earlier, she was trying to think of a reason to leave work. This is a damn good reason!

When we finally received word on his condition, it didn't sound promising. It doesn't look good. Just the vision of him dying and leaving her to raise their six kids, by herself. It sent chills through me. We have to do something. Since I'm in charge of the cards, birthday, sympathy, etc., I quickly got one started in rotation. Along with a collection envelope. Everyone can give from three to five dollars.

We want to get her something other than flower, so we decided on pizza gift certificates,. Enough to feed all the kids for at least two days. We raised enough to give her some spending cash also. Pizza doesn't help pay the bills, while her husband is down and out. I went out to the hospital to take her the gifts. She hasn't left the hospital for a week. Now, that's devotion! I walked in the door and I tried to be strong for her. Then I heard him continuously holler out in pain. He said, "Babe, babe, help me. It hurts so bad!" Then he started singing, "Jesus Loves Me."

I couldn't hold back the tears anymore! I discovered he depends on her, to do everything for him. He can't move any part of his body. There isn't any part of his body, that is not in a splint or cast. Some parts lay bloody and skinless! I feel so bad for them! I have to go. I don't want to intrude any longer.

His wife walked me to the elevators then she broke the news, "The doctor says, if the skin graph doesn't work. He will have to get his leg amputated. We haven't told him yet."

My eyes opened wide. Oh, my gosh. No! I hugged her and said, just pray about it. That's all you can do. I'll be praying too. I got in the elevator, shaking my head. It's always the good ones. A few days later the word came in. He is scheduled for surgery within days. He will have to get his leg cut off. We all hope he will recover soon! I received a Thank You card, from my supervisor. It says, "Thank you for going to pick up items for the team. You are doing a great job on the Great Place to Work committee. I also wanted to say, that it was really nice that you took so much of your personal time to make another teammate feel so special."

It feels good to be appreciated sometimes! I'm starting to feel more appreciated at home too. But I still stay on my toes. I check Rodney's caller ID every time I visit. He knows it, and it seems like he doesn't mind.

One day I stopped by unexpectedly. I caught him in the middle of using the bathroom. He cut it short long enough to open the door for me and then returned to the bathroom. We talked back and forth. I checked the caller ID while speaking. I stopped and stared at the screen. Here is a very questionable number! The same girl I'd had problems with before. Remember, there were two. Not the baby's mother, but the fat one.

When he finished using the bathroom, I asked, who's number is this? He said, "I don't know. If they called yesterday, I wasn't here anyway. You know that."

I replied, well, we'll just see whose number it is.

Boop, boop, boop, boop, boop, boop, boop, ring. She's not answering, just the machine. I hung up and called right back. This time she answered, "Hello?"

Hello? Can you tell me why, your number, is on Rodney's caller ID?

She said, "Daminika, don't act stupid."

I said, bitch, don't play with me! I asked you a question! We can do this the easy way, or we can do this the hard way! I know where you work at!

She sighed, and responded, "Because he called me. I missed his call, so I called him back. I told him don't call me anymore. I have a man, and I don't want him!"

I asked, why is he calling you?

She said, "I mean, we talk sometimes. We catch up, but yes, we did had sex. I know where he lives now. We had sex there, too. He told me y'all was broke up."

I said, Oh, we are, and hung up!

I looked at him in his face and hollered with tears in my eyes. If it's not one, it's the other, huh? I stormed out the door! I got to thinking, *All this time, I've been focusing all my attention on that one girl, and so he goes to the other one. How could I be so stupid? I've had both of their phone numbers for a long time now. I should have called them both, on the same day. Damn, I can't beat myself up about it. My world already feels like it is spinning out of control.* Literally spinning a whirlwind, all around, and through me. I never wanted to get back in the dating game, but I have no choice. I have to start over. I have to get over this man! How am I supposed to do that? I wanted to dig that love out with a knife!

He doesn't deserve me! I'm too good for this! This is what he does with his second chance!? He called with all kinds of lies. From, they only had sex when we were broke up, to he told her, don't call him any more. Out of all his lies, he couldn't come up with one good reason why, she knows where he lives at! He hasn't been living there that long. He's speechless, but I'm not! I really let him have it. I stood by your side, provided shelter for you. I trusted you, I was faithful and all. You don't appreciate shit, and you had the nerve to break up a happy home! Maurice and I were just fine until you came along. This must be one big fucking game for you! You are playing with people's lives, hearts and emotions. Rodney responded, "I'm not playing, and I haven't been playing. I love you, and even though I do stupid things sometimes, it doesn't change that. I don't think things out. I don't consider all the consequences, and I'm sorry about that. I never wanted you to get hurt." It's too late for that! Your apologies are empty! You are going to continue to do what you do. But you can continue without me! I do have one last thing to say, though. What comes around, goes around. I hope you get so wrapped up in a girl, that you want to marry her. She will cheat on you, break your heart, and leave. I hate you! I hate what you did to me. But I laugh, knowing it will all come back to bite you in the ass. HA!

Now it's back to sleeping alone and doing everything around the house myself. My attitude towards what happened, is reflecting towards my kids and at my job. I'm very snappy and touchy - an emotional wreck. I don't know if I'm coming or going most days.

DEVASTATING CONSEQUENCES

I used some FMLA time that I got for my son. Pretty much, it's time that you get if your child has a serious medical condition. Tayon had to get his tonsils and adenoids removed earlier this year. Even though my supervisor doesn't like it, it does entitle me to miss as many days as I like unpaid, and it's covered.

My supervisor is the type of person always trying to catch you doing something! She started investigating me, trying to find out how I was taking so many days off. Since she is so damn nosy, I refuse to let her in on the details of my situation. She doesn't seem as compassionate as my last supervisor. She snooped until she gathered just enough dirt, to try to hang me. She had already been approaching people one at time, seemingly trying to annihilate them. But I won't go down without a fight! I refuse!

This bitch is trying to weed out all the blacks first. Then comes the black lovers, like one of my little white friends. She goes with that fat black guy from my training class. The one who drove me home. We all came out of training together. She told me, "Watch your back; she's on a rampage!"

She called a meeting, including both supervisors, a lot of paperwork, and myself. She whipped out a calendar and pointed to it. She said, "How do you explain this?"

I looked at her and laughed, a pissed-off laugh.

I said, I was sick.

She replied, "How did you know ahead of time that you were going to be sick? These days were prescheduled."

I looked at her evidence, then I looked at her.

I said, I scheduled the days before I knew I was sick! I couldn't erase them, because I was out sick! It was going to be paid time off, then I just used sick time, since I was sick

. She replied, "So you were sick the whole time?"

I sarcastically replied, yep!

Then she whipped out some paper, that, in a nutshell, said, she has the right to make me fill out new FMLA papers every month. Only if she wants to. That means I have to take the paper back to the doctor, to say my son is still sick.

She said, "If you don't get the doctor to fill out a new paper, those days will count against you! You can be fired."

With a raised voice, I said, what? Let me tell you what I don't appreciate! I don't appreciate the way you approached me! For feedback purposes, you don't talk to nobody like that. You were so sure I was guilty before I even opened my mouth. You are trying to hem me up and take my job away! It won't be easy! I want another opinion! Go call another one of the lead supervisors in here! My male supervisor just sat there with his head down. I know he's not going to take up for me. She was flabbergasted when I said, call for backup, but she quickly obliged. It wasn't the one I wanted, but I proceeded with my story. I explained to her that I have FMLA and that the supervisor is trying to say I don't. She said, "Until you bring this paper back, you don't! If you look here, you see that we have the right to ask for an updated form."

I left that meeting hotter than a boiling pot. I saw the expressions on the faces of my fellow teammates when I left. I know I got loud behind that little screen. I can't go back and do my work after all that! I'll have to leave and get my paper filled out instead. That will be the only thing on my mind until I do. I am so pissed off that she would even question me. She doesn't have to challenge that paper; she just wants to. I went to the doctor and dropped off the paper. They called me back and said, I didn't list the exact days that I want covered. I told them the dates, and that's what they wrote. They told me if I need any other dates covered, I just have to bring another form.

I hung up and laughed in a cocky manner. Now bitch, that's done! Now I can really take whatever days that I want, and it will still be covered. My doctor knows the whole story, so he knows what fragile condition I'm in. I returned to work the next day with my paperwork. I think certain people thought I was fired, because I left after the meeting. I reassured them that I won't go out that easy!

13

I am going through so much. Between the problems at home, and work. Plus my grandma is in the hospital. I called a meeting with my supervisor, I pretty much threw the paper at her. Bam! Look at that. Check that out. With a sarcastic tone I said, so I don't have to worry about those mandatory days, right? She looked at it and meekly said, "Right. But if you miss any more days, I'll need a new paper. If he puts in a range of days instead of specific ones, it would be better."

Bitch, I know you are not trying to help me, or look out for my best interests in any way! But instead, I said, yeah, I'll let him know. I left all smiles. She had challenged me and lost. Now she knows - don't fuck with me! They all learn sooner or later.

Kam is trying her best to get back in good with me and the kids. I did let her watch them for awhile, when I didn't have any other babysitter. That didn't last long! Our attitudes clashed once again.

Another reason why she pisses me off is that she won't take the time to learn my kids' names. She calls them little boy and little girl. That is an insult! I feel as if, you couldn't be nice to me when I was a child. Why should you get a chance to be nice to my children?

She called me at work out of the blue. It scared the shit out of me! They said I have a call on the black phone. Usually people call me at my desk. It must be an emergency. I ran to the phone and when I heard her voice, chills went through me. I told her, don't you tell me anything bad, or I'll just pass out.

Panic rushed through me. Did my grandma die? She said, "I want you to go to the store for me. Call me when you get off, and I'll have the list ready of all the things that I want. Then I can describe to you how to get over here. I know you haven't been here before."

First of all, I haven't spoken to her in months, if not years. So we are not necessarily on speaking terms. Second, why the fuck would she think I would do anything for her? Third, why is she calling me on my job for something stupid? Like we are cool or something! Maybe she couldn't get in touch with her favorite niece, Shaun. Shaun would most likely do it for her.

I can make a mature decision to be nice and to do her a favor. I pondered for awhile, and even took a poll amongst my friends. I tallied the votes and more people said no, than yes.

Would she do it for me? No. Fuck her! I'm not doing shit for her! Since she got my blood pumping, about my grandma. That's the first thing I did when I got off work. I went to see Grandma. She's not doing her best, but she does recognize me. She can't talk that much, but she didn't have to. She reached out and grabbed my hand. She didn't let go!

My aunt pulled up a chair for me. I sat and held her hand for hours. If she doesn't want to let go, she doesn't have to. I didn't fight back the tears this time, I just let them flow.

We sat and watched the beautiful deer out the window. We could tell she really enjoyed it. One of my aunts has a roll out bed. She's been sleeping up here. My granddad should be up here with her too. He calls more than once a day though. We put the phone up to her ear so she could hear him, but could not speak. You can tell she wants to. The only reason Granddad's not here is because he is afraid of hospitals.

I do admire their marriage though. Not many people have a granddad around. They have been married almost fifty years, and raised nine children together. He still calls her, baby doll. That's the kind of marriage I want.

Sometimes I wonder, what in the world made her want to have nine kids? My two are more than a handful. Then I thought to myself, what if she didn't? What if she stopped at two? She'd been in a world of trouble because it's the youngest ones that take care of her the most. I left after a while to go home and think about all my other problems.

Rodney contacted me and asked if he could come over. He said he would make it worth my while. I know what that means - oral sex. Every way but up! I got to admit, I need it. I've been experiencing quite a drought lately. The dudes I have met, I haven't slept with. I don't want to be a slut, and where does that leave me?

He came over, and we sat in my room on the bed, smoking a blunt. We chilled for a while, just talking mainly about the movie, he let me borrow.

He said, "It's a real good movie, *The Butterfly Effect*. Kind of weird, but let me know how you like it."

I said, I'll watch it when I have some free time. Right now, I have only one thing on my mind, and he is good at it.

He was evidently joking when he said, "Can I get some ass tonight?" He means actual ass.

I looked at him and laughed. Yeah, right! You only got ass on a humble, when we was going together! Now, we don't go together. I know you don't think we are doing that! I walked out the room to the kitchen, to get my beer. When I walked out, I know I heard something that didn't sound right.

When I walked back in the room, he repeated it. "That's okay because I just got ass last Thursday. You know the girl we work with? The one you saw flirting with me at the liquor store? She let me fuck her in her ass."

What? How did you start talking to her?

He responded, "She gave me her number, before she switched shifts. Before I got fired."

But, while we were dating? You accepted her phone number, and saved it for a rainy day.

Fury shot through me, quicker than my blood could pump it. He continued talking, and I tried to push it to the back of my mind. This is not my man. I can not be but so mad. I tried to continue with our sexual plans, with no avail. Not on my part, but his. Since he had to wear a condom, his dick couldn't stay hard long enough to do anything with. Useless. We wrapped things up, and I walked him to the door. It infuriated me even more, to know that he didn't use a condom with her, while fucking her in the butt. I know he didn't, he couldn't, and she let him. That nasty, trifling, whore.

As if I didn't have enough problems sleeping, let's add one more thing. I tossed and turned most of the night, then I decided to watch the movie, maybe it will put me to sleep. Halfway through, it finally worked. I fell asleep.

The next morning came too soon. When I pulled up in the parking lot, I felt that fury again. I am determined to find this girl! Except I only halfway know what she looks like. From the moment I walked in that door, I looked at everybody differently. I see a girl that looks like her, and I stared to make sure. The stare turned into a grit. I have an idea of what my face might look like.

I turned away, at the realization that, it's not her. I feel desperate. I feel empty. I feel like a mouse in a maze. I don't know which way to go. I told my male supervisor, I'm not having a good day. I sat down at my desk, and it felt like all my problems sat right down on top of me. I turned the radio on and I broke down. "The First Cut Is the Deepest," by Sheryl Crow is playing. The first cut is the deepest, but the following stabs are just as painful.

I told my supervisor, I will not be able, to finish out my day today. I'm having an anxiety attack, and I need to go home. He told me okay, and he hopes, I feel better. I broke down even more upon hearing those words. I walked out, and I did feel better. At least a little bit. As I pulled out of the parking lot. I went home and relaxed. First things first, I need to leave this man alone! After I watch this movie, I'll return it, and be done with him. We can't even have sex anymore, he violated that privilege.

I watched that movie, and it scared the crap out of me. *Oh, my gosh. Whatever he has, I have!* Whenever I panic, my mind goes into hyper mode. Trying to prevent the worst. I think so much harder than everybody else. I know things, and it is so odd, that he was the one that showed it to me. A part of me feels grateful. He just doesn't know, how much this has changed my life. I'll get a head scan! That way, they can see what's wrong with me.

I must have panicked when I heard Kam is telling people that my brother has being touching on one of our male cousins. The family was outraged, saying things like, "Don't leave your boys around A.J."

I know he's being hanging with those gay men at church too much. You see, that's just the thing. All he is around is boys, little boys. He's never around people his age. Or girls his age, for that matter! He's going through puberty, and no one is around for him to go to for questions. He is curious, and I'll admit, I was curious at his age. Or even younger! I'm not gay by any means necessary, and I don't want anyone to assume that about him. Or discriminate against him for it, if he is!

While everyone was coming down on him, scolding him. I went to work, thinking of every possible way I could save him! I know how Kam is. You think she treats him like shit now! How is she going to treat him after he supposedly touched her favorite, beloved nephew? The one she spoils and treats like a son. She even lets him call her mom!

I didn't always feel like myself with every action and every decision I made. It feels like someone is working through me. I'm almost like a robot. I just know, it's my mom. I had a long talk with A.J. and told him what I came up with. I am going to call Social Services and tell them about your living conditions, and how she treats you. He added fuel to the fire, when he told me, "Make sure you tell them that she makes me help her wash up and get dressed! Along with helping her in and out of the shower. I have to empty her pot and be her personal slave, at all times of the night."

You have got to be joking! She makes you, help her, wash up? You see her butt naked? He shook his head, yes. That is disgusting! If I had to see that hippopotamus ass every day, and that's my only example of a woman, I'd be gay too. I let him know, he can come live with me. He gave me the go-ahead. I made the call, and Social Services responded promptly. We let her know about A.J.'s conditions, and the worker agreed to meet with us. She also said, she would be going over to the high school to meet with him. We told her that Kam lives right next door to my grandma's house.

Grandma has a key, and we know she won't be out of her room. She might not even be awake! Grandma let the social worker in. She walked into Kam's bedroom. They talked, and we stood at the front door and listened. She doesn't know we are here. I smiled bigger, with every moment that passed. They never give warnings that they are coming. As if, she could hide anything.

Ain't no way, that lady didn't smell the house as soon as she walked in. Kam couldn't cover up every one of her shit stains, before the lady saw the conditions.

After it hit her what was going on, she called her favorite sister, Maria. They are in shock! But she says, "I know who called. Uhm, I know my niece. Daminika called."

I laughed to myself. For a minute, I thought our cover was blown!

The social worker slipped up and said, "They are just concerned." She looked towards the living room.

Kam screamed, "Who's in there?"

The social worker said, "Here's your mama."

Grandma walked forward and explained her role in it all. I stood idly by, laughing on the inside. *Get up bitch! Get up and come find me! Yeah, that's what I thought*

Long story short, they took A.J. away from her. He went to stay with my grandma. The social worker thought that would be best until we go to court. I went to file for custody of my brother. We did have our day in court, and they wheeled in the whale. Because she couldn't walk that far into the courtroom. They left her in the aisle because she can't fit in the rows.

Before anything started, the judge stated, "You sure are dressed sharp, young man."

That's one thing about my brother - he can dress his ass off. He will buy a suit and some gators before he'll buy casual clothes. I gave my testimony as to why, he should live with me.

Because she didn't have anything better to say, Kam interrupted to say, "That's not even her brother; it's her cousin." She knows that cuts me like a knife. I began to cry, during my testimony. How dare she belittle the relationship that I have with my brother? I take that very seriously! I corrected her, and the judge jumped on her! Insulting her in away!

Now she's showing, those true colors! Now she's coming to the realization, that there is no hope for her. She said, "I want A.J. back."

I laughed. Yeah, right! I'm saving him from all to come, and in a nutshell, saving her life. We all have a snapping point! If A.J. stays there much longer, he is going to kill her. Then he'll go to jail. Just another statistic. I refuse to let that happen!

I made a promise to my mama! To never let my brother get taken away! That includes anything and anyone. The judged asked, "Is there anything wrong with where he is currently living? Do you have any objections to him staying there? Since you already have two young kids, it might be better that way. We really don't want him to be around young kids for awhile."

DEVASTATING CONSEQUENCES

I agreed, and it became finalized. I won, we won! A.J. doesn't have to live with that monster ever again! But in a way, I lost. I saw the smirk on her face. To her, as long as he is not with me, she won. But I know better than that! She'll have to explain to her friends why she lost custody of A.J., I'm sure she'll make up some lie. She won't get much more air time in this book, but to wrap things up.

Kam ended up going into a nursing home. She couldn't take care of herself. I am getting to that point myself! Strange things started happening! I would wake up in the middle of the night, sitting on the edge of my bed, fully clothed. Like I was going somewhere. Or was I coming from somewhere? That shit is scary as hell! It's like, I am sleepwalking! I open my eyes, confused, and scared. In this condition, I could do just about anything, to anyone! Or nothing at all. My lack of sleep, carried over into my day-to-day life! Cranky, irritable, mixed with coffee/caffeine. I never drink coffee, but it did give me an edge. Except for me, it was like falling *over* the edge! It gave me too much energy! It made me go faster, overanxious.

I am working so hard, just to keep up the pace of my fellow teammates! Sometimes, it feels like, I'm going too fast! Sometimes it feels like, I'm going too slow! I have these anxiety attacks, especially when I feel like I'm not going fast enough! Mix that with a new, cocky supervisor. Making new rules, rushing me, and always wanting more! Always just a little bit more, than you have! It started, my ticking time bomb!

My supervisor, is still poking and prodding,. Trying to get information out of me. She wants to know what's wrong with me. Subtly, she lets me know that I don't have to tell her. But yet, her prying is obvious. I let her in on a small part of it by telling her, I have anxiety attacks! I described the fact that when they occur, I'm not myself! I shut down! I don't know what to say or do! I stop. In a sense, panic!

My supervisor said. "It's called panic attacks. My sister has the same thing."

A part of me wanted to ask her, what happened to her? What was the outcome? Can she work anymore? But a bigger part of me, did not want to hear it. I don't want to be swayed by a probable outcome. Good or bad!

I don't know what happened to her. But I know it feels like I can't work anymore. I can only think about what my mind wants to think about! In a sense, trapped! In all of those dramatic moments in my life. She clung to my every word. But if she thinks I'm going to sit here and tell her all my business. She is sadly mistaken! I recognize nosy people. I know exactly how nosy she is! She loves to gossip with some of her other female supervisors. You won't spread my business around the job! I wrapped it up, by saying I witnessed something very traumatic!

She responded by saying, "Well, anxiety attacks are covered under short-term disability. You might want to talk to your doctor about that."

I admitted to her that talking to her, gives me anxiety attacks. She asked, "Am I that bad?"

I said, no, I can't help it! I left early to go to the doctor. But I forgot my regular doctor is out of the country, working as a missionary somewhere! He'll be back in a week or so. So I had to go into somewhat detail with a strange doctor! Mainly I addressed the issue of waking up, fully dressed. He looked concerned. I know, it's something wrong when you see a face like that! He looked scared! Which, in turn, scared me. A lot more things, scare me these days! Panic rears it's ugly face in all types of disguises.

The doctor prescribed some kind of medicine for me, antipsychotic pills. I began taking the medicine right away. Really, it seemed like I got worse! I can't remember anything. I have to write everything down. Everything, from calling into work to returning the movie. I have to return Rodney's movie. I don't want to see him, it will only hurt more! So I left the movie on his doorstep, where, ironically, I left my broken heart, so many months ago.

I called and left four simple words on his answering machine. Thanks, for the movie. Everything happens for a reason, and the fact that he helped to open my eyes, is to be commended. I do feel grateful in a way.

He called to say, "Why did you just drop the movie off like that? I would have loved to see you! Can I see you, please? I have to talk to you!"

DEVASTATING CONSEQUENCES

It felt like he knows, what I know, about the movie! He knows that I'm different, from a lot of people, and he understands me! He'll tell me everything, will be okay! He'll stick by me, if I need him to.

I need love, and to be frank, I don't care where it comes from right now! I need loving words, repeated often. I know, he'll give that to me. So, I'll go see what he wants to say. He opened the door and greeted me with a hug and a kiss on the cheek. He started off with all those terms of endearment, that make all women weak! "I've missed you! I miss you. I love you! How have you been?"

I responded with, I've been making it! I'm determined to do that. He came back with, "Well, I'm happy to hear that! I've been worrying about you! I had a dream about you. I dreamed that, I walked into your house, and you and the kids were dead! Y'all had been shot, blood was everywhere!"

I froze in horror, and like some of the scariest moments in your life. You are too scared to cry! Your body doesn't have time to think about that. I uttered the words, you had a dream, about killing me, and my kids? He said, "No, I didn't do it!"

Well who did? I zoned out, and anything else he said, for the next few minutes, I didn't even hear! A million things, raced through my mind. But the main one is, how do I get out, of this house safely? I know he owns a gun, and he has been violent with me before. Why wouldn't he do it again? Other than his freedom, he has nothing to lose. I feel as if, he thinks, if he cannot have me. Nobody can! He never said it. But he doesn't have to.

He has always stressed to me, that he always gets what he wants! I found that out firsthand about a year ago when a petty argument turned bad! He didn't get his way, but I thought the argument was over! I turned and walked away. I grabbed my cigars off the table and prepared to roll up. I turned my back for one second, and when I turned back around, he was charging towards me like a football player! I didn't know what to do! I tried to move out of the way! Our bodies collided, and my body went one way, and my ankle went the other! He proceeded to punch me in my face. I hit my head on the floor. He busted my lip, and I saw the blood pour out on the floor! I tried to guard my face against his humble un-aggravated, attack. He finally let up when he saw the blood.

The expression on his face, mirrored the look on my face, minus the blood. He looked horrified. He started apologizing. I can not believe he just violated me in this way! He snuck me. He begged me not to call the police! But with all the hollering, I'd be surprised if someone else has not done so already! You know how nosy these neighbors are. Neither one of us are fancy about the police. But that's no excuse! I should have called! I never would have thought I would take a step inside a battered woman's shoes! I am a big girl. I can defend myself! But not with over three hundred pounds sitting on your twisted ankle! I had to lie to co-workers, friends, and family about what happened.

It did help things, to have him escort me to the hospital. That's where the lying began. *I slipped and fell while mopping the floor! I bumped my mouth on the cabinet on the way down.* It can happen! My sister just had a freak accident like that. She had to have a plate put in her leg for the same reason. Mine is just accompanied by a busted lip and bruised forehead. I decided to wear bangs for awhile. The verdict is, a sprained ankle. No crutches, but a lot of pain! However, I did get a parking pass, so I wouldn't have to walk, from Egypt. When I parked at work.

Rodney nursed me while I was down. He did enough begging to get him right back where he started! Except, with a more hesitant me. I pushed his buttons a little less! I've got to admit. He said, "I will never put my hands on you again!"

So to this day, I tell him,. You don't have to put your hands on me to kill me! I don't ever remember getting a response from that statement. His dream sent my brain rattling! Panic! Just like on that movie I talked about. It made my head hurt from thinking so hard! All I can come up with is, *I have to move! I have got to get the hell out of this house! Move somewhere, somewhere that he doesn't know about! Somewhere he doesn't have a potential key.* I still remember the mystery entrance! When he was sitting on my bed when I got home from work - before I even made copies of the key! Who's to say he won't do it again? I nailed the windows shut!

Every night the fear intensified! Which meant more weed to calm me down and to help me sleep, with little to no avail! There is this program I want to make sure I watch. It's called, *Rebuild My Family!* It's about this black family that lives in Texas. The show is going to tear down their old house and build them a new one. I'm going to tape it because the husband on the special looks just like this nice guy that I met in North Carolina, on Shaun's birthday! They talk, just alike and everything with this cute little country accent.

I thoroughly enjoyed the program. I think I cried and shouted more than they did! That's the thing, though. It looks like every time I watch TV, I feel every emotion they feel. That includes commercials. And the later I watch TV, the more I feel as if, it includes subliminal messages! Every word is directed towards me! Every time I turn on the radio, the songs are playing just for me. All of my favorites! I read so much into these things. It seems like more than coincidence! Everything is just too much of a coincidence!

Shaun just happened to bring me along on a trip with her and her best friend. We met the dude that looks just like him as soon as we got there! She pretended like she was mad when I spent the rest of the evening with him. Instead, of going to the club with them. I don't know. Pretty good show.

Even so, it made me like the dude from North Carolina even more. When we talked afterwards. He said that everyone told him that he looks just like that man on the show! I laughed; then it's not just me! I feel so anxious, to be with this man. I have butterflies, in my stomach when I talk to him! My sister and I discuss moving there. I can't leave her! We both can transfer our jobs. I don't waste any time! I'm looking for neighboring houses, for me and my sister. Her best friend wants to make that move, too. It seems too good to be true.

I want to go back, and visit him. We are trying to get a trip together. I am starting to feel happier. Like things are turning around, things are looking up! I am still sick though. I have these panic attacks. My hands shake, and I just shut down. Like I'm, too fucked up to do anything else! I don't do this around my kids, though. I scramble around, cooking dinner, bathing kids, cleaning, and feeding the dog. Not to mention worrying. I put the kids in the bed. Probably, two seconds before I break!

I just need silence! I need to think. I have so many thoughts, it's hard to pick one thing to think about. I stare a lot of the time, and that scares me. It should be starting to concern certain members of my family. But I'm not around them long enough, for them to notice most likely. I've got to change that! I've have to show them how I am.

I received a call from my mother figure from work. We talked, and I told her some of my problems. She told me how concerned she is, about me! She had been looking for me. She realized I'd missed a lot of days from work. She harshly said, "Why don't you just get over it? Move on! Be single, and be happy!"

I told her, I can't do that! It's not that, I don't want to! It's just that, I can't ... She replied, "Why? Are you bipolar?"

I said, what's that?

She said, "You know what, Daminika? I'm at work, and I have to go! I'll call you later."

I said okay, and hung up the phone.

What is she talking about, *bipolar*? I wrote the word down, to make sure I don't forget it. I've had to do a lot of that lately. One more thought to be added to the swirling whirlwind of thoughts already in my head! I went to listen to music, it always helps me. Within no time, I began to cry. There could actually be a word, to describe, how I'm feeling! I've just got to know, I just have to! Out of nowhere, I just got this thought, to call my Aunt Maria. The aunt that is second-most hated, next to Kam. I don't know where the thought came from. But I went with it. I called my grandma's house to get the number. My Uncle Wilbert answered the phone.

"Hello, Dee. I heard you have been feeling bad lately. Do you feel worse than me? Losing a million dollar lawsuit?"

I said, I think I do! Anyway, I need Maria's phone number.

He said, "Hold on," and eventually came back with the number. "Why do you need Maria's number?"

I need to ask her something. We left it at that and hung up. I made that much-needed call. Maria answered, and I asked her, what does bipolar mean?

I didn't know if she had to look it up on the Internet or not, but she quickly came back with a response. "It means, sometimes you are okay, and sometimes you are not. Laughing one minute and crying the next."

I stopped. I gasped, and swallowed hard. Speechless, and uncomfortable silence followed.

She asked, "Why?"

With hesitation, and tears, I said, that's what's wrong with me. Pray for me, right now please!

She did as she was asked, and it did help me! At the end of the prayer. She said, "Dee, how do you know that's what is wrong?"

I said, I just know. I already know! It makes too much sense! She asked, "Who is there with you?"

I replied, no one.

She said, "I have to pick up the kids from practice. Then I'll be right over! Describe how I get to your house. You forgot, I've never been there before."

I gave her good enough directions for her to make it. When she arrived, we hugged off the bat. It's crazy, how things work. Her concern for me overwhelmed me! She toured the house and complimented me on how cute it is. I thanked her and invited her to sit down so we can talk. We sat on the edge of my bed. I told her that the zebras remind me, of my mama. I told her also of all my symptoms - sleeplessness, zoning in and out, missing half of all conversations and TV shows. The laughing and crying. The ability to stop crying if one, of my children enter the room. The fakeness! I just cannot do it anymore! The ability to smile when I'm dying on the inside, just so I can make somebody else feel good!

I caught myself asking someone how are you doing while I was crying! I can't help it! It's amazing how far, it's gotten me though! The class clown, has taken her makeup off! Now, I can't make myself smile at a stranger. Like the muscles in my cheeks, are numb!

She could relate, on a lot of levels! I felt this closeness, a bond emerging from thin air. I even admitted to her, that I smoke cigarettes, for my nerves. My grandma doesn't even know that about me. I don't want her, to look at me like that! Maria even admitted, to me that, she zones in and out. There was a time, in her life, that she almost snapped. But with some medicine, she got through it. She encouraged, me to go to the doctor! I told her, I want to get my head x-rayed. Just to prove, to everyone else, that I am bipolar! I already know it! Just like I knew, I was going to be sick. I planned time off at work. It freaked my supervisor out. I get these signs, that tell me what to do. Helping me make decisions! Warning me! I looked Maria in her eyes, and it's like she could read my mind, or finish my thought!

She said, "It's like, you just know."

I stared, at her and wondered. Maybe, she's bipolar too! Maybe, she's too afraid, to get a cat scan. I asked her, if she ever had one before. She said, "No."

But I think, she may need one. We could relate, on so many levels, while talking! Just like when two people click. Best friends, even! It's amazing, what it takes, to bring two people together! Kam, has been in the middle of us, the whole time.

I asked her, do I act differently? Do you think I'm bipolar?

She said, "Yes, but it's mild! We are going to be praying for you. You are strong; you will get through this! I love you, and call me anytime, day or night, if you need me!"

Thank you, I appreciate it. Then she left.

I really do feel closer to her now! What made me make that call? That's beyond me. But when something is meant to happen, it's going to happen, no matter what you do!

The lady from work called back. I told her that I am, bipolar! She asked, "And what are you going to do about it?"

I'm going to go to the doctor! I have to prove it! She responded, "If you know, why do you have to prove it? I am working closely with this girl, that is bipolar. She went to the doctor, and they ended up taking her kids away! You don't want that." I know I don't want that, and that's not going to happen! I take good care of my kids, and I don't get upset in front of them. I wrapped up the conversation with her because she really pissed me off!

Then Kam called out of the blue. She said, "I heard you are not doing very well."

I told her, yeah, I'm bipolar, and I need to prove it! A friend from work told me I shouldn't because a woman she knows got her kids taken away! Kam said, "Now, you know that's just the devil! That's not your friend, and you don't need to talk to her anymore! That lady she's talking about was probably on drugs, real bad, too!" I know, and if she, really knew me. She would know, I don't fool around with drugs, like that!

She said, "Yeah, I know it. Now, I won't hold you up. I just hope you feel better."

I thanked her and ended the call.

14

I tried to get some sleep, after this very eventful day! I tossed, and turned, like usual. Everything, that happened during the day, is relived in my dreams. If you can call them that. I'm never really sleep! My brain is like a TV with no off switch. I try over and over, to get it to stop. Stop thinking about anything! Start thinking about nothing. A blank, black, screen. It would work, but only briefly. I have to repeat it, when I become overwhelmed with thoughts, conversations with friends, Laughing at what I said. Regretting, the things I didn't.

It's becoming more evident, that I'm on the verge of breaking. Especially, when I start to cry, over picking out the kids' clothes. It's too stressful for me. I become panicked! I holler, I rush everyone else, but cannot stand to be rushed myself. I called Nettie and asked her, can she meet me at the house, after she gets off work. I have to talk to her.

She came over, and when I answered the door, she had tears in her eyes, for some reason. I have this crazy feeling, that I'm doing everything backwards. Maybe I already told her and don't remember. Maybe, she can sense something is wrong! At any event, I sat her down at the dining room table. I sent the kids in another room to look at TV, I explained to her that I have these panic attacks. I get real scared, my hands shake. I think something's wrong with my nerves. Or the official diagnosis, bipolar. I pretend to be okay around the kids, but when they leave, I break down!

My son walked in, and I sucked it up. I have to be strong for them. Just like I've had to be strong for everyone, all these years, especially my brother and sister. I don't know how much longer I can take this! At times, my brain gets confused. About whether, to be happy or sad. I've been both at the same time for so long.

Nettie really didn't have that much of an encouraging word for me. Yet, she didn't look surprised. Concern for me and the kids was evident. I do appreciate that. She is what I would label as a mother figure!

Although others labeled themselves as that. She loves me as if I were her real daughter! She even buys me more gifts than her own son for Christmas! Which is also appreciated and not taken for granted. She's the closest thing to a mom. And I love her for that ... But she doesn't even come close to my mom! My mom would know exactly what to say. She would have hugged and rocked me for hours, if that's what it took.

After I finished talking to her, I felt somewhat better, and somewhat worse. All at the same time! I need to get my hair done. That will make me feel better! I pondered most of the night, on a suitable hairstyle. I bought the hair and went to my regular hairdresser to get my hair done. She works out of her house, and she is good at what she does. The only thing is, it takes even longer than going to a salon. But for the price we pay, she feels as if it is okay to make us wait. We save almost half of what it would cost elsewhere. Just because we all are real close.

I do like going there, because she does catch me up on the latest gossip! Everybody's business, including detailed versions, of her own. Don't worry, she doesn't pry into your business much. She hardly gives you a chance, to get a word in edgewise. She told me that, her family doesn't know. But she had a nervous breakdown.

I said, I think I'm having a nervous breakdown myself!

She most likely didn't hear me, because she was talking over top of me. Talk about a chatterbox ... Don't let her phone ring, while you are getting your hair done. She will stop, and finish her long conversation. Or she has been known, to pull your hair, when the conversation turns abrupt! She is rude, and also very blunt at times.

She saw the broken hair, patch in the middle of my head. She said, "Ewwww! I don't know, what you expect me to do with this!" She played with it, back and forth, with her comb. She definitely, gets carried away sometimes!

I explained, I think my hair is falling out! Breaking off, or something. Because of stress... She only hears, what she wants to hear anyway. I got her to arch my eyebrows. I said, I want you to read my future. With the tarot cards, you've been talking about! I want to see, what they say about me. She was excited, to do it. I was reluctant, but kind of excited myself. She said, "Think of a question with a yes, or no answer."

I said, will I find me a husband ...

DEVASTATING CONSEQUENCES

She started laying down the cards. Then I finished my sentence, to take care of me, and ...

She said, "No, no, no, no! You have to think, of what you want, your question to be. Nod when you are finished."

She collected the cards. I began again, Will I, ever find, a rich man. To love and take care of me and marry me? I nodded.

She laid the cards down, then she said, "The answer to your question, is no! There is the queen card, that says, you are going to do it yourself. Meaning, *you will be rich on your own!*"

It sent chills down my back! That could only mean one thing: If I write the book, I've been saying, I was going to write. I will be rich - on my own! My life, has definitely been exciting enough. I remember, when I had started writing it, I was in the tenth grade. But it was accidentally erased. I guess, it wasn't quite time for it yet.

I left my friend's house, with goose bumps on the back of my neck. And the hairs on my arms, haven't laid down yet! At least I look good, real good! Which did give me a much-needed boost of confidence! But it didn't stop, the inevitable. I am still wrestling, with this feeling. Every night, when I go home to an empty bed. I want to find someone, to help fill it. This feeling overwhelms me, like an addiction. I have admitted to myself, that I am addicted to love. Which like many hard drugs. It can determine what you do, on a daily basis. It makes certain decisions for me. I don't want to *need* love so much! I want to be like the normal people, people who didn't have the ones they cared about most, in life. Ripped away, too soon. I wasn't ready for this breakup, and neither was he, for that matter. So, the only way to get *over* him, is to *replace* him. Being single is just *not* an option! I need certain things done around the house. Things that only a man should do, and until I fill that position, certain things will deteriorate!

I deserve, not to be, lonely! I've been through my downtimes. Everyone has those times, in their life, at sometime or another. Mine just happened to come back-to-back, for five years straight. Between the loss of my dad, my mom, and my first love. Then there's the evil stepmother, stirring it all up. I've been thrown enough hardships, to last me a lifetime. I know, I need to go to the doctor. Because what I'm feeling is not normal! I'm crazy half the time, and sane the other half. I have developed this fear of doctors. I panic, and I won't drive there myself. I am scared, of the outcome. That's the crazy me, talking. Because the sane me knows, I'll most likely be treated, with medicines, and released. The crazy part of me, fears hospitalization. I hate hospitals! It feels like jail. I not staying, in no hospital! I have things to take care of, on a daily basis. I can't be strapped, to no bed. I do *not* want, to sleep in a hospital. I don't want to stay there...

My objective for right now, is to convince my family. That they need, to take me to the doctor. Before the crazy me, can talk them out of it. I went to my Aunt Eva's house only because she is the most down-to-earth out of all our aunts. Plus, she doesn't work because of a bum knee. So she's the only one at home in the middle of the day. We laugh, and talk for awhile. Then we smoked a blunt, which, in a sense, made it worse. Again, I would go from crazy, to not crazy, all within a couple of minutes, sometimes seconds. I told Eva, that I need, to talk to her.

She sat in a chair, directly across from me. I explained to her not only that I think I'm bipolar. But I know, I am. It's scary! I see things, and I know things. I know what drugs you take, but I don't judge you. I don't want people to judge me! I need someone to take me to the doctor. Because I won't drive myself! It's like, I can't. My car won't take me there. That's scary too.

Eva has this look on her face, Like deer, caught in the headlights.

What? Was I acting crazy? Do you think I'm acting crazy?

She doesn't know if I'm joking or not. I laughed when I should be crying! She thinks I'm joking! I can't make her believe me. It's like looking at the TV on mute. She can't hear me! No, listen, listen. I'm trying, to tell you something! It's not a joke at all.

Damn, she didn't hear me. Did I whisper it? No, the knock on the door, distracted her. In walked a man, tall, dark, and handsome! He seemed like a stranger, but I do remember seeing him once before. To be quite honest, he looks like a fat version, of my dad. Older, but he did get a second glance.

The stranger sat down on the couch, next to mines. I spoke, but continued to go through the motions. I couldn't be as cordial, as usual. Because I don't feel, like myself. He made small talk with my aunt, then turned to say something to me.

DEVASTATING CONSEQUENCES

I told Eva, please tell him don't talk to me! Then I covered my face, to hide the tears.

He said, "I understand. I can tell you are going through something, but you'll be all right. I've been going through something myself. You see all these pills? Sometimes I don't want to be bothered either. I am the eldest, of a family of girls, and they all come to me, for advice. I'm there, for everyone else, but nobody's ever there for me! Even when they found out I was bipolar and everything else. I have nobody strong enough, to really be there for me."

I uncovered my face, and looked dead, into his eyes. Oh my gosh, did you say you are bipolar? What happened?

He responded, "They put me on a lot of medications, and here I am." I mean, can you work?

"Hell, naw, I can't work!"

All of a sudden. I felt this pain, in the bottom of my stomach. It balled up, into a real tight knot. Oh, my God, it hurts so bad!!!! I can't sit down, anymore. I jumped up! The spirit, got into me, and I shouted, all over that floor. Funny thing is, I have never shouted a day before in my life. Yet, it came like second nature. I guess I've never been this happy! I shouted and cried. He sat and watched, yet I didn't care. I jumped around hollering, Thank you, Jesus! Thank you, Jesus! I feel complete. I feel like, God has, sent this, man to, me. He is bipolar, too. We would make a perfect couple.

Eva was busy, on the phone, with grandma. I heard her say, "Mama, I've never seen her, like this before!" The pain only subsided, while I was shouting! When I went to sit down, it started again. I walked around the room.

He said, "Now that you know, you won't have to work. What will you do? Sit at home all day?"

I said, No, I'm going to write a book. I'll be rich! I started dancing and singing.

He said, "I knew you weren't crazy! She has a good head, on her shoulders. Now, does that sound like a crazy person?"

He watched me dance, around the room, like a plumb idiot, with no alarm. He's used to things like that. We would be perfect together. A large part of me, feels like, I found the man of my dreams! It's a reason, why both of us, came here today.

I think Eva went upstairs, to get squared away. Before we leave, to go to the doctor. I'm not stupid, or dumb. I know I scared her. So bad, that it blew her high! My dark stranger, called me out on the porch. He said, "I know that realize that I go with your aunt's friend. But we have been having so many problems lately, that I don't want to be with her, anymore! Honestly, I want to be with you! I like you, and everything I saw today. I want to know, if I can have your number, so I can call you later. You can't tell your aunt, of course. This will be between us, until we can make everything official!"

Yeah, I'll give you my phone number. I smiled more at that moment, than I've smiled in awhile as I wrote my number down for him.

When I gave it, to him. He said, "You really like me? I mean, you are so pretty! I like everything about you. I'm going to call you later, if that's alright."

Yes, it is.

We went back in the house and talked for a few more minutes. Like nothing, ever happened. Somehow, I ended up driving him to pick up his girlfriend and her sister. I drove them home. She is close to the family, so when she left, she hugged me. She said, she hopes, I feel better soon! To me, I took that as, "It's okay, you can have him. I won't be mad at you. Everything is turning into a game.

I think Shaun is trying to hook me up with the dude from North Carolina. But fate, is going to keep me here with him. It seems like more than a coincidence. That the dude looks just like and talks just like, the dude from Texas! I think my sister called the *Remodel My Family Show*. I have a man waiting in North Carolina, that's willing to marry me. They built this beautiful house, for me and my kids to live in. I don't want to spoil the surprise! But I think I found a man, on my own.

My whole objective was to find someone to unbreak my heart. I think I found a soul mate, and on a humble! Shaun will understand, I hope.

When I got back to the house, Eva was ready to take me to the doctor. One of her close friends was there. We struck up a conversation, and she told me that she is bipolar. I asked her also, can you work. She echoed the previous answer. It did make me feel better.

Eva drove me to the doctor, and we went in. I do not have an appointment, but they have to see me. The receptionist asked, "May I help you?"

I responded, I need to see my doctor. I'm bipolar!

With those words, my body shut down. I went into a trance. She saw the expression on my face. She hurried, to get the doctor. Evidently my doctor is finally back in the country. They escorted me to the back.

The doctor came in right away. It was like I knew, what he was going to say, before he even said it. "I wasn't expecting you."

I stared into his eyes. Scared, because it seemed like he said it twice! The first time was in my head. I told him, I am bipolar!

He said, "How do you know?"

I said, I just know; I see things. I wanted to tell him. I already knew, what he was going to say, before he said it. But I didn't want to scare him. My hair is falling out! I'm always trying to cover it up. This is weave."

"What kinds of things do you see?"

I see signs, that tell me to do stuff. Good stuff. And it warns me against bad stuff! I think I have, what the man, has in *Butterfly Effect*! I want a cat scan, to prove it! Have you seen the movie? He said, "No, I don't watch many movies." Yet, I knew he was lying. Then I saw him write it down. Without seeing him write it down. My back was turned. It felt like, I was the paper. I felt the pen dragging over me, to write the words! It's like, I can read his mind.

Will you buy my book? "Yes, I will. I know it will be interesting! I want you to go to this doctor, in the morning! I will write down the name and phone number for you."

I think the fact, that I only blinked twice. During our whole conversation, concerned him. He looked scared! Which in turn, scared me. Because I'm like ... what? What? Then I realized it's *me*! I'm scaring people! It's the way I act, and I can't control it! I can't do anything about it. I'm in control of every aspect of my life. A little bit of other people's too. I can't lose it now! But when is a good time? What's the perfect time to have a meltdown? A nervous breakdown. Now, I know what it feels like. My nerves are bad!

I got so scared when I saw a man crossing the street, coming towards me. It was while I was pumping gas. I rushed to finish! I barely screwed the top on the gas tank. Just so I could get in my car fast and lock my doors.

Scary things, remind me of the devil. I can see him, in their eyes! Which scared me! I can tell who's good and who's evil! Subsequently, leaving the gas top, too loose made my check engine light, come on. I had to pay over two hundred some dollars just to get it fixed! That was a costly lesson.

I went home to get dinner going for the kids. Something quick, during the week. Big meals, on the weekends. That's when I have more time. I'm not rushed, as much by kids, who might as well be banging on the table. Demanding dinner, as many times as they say, "I'm hungry! I'm hungry! Mom, I'm hungry!"

I whisper, I hear you! They know that whispering, is worse than hollering around here! I have to shut that up real fast. It can pluck my bad nerve! I try not to take out how I'm feeling on my kids. My frustrations of having to be a man and woman in this household in order to try to keep it running. This shit is hard!

Sometimes, I say, if I were on one of those talk shows as a kid that showed you how hard it really is to be a mother. I might not have. I love sleep! Since I've been a mother, my sleep has been cut, by at least forty percent! But with all it's hardships, I wouldn't trade them for the world! They are my world, and they are the only things that keep me going! I don't want them to live like I lived. Without a mother, or father, or loving caretakers.

Love, is a feeling, I don't want to live without. I think I found Mr. Right finally! Someone, to accept me, for me. I'm the yin to his yang. I'll be strong for him, when he needs me, and he'll be strong for me, when I need him! I put the kids to bed and relaxed, in my room. Then I got a call from him, and I was all ears. He said, "I told her, it's over! We have been over here arguing, and all kinds of stuff. I told her, I can't hide the way I feel! I told her, I want to be with you! She would have found out eventually! I need to get out of here. Will you come get me?"

I'm on my way. Panic set in. I panicked! I don't want him to have to go through that! I went in the kids' room, to see if they were still awake. Tayon is woke, I called Zay Zay's name. She didn't respond. It really hadn't been enough time for them to be sleep. It seemed like she was faking. Oh, well! I left her there, and the baby and I left. We drove, to pick him up. When he got in the car, he thanked me, for coming.

He said, "I can't believe that, you actually came! I'm so happy! I had to see you. Let's stop, at this store right here. I need some beer, after all that. Do you have a couple of dollars? Yeah, that five will be enough! I just don't have any money on me, right now."

He came out the store, and we headed home. To my house. He said, "I want to stay. So I can go, with you to the doctor, in the morning." That is so sweet! We settled in, and the first thing he did, was go to the bathroom. He took all his clothes off and used the bathroom - with the door open!

He said, "I just want you to relax, get comfortable! See, I can be naked around you because I feel comfortable. As if I've known you, for years!"

I know! I feel that way too. Then I took off all my clothes. He threw me on the bed and went to work! I said, wait! Let me wash up, first.

He lifted up his face and said, "I don't care; I like it natural."

Damn, okay! After that, he wanted to hold me. We talked a lot. He said, "Do you believe in love at first sight? I fell in love with you as soon as I saw you! You are different. I can't be with her anymore! She is on drugs real bad, and I never did want anything to do with that. I want to marry you! I will have to make you the cosigner on my check."

Wait a minute, calm down. Oh, my gosh! Are you serious? You want to marry me? He said, "Yes, Will you marry me? I mean, I haven't even met your kids, yet."

You would meet them. Yes, I will marry you! I want a big wedding, though. We could go to the justice of the peace, first. Then save up, for a big wedding! I just need, to get through tonight! So I can make the announcement, tomorrow. I think that's when Shaun is going to announce her surprise! I think she and my supervisor, got together. They are going to throw me, a going away party! Look at them! Everyone will meet me at the doctor, it will be perfect.

Shaun is going to be a little upset. That I didn't go with her guy, but I think she'll be happy for me! Everyone will know, I'm a psychic. When they find out, I knew about the surprise. They'll be pissed! They made it so obvious, though. Her little sister, is getting married! I did everything else before her, why not this? She is going to make a pretty maid of honor. Especially, with all the weight she has lost!

I snapped back to reality and kissed him, to commemorate the moment. I love you! He wants to have sex. My response is, we are getting married tomorrow. We can wait that long, I know!

He said, "I respect that! I respect you. I don't ever want to hurt you, and I know you say, you've had a hard life. I just want to make it easier! I'm a gentleman. Let's hold each other and go to sleep."

This feels too good, to be true! Fate is definitely at work here. He fell asleep. But not before he used the bathroom, four more times. That's probably because he drank the whole six-pack!

I can't sleep, in part because of his snoring. I am all to pieces, I have over a million thoughts, going on right now! I am so scared, about going to the doctor tomorrow. What if I die? Do I have my ducks in a row? Something as divine, as love at first sight, could mean my demise. What are the chances of that? I know too much! I'm getting too powerful! There is such a thing, as knowing too much! Some of the things I know, scare me to death! That's just it, scaring me to death! I can get so scared, that I might die. Oh, my God! Please, I don't want to die now! I can't waste one more minute.

I reached for my pen and paper, that I always keep by. I made a list of everyone, who had ever done me wrong! So that I could forgive them. I refuse, to let these people steal my joy! They won't keep me out of heaven. The paper read:

DEVASTATING CONSEQUENCES

Actual note written by myself in the middle of psychosis.

I jumped up out the bed, making sure not to alarm him. That's the last thing I need. When he has his attacks, I have to be there for him. Right now, I need to be here, for myself. I need to do something for myself. I walked through my living room, straight toward the paper. The paper that I keep encased in glass. When I picked it up, I drew it near to my heart, and started to cry. I don't read this letter often. Just the thought that *she* wrote this! *She* touched this paper. I want to touch it too. Just so I can be closer to her. Once the tears flowed, and passed, I read it ...

> What can I say to you. Mommy can't always be around to tell you or make you behave. You're a very intelligent & strong willed child. You will eventually find out that you don't know everything. Grow & learn. Remember everything I've told you, live by it. Help your little brother, teach him, don't yell at him. Support your sister & help her. Remember I'm always there in spirit. Don't let no one take A.J. it's my last request he's a part of us now. I love you

Love, Mommy

I did each and everything, she asked me to do! With no regard, for consequence! I love you, that much, Mama! I did it!

She said, "Now it's your turn. It's your turn to reap the benefits! For everything you've done. You will be blessed. For every one, you've helped. You will be blessed. I know you've found out some things, about yourself, that are surprising at best. What you do from here, is totally up to you. But if you write a book, telling everything that you've been through. You'll be set, for the rest of your life. All you have to do is write the book."

I went back in the room with my fiancé.

He woke up and asked me, "Is everything okay?"

I responded, things are better now. We embraced each other. We looked into each other's eyes. As if to say, just make the most of the moment. We began to make love, as a man and wife should.

"The more I looked at him, the more I saw Jimmy, my husband. He has put on some weight. That's okay, that's in right? The girls are in the bed and in case you are wondering this is Ethel. Dee, please forgive me. I have to make the most of this moment. I want to have sex with my husband, one more time. It feels so good raw. Just like you like it. But it sure did feel good, that night you gave me AIDS too! You killed me, because you are a selfish pig! I hate you!!"

He responded, "No, Dee, it's me, baby. It's me!"

I opened my eyes, Daddy! Oh my God, Daddy? Why are you doing this to me? No, I don't want you to. I'm going to tell my mama. He jumped up, and turned the light on. I snapped out of it, and squinted to see his face.

He said, "Everything is okay. We can stop, and go back to sleep."

You go to sleep, I'll be back.

I forgot to take out the trash. I have this feeling, that I just cannot explain. I want to test out a theory. I walked out of my back door and dragged the trash to the curb, butt naked. I waited. Traffic was slow, but a car came by. A white man was driving. He looked right through me! With no reaction. *Oh, my gosh. I'm invisible!* My feet started to feel cold and wet. I jogged back in the house. I put on my bedroom shoes, and grabbed my black dress. I went on the back porch, to listen to music. I listened to Boyz II Men, of course. They always help me. The song is, "In the Still of the Night."

It was then that my muscles started to tighten up. It feels like I am a robot. I didn't make my own moves. Someone else is one step ahead of me. Knowingly, moving parts of my body. Doing things, that it wanted. I think it's my mom. I *know* it's my mom. It's like she possessed my body. My arm and finger extended, pushing buttons until her ears were satisfied. I swayed back and forth, rhythmically. The music is absolutely as loud, as it goes. Bass and everything. Let's just say I have some nice parties. I guess my purpose, is to get sleeping beauty, to come out and dance with me. Make this moment magical! Okay, I'm going to close my eyes, and when I open them. If it's meant to be, he will be standing there. Ten, nine, eight, seven, six, five, four, three, two, one ... NOTHING!

15

The dog started barking excessively. "The End of the Road," by Boyz II Men came on, and she pushed repeat. We listened to the same song for hours. The feeling, you get, from hugging, someone. That's the, feeling that, I have. Just without, moving my arms. We played, "I Miss You," by Boyz II Men.

"I can't, let go! It's time for me to go back, but I don't want to. I told you, I was going to come back. You said, you can handle it! You're doing okay. One more thing! All you have to do, is one more thing. This thing is for you! Nobody else. You write that book for you! Like God says, you've run your course. For doing what I've asked, I'm going to take care of you, for the rest of your life ... You won't work another day, in your life! All you have to do is, dance, all the way to the bank. Get up and dance, baby. It's okay; you dance."

I danced and pranced, all around the floor. Laughing, and having a ball, with my mama. I love you, Mama! What an experience! We hugged, and I never wanted, to let her go! I said, no, mama. Don't leave me here with him! He raped me.

She said, "Your daddy raped you? First he's gay, then he's a pedophile! Oh, hell, no! He's not going to touch my baby, like that! That's incest."

I went and grabbed a knife. I burst into the room, and I said, Oh, you raped my daughter? You put your hands on my daughter? I will slice, your motherfucking dick off! Get up; I don't want to hear any more lies."

He said, "Oh my God, you are scaring the shit, out of me. Please!!!! I didn't rape your daughter! Both your kids are still sleep." Zay Zay, Tayon, you'll wake up! They are asleep. I'm sorry, I don't know, what's going on. Wake up, kids! Let's turn this music up, a little louder. It's almost time for everybody to come, anyways! It would be funny to show up naked. Like a joke on them, or something. It'll be funny! I'll take this dress off." The kids woke up and asked what's going on? To show everybody, that we already knew, about the new house. We are going to, color on the walls. Get your favorite crayons and markers, kids! Color and draw whatever you want. Something like this! This is fun, isn't it?

Zay Zay said, "Yeah, this is, fun. But why are you naked, Mama?"

That's not a big deal; you've seen me naked before. Firemen see people naked all the time. Just get ready for a whole new house! New toys and everything. You'll see! Okay, we can write on anything, on this side of the house. Don't go in my living room.

I found a pen and wrote, BIPOLAR WRITER! They'll come back to this house and see that I knew it, before anyone could tell me. What does that make me? A psychic. Let's knock down everything, out of the cabinet. I don't need that anymore. Ripppped the thermostat, right out of the wall. I wish I had a sledge hammer! "You know what? I want this man out of my house. I don't want him here anymore! Come on, Zay Zay, let's make a phone call. Let's call the police! You tell them, that someone raped, your mama. You know your address, don't you? Okay, let's call!"

She said, "Send the police; someone raped my mama!"

We hung up and laughed. "Okay, they are coming!"

I grabbed the knife again and told him to get his shit, and go. He ran outside, butt naked! Then the police pulled up. They walked to the door, and I growled.

They said, "Ma'am, you need to put the knife down."

I said, here, here you go! Then I tossed the knife down, right in front of my feet. This is no ordinary knife. It's about twelve inches long. A butcher knife.

The police, entered the house. They read the walls and asked, "How can we help?" I turned into myself, for a minute. Long enough, to be cordial. I saw one of the policemen's faces. I knew it was a guy, that I graduated high school with. Hey, how are you doing?

"I'm fine; how is your sister doing? Do you want a blanket, or something?" No, not really, but I'll take one. I can't believe, that I am sitting here butt naked, and he just asked about my sister. That's how I know, this all a game. I said, I don't want that man, in my house. He raped me! I'm bipolar! He said, "Well, we do need to get some clothes for him. He says, he also has medicine over here. Is that true?" I changed. "Only things, with his name on them! I don't really like the way your partner, is walking all through my house like that. I hollered, Excuse me! We are all in here! Let's wrap this up! Okay, thanks. Just take him away! Thanks, for coming out." I shut the door! Okay, kids, now all we have to do is wait, on the fire trucks. The kids asked, "When are the fire trucks coming?"

We have to be patient. I turned the TV on, and it said, "This house has been hit by lightning, and the fire trucks, are on their way." I turned the TV off and told the kids, see, I told you, they are coming. We sat quietly, and patiently, under the blanket. You could hear a pin drop. Then Zay Zay said, "I can hear them coming. Listen!"

Oh, my gosh! It's almost over.

Those fire trucks, never came! We still sat quietly, and patiently. My daughter interrupted, by saying, "Can we really have any toy, we want?"

With a big smile, I answered, "Yes, when this is all over, you will be able to have anything, you want." I called the police, so many times, until they got fed up!

They said, "What do you want us to do? We can't send fire trucks, if there is no fire."

That pissed me off! If they don't send the fire trucks. How will they get ladders tall enough to tear down and rebuild my house? Maybe they are redoing, our old house. Renovating the house, my mama left to us. We will live there! It's big enough, for me and Shaun. It's going to ruin, the surprise! But I can't wait any longer!

I'm going over there. Let's get dressed, kids. Throw on some shoes. Once I got in the car, I called Shaun. I can tell she is still sleep. I said, Since I already know, I'm going to meet you over at the house!

She said, "Okay."

So that is what I'm supposed to do?

"Yes!"

Alright! Well, I'll call you back later. Everything in me, feels like doing 95, just to get there! That's how excited I am! We will live in our old house, in our old neighborhood. Lord knows, we deserve it.

What if Shaun, lets me have it. To live in, with my new husband? The second part, of her surprise. My North Carolina cutie, is moving up here with me. She talked him into it. After all, I've been through. Being there for everyone, including herself. She wants to make sure her little sister, gets married, and is finally happy!

When I'm happy, she's happy. As is, a lot of others. I am a beam of sunshine, in a dark room. If anyone is sad, it's like, it's my job, to see if I can help! If they don't want to talk, about it. The least I can do is try, to make them laugh. Laughing, is good for the soul. With every laugh, I know my soul, is healed. At least a little bit. I've had enough blows, in life. Enough to knock my soul down, to the size of a little girl's.

There is a scorned, little girl on the inside of me, raring to get out. A little girl, who had her childhood ripped away! It was replaced by worry, and anxiety. There's a part of me, that resents that worry-free child. A child who's hardest decision is what color, to paint her toenails, and whose slumber party to go to. I couldn't go! I had to stay home, with my sick mother. She could die at any minute. That means every minute that I can be there, I need to be there!

When I rebelled, against that. My family took that, as an insult. Implying, that I don't respect, or love, my dying mother. That couldn't be farther, from the truth. I am the daughter, who mirrored her every move. Knowingly or unknowingly. She even gave me, her middle name. I am honored. I may not look the most like her out of my sister and me, but I did follow in her footsteps: smoking weed in the juvenile years, bearing two children, smoking cigarettes, drinking beer, full-figured, and an appetite for the finer things in life. Not to mention the two years, I proudly put in, at the same bank as her. She is the one, making this happen. There is some greater force, at work here. I hit every stoplight. The streets, with no stoplights or signs, there is a school bus, loading and unloading imaginary students. Lord knows, I didn't see any. That's the only thing, that made me slow down. I was forced, to do the speed limit. I finally arrived, and made the kids, stay in the car. I have to try the key. I looked at the two brand-new cars in the driveway. I knew they were mine. I told the kids, to look at our new van. I don't know what that other one is, but it sure is nice.

I opened the screen door and then realized. This lock looks like the one, they changed at my house. Let me find out that my landlord is in on this, too. I shoved the key in, and it didn't turn. My heart sank! I tried the door knob ... It twisted open, but it feels like, someone is on the other side, pushing against it. I stormed back to the car. It seemed like the blinds opened a little bit. Is this someone else's house?

DEVASTATING CONSEQUENCES

I called Shaun to curse her out. Why the fuck, did you tell me to come over here? Why did you tell me to come to the old house?

She said, "I didn't tell you to go to the old house! And why did you hang up on me earlier? Is that where you are now?"

Yes, that's were I'm at now, but I'm leaving! I started breaking into a hysterical cry.

The 911 operator called me back. I think they have been following me, anyway. She asked, "Where are you now?"

I responded, I am going home, NOW! I hung up on her too. I think my mama made me go there. Like she wanted to see the house one more time! Maybe she just wanted to go for a ride. That's all she had to say.

I got back home, pissed off and confused! A lot of thoughts, ran through my head. One of which was that, I cannot stay in this house! If I'm up at this hour, Rodney is to. He's on powder, which means he doesn't sleep much. He has lots of energy. I know he's mad. I haven't been talking to him. In a since, giving him the cold shoulder. He could pop up at anytime, let himself in, and do whatever he wants! I know he has a gun, and judging by the dream that he had, he's not afraid to use it! I have got to go, right now!

Oh my gosh! I don't have on a bra! We don't have time to change. Grab your shoes! I yelled at the kids, you just had them!!!!! Oh, well. I'll just carry Tayon. Let's go! I ran out the back door and jumped in the car, checking my back the whole time! He's a sneaky motherfucker!

I drove over Eva's house, surprisingly slower than last time. I do feel safe in my car. I arrived over Eva's, as she was getting her kids off to school. I walked in, and she looked concerned. I told her I panicked! I couldn't stay in that house any longer.

I was able to tell her a little about the problem. In concluding, I mentioned that I go from crazy, to not crazy, in a matter of seconds, and sometimes I can't control it! Eva left the room to hide her crying. Her close, female friend, who had previously mentioned that she is bipolar, whispered to me! "Middle. Middle. Just think about being in the middle. It will help!" I repeated it to myself. Middle, middle, middle, over and over again! It did help me ... but only for awhile!

Eva started arguing with her friend. They don't know but this is definitely not helping! In fact, it is making me worse. Zay Zay keeps making faces, trying to get me to laugh! It's weird, but I think subconsciously, she is trying to help me! All her faces and dancing piss me off after awhile. I told her to sit down.

My sister walked through the door and looked at us. She said, "Why do the kids have on pajamas?"

I said, I am sick, Shaun. I had a panic attack, and I had to get out of the house, right away! I felt like Rodney was coming to get me. I didn't sleep at all last night! I can't explain to you, how scared I was! You know something is wrong. I never leave the house without a bra! My boobs are too big for that. Just don't yell at me!

She said, "You still could have put some clothes on the kids! I don't understand that!"

I started changing! I sat down, overwhelmed. Almost like, my mom was coming out to scold her, for being so mean! I said, middle, middle, middle! This time aloud, unknowingly.

She said, "Why do you keep on saying that? You are scaring me!"

I stopped saying it, and it got worse! She calmed down, but I didn't! I had to start, saying it again. She got up and started crying. I don't want her to panic! I don't want her, to be scared of me! That made me worse too! I tried to talk to her and explain. That's the only thing that's keeping me sane right now! Hearing a crazy person talk, is like a teaspoon of salt in a gallon of water. It sure doesn't go far! She nodded and looked at me as if I were really crazy! Am I really crazy? I think so ...

Let's go to the doctor! I need to go to the doctor! But I won't go, without my daughter! Something keeps telling me, 'Don't forget your daughter. Don't forget your daughter!' What does that mean? 'Don't forget Zay Zay?' Or telling my mama, 'Don't forget me!' She has to hype herself up, to go to the doctor. So much so, that she might forget me. I don't know what it means, but I'm taking her! She might be what it takes to keep me sane in the car. Leaving my boy, was the hardest thing I've done in awhile! For some reason, I felt like it was the last time I would see him. As if, someone was dying! Is it him, or is it me? I don't want him to die!

Eva's friend reassured me, that Tayon would stay with her. He would be just fine. That's the only reason I walked away. What she said helped me so much before! I believe her.

Maria met us outside at the car. She hugged me and said, "I'm glad you decided to go!" She drove. My sister rode shotgun, while Zay Zay and I sat in the backseat. They fussed over where to take me. Shaun had only one responsibility, and she lost the paper! The paper with the name and address of the doctor. Bless her heart! She denied even being given the paper. Which in turn, made me worse!

Zay Zay started making faces again. I stared at her almost like she had hypnotizing eyes! Who knew a five-year-old child could have this kind of effect on me? I don't remember the journey there. But I do remember the arrival! We arrived at the same hospital that we were supposed to come to years back to get counseling. When Kam learned it would be unsupervised by her. She denied all requests. We did suffer from that, but now I'm here! Bitter sweet ...

How does a sane person, check herself, into a crazy house? She doesn't!! I had to convince my family to bring me here. In a sense, I was talking behind my own back. At times, I caught myself whispering, as if not to let myself hear it! Crazy, is a word tossed around way too often. Oh, you are so crazy! This time, it's not an expression or joke! To quote a line from one of my favorite movies, *Diary of a Mad Black Woman* ... "Mama, I think I'm going crazy! He hurt me so bad ..." No hurt worse than the amount you've endured. I continue to say, it's the ultimate betrayal! I think, I've tapped into the strength God gave us women, to stay alive. It's almost over!

You said, "Don't be afraid." Lord knows, I'm trying my best. We walked in, and I felt panic strike my whole body. I don't want to be here! Then I remembered, it's not my mama that doesn't like hospitals. It's me.

The counselor asked me a whole lot of questions. I went from crazy, to not crazy, depending on the setting. With my family in the room, I'm more relaxed. I told my sister, I hope you are not mad because I spoiled the surprise. I found a husband on my own! We are getting married tomorrow! We couldn't wait, so we had unprotected sex.

It's okay, Shaun. This was my first time doing it like that! You know, on the first date! I couldn't help it. It was love, at first sight! Plus, he's my fiancé. I tense up when my family leaves. I feel a little intimidated and overwhelmed. "What happened to bring on your condition?"

I think he drugged me.

"Who? Why would he want to do that?"

My ex-boyfriend. He's trying to kill me. Because I don't want to be with him anymore! I walked in on him, having sex with another girl!

"So, you think he's trying to kill you?"

Yes, he had a dream that me and my kids were dead. Shot to death. He says he didn't do it. I said, who the fuck else would do it?

The counselor left the room. I saw my family going through my purse, to get all the papers I had written on. I would write down things in my sane moments, so that I wouldn't forget them while crazy. After a lot of waiting and a lot of emotions, some lady showed up to escort me to my room. The most painful part, was saying goodbye to my daughter. Next, saying goodbye to the rest of my family. Preparing for the inevitable, we got on a locked elevator and rode to the top. The lady made small talk on the elevator. But since I have the ability to look dead in your face and tune out your every word, I didn't hear shit she said. The motionless stare, is what I call a zone. My visits to this zone, are also uncontrolled! We got off the elevator, and walked through a couple of locked doors, until we got to a room.

She said, "This is your room."

I walked in and looked around. I walked right back out, crying ... I can't stay here! I don't want to stay here! That room is disgusting! It looks worse than the sleaziest hotel room I've ever seen. I saw baby ants crawling around the cracked tile, on the bathroom floor.

My body tapped into that strength to cope! My mind said, "Don't sweat the small things!" Something my supervisor always said. It didn't help. I said, I cannot stay in this room!

The nurse ran over to help. She said, "Well, what about this room?"

We walked right next door, but it felt like I was in a different hospital. The bed is better, and the bathroom tile sparkled! This room is much cleaner and much better! Yeah, and next time, you better know, to give me a good room! Don't try to give me some old, rinky-dink shit! I don't know if I said that out loud just now, or not. But what I did say aloud is, I guess I can stay here!

DEVASTATING CONSEQUENCES

I looked up with tears in my eyes. I saw a lady. My eyes met hers. I stared into her eyes ... I see something familiar, in her eyes. She beckoned me near, with her arms wide open. I walked into her arms, and she hugged me. She hugged me like, she had known me my whole life! Mere words cannot explain that feeling! The nurse rushed me back to my room and handed me a small green piece of paper. On it was written: Call Maria, Call Shaun,   Call Eva.

The strange thing about it is, it's written in a familiar hand. It looks like, my mama wrote it! I tried to catch the nurse, to ask her who had written it. She was too busy, to respond. But looked up at me like, you know who wrote it! I do know who wrote it. My mama, wrote this note. They are taking this surprise wedding thing too far! They want to surprise me, and have my mama at my wedding! They have been keeping her in here! Keeping her away from me! She lost her mind when she found out she had AIDS! They've been keeping her away from me all these years!

I walked out of my room. I looked straight at the doctor. She started locking herself behind glass. Why are you keeping her from me? Where are you, Mama? Mama, please! Don't hide from me anymore! I walked towards the locked door on the right. I banged and banged on that door! I screamed, at the top of my lungs. Come out, Mama! Open this door! I have to get to her! You can't keep me away from her! Please, unlock this door! I need to get to my mama. I need her! I need you, Mama! Please, say something! God, please! You said, 'Stand at the door and knock.' I'm standing patiently, knocking! My knuckles hurt, and my voice is hoarse. I tried my best to claw that door down!

I'll sit here and wait! Minutes turned into hours until I came up with a plan! A plan to rescue my mama. I need to find someone with a key. The key is, to find someone with a key! I stood up, brushed myself off, and walked into my room. A nurse came in to check my blood pressure.

I asked her, do you have a key, to the room next door?

She said, "No, I don't have the key. Why is it so important that you get in there?"

My mom is in there. They are trying to keep her from me! They want to have her surprise me, at my wedding.

She said, "I'll bet she comes!"

Thank you, I appreciate that!

Then she said, "Did you make your calls yet? If you didn't, you need to go ahead and do that."

I will.

Just then, a sheriff, walked in. I remember going in and out of a zone. But hearing his final words, "Daminika Cunningham, consider yourself served. You are ordered to remain detained here, until the decision of the counselors." He handed me a paper and left the room.

With paper in hand, I stormed out the room! This paper says, you have to treat me! You can't kill me for what I know! However long you say, I'm going to be here. I'm going to do it in half the time! Thank you, Jesus!

I saw my family on the far side of Plexiglas. Once I prove that I am bipolar, I will be rich, and I'll dance, all the way to the bank! Thank you, Lord! I started dancing, shouting even! I am so blessed! My family watched in horror! They locked down the nurses station again. The doctor stared at me from behind the now-locked office. Everything, is becoming one long riddle. What does this mean? What does that mean? Proving this will be, one hell of a roller-coaster ride! But the countdown has begun.

A counselor walked towards me. She said, "I want to ask you a couple of questions." She did just that, but it was my response to one of her questions, that sent chills, down my own back. She asked simply, "What is your full name?"

I said, "It depends on who you are talking to." I can tell that scared her as well!

She said, "I want to talk to Dee."

I said, my name is Daminika. My friends and family call me Dee. You are neither. Don't pretend to be. The meeting ended there!

She told me, "You have to go in front of a committee and talk."

I don't know who these people are. But when I got in that room, I assumed they were from my job, and I told them, you don't have to fire me, because I quit! I stormed out, not being able to control my emotions any longer! I have uncontrollable fits of happiness and anger that do not exclude dancing or singing!

They let Maria in to see me first. She said, "I won't stay long, but

I'll bring you more cigarettes tomorrow." With that, she left. Then my sister and Nettie came in together. I sometimes say the first thing that comes to mind! I fought back an embarrassing thought. I was going to blurt out. *Are you gay, too?* Instead, I said to my sister who has dropped a dramatic amount of weight, You have AIDS!

She looked puzzled. She said, "Ohhhh!"

We talked a little bit, then the doctor came in. I growled at her! She gave me a shot. I came to reality for a split second and said something that made sense, and everybody laughed. The doctor said, "Do you feel suicidal?"

I said, no, I love myself too much!

She said, "Smart girl! She'll be fine, in time. For right now, she needs to eat! When is the last time you have eaten?" I don't know! I was doing so much other stuff, I forgot to eat.

They brought in a tray of, I guess, stroganoff. I said, what is this shit? I can't eat this. I hate anything cooked with milk! It stinks!

They urged me to eat. I picked the meat pieces out and forced that down. They said I need as much protein as I can get. So that's good! I drank juice, and that made me feel a little better. I am so sleepy, now! "She needs her sleep!" I crawled up in my bed and curled up. The doctor hit the lights on the way out. I went to sleep. It felt so good!

I slept for what felt like days. But turned out to be only hours. I woke up, confused and dazed. The lights in the hall seemed dimmer than earlier. Though, not dim enough. I squinted to see.

Can I smoke a cigarette, please? "Not yet. The smoking block doesn't open for another couple of hours."

I walked back in my room and laid down. I closed my eyes and slept about ten minutes, then jumped up again.

I need something! Some candy, some gum, or something! She looked in her burnt-yellow plastic goody box and pulled out three suckers. She gave them to me, and I felt as happy as a clam! Just as calm. I laid in the bed, eating candy and smiling. I can't really sleep that well. I got up so many times that night! I know I worried the shit, out of those nurses!

They changed shifts throughout the night. Most of the nurses are very nice though! One nurse urged me to talk to the doctor about getting sleeping medicine, to last through the night. The first thing I did was go smoke! I counted down the time. The next thing, is tackling this metal box, created to light your cigarette - but also to frustrate the fuck out of you! You have to blow out, before it lights, meaning exhale. You only exhale after you get upset! They have a camera to record, just how upset that lighter makes you.

I stood there puffing, to no avail. But as soon as you exhale, to give up in frustration, that's when it starts to work. I sit, and enjoy my cigarette, thinking with every drag, *This room is really cold! Almost like, they don't want us to sit in here very long or something!* I looked in the breakfast room. There is that mystery lady, with the familiar eyes. She's a white lady, with long brown hair, thinning a little at the top. She beckoned me in.

I got a plate of breakfast and sat with her to eat. Pretty decent food. We didn't say much, mainly talked of how I am doing. We lined up for medicine after breakfast. There's a little window, where someone distributes it. I downed mine and went back to my room. A nurse came in with a lot of supplies, including a toothbrush, toothpaste, lotion, soap, a comb, and waterless shampoo. She urged me to take a shower. I didn't realize I hadn't been doing that, either. I do stink! I ran the water and went to grab the soap and washcloth.

What is this? This little ass soap! I walked to the nurses station. I said, I can't use this! I cannot use this little ass soap! What am I supposed to do with this? This will get lost in the shuffle, before it cleans anything!

The nurses looked worried from all the ranting. They know I refuse to take a shower, without some bigger soap. They said, "Sorry, we don't have any other soap!"

I stormed back to the room. By this time, I really wanted to take a shower. I am pissed off, that I can't! Just then, my little friend that had made me feel so comfortable, when I first got here, rushed to my side. She heard what was going on. She said, "Don't worry, I have something for you!" She pulled a wonderful smelling, life-size bar of soap, from under her shirt! A name brand, bar of soap. It never seemed so rare, and valuable, until that moment. I thanked her! I damn near wanted to kiss her!

She smiled and said, "You just enjoy your shower! Do your hair. Make yourself feel pretty!"

I ran back to my room! I jumped in the shower, and let that hot water cover me! Exhilarating, is the first word that comes to mind. Scrubbing and squeaky clean, is the next. I felt some of my problems wash away. I do feel good and clean! I spruced up, my wet and wavy hair, put on my earrings, and I look like a different person! With all that jet-black, wavy hair, I look like a black Jesus!

My friend commented on how good I look. I know why her eyes, look so familiar! I see my mama in her eyes! Her quest, to take care of me. I looked at the door on the right of my room. Now it is unlocked! I peeked in. Empty! I sighed and turned away. A nurse said, "Who are you looking for?" Nobody, I'm not looking for anybody.

She said, "Well, the doctors are coming around to all the rooms. If you want to tell him anything. Think about what that is. You have a different doctor today, because the initial doctor is gone on vacation."

16

The new doctor came in and talked to me. He said, "Are you feeling better today? You weren't very happy to see me yesterday!" I don't remember seeing you yesterday! I have never seen you before in my life! I am doing better, though. I wish you would hurry up and release me. I have a wedding to attend! I know you are not going to make me miss my own wedding!

He said, "I don't want to do that! You be well!"

Thank you, Doctor. I walked out of my room and went looking for my new friend. Her name is Evelyn. She is working on some kind of picture web. She gave it to me when she finished. She encourages me to get some paper and write. Write about anything and everything that I want to say. When all you do is help people, your whole life! You'll get what you deserve! I'm getting married! I'll make a sign, telling everyone! I went to the nurses station. They gave me paper and a few pens. Just then, I saw a Bible! I asked, can I have the Bible. The response was, yes.

A nurse gave it to me. I opened it, and it said to dedicate this Bible, call a certain number. I hurried to the phone, and dialed the number. I said, I want to dedicate this Bible to, Ethel Darlene Cunningham! The person said, "Consider that done, and thank you in advance for your tax deductible donation of five dollars."

Thank you!

I hung up and hugged that Bible like a pillow. I placed it safely with the rest of my things. It did make me feel a little safer, and more secure. All of a sudden, a song popped in my head, that I just couldn't shake. It's a miracle, it's a miracle! Happening to everyday people. It is a miracle! I diagnosed myself. After hearing the name of this disorder for the first time, I knew it was me! I knew that's what I had. I'll call, It's a Miracle, and let them do a behind-the-scenes, interview with me. I am a miracle!! After that, I'll call the news station! I see news! I have a news story for you! That's exactly what I did.

The doctor learned of my intentions and detained me in my room. I have to let the nurse dial my numbers, from now on. They let me out, to smoke a cigarette. Smoking is contained to one room, with cameras. I tried to get Evelyn to come in with me, but she said, "It's way too cold in there for me! I'll wait outside."

I started talking to certain people in the smoking room. Mostly about, how they are being kept here. They don't know how long they are going to be in here. One guy said, "I don't have good insurance, and even though I need to be here, I think they might let me go today or tomorrow!"

I have a good job and good insurance. The man said, "Well, I heard the people with good insurance. They try to keep them, in here the longest!"

I don't want to be in here a long time! I quit my job! I forgot, I quit my job! I have to tell them! I'll let them know, I quit my job! I don't have any insurance, and they have to let me go! I walked right out of that smoking room and down the hall, lit cigarette and all. I walked to the furthest end of the hall. I saw reporters jumping out of the car, with cameras and all! Yes! IT'S TIME FOR ME TO GO!

I took a long drag, on my cigarette. I blew it out, as soon as the nurse, turned the corner. She has an ash tray in her hand and is walking towards me. She said, "Please put that cigarette out! Put it out, right here! You know you cannot smoke out here!"

I have to leave so I can go talk to my fans. They need to know the truth! I am a walking, talking, miracle!

Please, step back, fat black lady! Leave me alone! If I start a fire that will get you to open the doors. I took another long drag on my cigarette. Then I held it directly under the sprinkler head.

Open the doors! You better open the doors!

She said, "Please, don't do that! Walk this way to the smoking room."

I walked away. This shit doesn't work like it does on TV! Or it takes a long-ass time! I don't have that kind of time! This cigarette is burning down to the butt. I need to put it out! I walked towards the ash tray lady and after I crossed an imaginary line, a door locked behind me! *They are not getting me to the smoking room! They are trying to contain me!* With that thought, I turned to see a hallway lined with people.

I want to let you know, I quit my job! That means, I don't have any insurance. You can't keep me here! You have to let me go! Someone said, "We will. You just have to calm down!"

I walked two more steps. Click, Lock! There's another door. Shit! They are steady, closing me in! Okay, I don't want anybody to touch me! As long as nobody, touches me, we won't have any problems!

They said, "Nobody's going to touch you! We just want you to go to your room so we can give you some medicine."

Everybody started smiling. *Stop staring at me!* They started laughing. What is everybody laughing at? I don't like when people judge me.

They said, "No one's judging you!"

I am psychic! I can tell what's on some of your minds! This man stepped forward. He said, "Well, if you are psychic, give me the winning numbers!"

I said, I'm not giving you shit, because you are greedy!

More laughter! Some lady said, "Well, you are kind of greedy, Larry!"

I walked towards my room. I heard the final click, of a locked door. It sent chills through me. So much, that I had to stop walking.! I turned to the nurse and said, I'm only going in there, if you promise, not to lock me, in there. She said, "We are not going to lock you, in there! We just want you to take your medicine. That's all! You will feel a lot better, once you do! Promise." I like you. I don't really like your hair, but I like you ...

She said, "My co-workers have been saying the same thing! It's too big. How'd you know?"

I told you how I know. We walked in the room. She asked me to drop my pants to get a shot. I told her and her assistant, don't judge me, or my butt!

They said, "We won't judge your butt, sweetie. We do this all the time!"

They did what they had to do. I heard the nurse say, "I'll leave this bottle here, in the bathroom. I want you to use it, when you get a chance."

That medicine sure does work fast. I laid down in my bed and went to sleep. I woke up at what seemed to be dinner. I slept through lunch, it's still sitting on the table. I made it in the cafeteria, just in time to fix me a plate. Yes, good food! I heard Evelyn whisper, "Comfort foods." Nachos, ground beef, cheddar cheese, and the fixings. It seemed like, they made it just for me. That's a big step-up from that funky-ass stroganoff. They knew I wouldn't eat unless it was something good. I ate alone. Everyone else has already finished. I didn't mind. I preferred it!

Evelyn sat on the couch and flipped through magazines. They told me I have guests! Shaun and Eva came in and sat down. Right down, beside Evelyn. I gazed into her eyes and told my family what I had come up with. I said, my mama's spirit is inside of her! She is helping me.

They nodded, and I heard my sister say, "Ah hah."

They said, "The rest of the family, is waiting, down in the other room. Come on to the room. We brought you some clothes."

We walked to my room. They started pulling out all kinds of clothes. They have all the clothes that I got together to go out of town with! Plus, a lot of others. The clothes have been picked through, eliminating belts and any strings.

I said, What is this? What the hell is this? Why did you bring me so many clothes? You are acting like, I'm going to be in here, for a long time, or something! I'm not going to be here a long time! I told you that, however long they said, I would be here, I'll do it in half that time! You don't believe me! You don't even believe me! Get out! I don't want to talk to you! I'll go see the rest of my family!

I stormed out! I walked in the room with my family. I was overwhelmed to see my kids and my brother. Here's Nettie and her boyfriend, but not Maurice. That made me a little more upset! I hugged and kissed my kids with tears in my eyes. Then I hugged my brother, I told everyone that I love them, but I can't stay long. Then I rushed out of the room. I don't like the way I feel right now. Happy is one of the emotions, but often is heavily camouflaged, by the other racing emotions. Most of which is fear! I don't want them keeping me here, away from my kids and family!

Music keeps me in touch with the outside world. Let's see if they have cable. Videos might be on! I pulled a chair up in front of the TV, and turned the channel. Yes! I watched videos and bobbed my head to the beat for hours. Once they went off, I went to smoke a cigarette.

Wouldn't it be nice, if I could listen to music in my room. I wonder, if they have a radio. After I finished smoking, I went to ask. The lady said, "We are not supposed to have radios because of the cords. But I do have this from pediatrics. It runs by battery. You have to stay in your room with it, okay?"

Okay. I went back to my room and fiddled with it. I finally found a decent station. It seems like, every song that came on, even every commercial, was just for me. Like they were talking to me. Then a song came on. I can relate to it so much! I turned it up as loud, as it would go. I started singing even louder than the radio. "Locked Up! They Won't Let Me Out," by Acon. I felt every emotion that they sang about! I walked up and down the hallways, singing and dancing, wanting others to join in the chant! But all that got me, was a radio taken away. Damn! I just got so excited. I don't know.

They said, "Give me that! I don't know how you got that anyway!"

And you still won't know. I'll never reveal my sources! I am so pissed!

Just when I thought, there is absolutely nothing to do around here. A nurse, handed me a piece of paper, with a schedule on it. She said, "Try to attend as many classes as you can. The more you go, the sooner you'll get out of here."

Time	Monday	Tuesday	Wednesday
6:30 a.m. –7:00 a.m.	Wake Up	Wake Up	Wake Up
7:30 a.m.	Breakfast	Breakfast	Breakfast
7:30 a.m. – 8:30 a.m.	Personal Care	Personal Care	Personal Care
9:00 a.m. –10:00 a.m.	Medications	Medications	Medications
	Community Meeting	Community Meeting	Community Meeting
10:00 a.m.	Wellness	Spirituality	Expressive Therapy
11:00 a.m.	Process Group	Process Group	Process Group
2:00 noon – 12:30 p.m.	Lunch	Lunch	Lunch
12:00 noon – 1:00 p.m.	Medications	Medications	Medications
1:00 p.m. – 2:00 p.m.	Self-Esteem	Depression Education	Anger Management
2:00 p.m.	Free Time	Relaxation Group	Free Time
3:00 p.m.		Free Time	
4:00 p.m. – 5:00 p.m.	Life Skills	Life Skills	Life Skills
4:30 p.m. – 5:30 p.m.	Dinner	Dinner	Dinner
5:30 p.m. – 6:30 p.m.	Personal Care	Personal Care	Personal Care
*6:00 p.m. – 7:30 p.m.	Visiting Hours	Visiting Hours	Visiting Hours
8:00 p.m.	Wrap Up	Wrap Up	Wrap Up
8:30 p.m. – 10:00 p.m.	Medications	Medications	Medications
9:00 p.m. – 10:00 p.m.	Relaxation/ Personal Care	Relaxation/ Personal Care	Relaxation/ Personal Care
12:00 midnight	Lights Out	Lights Out	Lights Out

- Special arrangements can be made for out-of-town visitors-Please sp

Actual schedule given while institutionalized.

You mean, they want me to do everything listed on this paper? I'll tell you what! I'll do what I can, and don't you harass me!

My eye quickly went to the bottom of the page. *Special arrangements, can be made for out of town visitors. I spoke to the nurse. I told her, I'd like those arrangements to be made for my friend, from North Carolina.

She explained, "The visitor has to be here, and willing to stay with you, in here! We prepare the bed in your room, and they stay."

Yes! Now all I have to do, is get him here. Then there is the second part! Do I really want him to stay with me here, in the crazy house?

DEVASTATING CONSEQUENCES

Every time I turn around, they want to stick me in some kind of class. Talking about my feelings in a group, is not appealing to me. I don't want to be judged. That's the first thing a normal person does. If I said, I got paid yesterday and I'm broke today, without knowing the reasons, you are judging me. Everything happens for a reason! I'm the type, that will listen to the reasons and judge objectively. You won't find a lot of people like that. The only people that I may judge harshly, are crack heads. Mostly, I just feel sorry, for them, and sorry for the family members, who are inadvertently affected. Not to mention the household that goes to hell! They don't care about how they look, much less their houses. And you bet not leave anything valuable laying around. I won't comment on everyone, just the ones I've come across, and it's not a few!

I've been brought up with some of the finer things in life. In everything you do, try to make it bigger and better than what you already did! That's what I want to pass on to my kids. Those hard drugs are from the devil! No good, can come from it! That's not for me. I wouldn't want to do anything to jeopardize my relationship with my kids. I believe they help keep me sane ... Now I'm trying to keep my sanity, in a house full of crazy people. People who actually sit and pull their hair out, without knowing it! Maybe, that's what I'm doing. I don't have hardly any hair on the top of my head. It's either that or nerves. But my hair is falling out.

I went to one of the meetings where I had to fill out a questionnaire. I answered all the questions honestly ... How is your medicine affecting you? Great! I should have put that in all caps! I'm floating on rainbows, covered in dewww! It takes all of me, to even stay awake. The councilor said, "If you have any suggestions, or goals for today, list them at the bottom of the page."

Yeah, I suggest that I go home. I turned the paper in and left.

My feelings are based so much, on how the people around me feel. When someone's in pain, I feel their pain too. I can tell just by your expression, how your day is going. I had a run-in with a nurse that was supposed to be asking me some questions. She said, "Let me sit; my back hurts!"

From out of nowhere, I blurted out, stop getting up, on the wrong side of the bed!

She replied, "You know what, I think I did get up on the wrong side of the bed. I rolled over there, when my husband got up this morning."

I know you did!

She said, "Oh my gosh! That gives me the chills. I'll be back." She stood up. I think I scared her. I can tell by her face.

I said, wait a minute! Don't be scared; you don't have to be scared. Sit back down.

She did and fought away a tear. She finished her survey and hugged me, before she left. I think her back is feeling better now. I feel like Joan of Arcadia. It's seems like, I have the power to see what's wrong. Then I can help, to fix it. What if I am? What if I am the next in line? Why couldn't I be? With my hair like this, I look like a black Jesus! Every step of the way, has been a miracle. I might as well embrace this power! Like my mama told me, "Don't be scared. You don't have to be scared!" Soothing words from one of the best! It's a damn shame, how the best die young.

Jesus was one of them. He died and rose again. That's what it felt like happened. Like I died and my mama took hold of my body and mind. She kept me going until the next day, when I came to the doctor to get medicine, to reverse the damage. There was a lot of damage done! Anytime there is a good reason to be standing butt naked on the curb, you know something is wrong! I lost it ... I actually lost it! I don't know what's true and what's false anymore! I know I feel older, than they say I am!

I told my aunts Ann and Maria when they came to see me, I can't believe, I'm your sister. I'm 38 years old! You'll could have told me! I could have handled knowing before now.

Ann just shook her head over and over. She said, "Yeah, well, do you know my youngest son's name?"

I got the question right. She shook her head in delight! See ... I know what I'm talking about! Sometimes... I laughed! I didn't want to, but that happens a lot lately. And always at the wrong time - before and during, a cry. After a serious statement, to show offense or lack of appreciation, to a made statement. Right before, I light into you!

I try my best, to control those mood swings. But they come on so unexpectedly! It's like, trying to stop a moving train. It ain't happening!

I asked Maria over and over, have you heard from my friend from North Carolina?

She said, "Not yet." She encouraged me to just, write him a letter. I did just that. I like writing all of a sudden. Hence, the title, writer/author. Just like that, writer slash author. Anyway, the note went just like this.

9-25-04
Dear Anthony,

I know you don't know me, but I fell in love with you at first sight. I'm 38 years old, and I want to get married and have at least one child by you. Currently, I have two kids. But I have a feeling there are more kids hiding somewhere. Maybe if you see a picture of me, you'll feel the same way. We would be perfect for each other. All I need is some romance and your undivided attention. I can't handle it when a man does not give me that type of attention. As for those others that didn't, believe me, they can go to hell, for all I care. I need you, and I promise, I'll never do anything to hurt you. I'll give all my love to you, and if you need me, baby, I'll come running. Only to you. We can get engaged now. But I want the perfect wedding. So we can go to a Texas justice of the peace, until I plan out every detail of this perfect marriage. It might not be perfect to anyone else, but it is to me. Especially if Boyz II Men were there to sing, any song that I wanted them to. White doves would fly at the end of the ceremony. Pictures of my parents, at the front of the church. One long aisle, so I can walk down the middle. Come and Rescue me, Anthony Biggins.

Love,

Daminika Cunningham

P.S. I hope you like animals, especially zebras.

It got to the point that, I just want to leave! I will tell anybody, anything they want to hear, just so I can leave! I need a blunt, reeeeal bad! I'm counting down the days because, soon as I get out of here, I'm going to get fucked up!

I wrote a note and told the doctor, I've started writing my book, which I did! I wrote a whole page of things I want to include. I even came up with the title! *Devastating Consequences.* It's perfect! All the dire consequences that come from one man's actions. Devastated, is not a word tossed around too often! It takes a lot, to leave a person devastated. Without looking the definition up in the dictionary. My definition ... hopeless! It's nothing you can do or say to make the situation better. Nothing can turn back time, and the only thing that stops the clock is death.

I made a lot of realizations. I need to show these people, that I'm not crazy. I took the sign down, off my door. The one that said I'm Getting Married! Do Not Disturb! Whether that happens or not, I don't need to advertise. I'm trying hard to make it through the meetings. As long and boring as they are. Not to mention, how doped up the doctor's keep me. Sleep never felt better. I was getting up every five minutes, literally, until they changed my medicine. The more classes I go to, the faster I'll get out of here!

I got my diagnosis of manic bipolar. It felt great to have it verified and officially diagnosed. Even though I already knew it, and that's a feeling, that leaves you speechless. To all, who don't believe me, I wrote it on my walls before I died. Sane people don't draw on their walls. I did it to tell everybody, I am psychic! I already knew.

How does a sane person know what the cat scan is going to say, much less a crazy person? Yeah, that's it, I'm crazy! The funny thing is, I know things that actually come true. Not only did I write bipolar, but bipolar writer. And guess what I'm doing right now? Writing! I don't even like writing. I like typing, and that's exactly how I'm going to do it. I'll type it. I don't want to write it. My hand will get tired. I'll get a computer and officially start typing, in my free time.

I went around to all the patients and tried to say something to make them smile. Touching some of them, as if to share the wealth, in a sense. Sharing my powers, healing them. It sure seemed like it helped. Not only did it help them, but it also helped heal me. I'm a broken child, trapped in a scorned woman's body, dying to get out! Dying to be comforted, by my mother. Now I'm a mother, trying to comfort my own children, in an attempt to shield them. Keep them sheltered from hurt, pain, devastation, aggravation, and anger. I have so much built-in anger, I could smash a hole, in the side of a building. Because when you hurt that much, it starts to turn to anger. Anger toward those who could have helped, but didn't. Anger toward all the ones, that didn't do enough!

I'm in a position right now where I hate my ex! I think he drugged me in anger. Anger that, I won't take him back! I'm scared of him, and I just want to move, out of town and away from him! Somewhere, where he can't find me.

Fear has turned into anxiety, and it is killing me. I'm always watching my back, and double locking doors. Checking and rechecking. Paranoia set in, and all of that, combined with a broken, aching heart. That's what put me here. I won't let it keep me here!

The counselors see the progress and switch me to the other side of the hospital. This side means you are going home soon. I didn't have to say good-bye to my friends, because most of them, went with me. One didn't; her name is Evelyn. They moved her to another hospital the day before I moved over here. I was sad to see her go. I reflected on how much she gave me. Even if, she was a stranger, she was the nicest, damn stranger, that I ever knew! I know she was much more than that, though ... I can smile more now! More freedom!

The smoking block, is outside, and it's real nice. Gated, but nice. I think they have llamas on the other side of the fence. I might go look later. Right now, I have visitors. It's my sister and her best friend. Even my little white friend from work, came to see me. My visitors really mean a lot to me. We sat outside and smoked. We talked about how much better it is on this side. The staff told us, unlike the other side of the hospital, in this cafeteria, if you want two of something, you can get it! I ate like a fat rat, even ice cream. You weren't supposed to bring food back to the room, but I did anyway. They don't tell me what to do! I get hungry at night sometimes.

My sister managed to sneak in my cell phone. It was in her purse, and I guess they just assumed it was hers. Wrong! It's mine! This way, after light's out, I can lay in the bed and talk quietly. Maybe I'll go in the bathroom and talk, because they poke their head in every couple of hours, to see how I'm doing. Or to see what I'm doing.

I waited it out and didn't use the phone until after dark. I sat in the bathroom and called my friend from North Carolina. We chatted for a couple of minutes. He asked, "How are you doing?"

I said, I'm making it. But of course, I didn't reveal what kind of hospital, I'm in. It's kind of hard to explain, to someone. *I'm in the crazy house, but I still want you to like me.* It's hard for someone to judge, just how crazy you are! Most people don't care. They hear "crazy lady," and they run in the opposite direction.

I'm really starting to like this guy. He's so nice. I don't want to scare him away. I told him, I'll be down there this weekend. I can't wait to see you again.

He responded, "Every weekend, for the past month, you've been saying you're coming back down here. Every weekend, something comes up at the last minute. How about this. Don't call me until you are on the road, halfway down here."

He hung up. I melted and leaked under the chair I was sitting in. Even though I understand exactly what he's saying and how he feels, it still sounded harsh. And it still hurt!

I know what it feels like, to have your hopes up, week after week, only to be disappointed. Hell, my life has been full of disappointment. I didn't dwell on that though. I'm just ready to get the hell up out of here. That day finally came, after nine long days in the joint. I'm busting up out of this piece! They discharged me October the first. With prescriptions in toe, I went home.

My Aunt Maria drove me home. Walking through that door after nine days, felt like months. I can't believe what I did to this house. The walls are written and colored on. All my can foods, are on the floor. I had pushed the microwave off the cabinet. That's broke! I need the maintenance men to put up a new thermostat. I forgot that I jerked that, out the wall.

Maria stayed a while, helping me clean up. That's really sweet of her! She told me about the new Mr. Clean sponge. It cleans crayon off the walls. I hugged and thanked her, for all that she did to help me. We said goodbye, and she reassured me that she would stay in touch. She told me to call anytime, day or night if I need anything. After all those days of sleeping on what should be called a cot, rather than a bed. It's time to roll around on my king-size bed, a couple of times.

As I walk around, this house, it brings back, so many mixed memories. I love my little house, but it's time for me to go! I can't trust Rodney! He drugged me, and who's to say how far he'll go. I don't know how he got in before, so I can never be one hundred percent secure. My lease is up next month, so it's either be out by then, or live in fear for another year. I just can't see that! I want to move out of town, so he won't be able to find me. But after talking to some of my family, I realized that leaving won't just hurt Rodney. Of course, I'm taking my sister, with me! We vowed, not to leave each other. But what about Nettie and Maurice? Nettie is so obsessed with her grandkids. She calls them her kids. That also means I'm moving away from my babysitter. Maurice watches them faithfully! Every weekend! Not only on a schedule, but if I need him to watch them at the last minute, because of something important, I can count him. And since I talked him out of moving out of town, That's not going to go over too well. But if I decided to go, everyone would just have to get over it! But since I'm so damned concerned, with everybody's feelings, I'll try to find a place here.

It's really hard to adjust after getting out. I tried to stay on a schedule. Dinner, bath time, school clothes, wake-up, hair. Everyday, over and over. Shortly after I came out of the hospital, A.J. had some kind of breakdown, himself. My family didn't give me all the details, because they didn't want to worry me. I do know that it involved a knife. A combination of having no freedom, then too much freedom, and then having that taken away! He was rebelling against my grandparents, and they didn't know how to handle it. So he went to live with my Aunt Ann. I know he'll get the right supervision over there. She helped me out so much! Thank you to her, for both of us.

17

I gave my thirty-day notice. I got a newspaper and some packing boxes, then rode around, looking for houses. I want another house, not an apartment. We need a three bedroom. It seems like, it's about another hundred dollars a month. I got that! Then, when I find a man who's willing to put in half on the bills, it will be a lot cheaper!

Look's like, I have two objectives. I searched and searched. Then I finally lucked up. I found a reasonably priced three-bedroom house. It just so happened, to be right around the corner from Nettie's house. She's going to love that! Maurice is too. I'll be in walking distance from him. He likes to keep track of me on certain levels. I let him ...

He has this obnoxious charm. If he would just get his life together! Lord knows, I still love him! If he could help pay some of these bills, I'd let him move in. I called the number on the sign outside of the house, and set up a time to view the inside of the house. Just as I imagined, it is beautiful and convenient in a lot of ways! The house is backwards, not unlike myself. What I mean by backwards is exactly what I said - backwards! Self explanatory. The back of the house, faces the street. The front door, is in the backyard. It even has a one-way, private alley entrance, almost like my other house. That means, my car will be hidden from the street. It's perfect. I want it! I asked the owner, if I give you a deposit, does that take this house off the market? He responded, "Yes!"

I said, I'll have the money together by the end of the week!

Yes!!!! I got the money together and took it to him. He said, "I'll be adding a dishwasher before you move in."

I said, "I could shout in this kitchen, right now! That is great. Thank you! Everything is going a little too perfect. Oh, there is one other thing, though. They are currently, doing work on the house. Adding some last minute things, like electrical outlets, wiring, etc.

But the landlord said, they should be done way before I move in. Hopefully... Yeah, he added that word at the end. Low, but I heard it. It better be done! He don't want to play with my emotions! He doesn't have a choice. I already have the keys, and I already gave my thirty-day notice! You do the math.... I'm moving out of my house, and into a new one. I'm still worried though, because I want it to be finished!

That's not enough, to ruin my birthday, though. My birthday, is next week. I'm having a birthday/going away party! One last party at the old house, to bring in the new. The only thing about it is, that we have to keep the move and the location hush, hush! If I'm going to hide from him in Roanoke,, I have to be as careful as possible! Meaning, not telling certain people! Meaning, kicking down the for rent sign, that the landlord put up. He put it right in my front yard the next day after I gave my notice. Damn! I'm trying to be incognito! They don't understand that. They put the sign back up. I raked a pile of leaves in front of it. Fuck them and that damn sign! Whoever wants this info, will have to work for it!

I signed up for food stamps two days before my birthday. So, on October 23, my food stamps were ready to use. Happy Birthday to me! I bought food, and I bought liquor. To me, that spells PARTY! The only thing missing, is the music. Maurice said, "Leave that, to me!" That's exactly what I did.

Zay Zay helped me decorate. We had to put Happy Birthday posters on the walls and doors, to cover what Mr. Clean, didn't clean. Ink pen mostly. The crayon and marker came right off! It's was almost a shame to erase, those beautiful pictures.

The news spread about the party. All of my cousin's McNasty ex-boyfriends, are invited. Just not *him*! They all came, too. Even the troublemaker, also known as The Game. Word got to him real fast! Like a dumb ass, he came with his girlfriend. This is the same guy that has fought at all of my parties! I have one damn near every year. Rodney has missed every one of them, thus far, usually from situations beyond his control. He can't control this one, either!

We had the regulars - Maurice as DJ. Fat Rob, my sister, Eva, Deanna, TD, and they brought their drunk-ass aunt. She is always drunk and falling down! She made her nigga-late entrance. She came in with a liquor bottle, more than halfway finished. Evidently she started partying early this morning. Like it was her birthday or something! Well, bless her heart, she was partying for me. Thank you, girl!

She came in, dancing! We joined her. "Hey! We're going to party, like it's your birthday!"

Hey!!! It's my birthday!

We danced and drank, until I felt dizzy! I have to be careful, drinking on this medicine. I take it at night, but it stays with you all day! Let me sit down! I sat, and we laughed at almost everything! High, as a kite! Good times, good times! We had a ball, listening to music and chilling. The party started to break up after a couple of hours. My guests informed me that they are going to another party. How rude! No, I'm just joking. I had a good time. The guys were sad to see the women leaving. The cousin that came with his girlfriend. He left her in the house, and went outside, to see the ladies to their cars. Now, he knows better, but he doesn't care. He's nothing but a big flirt, anyway. Well, not just that. He follows through with it, to the end. Meaning, a nut! He is The Game!

The girlfriend saw his concern about the ladies. She went outside on the porch to stand with him. She said, "Where is my coat?"

He turned around, only to see his plan unfolding. He retaliated, "Don't come out here starting stuff with me, woman!"

We got up and ran to the door, to see what all the commotion was all about. Just then, he stole on that girl. Right in her face! Knocked her glasses clear across the yard. Dammmnnn!!!

We tried to get out the door, to break things up! She attacked him and jumped all on his head. They are fighting so hard, bumping up against the screen door! The door is pinned shut, from all the weight. They are actually going blow for blow, on my front porch!

I said, you'll need to stop that! Stop fighting! The next door neighbors are going to call the police!

Just then, pop! My screen door! The screen, and the glass, popped out. Well, I'll be damned! Ain't this, about a bitch! Plus, beer is wasted all over the front porch. The only reason they stopped, is because they were slipping around in it. She went and picked up her glasses. The guys held him back, while we talked to her.

She said, "He always has to show off! He hit me, and he was trying to break my glasses! This is the third pair, that he has done something to. I just wanted to know what he did with my coat. He had it last. Then he just ticked, and he punched me! Don't worry, I'll pay for the screen.

But I can't find my coat anywhere! I wanted to know if one of the ladies, might have picked it up, by accident. Let me tell you something, though! He told me before we got here, that he was going to start something with Maurice. All because Rodney couldn't come over here!"

I don't know why, he would want to do that. Every time he jumps up, he gets beat down! Maurice already beat the shit out of him one time! Sent him home with a bald spot, in his head. He know what's up! That's exactly why, he kept his mouth shut. But, I will ask my sister and her friends, if they have your coat. But I doubt it!

We tried to continue with the party. But he kept running in and out of the house, talking all kinds of shit. I heard one of his cousins say, "Man, you need to go on ahead. You are fucking up our high!"

He said, "I'm leaving! I just have to go to the bathroom first!" He walked past me, and he looked pregnant! Or like, he had gained thirty pounds. But I was too fucked up, to know the difference. I thought my eyes were playing tricks on me!

You have to cut through my kid's room, to get to the bathroom. I saw him go in there, and then I turned my head. I didn't think anymore about it. He left; everybody left, except Maurice. He chilled with me overnight! He made me feel safe. We made a night out of it! I know he enjoyed himself. It doesn't take much! I'm the one that benefits the most from it. Maurice just loves to spend time with me! I do miss this. I don't miss the snoring! I forgot all about that!

The next morning, he moved my stereo back. That was his excuse for staying. Yeah, right. I don't mind; just one night though! After the party, there's always the cleanup. Not too bad, this time. It could have been worse. A few days passed, and we concentrated more on the move. Throwing away everything that's trash, first. My kids got busy finding toys, that they never play with.

Well, what do you know ... What do we have here? Buried in the bottom of the toy box. It's that girl's coat! He actually hid her coat, just to start an argument. Unbelievable! I wouldn't put anything past him. That's what he had under his coat! That's that McNasty mentality! I dropped it off for her a day or two later.

Now who did I see, as soon as I pulled up, but *him*. I guess they have worked things out. Figures! He will continue to beat her, until she gets tired of it! Better them, than me. Once, was more than enough. At least this girl, does have some fight in her. She was boxing with his ass! The rest of his girls, just cut and stab him. I remember when my cousin burst his mouth open with a beer bottle. "When a Woman's Fed Up," by R. Kelly. That's a nice song to listen to now.

I'll wait until after Zay Zay's birthday, to move. It will be easier that way! I stripped down every room, including the bathroom. I think I have everything, I want. Maurice, Tony Bologna, and Eva showed up, to help me move, bright and early! Besides immediate family, I can always depend on Maurice to help me with the free shit. Meaning, he may not be there financially, but he's there for me in every other sense of the word. His heart is bigger, than all the men I've ever dated, combined!

He moved most of everything. I didn't hardly do shit. Me and manual labor don't mix. I'm more of a decorator. Tony is Maurice's right-hand man. Anywhere Maurice is, he's not far behind. He's a great helper! He's always trying to help. We became very close over the years. He feels something like, a little brother.

We moved everything within a couple of hours. Good timing! The only thing, was the rain. Pardon the pun, but it did put a damper on things! They slipped and slid everything on that truck, and we were out! It really feels good, to be out of there. Relief! I can finally sleep easy! I will try to keep this move, and my location as secret as I can, from Rodney! Hopefully, by the time he finds out, I will have my security system set up. Plus, Maurice and I have set up a signal system, since he can see my new house from his house. I'll turn on a red light, if I ever feel scared or threatened. He'll check every fifteen minutes or so, and rush over if anything goes down! That made me feel a lot safer, as well! He's doing all he can, to get himself back in there.

Maurice has a couple of issues, he has to work on before we get back together! The main problem, is his weight. He was big, when I met him. But he gradually blew up! Plus, he needs a job! I've explained all this to him. You would think this would change the way he feels about me. It didn't! Recently, he walked right up to me. He looked me dead in my eyes, and said, "You going to marry me?"

I always roll my eyes, and look away. I laugh, like it's a joke. But he couldn't be more serious! He wants us to be one big, happy family. With our two kids, a girl and boy. A big house, with a picket fence and car. All that's good and fine. But who will be paying those bills? When I say that, the look on his face always changes.

I'm sorry about that. But as I've stated, over and over. Love, does not pay the bills! I can love you all day. But your kiss, ain't going to pay my electric bill!

I said, you don't have a steady work history. Let me see you work somewhere for ninety days, without calling in! Can you do that?

Anyway, his dream of playing house again, has come true! I pulled up to my new house, and it is not finished. I still don't have a functioning, back door. There is a door nailed up there. Anybody could kick it in! As a matter of fact, we removed it with a simple hammer so we could move the furniture in easier. Even if I don't stay here, I'm keeping my furniture in here, while they finish the work. But I'm not leaving anything valuable! That means TVs, DVD players, and especially my zebras. They will stay in my trunk.

Nettie asked me if I wanted to stay with her, until they finish working on the house. I accepted, mainly because it was more convenient for the kids. There's not really enough room for all of us, at Shaun's house. We would have gone, if we had no other options. So we walked in, bags packed, the kids scattered, running and screaming with delight. They love it over here. I'm not so sure. I looked up to a smiling face. "Welcome, welcome, this is a celebration!"

I said, you are so crazy, Maurice!

He quickly established the sleeping arrangements! "The kids will be sleeping in the bed with my mother. That means you will be forced, to bunk with me. Make yourself comfortable! Let me know if you need anything. I'm going to start dinner."

That's my boo! He is absolutely, loving this! I like my own space, but I appreciate the hospitality. So, I'll make the best of this, until it's over! My house better be finished soon.

I called and cursed the landlord out! He said he will try to finish as soon as possible. The days turned into weeks. I started counting hours! Certain things, are starting to get intolerable! We are now in a joined household, so the head count doubled! It was hard enough competing for the bathroom with just me and the kids! Now, every single time I have to go to the bathroom, someone else is in there!

Maurice's brother brushes his teeth for fifteen minutes, every morning. He has to brush his teeth before I do my morning bathroom run. He takes his precious time! I think he brushes his hair while he's in there, too. I don't know what he does. I just wish he'd do it faster!

As if the waiting, weren't bad enough. He plays his music, as loud as he can! At seven o'clock, in the morning, he says it gets him going. It gets me going, too! I have to wake up, to get the kids dressed. My head pounds until he leaves for school! Then the music stops! Then it got to the point where he would forget it was on. He just left. That means continuous noise, until somebody went in there and turned it off.

This is not my house, who am I to complain? Speaking of complaining, Maurice snores loud. Damn! I have to take my medicine and beg him to let me go to sleep first! Most of the time, I was too zonked out to notice. But those nights, when his pretty boy qualities and his charm took over. He got everything he asked for, and he was asleep first! I have that effect on people. Although, I can't complain afterwards, either. Maurice is the best kind of baby's daddy. The kind that can be a friend, despite everything! We talk about anything and everything! For him, nothing has changed. He would kill, and die for me. He said, "The only reason I didn't come see you in the hospital, is because that shit, really tore me up! I couldn't see you like that! Ask Fat Rob; he came over and comforted me. He saw how fucked-up, I was. Because if I ever lost you ... I'd be lost! Daminika, you know I'm still in love with you!"

I stopped him, right there! I may not be in love, with you. But I love you, too. I told you, I will love you for life ... I meant it! You are the father of my children. Most likely, there will never be another! You are special to me! You have special privileges. I don't know if we will get back together or not. You work on those things we talked about, and we'll see! That was enough for him. As long as he has a glimmer of hope, he's happy! I just can't break his heart, and tell him he has no hope, for more reasons than I have time to list. But most of all, his facial expression! The heartache, devastation, despair, and depression. I feel the emotions of others. Especially the ones, I'm the closest to! So not only would he feel that. I would, and the kids. The best thing to do, is exactly what I did. In a perfect world, we'd be married by now! But everything happens for a reason.

I walk around in clothes suitable for the people who live here. That's when I discovered the visitors! Every now and then, we have a visitor sleeping on the couch. Even a visitor sleeping on the porch, in the middle of winter. He came in to use the bathroom. What the hell? At one point, we had a kicked-out husband/uncle sleeping on the couch. Oh, excuse me, moving in! What the hell? He just moved the fuck in! It ain't gonna be no room left for a nigga.

Nettie is as nice, as she can be. She just has a problem saying no! Ever since I've known her, she has always had somebody extra, living with her. From nephews, to nieces, and a brother. Nice, is one thing. Not being able to say no, is another. But I've seen her in situations where the load could be easier, and she chose otherwise. She wants to feel in control of as many things as she can. She doesn't want to let go of anything. She has separation issues, not unlike myself. Add that with a pack rat, equals a big fat rat! Make that a couple of big fat rats.

One of my fears, was confirmed. When they informed me that we do have mice/rats - whatever you want to call them - Nettie said, "Look at that fresh bread right there. Damn! We just got back from the bakery about an hour ago."

The mice had chewed through the bags. They ate their <u>due</u> of bread. Then they, left their <u>doo</u>, behind. Doo-doo! Little black turds lay where our fresh bread had lain not but minutes ago. Oh, my gosh! I'm so grossed out *and* pissed off. I don't want to stay anywhere with mice! Looks like, I don't have a choice right now! I started finding more evidence of the mice. They chewed through brand-new clothes that the kids had. Most of all, we can hear them in the walls! I sat, taking a shit, in the bathroom. I wasn't relaxed and flowing, but tense, scared, anxious, and constipated. Damn! I just wanted to get the hell out of there. Those mice scare me!

The only way I got through some days and nights. Was to stay doped up, on my medicine. I tried not to think about! The thought, that mice can climb stairs, means they could climb in the bed, with me! I have to try not, to think about stuff like that. Psyching myself out, almost worked --- until in the middle of the night. I was on a drink run, and then a mouse ran right in front of my feet. I know I screamed loud enough to wake everyone, even though I didn't. Maurice came to see what the problem was. He laughed and told me a story.

He said, "I was eating in the middle of the night. Then I did a double take. I saw a rat! I stared, at him. He stared back at me! I jumped at him, and he didn't move! I left him alone. I finished eating, and he was gone. We tried putting down sticky traps. The mice just chewed through the sticky paper. They only left fur behind! We did catch, a couple, with the snap-back traps. But one mouse was so big, that it just stunned him! It plucked, that head, though! I had to finish him off, with the broom!"

As if all that, wasn't bad enough, the next door neighbor came over the next day. He said, "I see y'all are having a problem with rats, too! Yeah, they are bad next door, too! I think it's this whole neighborhood. They are so bad next door, that we had to put down poison pellets. Don't give them anything else to eat! You know, like peanut butter, or cheese. They eat it off the traps, then go about their business! Those motherfuckers pulled my daughter's doll up through the wall. We just sat and watched!"

That's some scary shit! I can picture it, too! I couldn't make this shit up, even if I wanted to!

Meanwhile, I am trying to get the fuck up out of here, as soon as possible! But the status on my new home looks bleak! Turns out, he's a slum lord. That took my money and didn't even have the house inspected yet! I signed a lease and received keys to a home, that was not yet approved by an inspector. He admitted that the house keeps failing inspection, for one reason or another. Minor things, but they do add up. Instead of disclosing this information to me before he took my money, he disclosed it after.

It is getting close to Christmas. That means, I won't even be able, to put up my own tree. With my own lights. and decorations, in my own house! The landlord promised to give me one month's free rent, for my troubles! Good. That will pay for the first month, of my three-month lease. If I like the area, I'll stay. If Rodney finds out where I live, I'm moving. Win-win, situation! The only thing is, the wait!

Christmas came and went. Nettie put up two Christmas trees. A big one for the house, and a little one, for the kids. She asked me to help decorate the little tree with the kids. Excuse me, if decorating a two-foot tall, artificial tree doesn't excite me. I'm used to decorating the biggest, fullest, pine tree on the lot, with Christmas music playing in the background. It's a tradition, that we've had since, we were little girls. I've yet, to let it die! I don't like fake trees, and I refuse, to decorate one. Where is the Jackson 5 Christmas album? I said it nicer to Nettie, though - No, thanks.

Well, Christmas broke me. But I didn't realize how broke I was, until I realized, I can't even afford the house I'm supposed to be moving into. They cut my short-term disability. I'm waiting on the news of my long-term disability. That means a pay cut, if it's even approved. I didn't rush to go get my furniture, because as long as the landlord holds my money, I'll have storage! Where am I, going to put my furniture if I go get my money back from him? That means, back on welfare.

The food stamps were nice, though! We ate good. But I didn't want to fill Nettie's freezer, then I move and either have to take it, or leave it. Both could prove detrimental! I gave her money when I could, because I know what it's like to have a visitor and to be a visitor. She treats me like family, like a daughter. I have to force her to take the money. We both know she can use it.

Everything is all good, until it comes to cleaning, washing dishes, especially! Everybody scatters like cockroaches. I don't like to wash dishes, either! So in my house, everything is paper or plastic. If I could, I'd have plastic pots and pans! I would. But since I can't, I have to wash those. I told Nettie about my method. She looked at me like, she was too good for that! Okay, that's not good enough for you! Then you should be in here, every day, washing dishes! These rats are having a field day! Come on now! They are smart enough to eat the peanut butter off the traps, without getting caught! These motherfuckers have a leg up, on us! Evidently, she doesn't care.

She has two full cabinets full of dishes, and they use every single one before they wash dishes! You are forced to wash them, because there's nothing else clean. Damn it! I tried to start a wash-as-you-go policy, that didn't work. Because her youngest child, doesn't like to follow rules.

DEVASTATING CONSEQUENCES

There are no consequences! He doesn't care! I tried to alternate days with Maurice. That didn't work either! On his days, he did half, and promised to do the rest later. They sat until my day! Damn it! I do feel somewhat responsible. I do eat here, and so do my kids. I went in there, guns blaring! Let me knock this out!

Usually, at my house, there are two to three sinkfuls of dishes. Then you are finished. I washed four sinkfuls of dishes. I looked around, and it didn't look like I had did shit! There is a never ending table of dishes. All these damn Tupperware containers! Who the hell owns this many damn Tupperware containers? I hate Tupperware containers, especially cleaning them. That is just too much for me!

Maurice promised to rinse everything I washed. Which sounded good, but if your other half is as slow as molasses, the momentum changes! The blaring guns that I had, turned to sling shots. I don't feel like doing anymore! I found myself slowing down, then stopping for good, but promising more. The next time the dishes were washed, Maurice did them. I agreed to rinse. Again, the pattern was the same. He didn't wash them as fast as I would have desired. He wants to drag this out for hours. I want to get it over with. As frustrated as I get with him, he always manages to make me laugh with something stupid! Arguments don't last long, between us ... But when we were together, we would celebrate a week of not arguing! He's so crazy.

If you were noticing a pattern, of the people who actually wash dishes around here, then you'd be right! It consists of Maurice and myself. I have been here two months, and I've seen Nettie wash dishes once. You probably said, "Damn, that's not a lot!"

I agree, but it is even more of a shame, that her younger, more vital son has surpassed her lack of cleanliness. He hasn't touched a dirty dish, or the dish detergent since I've been here! Most likely, longer. She doesn't make him do it, and he doesn't. Maybe he'll get his new jersey dirty! Take it off and hang it up with the rest of them. Then get your ass in here, and wash some of these dishes. All them damn jerseys. They cover his walls like trophies. A different one for every day of the week for a month, damn near! She harasses her older, unemployed son for money. Then doesn't open her mouth to her younger, employed son. That's seems backwards! Especially when he has nothing more to spend his money on, besides more tennis shoes, to match the new jersey that he bought! He has more tennis shoes, than the above-average lady has pumps. I mean a lot! He manages to keep his room clean, but he doesn't want to contribute to the cleanliness of the house.

When I saw that, I decided to put my foot down! I went to the store and bought everything that I would buy for my house, like toilet tissue, which is important. Because I hate to run out! But most of all, plastic forks, cups, and plates. Then I made an announcement. I bought these items for the house. If you choose not to use them, that's fine ...

Days went by with an empty sink. Even though she never admitted it, I saw the smile on her face. Nettie saw how smooth everything was going. Honestly, I don't think she'll stick to it. It's like taking the easy way out. Like she's selling out or something! She doesn't want any part of it. I saw her eat on a real plate, and then put it in the sink and walk away. You can't change some people. Fuck that, you can't help some people! The ones that don't want to be helped, the ones that don't want to change, even when they see that their way isn't working! And it's like pulling teeth, to get them to admit it!

18

My long-term disability kicked in. Yes! I started looking for somewhere else to move to. If I time it just right, I can find a place, get the deposit back from the slumlord, then use that for the deposit, on my new place. All before, he makes me move my furniture. I'm not paying storage, not even for a day! I exhausted all possible leads to reasonable, three-bedroom houses. I checked duplexes and apartments, too. I either can't afford them, or don't want to.

Some man tried to pass off a three bedroom, for a two bedroom with a walkway. He said, "And here is your third bedroom!" He sounded excited about it.

I said, where? Behind this wall? Because I can't fit anything in this area, but a coat rack! It's right beside the front door. Talk about a draft! It's warm enough, and big enough right here, for a pile of coats, on the coat rack that I could keep right here! I have a growing, three-year-old little boy, with a lot of things. His basketball goal wouldn't even fit in this space, much less his bed. The nerve of him, and he is charging three-bedroom prices! To me, that is false advertisement! I worked my way through the swindlers and slum bags, then God blessed me! He put a thought in my head, and I pursued it. He reminded me of an apartment complex that is reasonably priced. It is not labeled as the projects. To me, that is like going backwards. I made a promise to myself to never go backwards! In everything you do, let it be an upgrade! Anything is an upgrade, right now. But I'm judging my own merits.

I went from a three-bedroom, roach-infested apartment in the southwest projects. To a, just-my-size, two-bedroom house in northeast. I don't even know anyone who has ever had the same zip code. I don't know anyone twenty-two years old owning a home, much less renting one! I started by renting. But I'm working my way up. I am determined to upgrade to a three bedroom. My kids are getting older now. They definitely need their own space. Plus, there's some kind of law, that a male and female child can't sleep in the same room together, after a certain age. I think it's seven. I'm not just doing it because it's the law. Fuck them! I'm doing it because that is nasty. With all that children witness on TV and PG movies nowadays, you need to keep them apart.

I witnessed my four-year-old nephew, Smelly. He had a sleepover with one of his best friends, his best playmate. It just happened to be a girl. They slept in the same bed, with no concern from my sister. Hey, they're four. In the middle of the night, I walked to the bathroom, passing by his room. I spent the night with them from time to time. I had to do a double take. I threw it in reverse. I scooted back, far enough to be hidden by the darkness. The door was cracked, and I watched him laying on top of her, talking to her softly! I heard her laughing ... What the hell? Did he throw her a line or something? What the hell is she, laughing at? He leaned in for the kiss and stayed there awhile! Then he rolled off of her. She got up and straddled him. What the fuck? I wanted to make sure that I'm seeing, what I'm seeing! This is some crazy shit! Yeah, I am high. But not that high!

I said, break it up! What the hell is going on in here? I flicked the light on. Get up! I cannot believe what's going on in this room! Innocent, my ass! It won't happen in my household, and it won't happen in this one. I made her sleep in the living room with me. I tried to wake up Shaun. I tried to, tell her. But she was out of it. Like always, she didn't know what was going on! I had to tell her in the morning. She scolded him, and that little girl never spent the night again.

DEVASTATING CONSEQUENCES

RahShaun Alique Poindexter, my one and only nephew.

Anyway, back to my good news! I am approved! Approved for a three-bedroom apartment. With a balcony. Nice! I passed the credit check and the background check. Well, the background check hasn't actually come back yet. They said I can move in, as long as I promise that I don't have anything on my record. I assured them that I don't. I paid my deposit, and they gave me the key. Yes! I can't let this opportunity pass me by even though, I do have something on my record. If they find out, they will put me out! But even if I only get to live there for a month or two, that will be a month or two away from the rats! I have got to go! I'm starting to go crazy, just being around them too much! I'm talking about Nettie, Maurice, his brother, and any unexpected visitors. They were always good to me, but I'm the kind of person that needs my own space. There is nothing, absolutely nothing, like your own space! I have a king-size bed just waiting for me to roll around on it!

Maurice was kind enough to sleep in the living room sometimes,, leaving me his room and his bed. It was mainly so I wouldn't have to hear him snoring! He obliged, willingly. That's just what kind of person he is. Who do you think helped me move? Move number two! You better believe it! A couple of other family members helped too. They made sure, I got my money back from that slumlord. Surprisingly, the slumlord even helped me move my stuff. He better have; he had my stuff stored somewhere else. They had to move my furniture out of the new house, in order to have the house inspected. It didn't make me, no difference. As long as, I didn't have to pay for storage.

I moved in, and it is absolutely, wonderful! I put my bed together first. I made it up with brand-new sheets. I rolled around on it, for hours. Slowly, but surely, I pulled everybody's else's room together. Even though I had lots of help bringing the stuff in, nobody helped set things up! Not even Maurice. I didn't have a problem with that, though. I appreciate, the hardest part being done.

The couch was the heaviest thing to maneuver. But, I did it. Even though I am still paranoid about the result of the background check, I still feel this uncanny peace. I prayed, and I asked God to open my eyes, to show me what to do and what to say.

We didn't get to spend Christmas in our own place. But it sure does feel like Christmas! I am still leading a secretive, double life as far as Rodney, is concerned. Even though I did make contact with him, after many months. I will not let him know where I live. Months to us, feel like years. The only reason those feelings returned for me, is because I got word from my doctor, that Rodney did not drug me, after all! I thought he slipped me something. I thought he slipped me ecstasy, the reason why I went crazy. But, no! In laymen's terms, I had a nervous breakdown. How many twenty-three year olds have nervous breakdowns? My sister was there when the doctor told me. I'm glad, because I don't know if my family would have believed me!

I started looking for him in everyday driving around, just seeing if I see him. After weeks of searching, I saw him! I blew my horn, made a U-turn, and went back. He stood outside the car. I got out and looked up at his face. We spoke to each other, then stared at each other. He said, "Long time, no see."

I know! Can I have a hug?

We hugged, and I almost cried. But I kept it in. He told me, "Come see me some time. I missed you! I've been worried about you. Are you doing, okay?" He told me where he lives, now. I visited him, and we talked. Before I knew it, he was buying me all kinds of stuff. He bought me a cell phone, so he could keep in contact with me. On New Year's Eve, when I got stood up by a guy with a bobble head, he was my rebound guy, there to take me out. It was great to be all dressed up with somewhere to go! I knew spending New Year's with this man meant I will have to deal with him all yearlong. We had a ball, though. A real nice time.

I ordered a lot of food. Just to make him spend money. We ended up getting half of everything for free, because they messed up our order. From hors d'oeuvres, to drinks and dessert. All free! He laughed and said, "Only with you! The only time I ever get free stuff, is when I'm with you." Which is, true. It's occurred with us, more than once. He also told me that he came into some money recently. He doesn't have anybody to spend it on. He didn't have to tell me more than once! I milked him for everything I could. All the while not letting him get too close. We did get back together sexually. But that's about it. That's all he can get. I did miss the sex! He is a great lover! But he has too much drama with him. Remember, his dick doesn't stay hard with a condom on! He would pull it off during intercourse, then pick it up after he nutted! Like he just now, took it off.

Oh, hell no! You fool me once, shame on me. You fool me twice, shame on you! I cut the sex out. I limited it to, desperate times. Even then, I followed the condom from start, to finish. I put it on, and stopped to feel for it, during intercourse. I even told him, I want to take it off. That way, I can exam it and make sure, everything is where it's supposed to be. He's a sneaky, little bastard. He even resorted to ripping a hole in the condom. By time we finished, I looked up, and all he had was just a little white plastic ring, around his dick. Head poking out, and a mess to clean up. I have to be careful and cognitive, every time we have sex, and that's sad. But it's worth it! I haven't met a man yet, that can top him!

Before long, his money ran out. I would holler at him on payday, which may sound shallow, but if he don't have no money, he's helping to spend mine. I don't need no help with that. Instead of renting movies for me and the kids, I caught a sale on buying them. And just for the irony of it, I bought the movie, *Willard*. The movie, about rats. My daughter is still too afraid to watch it. I couldn't watch it until I was away from the rats.

I finally got all my zebras exactly how I wanted them. The living room looks beautiful! The whole house looks beautiful. I am so happy right now, and I give God all the glory. But my happiness, soon turned to despair, when I returned home to a notice, on my door. A notice to vacate, the property. Damn! I failed the background check, and now I have to move. My misdemeanor, weed charge, has come back, to haunt me! I can't believe this! I had enough trouble getting a moving party together, for the first two times. This is really, a nightmare!

I cannot go back over Nettie's. I just can't! I just left. I'm going to have to start looking for other places. I just cannot bare all this stress, all over again! I asked God, why? Why would He bless me like this, then turn around and take it all away. I really had good signs and feelings about this place. It's just right for me, right now. Damn! Instead of opening up and sharing my problems with my family, I did like usual and kept it to myself, slowly tearing down what I just built up. I made a vow to myself. That if this ends badly, I'm going to check myself back in, the crazy house. So I won't have another nervous breakdown! If need be, the kids can go back over Nettie's house. I just can't! The last line of the letter said, to appeal this decision, schedule a face-to-face appointment with the manager. Appeal, for what? What is there to appeal? They should have said … To look like an asshole, schedule an appointment with the manager! That's just a waste, of my time.

I kept that secret for days and weeks, until I had to confide in somebody. Rodney was there to listen and to comfort me. When he found out that I was living with Nettie, he let me know there is always enough room, for me and the kids at his house. He re-extended the offer. He just wants to take care of me. Which is always a fallback plan. But I just don't think I'm ready for that right now. He made me feel so comfortable, that I told him where I live. I even let him come over. Fuck it! I'm moving. He thought it was rude, because that was the only reason why I invited him over. So what? Even though, some of my fear of him, is gone. I'm still somewhat scared of him. I know what he's capable of. That's why I don't sleep around him. That's the time when my guard is down. Those are my most vulnerable moments.

I don't sleep with my door open, ever. First of all, because I'm scared of hallways. Second of all, I don't like for people to see me asleep! I could be doing anything. Drooling, mouth wide open, or whatever! I don't want someone staring and judging. Or giggling and laughing. I've been like that for years. I always sleep with my door shut and locked. With all the medicine I'm on, I don't trust myself at nighttime. I could sleepwalk, sleep talk, or sleep eat! If someone scares me while I'm sleep, I don't know what I'll do. That's why I try to limit that, by locking my bedroom door at night. I don't want one of my kids to come in there and scare me. My scared, is not like others'. I have panic attacks! It feels like, I'm having a heart attack, an asthma attack, and a stroke, all rolled into one. And I don't even have asthma. I just can't breathe. That's not fun, not by a long shot! I can't even watch scary movies, or go to haunted houses, like I used to. I'm too scared! I'm scared of things you wouldn't even think about! Crazy things! Way too many to list!

I stay in touch with my Aunt Maria. She just happened to call on the first day of my journey, to ride around and look for houses adventure. She asked me how I was doing. I confided in her. I told her everything. I can't keep stuff from her. It's like she knows, anyway. She heard the distress in my voice. I heard the concern, in hers. She said, "I will drive you to look at some places."

That's exactly what she did. We talked while we rode. She confided in me.

She said, "Your situation, mirrors my situation. The reason I have so much free time to help you, is because I lost my job. Something I did more than fifteen years ago, came back to haunt me! I had settled into the job. I was really excited about it. Then, all of a sudden, it was all ripped away!"

I empathized with her. That's a shame. Damn those last-minute, background checks! I told her, I'm going down to the office. I want to ask them how long do I have before they sit my stuff outside. I want to act before then!

She asked, "Can I come with you?"

Sure, I'd love the extra mental, support. We went down there. There are other people in the office. The manager asked, "How can I help, you?"

I started explaining, I want to know, when is the last day, that I have to be out of my apartment? My aunt interrupted, "Just wait until they leave."

She doesn't want me to be embarrassed. Or either, trying to limit the amount of people involved, so no one extra would be aware of what's going on. That's why I think she is bipolar, too. She thinks just like me. She reacts the same way I do, on a lot of things. Certain things she does, certain things she says, the way she looks at you! And the tone of her voice. She always talks real calm to me. That's exactly, what I need. She hasn't been diagnosed. But I know, and I know she knows.

The office cleared out. We had a seat. The manager verified who I am, where I live, and what the situation, is.

I asked her, how long do I have before you'll put my stuff out?

She asked, "Why didn't you just disclose your misdemeanor? Why didn't you appeal this?"

I figured it would be a total waste, of my time. I can't deny that it happened anyway. All I know is, when I admitted it to the lady, at the Section 8 building, she told me it wasn't on my record. But since I had already admitted to it; I couldn't get Section 8 for three years. So that's what I went by. I don't know the lady's name, but I know what she looks like. I can find out who she is. That is the God's, honest truth! She said, "That's not necessary even though it's past the day to appeal this. As long as you write up a statement saying exactly what you told me, I'll let you stay."

I heard the words, but I said, what did you say? I can stay? I can stay! Maria and I got up and embraced each other. I'm happy! I'm overjoyed! I'm blessed! And even though the tears flow today in happiness, that day I was so much in shock, that I couldn't react. It's like, it was too good to be true, when that lady delivered the news. I looked at her like one of those people, that God put on earth, just to help you! Seldom seen, something like a guardian angel. A white lady, that thought to herself, *Maybe her marijuana conviction is not that bad*. She even said, "Everyone makes at least one mistake, at some time or another, in their life."

Now, how often does something like that happen in today's world? I wasn't expecting that at all! I know that lifts a tremendous burden, off my shoulders! Thank you, Lord! I can't thank nobody else, but Him. He's the only one that makes sure, that I have each and everything that I need, on a day-to-day basis! If I started the list of things I'm thankful for it would include..... a lifetime of happiness, joy, pain, tears, heartache, blessings, and the lessons, from all of that! It would be enough words to finish this book, for me. So I'll do my best to summarize ... I hope you feel what I feel, cry, when I cry, and laugh when I laugh.

I started this book when I was in the tenth grade. I worked on it in my spare time, while in my computer class. I started to pour my heart and soul into it. But somehow, it was deleted. I was heartbroken! I even cried and gave up on that idea. I never once said, I wanted to be a writer when I grow up. But everything happens for a reason. It just wasn't the right time to start writing my book.

After everything that has happened in my life, I didn't have a choice. I had to write this book. After my out-of-body experience, where God told me to be one of the first Black, female, bipolar authors in the world! I wrote it on the walls when I was crazy, so I could read it when I was sane. I'm sane now! You can't make the signs any clearer for me. That same night, my mama showed me that I could be rich. I would never have to work again! All I have to do is, write the book! Tell the story! People love this kind of story! Deceit. Adultery. Death. Life. Love. Pain and Scandal. Juicy gossip, and scandal!

I'm in a place in my life where I have enough peace, to start typing my book. I heard that God gives us peace, to do His will ..... I believe that! I was blessed to be able to purchase a computer. I started my book officially, on March 23, 2005. The first day's work, four hours' worth. Deleted by accident! Some kind of freak accident or system glitch. I was disappointed, but not discouraged. It just gave me more determination than ever, to go on! That made me go out and buy a printer. I'll just print as I go. I double disk saved, my work. Just in case! In determination, to get this going.

The next night, I pulled eight straight hours on the computer. I think I managed to get back what I lost, plus some; at least, I hope, so! We settled in and I started listening to my music. Loud, like old times! Smooth, soothing, slow music. Like Mary J, Jodeci, and Blackstreet, just to name a few. Before long, I had a notice on my door about my music. It wasn't even that loud! They called the police on me and everything. That really pisses, me off! The apartment manager sent me a 21-day notice, meaning I have that long to leave the apartment. Just because I was playing my music too loud. What the fuck?

Okay. Now, they let me stay after my drug conviction. But they are going to put me out over some music. That's some real bullshit! I addressed the head manager with my dilemma. I said, you'll don't have to worry about me playing my music anymore. Just don't put me out over that!

She laughed and said, "What are you talking about? You don't have to move. This is just a warning! It can't occur again within 21 days, or you can be put out."

Oh, okay. Y'all had me worried. Okay, here is my rent. They wasn't getting shit until I knew for sure.

To be on the safe side, I unplugged the stereo in the living room, to prevent me from listening to music in the front room. I don't even want to be tempted by the lights. I'll just limit my music to my bedroom, on my computer. As I work, I have on a headset. I'm in my own little world, listening to all the good stuff, like "If I Had to Do It All Again," by Faith Evans. Looking back on my entire life, I can sit and tell you if I had to do it all again, I would! But I'd be, lying ..... I just want my mama back! I would have done anything in my power, to save her.

As far as Rodney is concerned, I wouldn't change anything, even though he hurt me. We had over three years, of good times. I know I can't go back, and change anything in my past! I've accepted that. Everything that didn't kill me, made me stronger. It made me into, who I am today. Now, I just have faith the size of a mustard seed. I believe it will all pay off ...

What's the total of all the money, that your parents gave to help you, over the years? Even into your adult years. Where Mom is there, to bind you out of a jam. When dad's wallet is open on your wedding day, to pay for all the frills. Over a million dollars? Well, somebody stole my million dollars! Your parents, are priceless .... My parents, were priceless ....

I plan to put a price on this book, though. I'll see where it goes from there. As much as you might not want to admit it, rich orphans are a lot happier than poor orphans. The money helps! Money will bring needed joy back in our lives. I use the word, *our*, because the few people who showed me unconditional love, over the years ... will be glad they did! The ones that didn't, will feel my rich, powerful, wrath! I do want to take the time, to thank my Aunt Maria. Through all this, if I forgot to say thank you, Thank you! I think all our problems in the past, were just a misunderstanding of two people, seeking the same thing. Trying to save, what we do have left. The things and people that matter most. I know who you are trying to save. I know you have your reasons.

One of the few things, that I would not do again. Would be to tell Rodney where I live at. Damn! I thought I was moving. I said, fuck it! I let him come over. Now, I'm stuck! I wanted to pretend, pretend like I was still moving. I told him, I'm not going to tell you, where I'm moving to. That didn't last too long. He started opening up to me, so I shared that with him. He just looked so concerned! I have been so blessed in life, to be a big, beautiful woman. He is one of the many, that are still crazy about me, even after a breakup. It's like, I have this certain hold on men, that lasts damn near a lifetime! But this one in particular, is head over hills in love with me. He will do almost anything for me, any little thing I ask for. For God's sake, he bought me a car plus, a TV! I know I can work with this. I kept him on a dangling string. I made him think there is a possibility that we could get back together. That was enough for him to keep buying me stuff. Of course, he was doing the free shit. Like, taking my trash out, bringing my groceries in, Plus, helping me with those heavy-ass laundry baskets. I gave him pussy whenever he wanted it, which was still a win-win for me. He has good sex. Plus, he's not shy with his mouthpiece. I keep him close enough to get what I want. But far enough to do what I want.

I don't trust him enough, to sleep around him. He says things that scare me, sometimes. Like, I told him that I have three locks on my patio door. He told me, "I know how to get around stuff like that."

I looked at him like he was crazy! What the fuck, is that supposed to mean?

He laughed. Like it was a joke, or something. I didn't think it was funny. Not in the least bit!

Meanwhile, over all these months, ever since I left Nettie's house, I've only been back once. That time it was just in and out. This time, I decided to sit, to talk to Maurice for awhile. We smoked a blunt and talked. The conversation was unlike none other that we'd had before. None of my family members know about Rodney. You know that I talk to him again. But I admitted to Maurice, that he'd bought the cell phone. I told him that I mainly just like his money.

He admitted some things to me, also. Things about some girl, that he was going to move away for. He told me why they didn't work out. The conversation got deeper. I don't know how we got on the subject of my first, Jason. The guy that took my virginity, and I took his. Oh, yeah. I told Maurice that I'd talked with him. After all these years, I thought he may have been lying, about being a virgin, too. But, it was confirmed! I kind of tested him, asking how old he was when he lost his virginity. What grade he was in. I found out that the coincidence, that changed my mind about having sex with him, was as true as it sounded, on that day when I heard it, years ago. Back then, I didn't know guys could be virgins, too. I thought only girls guarded this jewel, that every man wants. It blew my mind back then!

I let my guard down. He made me not have sex with another man for one year. I didn't see what all the hype was about. It hurt more than anything. Now that I'm grown, I see why! I gave him a shot at round two. I gave his brother my number. I told him to give it to Jason. He called, and we hooked up. I got to tell you, I thought Rodney was good. Jason is great! His dick is bigger. Plus, he knows how to use it. He came over my house, looking like Wanye', from Boyz II Men, my absolute favorite singing group. I felt the wetness. I felt like I was fucking a celebrity. Took it to a whole nover level!

For a big girl, you would think I weighed a buck twenty, the way he was tossing me around my bed. Dammmnnn! We did it on every square inch, of my California king-size bed. It felt so good, until it started to hurt. I don't know. I never felt that before! Almost like, he was going too deep. I felt it in my stomach. But, I think I like it, though. Oh, my gosh! He did it so good and for so long that I asked him, do you need to take a break, a breather, or something? I wasn't used to all of that.

He smiled and said, "No!" He kept right on going! I see exactly why, he left me hurting for a year, the first time. He got that good stuff! I didn't give Maurice that much detail, though.

He said, "You did it to him? It was good, wasn't it? I know. You know what? Out of everybody, I would want you to be with him ... Pretty, motherfucker!"

We laughed. I said, you are so crazy! I'm laughing, but in the back of my mind, I'm crying! I cannot believe those words, just came out of his mouth. He can actually see me with someone else besides himself? I reassured him that Jason has a girlfriend, that he lives with. He just works me in whenever he can. I can't make no demands, on that man. I don't even try. I'm happy to get in, where I fit in.

We continued to talk. He shared things with me about himself, that I never knew. We also talked about both of us taking our medicine everyday, as needed! He takes fluid pills. We promised each other ... That same day ended up turning into a big family function. Zay Zay came into the back room. She asked if we wanted to ride and get banana splits. We haven't been on an outing like that, in a long time. I'm game!

Maurice got dressed and we all loaded up in the back of the station wagon, on the way to get ice cream. It feels so good, for all of us to be together! I know Maurice is in seventh heaven! He wants his big happy family together again. I haven't met anyone yet, with a bigger heart than his. We watched as the kids spilled ice cream all over the seats, in their grandma's car. She laughed, I laughed too. It wouldn't even have popped off like that, in my car. Oh, well! We ended the day on a happy note. With a memory, that will last a lifetime.

After that day, Maurice almost never left the house. He said he is too big to get in a car. He is getting bigger! But it is mostly from fluid, which can be helped with his pills. Fat Rob and Maurice had already planned to go to the show, with a whole lot of friends. Some concert, coming to North Carolina and they already have their tickets and hotel room reserved. Fat Rob said, "At the last minute, Maurice said, he wasn't going! I said, Oh yes, you are! Get your shit, ready, and let's go! You will ride in the jeep. You will have plenty of room!"

They went, and they had a ball! I know, because I was on the phone with him the whole time! I don't know why. He just kept calling me, describing his good time, minute by minute. He is crazy! Yeah, crazy about me ... Me and his kids. His daughter that looks just like me, and acts just like him! My son, that looks just like him, but acts just like me. You can put a value and total, on child support. You can't put a value, on the time, that a man spends, with his kids. Maurice has his kids <u>every</u> weekend, rain, snow, or shine. Friday through Sunday afternoon. How many men watch their kids <u>every</u> weekend? When I needed him, during the week, he was there and willing.

I pushed Maurice to the back burner somewhat, because I have big problems that he cannot help me solve. My job is cutting my long-term disability money. I don't know what I'm going to do! It feels like, the world is closing in on me. I feel like, I'm having another nervous breakdown! I let my family know. I couldn't keep it in. I told them of the one idea that I do, have - to check myself back into the hospital. They will have no choice but to pay me, if I'm in the crazy house …

Well, I psyched myself up. I packed my stuff, then I got Shaun to take me to the same hospital that I'd been to before. We cried a little. Then we went in. I filled out some forms, and then was seen by a worker. Yeah, about 45 minutes later! She asked me a series of questions. I answered them to the best of my ability.

After we were finished with the questions, the lady said, "You are in luck! Your doctor is on call tonight. She was just about to go home."

She left out of the room. My sister and I waited and waited. Shaun was half sleep, like always. The lady finally came back. She asked me three, straightforward questions. "Do you feel suicidal?"

No.

"Do you want to kill anyone else?"

No. Who am I supposed to kill? My insurance people?

"Have you been taking your medicine?"

Yes.

"Well, then, you don't need to be here. Your doctor, said no!"

What do you mean, my doctor said, no? I don't need to be here? I feel like I'm having a nervous breakdown. But my doctor is turning me away! I guess I'll be back in an ambulance, then! I wasn't suicidal before! How is she going to tell me no? I know how I feel! Come on, Shaun. Let's go! They would prefer for me to be writing on the walls, and tearing my house up, before they take me. That is real bullshit! I wasn't expecting that in the least bit. I've never been suicidal! Now, I have to be ready to kill myself, before they take me! We left disgusted, and unaware of how to fight this. I took retroactive measures, just in case it doesn't pan out. I went to Social Services and got a package deal.

19

Instead of letting the kids remain with Maurice, I decided to go pick them up.

Nettie said, "Maurice is in the kitchen, fixing the kids something to eat."

Good! Well, at least, he's out of his room. He hardly ever comes out any more. I didn't see him that day. The kids grabbed a sandwich and left.

The next time I saw him, he was coming out of his room to go to the bathroom. Looks like, he is losing a little bit of weight. That is great! Now I can be more concerned about myself. He is doing good.

One weekend that Maurice had the kids, I received a message on my answering machine. It was my cousin, calling to tell me that she had her twins. She'll be in the hospital for one more day, if I want, to come see her. I am real excited about this. I want to see those babies. I want to show her that I can be there for support, whenever she needs me. She came to see me when I had my children.

I also want to see if those babies look like, her light-skinned ex-boyfriend, or her dark-skinned new boyfriend.

About thirty minutes after hearing that message, Nettie called me. She said, "Maurice fell in the shower. He was probably asleep in there! You need to come pick the kids up early, so I can take him to the hospital."

I hurried up and got dressed. Then, I received a second call from Nettie, this time to say, "Never mind. Maurice says he is fine. He doesn't want to go to the hospital! I keep trying to make him, but he says he's just fine. You know how he gets! I'm not going to worry about it."

Okay. Well, I was going to go to the hospital to see my cousin and her twins. We started talking about that. Everything seemed fine, so I went on with my plans.

I got to the hospital and surprised her. We hugged, sat, and talked.

The babies wouldn't be ready for about an hour, so we waited. Her boyfriend came back in the room. You want to talk about drama, they have enough drama for all of us, combined. She always has some kind of soap opera shit going on. First of all, she has children by two guys that are cousins. You are going to have drama with that combination, anyway!

The argument started small and escalated. It started with what he brought her to eat, or how long it took or something. Next thing I know, he's threatening her with "If you don't give me the car keys, then I'll just go to Plan B."

Plan B, which evidently involves his ex-girlfriend, and *her* car.

I can't believe he just said this to the face of a woman, that just bore his twins, less than 24 hours ago. Just like the saying goes, and exactly what I've always believed: A man will only do to you, what you allow him to do to you.

Before long, I saw one of the twins; the one who's health, permitted. I held the baby for awhile, then got ready to leave. After about two hours, my cousin asked, "Can you drop him off around the corner? He is going to handle some business, then walk back."

I said, yes. Before I knew it, we were in the parking lot. They are fighting, and I am just trying to leave. I don't know what the fuck, they are arguing over. Car keys, house keys, or something. All I know is, he was trying to shut the car door, but her stomach was in the way. The same stomach, that had not quite gone down all the way, from having his two sons in it. But he didn't give a fuck!

She was trying to get the keys from him. He tried to get me to pull off, with her standing in the door. She finally gave up, and moved from in front of his door. He jumped out of the car and started walking. I told her to get in. I'll drive her back to the hospital doors. I can't believe, what I just witnessed here. She said, "I can't believe that he left with my keys. No telling who he's going to have in my house, while I'm here. It's a shame what I have to go through."

It is a shame, what she has to go through! But as I've said before, she allows it. It ain't the first time that he has disrespected her. I have a feeling, it won't be the last ... Some people are so used to bad; doing bad, and being bad off, that they don't want anything better. They don't strive for it. They're not used to it.

I left after that and went to pick up my kids. When I got there, Maurice was sitting on the couch, with a sheet wrapped around him. One of his friends was sitting on the couch across from him. Nettie was sitting next to the friend. Maurice said something to Tayon. I listened carefully. I said, talk again. His voice sounds funny. He said something else. I listened harder! It sounds like, he has fluid on his throat.

I told him, you need to go to the doctor!

He looked into my eyes, and said, "Why?"

I said, because you sound bad!

He looked at me, dead in my face and said, "I just caught a cold from one of my friends. That's all, that is."

I said to myself, okay. Well, that's possible. I didn't push the subject, but I made a mental note to myself, that if I heard him talking like that next time. I will personally, make him go to the doctor. If anyone has a way of getting through to him, it's me!

A week went by. I dropped the kids off, as usual. I didn't go in. I watched them go in the house, then I pulled off. When I picked the kids up that Sunday, I was in a bit of a rush. But I still went in, instead of just blowing the horn. I walked in and spoke to everybody.

Maurice is sitting in the big chair, the one closest to the door. His uncle is in there with him. They were talking about something. He sounds much better today! I sat long enough for the kids to grab their dirty clothes. They threw them in a bag. I got up to leave. I got to the doorway, where Maurice is sitting. As I walked by, he pinched my butt. I turned around to look at him. He looked into my eyes, then he said, "You going to marry me?" He held on to me as he asked.

I jerked away and laughed. I turned around to see his uncle staring at what had happened. I was so embarrassed! I hit Maurice on the arm and left, still laughing. He is so crazy!

Once I got home, I was talking with my sister on the phone. She had somewhat of a somber tone, in her voice.

She said, "I have been wanting to tell you this. Ever since, I went over Maurice's house the other day, to drop off those clothes. When I went in, I saw Maurice laying across the couch. I called his name. I said, I have some clean clothes for the kids. He turned his head, but he never turned all the way, around. Then I said, what's wrong? You can't get up?

Then I laughed. I thought he was laughing too, but he wasn't! He really couldn't get up! He struggled for awhile, then just gave up! I tried to fight back my tears, as best as I could. But you know me. I dropped the bag down and left ... I sat in the car, crying! He looked so bad, Dee!"

I know, I know ... But what can I do? He is so damn stubborn! I can't force him to take his medicine every day. He says he's taking it! It takes time, for it to kick in. Once he starts back taking it, after missing a couple of days. He lets himself run out, then pays for it later, when he's all cramped up, on the couch. I have talked to Maurice, I told him more than once .... 'You are disabled. You need to, accept that fact, and get a disability check. Or you need to prove that you're not, and get a job. One, or the other. But you need to help me take care of these kids! Because if you die, we will get a government check. It's a shame it will take that, before I get some help with these kids.'

We sat on the phone, just crying, for a few minutes, and sniffling. He's scared to have the surgery. He doesn't want to be too skinny, like his cousin. But his cousin didn't even have the surgery. He just lost weight on his own. I would say that he lost too much weight, so much weight, that he looks like a totally different person. Maurice won't lose that much weight. I told him don't compare himself, to his cousin.

I said, we'll just pray for him! Prayer has the power to change things!

Shaun said, "I've been praying for him, ever since that day!"

Two days later, Maurice died. It hurts just as much, to write it! As it does to say it, and hear it! NO! No! No! This can't be happening! Why couldn't we be, "Happily Ever After," by Case. That's the perfect song for this moment. Maurice would sing this song to me, if he could.

I got a call on my cell phone at 4:30 in the morning. I never, hear calls at that time of night. But I heard this one, for some reason. I answered the phone, and Nettie said, "Open your door."

I said okay, got up, and threw some pajamas on. Then I went to open the door. I saw her with Maurice's brother, his uncle, and another close friend. I broke down. Then, I went into denial mode.

I said, I really don't want all of y'all in my house. I knew, what letting them in my house, meant. At 4:30 in the morning. It's not a social visit. What else could it be? Maybe, he's in the hospital. Okay, I'll let them in.

Nettie said, "Come sit down, right over here ... He's gone, Daminika. He's gone."

The tears started, and they never stopped. No! No! No! Why? Why did he, have to go? My kids ... I'm going to have to tell my kids. This is a fucking nightmare! He was my closest male friend. We had a friendship, like none other! Like none other.

I sat in a daze, thinking about every aspect of everyone's life, with this big, loveable man gone - taken from us way too soon.

Then I thought to myself, *Why didn't I see this ahead of time? Where were my signs? Why wasn't I able to save him? Why wasn't I able to save him, like I'd saved so many other people in my life? He hid it from me. He acted like he was just fine. Every time I came around, he'd come out of his room, so I could see him like that, not trembling with pain, in the back room.*

Nettie said, "His brother and friends found him butt naked, on the floor in front of his bed. His head had fallen, to the side and he was barely breathing. They called 911, but he died before they got there."

The rumors that I heard after that, was that the ambulance crew didn't even try to revive him. I heard it took both the ambulance crew, and four or five friends, just to get him up off the floor and out of his bedroom. He had so much fluid on him.

Nettie and the family left. I called some of my family members for support. I don't know why my sister heard the phone, at 5:30 in the morning, but she did. I told her what happened. She started boo hooing, crying. She has to go to work in a couple of hours, so I let her go back to sleep. Then I called my aunt, and she answered. Thank you, Lord! I told her what happened. She is so concerned. She got out of her bed and was at my house, by 6:15. We sat and talked. The moral support really helps! She left about 45 minutes later and told me to call her once I got to Nettie's house, then she'll come over.

Afterwards, I called Rodney, to kill some time. Plus, I wanted to tell him how I'm feeling right now. He answered, and he was shocked when I told him the news. He sounded like, he was getting ready to cry. He said, he'd call me back. I hung up, then I prepared myself to talk with my children. I know how I felt when I lost my father. I can't believe, that they have to go through this, too.

My kids woke up, a couple of hours later. I braced myself, to tell them the truth. My daughter could see the despair, in my eyes.

I told them, I have to tell you something important. I took a deep breath ... and said, your dad died last night.

The tears started again. Zay Zay's head dropped. Her tears started.

My son said, "I'm not going to cry."

My daughter said, "I knew you were crying about that. I knew he was going to die."

My son's head dropped. He started to cry. He looked at me and said, "Can you tell Dada he's okay?"

I cried even harder. I hugged, and embraced my children. Rocking back and forth, as some kind of comfort. When we finally stopped embracing, my son said, "I'm glad I was born, before my daddy died."

Words from a four year old! They rocked my world. I knew I had to get my pen and paper, to document exactly, what came out of these kids' mouths. What a smart thing to say. *I'm glad I was born, in enough time to spend some quality time with my daddy. I'm glad he didn't die before I was born. I surely enjoyed spending time and getting to know him.* As adults, we might say that his father would have to be alive, for you to even be born! But not necessarily. Think about it. I could have conceived and *then* Maurice died. So in actuality, it really was a smart statement.

We got dressed and grabbed enough food, for us to sit down at Nettie's house all day. I don't want to be alone right now! We got Tayon's bike, and Zay Zay's scooter, so they will have something to play with. Then we went over there and sat. Family members came in, one by one. Some were cleaning, and some were cooking. All I can manage to do is sit, stare, and cry. The people who cleaned went in and stripped Maurice's room down. They bagged up his unwashed clothes, sheets and towels and threw them outside. With him being sick for so long, it stinks back there. They sanitized everything and even rearranged the room. I can't bring myself to go back there, just yet.

We pulled out pictures, and started going through them. Memories you didn't even remember you had, until being refreshed, by Kodak paper. Beautiful memories, of when we were in love, a rebellious love. There was no stopping us!

Nettie paused, and got up. She said, "I have something for you! I better give it to you now, before I forget. Or lose it in my jungle of a room, that I got going on, in here." She went into her room. Within seconds, she was walking out with a large, white bag with a box inside. The box is transparent. So as soon as I looked in the bag, I saw that it is something zebra! I opened the bag, only to see a big, fat, round zebra. I opened the backside of the zebra. It's a candle on the inside.

I had already said, that I was going to name my next zebra, Maurice. But this big, fat zebra, takes the cake. It's perfect! Maurice died in this house, and this candle was in the house at that time. I feel like, a little piece of his spirit, is in this candle. I'll light it, when I want to feel closer to him. I hurried and put it in my car, so it wouldn't break.

Then I asked, where is Fat Rob? How is he doing?

Someone said, "He is all fucked-up! He hasn't left his house."

I just shook my head. That was his ace boon coon, his brother. Certainly close enough, to be his brother. As they say, "That's my other brother!"

We sat for hours. Everyone was affected differently. I made an announcement that I want, to get some tee shirts made, with Maurice's picture on the front. I'll get the prices and let everyone know. This is the picture, that I want to use. This is the best one of him. I want everyone to have the same picture. Nettie said, "Good idea! Are you going to do that tomorrow?"

I told her, yes. She's all fucked-up, walking around with Maurice's baseball cap on. It's the one he wore to the concert, which makes her feel closer to him. I totally understand that. It's this song, that makes me feel closer to him. I haven't even heard it all the way through. There is always a song that comes out whenever someone I love dies, that sums it all up. All I know is they say, "Even when those spinners, stop spinning." They are talking about rims. That's one thing that Maurice took the time to explain to me, when we were going together. All the names of all the different types of rims and tires. This song is sung by someone who sounds like a hustler, a thug. It's nothing like when a thug sings a sad song. It seems so much sadder coming from someone so hardcore. I don't even know the name of the song. But I know it when I hear it.

I went outside when they said that my Aunt Eva arrived. I sat outside on the wall, and we talked. We even listened to music. Her boys sat in the car to control the music. A few minutes, later while we were talking, I just stopped. That's the song! Turn it, up!

The boys turned it up, as loud as it would go. It still wasn't loud enough for me. The song was almost over, but I still jogged across the street, jumped in the front seat of Eva's car, and listened to our song. I sat cramped, in a little car where the seat wasn't slid back quite enough. I listened, and cried. As I rocked back and forth, I imagined Maurice saying, what he'd said so often, in a sarcastic way - "Must be nice."

The song went off too fast. But in a way, I'm glad it's over. The cramps in my stomach, are unbearable! I'm on my period. Which is funny. Because I've been late for so long, that I thought I could be pregnant. That fact was resolved the day Maurice died, when my period started. It's like he made sure to hold it off long enough, to assure that I wouldn't have sex with any other man, during his week. Or like saying, "You are not having a baby by anyone else, especially that motherfucker!" It would have been, Rodney's.

I socialized a little longer. Then we went in the house. By this time, they had music playing in the house. We sat down and looked at more pictures, comparing Tayon to Maurice's baby pictures. Al Green came on. "For the Good Times." I just broke down! This is the song that Maurice mouthed the words to at every party, or holiday gathering. I actually broke down. It felt so good to let it out. I miss him so much! The day turned to night. Everyone started going home.

Nettie pulled me to the side, in the kitchen and said, "I want you to know that Maurice stopped taking his medicine. He hid the pills. I found two months' worth of pills. Daminika, he wanted to die. In a way, he killed himself. You might not want to believe that, but it's true. He told us he was taking his medicine. I prayed for God to knock him on his ass, to straighten him up. But not this!"

She went on to tell me about him knowing he was going to die, like calling for some of his friends and family to come see him after months of separation. She said, "I talked with one of his friends that came by. She told me, that he said he was tired."

I just shook my head. I rocked from side to side, to comfort myself.

DEVASTATING CONSEQUENCES

This is way too much! I thought to myself, *Why didn't he call for me? Why didn't he call me?* As fast as I thought up the question, I figured out the answer. He didn't call for me because he knew, I would try to stop him. He tried his best, to hide this from me. Coming out of his room when I came by, so I'd see the good side, and not the bad. But, in his own way, he was reaching out to me. I just didn't catch on. I think back to that day that he grabbed me, when I walked past. He loves me so much! He was just trying to show me ...

Then I think back to the day. When he said his voice, or lack thereof, was due to a cold. If only I'd said, I'd prefer for a doctor to tell us that! I could have pushed more! I could have done more. But now, I don't have a chance. I broke down even more. I told his mom what I regret.

I regret, that I didn't tell him, that I thought maybe, if he got the surgery done, got a job, or just some money coming in, we might have actually gotten back together. I thought maybe, since God hasn't showed me my husband yet, that it was meant for Maurice, to be my husband. Nettie, I was going to tell him! But, I didn't want the only reason for him going under the knife, to be me. I wanted him to do it for himself! But maybe if I would have told him that, it would have given him some motivation to change; a reason to go on. But I failed. I failed miserably! I was unable to save my best friend, my one and only male best friend.

In the midst of me beating myself up, a thought popped into my mind. *Maybe, I wasn't meant to save him. Maybe, everything happened the way it did, because it wasn't meant for me to save him. If it was meant for me to save him, I would have! God doesn't make mistakes.* Now, I'm just looking for the reasons, why!

We got the orders together for the tee shirts. I have to dish out enough money for four shirts. I'm paying for his mom's shirt, too. I want to make sure she has one. Her shirt will say, "My Big Teddy Bear" on the front. We'll put "Mama" on the back. Even though, I can use every dollar at a time like this. It just seems like something, I have to do. Just to show him, how much we all love him! Tayon's shirt will say, "Lil' Maurice." Zay Zay's shirt will say, "Daddy's Little Girl." My shirt will say, "I told you, I will love you for life ... I meant it!" On the back, it will say, "Baby's Mama." I want everyone to know exactly who I am. I was going to write "Maurice's Dime" on the back, but I didn't want anyone hating on me. Thinking that, I'm putting words in his mouth. I know the truth, though. I'm going to always be his dime!

We sat with the other family members. Every day, just counting down the days until the funeral. I spent the night, that night over Nettie's, since I had stayed so late. I slept on the couch, if that's what you want to call it. I didn't really sleep. I tossed and turned, because I don't have my medicine with me. Just as I got real comfortable, I saw Nettie's next door neighbor, walk down the hall. He stopped and stared at me.

He said, "If you are not sleep, I have something to help you sleep."

I saw him holding up a blunt. Oh, yeah! As if I hadn't smoked enough, during the day. I always go to sleep on a blunt, though. I jumped up and went out on the porch to smoke with him. He is a real nice guy. He and Maurice were close. We talked for a long time. Then he said something, that I didn't expect. He said, "I know for a fact, that Maurice loved you to death. He told me, and I could tell. He didn't do too bad, either. I told him that. You are the prettiest girl your size, that I've ever seen around here. In all of Roanoke."

I do take that as a compliment. Especially, coming from a skinny dude. It usually takes a big dude to appreciate, this kind of beauty! I am flattered. After awhile, he just started to talk my head off. I politely excused myself, and went in the house, to go to sleep.

One more day to go, until the funeral. The kids have been begging, to see their daddy. That's where we are going today. At the last minute, Nettie said, "I don't want the kids to go. He might look too big."

I said, that's all the kids have been talking about! They are going! They've seen him worse. That was that, and we went on.

We pulled up, and I have this uneasy feeling, in the bottom of my stomach. They said that Maurice's dad finally arrived from out of town. They are all in the back, talking business. Nettie joined them, along with her sister.

We sat in the lobby, patiently waiting. We waited ten minutes, or so. Then formed a line. The staff opened the door to where Maurice lay. I caught a glimpse of him. I wanted to cover my eyes, and my kids' eyes, but I don't have enough hands. I turned them around and explained it to them. Your dad looks bad. You don't have to look, if you don't want to. Do you still want to look?

They said, "Yes."

We made our way to the coffin. I hollered out, that's my baby!

That's my baby, lying in a double-wide coffin. His face looks like two faces, stuck together. His gigantic body filled every inch, of that coffin. I've never seen one like it! I held Tayon up, to get one more look at his daddy. My daughter broke down. I did my best to comfort her. Only, I can't even comfort myself. I had a quick side bar, with one of the attendants. I asked, can you take some more fluid out of his face? Or his body?

She shook her head no. Nettie started hollering and crying! "That's not my baby! My baby didn't look like that! He's too big! That's not him." She shook her head and walked away. That is him, though. If it was meant for him to look like that in death, then so be it. We remember him a different way.

She said, "I want to bring pictures up here to display, before anyone else sees the body. That gives us a couple of hours."

Whispers were heard about having a closed casket funeral. I definitely do not want a closed casket. I'll make sure my wishes are heard, too.

Even though when Maurice died, he probably weighed 500 lbs. But with all that fluid on him, he looks like, he weighs 1000 lbs! We went back to the house, with sad stories to tell to those who didn't come. In disbelief, they went to the funeral parlor shortly thereafter. Even his cousin, the one that didn't even want to go to her own daughter's, funeral. She mustered up enough courage, to go see him, one last time. She said she won't be at the funeral, though. I let her know I am proud of her, for doing as much as she did. That took a lot, of courage. Especially considering, how tight they were growing up.

The day turned to night. Lots of people came by, after viewing the body. I saw this somber look on everybody's faces. If it was somehow possible, for all of them to feel even sadder .... they do. Like it wasn't bad enough, that he had to be dead. But he looks bad, too. That's not like Maurice. One of his close friends approached me, an old head from back in the day. He said, "Tooooo smallll!!" Which may not sound like much to you, but he would yell this same expression, every time he saw Maurice and I together. Every time he saw Maurice. I started laughing, then boo hooing, crying, all in the same breath! He grabbed me, and hugged me tight. We rocked back and forth for a long time, until I was comforted enough to let go! He spoke comforting words. He said, "I remember, baby. You'll used to be together all the time. Yeah, I used to call him and Fat Rob, washing machine and dryer." He really made me feel better. Unexpectedly. I really appreciate him taking the time to help me.

He walked away and started talking to one of Maurice's aunts. They used to date. That's when I heard her say, "He was so depressed. He didn't leave the house for months."

Depressed? That's not a word that I would associate with Maurice. It made me cry, just thinking about what he might have been depressed about. Was it me? Was it his weight? Whatever it was, it just kills me, that he had to feel like that! Maybe that's why, I haven't seen him smile for a long time. That beautiful smile ... Even though he was big, he never acted like it bothered him. That was, up until the past few months. I thought the reason why he didn't leave the house, was because he said that he was too big, to fit in just any car. It would have to be a jeep or truck.

20

We moved the gathering to the back of the house. Everybody decided to match a blunt. About seven blunts went around. We sat and reminisced about the good old days. Fat Rob finally left his house and came over to join us. We tripped, like always. I said things to make him feel better. He said things to make me feel better. We have always had this bond like that.

In the midst of all the laughter, through the smoke, up walked archenemy number three. I'd already listed two of the enemies, to Maurice's cousin. I let her know, I forgot one! The girl stood behind someone else and stared at me. She doesn't think I know who she is. To her surprise! Maurice already informed me about her, in one of our long talks that we had before he died. He told me everything. Bitch!

I asked her, what the fuck are you looking at? Don't be fucking staring at me, like I don't know who you are or something!

She looked confused and insulted. She said, "Daminika, I don't have anything against you."

I said, Bitch, don't say my name like you know me or something! Oh, you know my name. That means he must have talked about me, a lot! He sure did talk about you a lot. I laughed in her face. That's why, I know exactly why he broke up with you! Seems as if, she has, some kind of daily incontinence problem. She is way in her twenties, too. I didn't say it out loud, but she knew exactly, what I was talking about.

Embarrassed, she jumped up. I prepared myself to whip that bitch's ass. She started dialing numbers on her cell phone. Then she walked away, real fast. She has a twin sister, and even though they don't look alike, I really didn't know which one it was. I don't give a fuck, though! If it was the wrong one, then ... give that message to your sister, bitch!

Everyone told me to calm down. They said, "At least, you know about her! We didn't even think you knew."

Fat Rob grabbed my leg, and looked into my eyes. He said, "Daminika, chill the fuck out! Come on, now, don't embarrass that girl like that! Leave that shit alone. You know who the fuck it's all about! Who's the one, here? That's all that matters. Do you know how many girls in Roanoke are jealous of you? You are the only one that my boy would say, 'Naw, I ain't going!' for …. We need to talk anyway."

It seemed like, it really hit me. I took what he said to heart ... I let it go. I enjoyed myself, then I went home.

We went home earlier than usual, to get things together for the funeral. The next morning, we got dressed early, then went over Nettie's house to line up. We got in the limo, and ride to the funeral. My son looks like a big boy. He has on the same kind of outfit, as Maurice. His brother is also dressed like him. We finally arrived at the church, got out, and lined up, two by two. I need a man to walk with me. I might pass out, or anything.

I found my uncle and asked, if he would walk with me. He obliged. We filed in down the aisle and up to the casket. I saw all the beautiful pictures. They brought back memories of a happier time, a time when we were in love, head over heels. A love that bore, two beautiful children.

I looked at Maurice, and to my surprise, he does look better! His face and his body, went down some. Thank you, Lord! I rubbed his arm continuously, as if to keep him warm. I kissed my hand, and touched his face. I wish I could kiss your lips, baby!

I mouthed the words, I love you. Then I walked away. I took my seat because I didn't want to hold up the line.

I asked my brother to sing. He thought of a couple of selections, then came forward to sing. He sang, "I Won't Complain" by Rev. Paul Jones. One of Maurice's boys came up, crying. He put his gold chain in the coffin. I think that is so sweet. Then A.J. sang, "There Is None Like You," by The Toronto Mass Choir. It is such a beautiful song. It spoke to my heart. It also compelled me to get up. I excused myself across the knees, of those sitting nearby. I walked to the coffin, to see him, just one more time. I stood and stared at him. I heard more, of the lyrics, "I could search the whole world over. There is still no one like you!" I grabbed his arm. I rocked, back and forth, getting more and more into the song. I rocked so hard that I felt his arm SNAP! *Oh my gosh!* I felt myself becoming faint! I started falling backwards. All of a sudden, there were all of these people behind me.

I heard someone say, "She's a big one. Don't let her fall. Get behind her!"

I didn't fall, but I do resent that. I heard my Aunt Ann's voice say, "I got her. Come on, Dee. Let's sit down, right here."

We backed up two steps and sat down. Those same people who were behind me, are now closing the coffin top.

Oh, my gosh! They are closing it! I hollered, I love you, Maurice! There is none, like you!

My aunt sat and comforted me. She hugged me and sat beside me, for the rest of the service. The preacher touched on the fact that, it's a shame what it takes to bring us all together, in the house of God. Sometimes, it takes a funeral. But whatever it takes, you want to be ready, when He comes for you.

Nettie said, "I really think Maurice made peace with God. He grew closer to the Lord in his last days."

It doesn't matter, anyway. His heart, alone, will get him into heaven. He has a guaranteed spot. Right next to my mama. I'm sure she likes him.

Before we knew it, the funeral was over. They rolled him out, and I dropped my head. You left me to raise these kids by myself. We filed out after the casket.

One particular member of my church, made sure that I saw her. She stopped me and gave me a hug. Her love, and support over the years, actually leaves me speechless …. I appreciate, her coming. More than, you know! But, as long as, she knows. Then, I'm fine. I thought that more people from my church would have come. I guess since we weren't married, they didn't announce it at church.

The limo drove us to the burial ground. Seven of us got a chair, to sit in. They prayed, and we paid our last respects. They handed each of us, a red rose. Then the preacher said, "Please stand, and put your rose on the casket."

Everyone stood but me. I just couldn't bring myself to say bye. I closed my eyes. I pictured that I was somewhere else - anywhere else! I felt a hand on my back. I felt rushed.

I wanted to holler, Don't rush me!!!!!

I clinched the rose tighter, and stood up. I kept my eyes closed, and my head down. I took one step, then looked up. I saw that big casket, draped in flowers. Slowly I walked closer; I kissed my rose, and dropped it down, then walked away quickly. In denial of what just happened. I saw the faces of friends and distant family members, all concerned and somber. I expected to see more people from SW. That was where we lived, in the projects for years. Where are all those SW niggas? All Maurice's boys, that used to come by the house everyday. There was only one that stopped by Nettie's house - a drunk, a man that would stumble down the street. But he was always alert enough to speak. A very sweet man! I was humbled to see him sober enough, to walk through her door. He stopped by, just to show his love! One more showed his face at the burial ground. He saw me and grabbed me! He hugged me and whispered, "You know, that was my boy. I had to come out." I cried even harder. They helped me into the limo.

Even though I shouldn't be surprised, at some people's reaction to death, I am. Funerals just make some people, too sad. They don't want to even deal with those emotions, especially men. The hard-core motherfuckers! The drug dealers. They have an image to maintain. They can't be caught balled up, crying at a funeral. They grieve at home. They pour out a little liquor, for each one gone before. I respect that, though.

More people got shirts made than I thought. Some of them wore it to the funeral. We planned to only wear ours afterwards. Oh, well.

Once we got back to Nettie's house, we quickly changed. It was the first time I'd been in *his* room since he died. They moved things around, so it doesn't have the same feel that it had at first. Especially because, they moved his dresser. It was the first thing you saw when you came in. It does still have an aura of him, though ...

The kids were proud to put their shirts on. Everybody looks like a mini army, with their shirts on. After sitting and staring at so many shirts, I realized that having his face on the shirts, makes it feel like, he is right here with us. Like he is puffing every blunt, and laughing at every joke. I like this feeling! Since the majority of the shirt is white, I made sure not to eat or drink anything! I guarded it like a trophy.

I'm not eating, anyway. I've only eaten enough to keep my stomach settled and to keep me from throwing up. I have to eat something when

I take my medicine, though. I asked Maurice's cousin to put a plate up, for me. With so many people showing up to eat, I wanted to make sure I had something to eat, for later. That will be my first full course meal, in almost a week.

I joked and said, that I have Maurice to thank, for my new figure, we laughed. We all sat in the front yard, on the wall, displaying our shirts proudly. People walking by stopped, to try to read what my shirt says. But trying not to stare. I didn't mind. I know what the extra looks are for.

Maurice's cousin got out of the car and walked towards me, holding a stack of pictures. Pictures that I've never seen before. I flipped through them, until I came to a picture, that took my breath away. It made time, stop!

It's a picture of Maurice and Tayon, together. The only one, I've seen. I sat, holding it. Staring, at it. I held it close to my heart and cried. I don't know how long I stared at that picture. But, I noticed the world moving around me, yet I was standing still. I don't need to see anymore pictures. I'm in love with this one! Out of all the pictures we've been through, in the past couple of days, I haven't seen any with them together. I told her I want a copy of the picture.

She responded, "You got it!"

She let me hold on to the pictures. For one because, I didn't want to give them back. Another reason is because; she didn't want them to be messed up. She knew they would be safe, in my possession. I tucked them safely in my pocketbook.

Just then, through the sunshine, raindrops fell. Everyone rushed up on the porch and into the house. I sat …. Feeling the raindrops, one by one, get bigger. I laughed, and continued to sit in the rain, like a crazy person ….. knowing this is the perfect moment! Maurice's tears are raining down on me. Cry, baby, cry! I don't know if they are happy tears, or tears of grief. All I know, is that they feel good! I'll sit out here all by myself, if I have to …. The rain came down harder. The only reason I got up, is because I didn't want the ink from his picture, to run all over my white shirt, ruining it.

I walked through the house to get to the backyard. We have a covered place to sit and smoke. When I opened the back door, I was greeted by one of Maurice's uncles on his daddy's side. He introduced me to one of his friends.

He said, "She's his baby's mama." Then he referred to me as Maurice's, common-law wife. Saying that we were together long enough, and that legally, we are married. He said to his friend, "Fuck that! That's his wifey."

Well, I'm honored. I didn't know he felt that way. Then I thought about it. All this, coming from the man that didn't even claim my son, as being Maurice's child.

I saw him at the store one day. He said, "How is your daughter doing?"

I said, *they* are doing just fine. I am used to people saying, "How are your children doing?" My answer came out without thinking. But afterwards, I thought to myself. *What are you trying to say? Now that Tayon looks just like Maurice, there's no denying it! Now, they are trying to claim us. Fuck that! We don't need your fake love!* I laughed a fake laugh, then walked away.

A group of us sat in the back of the house and smoked, like usual. After the munchies set in, certain people went in, to get a plate of food. I watched them eat some of my favorites, and made a mental note to eat after I take my shirt off. The kids are having fun playing football in the backyard. All of a sudden, a football came flying through the air, and landed in the middle of this girl's plate. Damn it! The plate flipped up, and the food went everywhere! *Especially,* on the back of my new shirt. I am so pissed! I cannot believe this. After all my efforts, to keep this shirt clean! I didn't even eat my own food, but somebody else's food, is all over my shirt! I just shook my head. I sat pissed off, with my mouth still open. They saw my reaction and ran to get wet cloths.

I laughed. Knowing, it wasn't funny. I wanted to cry. It felt like Maurice was telling me, "Loosen up, gal."

They cleaned me off, as best as they could. Then they tried to make me feel better by saying, "You can hardly see it."

Green beans, and macaroni and cheese? I *know* you can see it! I sat and finished the blunt. I'm ready to leave, but I don't know how to say goodbye to everybody. I just got up, like I was going to the bathroom or something, and walked in the house. I asked, where did you put my plate?

The response was, "Oh! I forgot to fix your plate. I just had so much going on."

Long story short, I had to fix my own plate. I got the last few of the big pot of meatballs, that *I* paid for. Tiffany made them. Nettie had asked her to, but she didn't have enough money. I didn't want it to not be enough variety, of food.

There were two helpings of macaroni and cheese left. I got one of those and the rest of the fixings. I know, you're probably thinking, *Where's the chicken?* Of course, we had chicken. All black people eat fried chicken, at a funeral. I found me a breast, wrapped it all up in aluminum foil. I said, I'm going to put this in my car. Then I walked out the front door. I jumped in my car, and pulled off. The kids had already gone with Nettie somewhere. At last I can relax for a few minutes.

I turned the corner and turned the radio up. The song that I have been waiting for came on! "Must Be Nice," by Lyfe Jennings. I get to hear the song from the beginning, through it's entirety. It's like Maurice is playing this song, just for me! It's like, he is singing this song to me. A song about himself. Like he wrote it, or helped write it. And I was able to get in the car at the exact moment, to be able to hear this song from the beginning. I began to cry. I cried so hard, that I could barely control my car. I banged on the steering wheel, through all the intense moments in the song, driving with tears in my eyes. The lines on the road all blended together. Finally I pulled over and sang aloud, right along with the music!

After I composed myself, I drove the rest of the way over Rodney's house. He said he'll be there, sitting and waiting for me. Today is his birthday. Maurice was buried, on his birthday ... Well, I haven't been with a man in awhile. That's why I need some of that male type of attention. Not just sex, even though I know we are going to do that. But just cuddling, laying around, and talking.

When I first went in, he gave me a hug and a kiss. I followed him upstairs and made sure he saw my shirt completely, before I took it off. I really didn't feel right wearing it in front of him. I told you, it's like Maurice is staring at you. I didn't want to make him feel uncomfortable. After I took it off, I draped it across the door to the extra bedroom, face down. I didn't want him watching us in the bedroom. Rodney gave me another shirt that, ironically, used to be Maurice's, anyway.

We sat, smoked, and talked. He comforted me just right, then asked, "What did you get me for my birthday?"

Nothing. We discussed going to the grocery store, using my food stamp card, to buy ingredients to make him a cake. Mmnn! That sounds like a good dessert to go with my dinner. I get so excited about food! We decided to go. But that reminds me, I'm ready to eat now! I don't want to wait until we get back. But I did anyway. I haven't eaten in this long. What's another thirty minutes? He ran in the store, and we were back, before I knew it.

I made myself comfortable, unwrapped my plate and heated it up for a few minutes. Then I dug in! Rodney, is asking for food already.

Damn! I haven't ate. I'm hungry! *Just wait a few minutes. Until, I'm almost full. Then I'll give you some. The macaroni and cheese is delicious!* I tried not to let on, to how good it was.

He said, "How's the macaroni and cheese?"

I said, ehh.

He said, "Shut up! I know it's good, because you haven't stopped eating it."

I laughed.

Then he said, "All I really want, is one of those meatballs."

Shit. I gave him one just to shut him up! Then I started working on them myself, right along with my chicken. Eww! These meatballs, are disgusting! Just then, Rodney came out of the kitchen, making an ugly face! He had already chewed his up, and swallowed it before he realized how nasty it tasted. We agreed that it tastes burnt. I told him that Tiffany cooked them. She said she left them on all night and when she woke up, there was grease and barbeque sauce all over the cabinet and floor....

I guess so, bitch! You are supposed to cook them for twenty minutes! She also said that she makes her own barbeque sauce. It tastes more like tar, to me. Plus, it's the same color. Damn! She's ugly, *and* she can't cook! I don't know what man in his right mind, that would ever want her. We laughed about it. We even joked her, for awhile.

I ate as much as I could, then sat back to enjoy my fullness. I heard Rodney working away in the kitchen. I yelled, whip that cake up, boy!

DEVASTATING CONSEQUENCES

My stomach is so full and gassy. I felt myself getting ready to fart. I sat still to let the gas pass smoothly and quietly. All of a sudden, a big squirt of doo-doo, came straight out. With so much watery intensity, that it went straight through my clothes, even my jeans! Right onto Rodney's suede couch. Oh, my gosh! Just then, he came in there to talk to me. I tried to sit still, knowing that I had to get up. Damn it! *Why are you talking to me now? Go back in the kitchen*!

I said, I have to go to the bathroom. I just have to work up the energy to get up. He stood there reading the directions on the cake box. I squeezed my butt cheeks together, then got up. I looked at the stain on the couch. I just shook my head. I quickly jogged up the steps. Ensuring that he wouldn't be close behind. You do not want to be close behind, my behind right now!

Once I got in the bathroom, I stripped down to access the damages. Oh, my gosh! That is so nasty! I called Rodney on his cell phone, to explain what had happened. Also, to apologize for his couch. He laughed and said, "Those nasty-ass meatballs made you shit on yourself!"

I said, I know! Either that, or the fact that I ate a full course meal, for the first time in almost a week. It went in, and came straight back out. I said, now, I'm hungry again!

He laughed. I'm just kidding. We hung up, and I folded up my funky clothes, good enough to not see the stains. Rodney peeked in and gave me some clean clothes. I got in the bathtub to clean up.

When I finished, I rushed downstairs to clean his couch cushion. It is propped up against the wall. He had already cleaned it! Oh, my gosh! That says a lot about a man - a man that will clean up your shit! I'm impressed! I don't even clean up my kid's vomit, much less anything else! From anybody, else. I merely point and say, clean that shit up! It makes me sick just to look at it. My kids have better aim now.

I said, thank you for doing that for me, babe.

He nodded.

I told him, I'll be waiting for you, upstairs. Come on up after you put the cake in the oven. I'll frost it for you, when it gets done.

He said, "You better!"

I laughed and said, whatever. Then I went up the steps, and sat on the bed. As soon as I sat down, I felt this cramp, in my stomach. Not a shit cramp! More like a muscle spasm. Oh, my gosh. I looked up and saw Baby's Mama, reflected off the mirror, on the wall. *My shirt!* The muscle spasm moved, right down into my thigh. I feel Maurice's presence.

He said, "What are you doing over here?"

I whispered, I know you don't want me to be over here. But, if you want me to be with somebody else, then *you* need to help me find him! Just leave! Don't talk to me now. My pains went away. Just then, my foot jumped! Like he grabbed my toes. Something he always did. After that, I felt his presence leave. That wasn't the first time that he tried to talk to me. The last time, I was at home. It almost kept me there. He played, "How to Deal," by Frankie J., for me. Then he played a special song, for the kids. Back-to-back songs, by their favorite artist. I've been looking for ways to control this. I hope that worked!

I spoke to Nettie on the phone. She said, "I will be keeping the kids all night. You need some time to yourself. But I don't want you to be alone."

I assured her, that I'm not.

The night went on. We cuddled for hours. Then we wanted to have sex. I assumed the position, but immediately felt that muscle spasm come back in my thigh. *Oh, no. Not now! I need this!* Maurice is going to, make this impossible. I started getting into it, anyway. I felt Maurice release my thigh. In a way saying, "Go ahead, have an orgasm. I just want you to be happy."

I felt one teardrop, fall. Then I thought about how weird it is, with Maurice watching me. I hesitated, wanting to stop. Then, I thought about it. All dead people could be watching. So, never mind then. I finished my business.

We ate cake, and I told him, I will be leaving soon.

He said, "You ain't going nowhere! I don't want you to go nowhere. I want you to stay."

My heart melted with the first sentence. By the third, I had already fluffed my pillow. He is a Casanova. This is weird, because I haven't felt at ease enough, to sleep around anyone, besides close family members ... Something happens to me at night, and I don't want just anyone around, to witness that. You could say, I sleepwalk, talk, and eat. I knew if I spent the night, that I wouldn't get much sleep. I don't have any medicine, so I listed my rules to him, in order for me to stay. The main one is, <u>DON'T SCARE ME!</u> I don't care if you think it is a joke. Or that it's funny, I don't! I scare very easily.

He followed all of my rules, so we had a nice night. One night turned into every night since then. I opened up to him, a lot.

He asked me, "Will you be my girl?"

I agreed, but not before I ran the plan by Nettie. I told her I need his help right now. Not a lot of other men, are offering to move me in with them. Adding me to his Section 8, so that we can get a bigger house. At this time, there is no other man willing to do that. He's going to give me money, and get my hair and nails done. I want that.

She said, "I don't think that is a good idea. I know you want someone around. But you don't have to go with him. You see, I have my ex around. That doesn't mean I'm going back with him."

I explained to her that if I don't have the title of girlfriend, then I get nothing. I'm going to give him that. I'll let him call me his girlfriend. I'll let him pay for me to get my hair done and a pedicure. But, I won't get seriously involved with him. I won't trust him. I can do this. I'm still The Gamette!

She said, "Okay, because, you know he is sneaky. I heard that he was messing with Tiffany. You know, your friend."

Sleeping with, or talking to? I know she's friends with his cousin, but I really don't think she was messing with him. All of a sudden, I felt this rage take over me! What if he did mess with her? He knows the list of people to stay away from! I thought about the two of them together and laughed. She is so ugly! Why would he want to mess with her? Ass? Ass has no face. I remembered him saying that before.

Nettie continued with her conversation. It was like, I was on Charlie Brown. Womp womp, womp womp! I nodded like I was paying attention, even though I'm really not! I hurried off, got in the car. Then dialed her number.

I called her at work and asked, Tiffany are you messing with Rodney?

She sounded shocked, and said, "No!"

I said, well, that's what I heard! Do you know how I feel about him?

She said, "Yeah, you still love him!"

Yeah, and if I find out that you've been messing with him, I'm going to fuck you up! I'm going to call and ask him. I can tell when he's lying! If he denies it. I hope we can still be friends ... If not, oh, well! Goodbye!

I hung up, then went home and waited for him to return from work. He finally arrived. I waited around a little, before I asked him. But I can't hold it in any longer! I told him what I heard.

Then I said, did you fuck her?

He denied it. Then he angrily said, "I want to know who said that! Who the fuck is trying to pin that ugly girl on me? That bitch can't even cook. She don't got no money!"

I know; that's what I said. I believed him. Now that I have the title of girlfriend, he did everything he promised. I got my hair done, and my toes. He pays special attention to the kids. He took all of us swimming, on several occasions. Everything was going just fine until, I actually did start getting into him. Becoming possessive, wanting him around all the time, having to actually trust him. This is a whole lot harder than I thought!

I wanted to be a fake girlfriend. But I feel myself becoming a real girlfriend. The more that I cooked his favorite meals, the more I realized how much I'd missed doing that. That only made me want him around more. To enjoy the meals and to help with the clean up. I feel myself getting stressed out over this man, again! I let it take over me. Or should I say, it consumed me! I found myself keeping track of his movements on paper. *Why? Why am I putting myself through this? He is sooo good to me. He treats me like a queen! He is always exactly where I want him to be, when I really need him! He's helping me pay my bills.* Yet, I want more.

21

I have to demand more, in order to keep him on his toes. To let him know that I don't take no shit! I never did, and I never will. My illness has changed a few things. But me being lenient, it's not happening! I told him I want to meet his mom, something he'd been dangling over my head for years. He agreed, so I made him set a date.

I told him, if you are so serious about me, you want to marry me. You can't live without me. Then I should be able to meet your mom.

He set a date about three weeks later, that we both agreed upon.

I said, I know that you have been working to try and restore your trust. You have been doing great, while you are around me. But, I want to know what you are doing, when I'm not around?

He said, "There is not a lot of time, that I'm not with you."

I said, I know. But you do go over your uncle's house for hours. Do you know how long it takes, to make a phone call? I do! It only takes a couple of minutes, seconds, sometimes.

I said, I haven't contacted any of my little, boy toys, and I can, prove it! Can you? This is the ultimate anty up! I continued, I want to see an itemized copy, of your cell phone bill. Only starting from when we got together. If you haven't been doing anything wrong, then you won't have a problem with this.

He replied, "I don't have a problem with that. You can get that."

I smiled, and we kissed. Later on that night, I gave him a special reward. I let him stop wearing a condom. I told him, as long as you don't cum in me. Then we won't have a problem. All the disease is in the cum. We had incredible sex that night. I can see he is really trying! He wants this to work. We are still waiting on his results, to come back. Yeah, I made him get tested! I even went to get myself checked out. The whole nine yards, a physical and everything. I haven't had one of those in years.

My illness has affected my sleeping habits, my eating habits, and my driving habits. By the time I come out of my self-induced medicine coma, I'm playing catch-up! I always feel at least a day behind everyone else in the world. I stress to Rodney the fact that, I have to take my medicine everyday, for the rest of my life! It's not an option. When I don't, things aren't pretty. I don't ever want to be like that again!

At first he thought I was some kind of pharmacy, that would just dispense drugs to him, at will. I let him know, it does not work like that! I don't want him to take any of it around me. Not even one! I'm so scared of what his reaction will be. I had mixed reactions; with every medicine those doctors tried on me! I don't want to be around anything like that. It scares the shit out of me!

For the first month, I hid my medicine from him at night. Then it got to the point, where I did trust him more, so I started leaving it out. We talked a lot about my condition. I told him what I wanted him to know. I still haven't told him exactly, what's wrong with me. You know, the medical term. But we had a heart-to-heart, one night. I revealed to him the actual clinical word for my disease. Manic Bipolar I. The worse kind of bipolar. I asked my doctor, what are the differences between I, II, and III? She said, "With Bipolar I, you are always hospitalized, and you'll have to be on medicine, for the rest of your life."

In a way, I think he already knew, but wanted it to be verified. It felt good to get it out in the open. I feel so good about his change. I actually let him read a page of my book. I have never let anyone read it! I let my family members look at how big it was getting, but never let them get a peek! I made him close his eyes and pick a page. He just happened to pick one of the juiciest pages in the book. I am embarrassed to have him read it right in front of me. I feel vulnerable, as I await the word of what he thinks. He was at best, captivated by it! He wants more! He clawed and begged for more, for the next page. His page had been cut short, abruptly. I'm sorry. I denied his request. I returned the page, and tucked the book away. I am liberated at his surprising, but much appreciated reaction! He is not one to fake a reaction, either. He doesn't tell people what they want to hear. He only tells you the brutal, honest truth! So, thank you. I feel much more motivated, to finish.

Time passed and his comforting nature, turned to desperation - desperation to get away. I guess he wanted to go out with his cousins, but didn't know how to ask. Oh, I mean, tell. What had happened was ... After he got off from work, he took the bus to his house to get clean clothes. I agreed to pick him up there. I called to tell him that I am around the corner, from his house and to please be ready.

He said, "I am not at home! I decided to wait until tomorrow to get clean clothes, since I'm off."

Okay. Well, where are you, so I can come pick you up?

He said, "I'm chilling right now. I will be home after while."

I said, no. I don't think so. You told me to come pick you up. You just wasted my time and my gas! If you wasn't coming home, then I could have made my own plans! I'm coming to pick you up! Where are you, at?

He said, "I'm not telling you where I'm at. I'm just telling you that, I'll be home after while! If, I come home!" Click.

If you come home! If you, come home! I got that! All day I got it, right here! I pulled up to my house, frustrated and boiling mad! *You want to hang up on me? You don't want to tell me where you're at?* As I walked into the house, I saw a big black bag full of Rodney's belongings. I grabbed the bag and walked to my bedroom. I unzipped it, and dumped it's contents on the floor. I grabbed the scissors, then dialed his number, one more time.

He answered by saying, "Why are you tripping? I'm always in the house with you! I wanted to spend some time by myself."

I said, there were better ways, to go about it, than this! I told you, don't fucking disappear! Don't leave and not tell me where you are at! You are by yourself every day that you go to work. We are supposed to discuss the other times. You changed the plan and didn't call to let me know. And you wonder why, I'm pissed? Now, are you going to tell me where you are?

He said, "No, not yet."

I hung up. Then I started cutting shit up! Oh! You don't have to tell me where you're at! I started with the small stuff, socks, underwear, shorts. I cut that shit into a million tiny pieces! Even though I saw his favorite jersey laying in the pile, I pushed it to the side. I'll wait on that. I'll give him one more chance to fix things, before I cut that. I know how much he loves, that thing! He better call back! I bought it, but I won't think twice, when it comes time to cut it. Maybe I'll mail him a little piece of it. I feel that evil laugh coming on. *Ha, Ha, Ha, Ha, Haaaaaaa!*

I sat puffing a blunt, staring at that jersey. The phone rang. He said, "Come and get me. I'm right around the corner from my old house."

I dropped the scissors, and went to pick him up. We argued for a little bit, but I let it go, since he did tell me where he was.

He said, "I didn't know how to tell you, that I wanted to chill with my friends, for a couple of hours. I thought you would have been mad, then cause an argument so I couldn't go."

I said, all you had to do was tell me. Also, tell me what time you were coming back. That's all I ask. I want you to go out just as often, as you would like me to go out. Later that night, I asked him. Where is the print out, of your, cell phone, bill?

He said, "I haven't ordered it yet."

I said, well, we can call on three-way, because I'm tired of waiting for it!

That's when I broke him down. He gave me his version of the truth.

He said, "The reason why I can't get a copy of the phone bill is because, the bill is not even mailed to me. The phone is in another girl's name. But, as long as I pay the bill, the phone stays on. I don't have any codes or anything, to give the operator so the phone company won't let me get an itemized bill."

Wait! Wait, just one minute ... You have a cell phone in another girl's name? And you pick now, to tell me? You could have told me this, when I first asked for the statement! But, noooo! You want to hide it until the last minute! Who's the girl? Who's the dumb ass, that put a phone in her name for you?

He said, "You don't know her. And you don't have to worry about her." He laughed. "She's in jail, for five to ten."

I can not believe this. You should have told me before now! I want you to take the phone out of her name!

He said, "Unless you are willing to put it in your name, then I can't do that. I can't put it in my name, because the deposit is too high."

I checked on the cost of adding him to my bill. That cost is also way too high. That's when I told him, I want your phone number changed! *I want it changed, today*!

He agreed, and changed it promptly.

I feel good about his honesty, so we moved on.

I let him know, since I am his girlfriend, I do have the right to answer, or check, any calls that come in.

He stated his right to do the same.

I don't care. I don't got shit to hide.

He said, "I don't, either!"

As time went on, our relationship did get better. The communication is there. He goes to work, then comes straight back home, to a hot, delicious meal, hand delivered to him in the bedroom, every night! Just like old times. He enjoys all of his meals, prepared by a head chef! That's what I feel like, except I don't get paid. But in exchange, he took out the trash, brought in the groceries, and helped with the laundry. Plus, he washes whatever I need, to make the meal.

On Sunday, since Rodney is off from work, he agreed to go to church with me. Sunday morning came around. I got up to start getting dressed. I turned the light on to help wake him up. He hollered at me! I told him to get up.

He said, "Turn the light off! I'm not going."

Oh, yes, you are! So get on up!

He said, "I changed my mind. I stayed up real late, playing the game."

I don't care! You knew exactly what we were supposed to be doing! So throw on some clothes. I'll take you to your house, so you can get some church clothes.

He said, "I told you, I don't got nothing to wear!"

No, you told me you do. So, stop making excuses and get up! You are not staying here, and I'm leaving. So that means, you're going to have to make some kind of move. Because, I still don't leave him in my house, by himself.

He jumped up with an attitude, and threw the covers off. Then he shot me a look from hell! Damn! I watched him get dressed. Then we all left out the door. We went to his house, where he took a long time, but finally came out, dressed. No church clothes, huh? But he still looks neat. He smoked a whole blunt, before we even got there. I guess he was thinking, "If I am forced into doing something, that I don't want to do, then I'm going high as hell."

Speaking of hell, the same look from hell that he shot me, when he woke up. That's the same look, that he kept on his face the whole time, that we were in church.

The more time passed, the more I got into the service! I hoped that he was doing the same. I looked over at him again. It's that same look. Is he that unhappy to be here? The more I looked at his face, and into his eyes, the more I saw the devil.

Oh, my gosh! Have I brought the devil, to church? I saw his aura start to rub off on certain members, of the congregation. Like, he is making them uncomfortable. A beautiful song began to play. The choir rose to sing. I closed my eyes, and began to sway. One verse in, he tapped me and said, "I'm ready to go! Give me your keys."

I turned and looked at him like he was crazy.

I said, we can go in a little bit.

He stood up and brushed past me, hard and fast! He walked out. I tried to compose myself. I know people are looking. I can't get up right now. I waited until the song finished, and I told the kids, come on.

We left before the sermon even started. He was only in that church for about an hour. He acted like it was never going to end.

I got in my car and drove around, looking for him. He's not at the park right across the street from the church. I drove across the bridge and saw him walking towards the store. He got in, and I didn't say a word about what just happened. I left it alone. At least he went. I can't expect him to be as into it as I am. I can't force that. Nevertheless, the relationship progressed. I started to trust him more and more. But, I still kept an eye on his cell phone. I never noticed any strange activity. We really have some good times together. We often talk of marriage. I told him that I want at least a one-carat ring, by Christmas.

He said, "Maybeee."

I do love him. I made it a point after Maurice died, to tell him, I will love you for life. No matter what happens, you'll always have a little piece of my heart. We click on so many levels. We make each other laugh! He's everything I've ever wanted. If he can just cut out the cheating, he would be my perfect man. We talk about being married and rich! I told him that I want my husband and I to have matching SUVs. I want mine to be pink, with sparkles on it and with spinning rims.

He said, "Mine will be white."

He is actually including himself in the fantasies. I let him know point-blank, I will only marry you if you pass a lie detector test. So don't include yourself in my fantasy, if you know you can't pass a lie detector test! The test will include, but not be limited to, questions like ... Have you ever cheated on me? and Did you have sex with my best friend? If you fail, then you get nothing!

I even called the *Maury Show*, to see if we can get on there for a test. If not, I'll pay for one myself, once I have the money.

I told him, I don't want you if you did it to anyone on that short list. You know; the list of people that I gave you. Because if you do, then you can't have me!

He continues, to include himself. I take that as a good sign! I haven't talked to Tiffany ever since I confronted her. So either she feels guilty, or I really hurt her feelings. I did come off on her! I joked with Rodney, saying, maybe I should call her and apologize.

He said, "Maybe you should."

Long story short, I didn't.

One day, Rodney called me earlier than usual from work. He said, "Come and get, me." So I did. When I pulled up, he was walking out of the parking lot, down the street.

I asked him, what's wrong?

He said, "Nothing! I just got off early, and I didn't want to just stand there. I was glad to leave, so I started walking."

Oh. Because of the unusual circumstances, I asked, did you get fired?

He said, "No!" very defensively.

I said, well, did you quit?

He said, "No. There were too many people there today. I volunteered to go home. But they are fixing the schedule, so that won't happen anymore."

Oh. Well, sorry ... I let it go.

The next morning, he slept in. When I woke up, I said, what the fuck are you doing here?

He said, "I was off today. I go back to work tomorrow."

You haven't been off on a Friday, for awhile. We made the best out of it. We went to play cards, with some of my family. We stayed up late, since he doesn't have to go to work until noon, tomorrow.

Saturday morning came. I am glad to sleep in. My kids are gone with their grandma. Rodney said, "I'm taking the bus to work."

He gave me some money to get my toes done, plus bill money, then he left. I'm happy! I enjoyed a nice, relaxing visit at the toe shop. I feel even more like a pampered princess. Forget that - a queen! He called me to pick him up, a little bit early. He already got a ride over his uncle's house. That's, right around the corner from his job. But when I picked him up, I noticed he has on street clothes, with a matching hat! I mean, g'd-up! He got in the car. I looked him up and down, then I said, why are you so dressed up?

He said, "I had this on this morning. I just had my work shirt on top of it."

I tried my best to remember exactly what he had on this morning! All I can remember is, the money. Damn it!

I really don't think he had that on though, especially the hat. I asked him, so, where is your work shirt?

He said, "I left it over my uncle's house."

I started to make a wild U-turn, to go back and check. But, I didn't want to look like a major bitch, overly possessive. I had already done it before, when we went to Hardee's. He came out with all this free food, after he'd been in there for like fifteen minutes.

He called me on my cell phone, to tell me about the wait. I thought it was okay, until I *really* thought about it. He just doesn't want me to come in. That's why he called me.

When we first pulled up, he insisted on going inside instead of using the drive-thru. He was in there talking to a bitch, and she hooked him up. I wasn't going for that shit! We had already pulled off; by time I came to this conclusion.

I made a wide U-turn, pulled up, and went inside the building. I asked for someone named Brian. That's what he said the boy's name was. Some big-lipped lady at the cash register said, "There is someone working here named Brian. He's in the back, right now. Do you want him?"

I said, no, thank you. I turned around and walked away, feeling a little bit like a fool. But, at the same time, feeling satisfied.

I got in the car, and he started to mock me, "You should be ashamed."

I told him, I'm not ashamed of what I did! If you are ever ashamed of what you are doing, then you shouldn't be doing it.

That's just one example of where I ticked and went crazy. I smell him, too. Let him be gone under shady circumstances, he better not smell like sex, when he gets back. And he better not smell like soap. He knows what's up. Sometimes he acts like he is suspicious of me, too. But he knows I'm true blue. I never cheated on any of my boyfriends, until I was given no other choice.

Regardless, he said, "I want you to get your phone number changed, too."

I told him, point-blank, you got your number changed so that your little bitches won't be calling. If I want my dudes to stop calling, all I have to do is tell them, which I have ... I didn't erase their names out of my phone because, if they do call, I want to know who it is, so that I won't answer. Also, more people have my number, like schools, doctors, and important companies. It would be more of a hassle to change it, then anything. It's not necessary .... Plus, I knew I didn't have to. He won't insist. That's a fucking joke! I run shit around here. Plus, if it doesn't work between us, I want my men friends to have my number. The reason I didn't erase them from my phone, is because I didn't want to. I could have written them down somewhere else, and hid them. But, why go through all that trouble? I don't have to do all that, believe me. Obviously ... He doesn't want to say anything to cause an unnecessary argument. This man is crazy about me! He'll give me his last dollar, where he wasn't giving those other bitches nothing. They were buying him shit. He treats me like, I'm, beautiful! When I dress up, he calls me his 9.75. Not quite a ten. That's good enough for me! I'm flattered.

Maurice used to flatter me in the same way. He got so tired of telling me that I looked pretty, that he just stopped. I was dressed up real nice one day, but Maurice said nothing.

I said, Maurice, you didn't tell me that I look pretty.

He said, "I know I didn't. I stopped telling you, because you know you look good! You know exactly when you look good. You know what I like. That's why I stopped telling you."

I took it as a compliment, of confidence! One that will stick with me, for the rest of my life …. I'll also treasure the letter that he wrote to me, before he died. It's contents I'll keep private, and sacred. A poem he calls "Just Wishing." A poem that tells, and shows me, how much he really cared.

Now, I want to take this time to show him, how much I really care. I want to dedicate two songs. Two songs for a man befitting, of two songs! The first is a song by Fantasia. "You Were Always On My Mind." I want you to know that through every decision, that I've made recently, you were always on my mind.

The second, is a song that tells you, I know where you are. I know you are looking down on me, from heaven. I feel your spirit. I know that you feel better now! You are running and jumping now! I'm just glad, to have known you. I will never let our kids forget you ….. You have changed my life, forever … R.I.P., Maurice Dominic Fitzgerald Hunter. "You're In The Arms Of The Angels." May you find some comfort here, by Sarah McLachlan.

DEVASTATING CONSEQUENCES

Maurice Dominic Hunter, passed away at 24 years old.

Tragically, I'd told Maurice beforehand, if you die, I'm going to get a check. You should support your kids while you are living. Get disability if you have to. He didn't live long enough to see that through. But as I had predicted, I did get a check for the kids. Despite, the overwhelming feeling, that I wouldn't, get anything at all. I didn't think he had worked long enough.

My friend told me that she didn't get a check when her mom died, because she didn't work enough. Then I remembered when my dad died, they said we didn't get a check from him; only my mom. But he worked his whole life. Considering who that information came from, I know I can't trust shit she said.

I was overjoyed when they said, I will get a check. Yes! Enough to pay my rent every month, with a little spending change. Thank you, Jesus! At least he's seeing that the kids are being taken care of, from the grave. I have to work like a slave to actually get the check, though. I will have to prove that they are Maurice's kids. I need something that he signed, acknowledging that they are his. I have, several papers from Zay Zay, but nothing from Tayon. I haven't even ordered his birth certificate, yet. I went through every paper that I have, looking for something, anything. Then, I got a thought: I'll go back to the hospital. I know Maurice signed something when Tayon was born.

A hospital clerk found the paper that I'm looking for. But, it doesn't have Maurice's signature on it. He didn't sign anything at the hospital.

The clerk said, "That's not a problem. I'll give you a new form. You take that with you and get him to sign it."

I looked at her with despair in my eyes. I fought back the tears, as I muttered, He passed away. I left feeling defeated. I might not be able to prove that Tayon is Maurice's, even though he looks just like him. They don't care about none of that. They want to see something in writing. And I don't have anything. What if we have to exhume the body, just to do a DNA test? I don't know what made me think about it, but I decided to go to the courts. I know he had to have signed something in court, in order for them to come after him for child support. Something that said, "I don't want a DNA test. He is my son."

The court secretary looked for awhile, then she started shaking her head no. My head dropped. Suddenly she said, "Wait a minute! Is the child's name, Tayon?"

Yes! She handed me a paper and smiled. I said, Let me just take a minute to read over this. I read the exact words that I needed, smiled, and fought back more tears. I told her, thank you. This means more, than you'll ever know.

That money came right on time, at a time when I was depending on Rodney to add me to his Section 8. Fuck him! I don't like depending on nobody. They always let you down. I got enough money to pay my own rent.

My disability stopped a few months ago, all because I smoke weed. I wasn't complying with the doctor's orders. Weed is like, my medicine. I take it every day. I don't feel happy without it. The doctors, don't understand that. I thought they'd be trained enough, to handle that. But with all that I've been through in my life. They better be glad I don't smoke crack. I don't shoot up. I don't sell my body. I didn't kill myself!

And I'm not dead! Thank you, Jesus! If they are not glad about all of those things. I got to tell you, I am! I don't see anything wrong with relaxing with a blunt. That's what it takes for me to relax. Just like most people need coffee to start their day, I need weed!

Those suckers, want me to come back, to work. I know, that I can't! I admitted it to myself, a long time ago. But I was finally able to say it to my supervisor. I got up enough courage, to finally go get my box of belongings, from work. I drove, and Rodney went in, to get it. They didn't want to release it to him. I had to go in and get it. I walked in with my head down. I don't want to look at anything. It will only make my anxiety attack worse! I showed my ID and signed for the package. Rodney carried it out.

I opened it alone. It contains, a lot of good memories. But some of them are bad. The boss refused, to give me my nameplate even though it would have made me happy. I don't know what else, they can do with it. But that's okay! I'll just have to get me a bigger and better one!

22

Rodney and I started to argue more, because when he gets off from work, he goes straight over to his uncle's house, almost every day!

He said, "Well, if you don't like me going over there everyday, then you should be out there to pick me up!"

The only reason I'm not, is because Zay Zay's bus comes around the same time since, school just started back. I had to get used to the schedule.

I said, well, I'll start picking you up. I'll pick you up first, but we have to come straight home. The next day, I called him at work, right around the time for me to get him. I want to know if he wants me to be there at 3:15 or 3:30. A manager from the dish room answered the phone.

I said, "May I speak with Rodney, please?

He said, "Rodney, does not work here anymore."

I said, are you sure? A tall, light-skin dude. Darnell, that's his alias/ middle, name.

He repeated what he said. I am in denial. I know that Rodney woke up at 5:00 am, put his clothes on, and kissed me, like he was going to work. And he doesn't even have a job? I wonder, how long this shit, has been going on. Probably ever since I asked him about it.

He called me fifteen minutes before time for him to get off. Calmly, my first question was, where are you? His response was, "Downtown, at the bus station."

My reply was, where, are you, coming from? He said, "Work. I got off a little bit early. I'm on my way home."

I'll see you when you get here. I don't want to ambush him over the phone so that he won't, come home. I can wait until, he gets here. I'll drag this one out a little bit. Pump him for details. I got up and dragged my chair right in front of the patio window. I opened up the Venetian blinds, but not all the way. Just enough, for me to see out of, but not enough to not let anyone look in. Then I timed him. I watched to see if he is really getting off the bus or not, and the exact time that he gets off that bus. That will, narrow down a possible time line, so that I can see where he really came from. I usually don't pay attention to all that.

I watched him get off the bus, twenty-three minutes later. He didn't see me. I left the front door unlocked. Then I went into my bedroom. He doesn't have a key. Yeah, right. He asked me recently when he will get one. I said, when I get a key to yours and ours - our new place. I haven't seen any initiative on that!

He came in the door and little does, he know. I am watching his every move, like a hawk. From the time he took his shoes off, to the time he lay back on the pillow, moaning like is tired!

I said, rough day at work, babe?

He said, "Yeah, they tried to work me like a slave! But I finished up early, so I left."

I said, oh, yeah? I sat watching TV, rocking back and forth. Looking at this motherfucker lie, right to my face! I want to make sure that he didn't go to work, and then get fired. That's better than already being fired. But getting up anyway, acting like, you are going, to work ... Let me ask you a good question. What was he doing to fill his time, while he wasn't at work? *That* is a good question. I know....

I can't keep my anger in, any longer! I looked him in the eye and said, why is it, that when I called your job today, the manager said you don't work there anymore?

His head dropped down on the pillow, and his hat fell in front of his face. He said, "I don't know."

Of course, you know! Oh, you know! You got up on time, this morning. Like you were going to work. And you didn't! Where were you?

He said, "I was at home this morning. Then, I went job hunting. I was too ashamed to tell you, that I don't have a job. Because, I'm going to have one by the end of the week, anyway!"

Yeah, I'm sure you went job hunting.

Just then, he pulled out some kind of papers and threw them on the bed. He said, "That shows you I was at the Unemployment Office today. It also shows what time."

DEVASTATING CONSEQUENCES

I picked up the papers and read them. Then, I said, don't you think I would have noticed once the money stopped? Why did you get fired, anyway?

He said, "They found out that I was working under my alias and a phony social. It was just one digit off! But I don't want to talk about that anymore."

I do let him feel like a man sometimes, just by letting shit go. I just let some things, go over my head. He thinks he wins! *Yeah, right. You can never win when you do dishonest stuff like that.* I thought he was doing good. because when I got with him, he already had a good job, making decent money. But, the job was obtained through dishonest, means. That means, every job in the future will be the same way. He's trying to get over. He's trying not to pay child support! Back, child support.

I'm glad I don't have any kids by him. Me and my IUD are doing just fine! He's a deadbeat dad in every sense of the word. His daughter lives with his mom, the grandmother. They share custody. Yet, he only sees her on special occasions. I asked why she doesn't participate in activities with us. He doesn't want her to. He barely pays attention to my kids.

I will give him some time to get his job and money together. Not that long, though. Days passed, and it got to the point, where he couldn't contribute on any level. No weed, cigarettes, or food. I need my hair done, and he don't got no money.

All of the above took a toll on me. But I still want, this man. He is so good to me. But I can't trust shit that he says, though. It made me want to go to the *Maury Show,* even more! Give him a lie detector test so I can see if it's even worth saving. Then I thought about something I wanted to tell Rodney. But then I changed my mind. *Maurice will tell me, if you are cheating on me.* I said, I really hope, you are not, cheating on me. I hope, you are serious, about this. About us .... Shit, I don't want it to go back, to the way, it was. I'm going to have to take my own trash out. Well, I don't know. Zay Zay is getting big enough. She better put some elbow into it.

Then it all hit me, like a ton of bricks. When I walked into my bedroom, I looked into his eyes. He is sitting on the side of the bed. I called his name, and even though he is looking me straight in the eye, he didn't respond. I repeated myself. But the more, I talked. The more, I knew. *I am, talking to, the devil! I can, see it, in his eyes.* That same look that he gave me at church. It scared me! When I have a feeling about a person, I'm not wrong! I see the devil in him, and that can't do me nothing, but harm! I can't even look in his eyes anymore.

He's not talking to me? He's not talking to me! I didn't do anything to him. How dare he not talk to me! He's acting like he doesn't want to be here. Like, I'm keeping him from something! I told him, if you don't want to talk to me, then you don't need to be here! If I have to act like, you're not here, then you might as well not be here! You can go. It's over!

He packed his crap to leave. On the next thing, moving! I don't care, how you leave! You just need to get the hell, out of here!!!!!!! I try to avoid the devil, at all costs! Everything and everybody associated with the devil. I sure as hell won't have him sleeping in my house! I don't even dial phone numbers with the numerical symbol for the devil. Only 777 numbers. I'll consider it to be a sign. I'll consider it to be a blessing, to be away from him, having somewhere to send him! I'm glad that we didn't end up living together, in one big house and having nowhere to send him.

I guess I just experienced two and a half months of façade. Meanwhile, on top of, all my other, blessings. God decided to bless me again. I went in for my first yearly review at my apartment complex. Two months before I'd been here a year, we did a review, of how much money I make. I was on welfare at the time. Not even enough, to pay my rent.

The manager said, "Well, how are you paying your rent, darling?"

I explained it to her that I supplemented the difference, with the money I'd saved from my disability. But the money was running out, and the money from Maurice had yet to kick in.

She said, "Well, why didn't you come sign up, for the Section 8 program through us?"

I said, Because I didn't know you offered anything like that! I thought I was paying the lowest rent possible. That's why, I didn't report my drastic income drop. It wouldn't have made a difference, anyway. Either, I have it, or I don't.

She said, "Well, the other family, that I was dealing with. It seems like, they are not, going to qualify. That would make you next on the list."

DEVASTATING CONSEQUENCES

The same list, that if I had the privilege, of putting my name on through the city, I'd be waiting, for a minimum, of 2-3 years for assistance! But, I just walked into this office and was handed my second big blessing, from this establishment. On and off a list, within fifteen minutes! I can't call it anything else, but a blessing!

Have you ever not been able to pay your rent? Have you ever had your landlord say, "That's okay. You just pay half. We will reduce your rent by over, one half. Just pay us two hundred." Not unless, you live in the projects. Well, I don't live in the projects. Thank you, Jesus! I have a nice apartment, with a balcony, wall-to-wall carpet, and very spacious rooms. But when you move in, they don't tell you that if you lose your income, it's no problem! They don't want to influence you.

I stay in contact with Rodney. He's begging, as usual. He said, "I was having a bad day that day! I was tired and just wanted to go to sleep!"

I told him that's what he should have said. Or, that's what he should have done! I tried to cut him out all together. Especially, when he missed my birthday party! I was supposed to have it over his house. Since, I can't play loud music here. He started acting funny, the closer it got. I feel myself trying to kiss his ass, just to stay on his good side, until after the party. We have never partied together on my birthday before, because he always got locked up, just before it. Then I came to the realization, that my lips are chapped! I'm tired, of kissing his ass! I don't have to. I'm too good for that!

One of my friends don't have a babysitter. But she does have a big house. She can't come out to party, so I said I will bring the party to her house, if that's okay. She agreed. We ate, got drunk, and we laughed all night! People are hilarious when they are drunk! The drunk aunt, is back at this party, too. She watched as I got a lap dance by a sexy-ass neighbor, totally unplanned. I'm glad, Rodney, is not, here! By time the entertainment finished, the drunk aunt was eyeballing him, like he was her unfaithful mate! The anger grew in her eyes. Finally she jerked him up! I don't know what she said to him, but I'm sure it was hilarious. But the funniest part of it all. Is that she never saw that man, a day before in her life. We laughed and had a ball, as always, at one of my functions.

My sexual needs outgrew my anger about a week later. We hooked up for some fun. When I walked in, I noticed that he is playing slow music. My favorite! The more we talked, the more, I got into, the music. With hesitation, I looked for the devil in his eyes, even though I am scared of the outcome. I did it anyway. I have to prove myself right! I don't see it. It made me want to stare into his eyes. He said, "Happy Anniversary! Four years ago today, is when we first started going together! You remember, 10-29." That's not today, is it? Oh, my gosh! I didn't even know that ... The music helped the mood. We went upstairs and got comfortable. He can control the music from upstairs. He put it on my song, then he went down, on me. Something I was hoping he would do. He had stopped doing it, ever since we broke up because, he says, he doesn't know for sure what I'm doing.

But not tonight. I said, go for what you know! He licked every crevice of my body. It is, so hot, and intense! We don't usually, have sex to music. That takes me back to the Adrian days. I forgot what music does to me. I lost control. I'm having unprotected sex, with this man. And it feels, so good. The intensity! We are, making love, which is something we don't usually call it. He moaned words telling me how much he misses, me. And how much he misses this. I have to admit, I do to! The night ended perfect! Now, I'm confused about the signs God is, sending me.

Two days passed. It's, Halloween, a holiday that I usually don't celebrate. My mom never took us out trick or treating! I work strictly off tradition. We used to make costumes and go to a big party. Never door-to-door. I just buy my kids some candy. That's the point, right? Yeah, some of it is dressing up. Blah, blah, blah. I don't have the money for all that, but my sister convinced me to go with them trick or treating. She will give my son an old costume. I put makeup and a wig on my daughter. We went out, and my Uncle Wilbert took them door-to-door. We sat in the car, watching and smoking. Let's face it, I wasn't going to do much walking anyway. At the end of the evening, I received a call from Nettie. She said she has lots of candy over there and wants us to stop by.

Shit! I rolled my eyes. Now I have to take them over there. I am ready to go home, but if I don't go, she'll make me feel guilty. I convinced my sister to go with me. We all went over there. By this time, the kids' bags were so full with candy, that they were too heavy to carry. They got new bags for Nettie's candy. My sister left promptly. I had small talk with Nettie, I told her about the new guy that I met, the one that the kids say, looks like Maurice.

She said, "Well, I'm happy for you. But what about the other one?"

I said, I kicked him to the curb. He didn't have a job, and you know that don't last too long with me. If you ain't helping me, you're hurting me.

She said, "Ain't that, the truth! But you know, I heard, he is still messing with that Tiffany girl. You remember what I told you before? It's true."

My stomach turned. I looked at her with concern. Damn. I can't hide my reaction. I can't pretend like I don't care. I don't *want* to believe her, but this is the *second* time she is saying this to me. She knows something! I feel weird, pumping her for information, about her resources. But it feels like, I have to. I can't just take her word for it. I need some undisputable facts! I asked her who told her that. Also, how much detail she knows.

She doesn't know much. But once she told me who gave her the information, I knew it was true! I now know that he was fucking a wildebeest on the side and still begging for my hand! I started to question his motives. He knows that everything I've said I was going to do in life, I've done! I have two beautiful children, a boy and a girl ... I got my dream job, a house, and a car that's paid for. All by the age of twenty-three, when no one thought I could. They thought I shouldn't even try. But with no parents and no backbone, I pulled it off! I won't say, I did it all by myself. Because, I'd be taking too much of the credit! I'll just leave it at this. Rodney knows what I'm capable of,. I told him that I'm going to write a book, and that I'm going to be rich! He believes me. He believes in me. And above all, I appreciate that! But what if he is just trying to use me? Yeah, he wants to marry me because that means, he will be set for life. If I die, he gets everything! The least that he would walk away with is, half of everything.

I wouldn't ordinarily have a problem with that. But I'm only going to share my life and my wealth, with people who deserve it! He's proven that he doesn't deserve it. And if I have even one thought, in the back of my mind That he might, want to kill me, over it - no way! He could kill me, get away with it, and live off my riches, with all those bitches that he decides to fuck. And even if he didn't have sex with her while we were together, he knows that *any* time is a big no-no! I don't want to touch anything, that's been near, her pussy, that disease factory! And as her ex-best friend, you know I'm privy, to all of that information.

She tried to be my friend again. After all this time, why? Why would you want to be my friend, if you are fucking, my man? To pump me, for information? I realized that, I never told her much, thank goodness. But she always wanted to know when I was going to be with him, so that she'd know when to be with him. That's dirty! You nasty, dirty bitch!

I went home to ponder things. To try and figure out what I'm going to do and how I'm going to do it. I have to get him to admit it, to me. I'll pretend like I know everything to see what I can get him to say!

I ate more Halloween candy than normal that night. Good candy, too! A lot of chocolates. Then I went to sleep. When I woke up the next morning, I could hardly open my eyes. My eyes are, crusted over. Especially, the right one in particular. I went to the mirror and cleaned it off, as best as I could. Damn! I have, pink eye! It made my eye red and very puffy. You can call it, swollen. Luckily, I have some medicine leftover from my daughter's case of pink eye. It has a tendency to infect both eyes, if you let tears run from one eye into the other. I don't want it to spread! I want to cure this right away! It's making me look ugly.

As a matter of fact, it looks like, I've been in a fight. I wouldn't want certain people to think that, with all their questions and so forth. I'll have to choose an outfit with matching sunglasses. I'll try, to hide it as best I can. I have to do my hair up real nice and be g'd-up, just to compensate! And that's exactly what I did.

Then I got to thinking. You know who the main person, in this world who I would love to think that, I did get in a fight is? Rodney! So, thank you, Maurice. We'll put this to the test ... I went over his house, g'd up. Which messes with a man's mind, anyway. He thought he was getting some. We went upstairs and sat on his bed. I went in my pocketbook and pulled out a blunt. I sat it down on the bed and lit a cigarette. Another way to mess with his mind. He got excited about the blunt. I don't usually come over and just smoke with him. He should have known something was up.

DEVASTATING CONSEQUENCES

I struggled to act normal. Calm, even. I passed him the cigarette and lit the blunt. I see, his excitement because he is so broke that he doesn't have either.

I puff, puffed, and passed. We switched. Then I took my sunglasses off. I looked at him in the eyes. He got up and walked towards me. Then he held my face in his hand. He said, "What happened to you?"

I said, I got in a fight. He stared at my face, in disgust! As if he were staring at a shattered, porcelain doll.

He said, "Which one of your niggas put their hands on you?"

I jerked my face away. He went back and sat down. I said, I didn't get in a fight with no dude. I got in a fight with a bitch!

He sat smiling and laughing. He said, "Whoooo?"

I said, I'm only going to tell you if you are ready to tell me the truth. If you're not willing to tell me the truth, then don't waste my time. The only way I can start getting over this, is to talk about it.

I saw his smile, drop down, to a frown. He said, "The truth about what?"

Don't answer, my question, with a question. Just answer, my question. Are you ready, to tell me the truth?

He said, "Yes."

I said, I got in a fight, with one of your, bitches!

Before, he could ask who, again. I said, Tiffany! Why does, she have, your phone, number?

He dropped his head and said, "I don't know."

Oh, my God! He just admitted it to me. I can't believe it! I tried hard not to cry … Okay, I have to make myself laugh. I have to act like this is old news. He knows when I'm pissed off. I always hold the blunt and never pass it back to him. But I didn't do that. I kept smoking. He is surprised, confused, and a little bit dazed. By now, I'm sure he doesn't know if he is coming or going! He don't know what's going on. He don't know what to expect! I want to see how much he is, going to admit to. But first, I have to live up to my end of the bargain. I have to, tell him a little about the fight. I said, yeah, my eye might look bad, but you should see her mouth! I busted that bitch's mouth open. I think I might have knocked a tooth out. I started laughing, but tried to contain it.

He said, "Dammnn!!!"

Now, how long, have you been fucking that, ugly bitch?

He said, "I don't know."

Okay. He just verified, his first statement. But I need a little bit more. I said, so, you been fucking her raw? In that disease factory!

He said, "I have not been fucking her raw! I wrap up every time!"

Now, it's no disputing it! I stood up, and grabbed my purse.

I said, well, you just keep on fucking her! I turned around and walked down the steps with care, but faster than usual!

His steps are so narrow. I can't, hold the tears back any longer! I put my sunglasses back on, but because of the way that they are made, the tears started to pool up at the bottom. I remembered how contagious my pink eye is, so I took the glasses back off, to let the tears flow free.

He ran down after me and told me to stay for a minute. He saw me crying, not knowing that I just walked in here with nothing, and he just gave me enough information to hang himself. By then, I had already walked out the door. But, I stepped back in. What else could he possibly have to say? Maybe he's going to say something that will, in someway, make me feel better.

I said, talk fast, and let's keep this door open. I need witnesses. I am trying to think of things that he could say, to make me feel better. Something like he only fucked her in her mini van, or in an alley. That he disrespected her and treated her like she was ugly!

He didn't say any of that. I asked, so, do you give her special privileges? Like, letting her come to your house? Fucking her in your bed?

He said, "I wouldn't call that a privilege, but, yes."

That's all I needed to hear. It was over before it even began. I already knew that. I just needed confirmation. I put my shades back on. Fuck it. I'll just treat both eyes. With that, I got in my car and pulled away, shaking my head and laughing. The professional liar, has just been dethroned. He fell for it! Looks like, I tricked you! Talk about a trick or treat. I can't even have sex with him anymore. No exceptions! Our anniversary was officially the last time that we had sex. What a way to commemorate it, though. In a way, going out with a bang! Looking back, I don't see how he fell for it.

There were a couple of holes in my story. I didn't know what I was going to say. I was ad-libbing! I knocked the girl's tooth out and everything! But then again, he did see me beat down his baby's mama. But I was dressed up, when I went over there. He should have asked when the fight went down. I guess he considered, an honest person like me ,wouldn't make anything like that up. It was more plausible than not. Even though I was a skeptic, honesty really does pays off …. sometimes!

23

About ten minutes later on the car ride home, he called and I answered, just because I thought maybe now he has something to say, to make me feel better. He didn't. Evidently in those ten minutes, he managed to call her and asked if we got in a fight. Once she said no, he knew that he just fucked up! He told on himself. And this is the best, that he came up with.

I said, hello.

He said, "I don't know, what you are talking, about!"

I said, I don't know, what you, are talking about! I'm not talking about, nothing. I'm listening, to music. I saw his last desperate attempt, to cover up the truth. His way of keeping my rose-colored, glasses on. A coincidence because, that is the color of my sunglasses, today. Nice try! I hung up on him. I don't want to hear shit, else. That he has, to say! It's nothing he can, say.

My sadness quickly turned to anger, anger towards both of them, but especially her! First Maurice, then Rodney. Maurice had enough sense to know better! I think she wants, to be me. *You want to be me, Tiffany? You envy me? A beautiful, big girl, getting, as much attention as the skinny girls! Getting money, instead of buying men. I have a nice car, and a nice house.*

Bitch, you still live with your parents! You have a crappy job, where you wipe people's ass. That's shitty, huh? Somewhat like, your life, right? God made you ugly on the outside, because you're ugly on the inside! Beauty is what beauty does. You look at your life and realize, that you have nothing! And that's exactly what you'll always have. *Nothing!* You have to take what you can get. And what you can get is my pity ... You've never had a boyfriend, but managed to fuck at least thirty people, before we left high school. You are a whore! All those times when we went out and I came back with numbers. You wasn't happy, for me! You was, jealous! You are, jealous. Because, you know, he ain't, gonna be no more to you, than a bootie call. But you are willing to settle, for that. You have no standards! You are nasty, and I hope you die, from AIDS! I hope you leave your child, motherless. That's how much, I hate you! And I'm going to get you!

I'm not going to her house, but I will, go to her job! I'll leave a note. Saying, half of what I'm going to tell her, once I see her face. I'm going to, carry the shit out of her. Embarrass, her! Whether we be, in Wal-Mart or at the gas station. The only place that she is safe, is church. I have too much respect, for that. I dropped off the letter, a few weeks later, when I finally caught up to her. She even taught me a good way to recognize her car. Thank you. She can, take this however she wants, to take it. But I'll tell you this, I'm too smart to threaten somebody in writing. This is exactly, what my note said. I addressed it to, Biz Markie. That's what we called her in high school.

CARMA IS A BITCH,
AND SO ARE YOU!

Dogs deserve leftovers; you can have mine. You are the nastiest, most trifling so-called friend I ever met. You are also the ugliest. That's exactly why the *only* boyfriend you ever had, was your husband. You and I both know that your marriage was a joke. I'd marry a wildebeest for a green card too. <u>Instead of</u> smacking you in your face, I'll smack you with the truth, it hurts more. What you think you have, you don't! He'll never feel about you, the way he feels about me. He's going to continue to *use* you, and I hope he does. I want y'all to enjoy each other and share diseases, like chlamydia and gonorrhea. I let him in on that secret. Did you tell your mama? Did you tell her your pussy was burning? Did you tell her you was fucking my man? You tell her everything else. Oh, I almost forgot - he has a camera in his room, and you're on tape. Stupid Ass! Since you are hiding out, if you are a woman and have anything to say. Say it to my face! You know where to find me!

I'm going to see her out here, somewhere! And when I do, she is going to wish that she didn't see me. Time passed, and every time I went to Wal-Mart, I looked around for her, but I was never that lucky. I thought about flattening her tires. But then, if she flattened mine, I would be pissed. Then I'd have to think of something even bigger! You know I'm crazy! Then we'd go back and forth until someone went to jail. I don't have time for all of that! I'm too damn grown, for all of that! He's not worth it anyway.

24

It tells me a lot about his character. I'm just glad I found out before the marriage! I'm holding out for Mr. Right! I have FAITH that God will bring him to me. Something told me that after I finish writing my book, I will, find him, or he will, find me. So I've been trying to hurry up! But then, there's always something else I want to say. I've always believed that if you are not going to do it right, then don't do it at all! So, I won't rush it. I'll just let it come to me. When I think of what my doctor said, "Most bipolar people, don't write books. They can't concentrate for that long." Which is, true. Because, I can't concentrate long, on much else. The medicine keeps me so doped up. All I want to do, is sleep. But just like I said, God gives us peace, to do His will ... No amount of medicine, can hinder God!

She looks at me like, I'll fail. That just makes me try even harder! So, thank you. I'll be able to look at you with disgust one day. Only if, I want to. Disgust, for not believing in me! I already proved you wrong, once. You said I'd be institutionalized for 3-6 months. I was out in nine days! Any longer and I think I would have been, even crazier! If that's, at all, possible.

Recently, I was surprised and somewhat horrified, to know that Rodney actually took time, out of his day to program the TV in my bedroom. I don't have cable, so there are only a few channels to choose from. I was used to just pushing the exact numbers, to get the stations instead of scrolling through all of them. But, he had deleted the gospel station! He deleted a station that I never knew about. That was, until the power went out, and I had to program my own stations. Then I realized that I had a new station. But it's not, new. I saw T.D. Jakes preaching. I'd heard of him before, but never had the pleasure of hearing him speak. I was both moved and disgusted, all in the same breath - disgusted that Rodney kept this from me. I could have been moved a lot sooner. I didn't want the show to end. I got hip to the game and started taping it. Just so, I could rewind it and watch it, over and over. I cry, on every episode! I feel like, it's me, specifically, that he is, talking to. Just like millions of others. But I am, one in a million! Now I get up before 7 am, just so I can see the show and to press the record button, because I don't have, tivo. I can't program, the VCR on a timer. Even if it does record, like that. . But I can set the alarm clock.

So much of what he says, relates to my life. I am stepping into my vision. He said, "Where do you want to be ten years from now? Stop dreaming, about stuff you can finish in a week ... It means, your vision is too short." I really took it to heart.

I finished my book three days later! After ten months, I am finally finished! If I had the money to buy Bishop Jake's series, I would. I have faith that if I hold out, I'll be on his show. Then I'll get the taped series for free! I'll send him a copy of my book. Written by: A projected failure, from the projects, turned meek, profit.... God gives some of us a little. He gives some of us a lot. He even gives some of us nothing at all! But he gives all of us the ability to get something! Whether or not we use that ability is up to us. But when we do get what we long for, if we don't appreciate it, He can take it all away! That's when the devil takes over. That's why I appreciate, each and everything I have. So I say, I rebuke you, devil!

The two people that I think believed in me the most was my mother and God. But if either of them were here in the flesh to encourage me, then I wouldn't have much of a story to tell! Through everything, the only words I've always longed for someone to say were, "You deserve it! You'll get what your heart desires, because you deserve!" But I never heard anyone say that. Or anything close to that .... But I know! I deserve it! Then I thought to myself, *I'll have to be rich before anyone recognizes and acknowledges that I actually do deserve this!* That's when I spoke to my longtime friend, LaTonya. We haven't had a heart-to-heart talk in awhile, for almost a year! I told her that I finished my book. She expressed how happy she is for me. We talked about it in length.

Then she said, "Daminika, you deserve it! You deserve it."

I made her repeat it, just to make sure that I heard exactly, what she said. I told her, that is so nice! That you would say that.

She said, "I didn't say it to be nice! I mean it. You deserve it."

I said, thank you so much, for saying that! I started crying. You just don't know how much that means to me! We also spoke about my mental health. That's when I found out that she is a therapist. That is her career! I am so proud, of her! All those years that I should have been in counseling, I actually, was...God, made sure, of that. I had so much going on in my life, that I didn't realize what my best friend was doing with hers. All those years, all those nights, we sat on the phone. Talking, crying, and discussing feelings, we were counseling each other. She was my therapist, and she said I was hers. I gave her just as much advice as she gave me.

I always thought, I'd be the therapist. In a way, I still am ... What made me pick a therapist for a best friend? Or is she only a therapist because of me? She works with people like me all the time! She knows some of the same things I know. But since I've been there, I can give an even better perspective swing, on things. If she ever needs advice, I'll be happy to help. She doesn't write prescriptions, but she does talk with the patients. That's the second most important thing. The most important thing is the medicine. I know she'll give an impartial opinion. She's done great at that for over 12 years. She should be able to add that, to her résumé.

LaTonya asked if I would be interested in coming and speaking to some of her patients. I said, I would love to. She lives in North Carolina and said she will come and pick me up, so I can speak. I said, I would, love to. She got real excited, then she asked, "Daminika, why don't you become a peer counselor?"

I said, because I can't work an eight-hour job!

She said, "No! When you are a peer counselor, you make your own hours."

I thought that's too much like working. I don't want to do that. She said, "Peer counselors are people who have been diagnosed with something themselves. They come and speak to other people, who have been through the same thing."

My stomach started to tighten up! I have this strange feeling, in the bottom of my stomach! I started to cry. Thank you, Jesus! She just verified, what I already knew when I was crazy. I really wasn't as crazy, as some people made me feel.

Then there were the other people, people who worked there in the hospital. People with charts and pens. In plain clothes, that assumedly, worked there! But in private, these people acted just as crazy, as I was acting! All of them would crack their neck, from side to side, before or during the conversation, just like me. And like a yawn, it's contagious. It made me feel crazier because I thought they were crazy, too. Then, I started thinking. Well, if they are crazy, then I must think everybody is crazy! But it wasn't that ... I now know, it was some type of sign. It was really something wrong, with them. They just took the time, to come back and speak to me.

I believe the more friends that you make on earth, the more friends you'll have in heaven. Except there, they won't have the ailments, that ail, them ....

So, to the lady with the bad back, the black lady in a hurry, the sad lady in the hall, the man in the wheelchair, the lady with the radio, the generous, cute white boy, the tall girl, the fidgety man, the scared woman, the man with no insurance, and Evelyn, I would love to come back and speak to you all again. But if I never see you again on earth ... I'll see you in heaven!

I ended my conversation with LaTonya, by telling her that I am right, about what I know 95 percent, of the time! I won't say, 99 percent. I'll give myself some leeway. I reminded her of the fact, that I am a psychic. If you know a better word to use, let me know. What do you call something that you don't have a word for? The closest word to it! I wouldn't say it if it wasn't, true. Just like everything else in this book. I can't tell you what is going to happen in your tomorrow. I would never have a one eight hundred number. It only works when it wants to work. It mainly affects my life and the close ones around me. Sometimes, with people, that I feel like I've known my whole life. Some people don't like it when I use the word *crazy*. I don't have another word to call it! I know that I'm crazy. Just like with the people in the mental ward.

I now realize, that the people who worship God like myself, get out of the crazy house! The people who worship the devil, don't! I know the difference. As real as God is, that's how real the devil is! I wasn't wrong about the feelings, and vibes I got from them. I bet they are not allowed to tell you, even when you know! I knew. I didn't mention many of them by name, because I don't know many of them by name. They still know who they are.

At some point, I thought about the *what if's?* What if the doctors or peer counselors told my family that bipolar people always get what they want, whether it hurts them or not? That's why they are so few and far between. But if you tell your loved one that they are going to get it regardless, they'll be so overwhelmed that they will never get it! You have to figure out how badly you want them to have it. I bet it killed my friends and family to know that secret!

These, psychic powers have traveled with me through life, preventing some of the worst outcomes! Avoiding, tragic situations and enabling me to defy the odds! Just like I can fast forward my mind, at times. It also allows me to, rewind my mind. I have more, than memories ... It's my home movies! Nobody can take those away from me! Nobody can throw those away! I am honored to be able to share them with you.

I'm normal most of the time. But sometimes, I'm not. That is not my only symptom from all of this. Here is a list of some of the others:
1. Panic attacks
2. Lack of concentration
3. Mood swings
4. Decreased need for sleep, hence, medicine
5. Drousiness
6. Inability to handle stress
7. Feeling at least a day behind the world
8. Double-check everything twice

Either I'm happy, or I'm sad. There is no in between. Everything is always one way or another. No in betweens. Either I look good, or I look like shit! That's hard to deal with sometimes. I can only go around people, when I'm happy. If I'm not, then I have to fake it. And I don't like that! Nowadays, I say exactly, what I feel. I can't help it! So if you don't like it, then, oh, well. Here are some more people, that I'd like to tell exactly, how I feel.

There's nothing that I won't say or do, for my kids. Just, to see, a smile. Why not? Smiles are free! We have them all day long, in my house.

We love free stuff. Speaking of free stuff. Let me tell you a funny story about my grandma. She's eighty years old now. She has done everything that she ever wanted to do in life. We talked about one of her friends that just turned one hundred.

She said, "I don't know if I want to live that long."

It humbled me because nowadays, so many of us are striving to add two or three more years onto our lives. She is saying she is ready at anytime when God sees fit to call her. She knows where she is going, and she is not afraid. I see why. Heaven is a beautiful place that we should all strive to reach. It solves, all of our problems. However, I know I won't be ready for whenever her time comes. I don't want her, to go! That's why I try to spend time with her whenever I can.

She has Alzheimer's, and I want to try to understand it. I want to know exactly what she's going through. She tells me the same thing over and over again. I act just like I'd heard it for the first time, but it really hurts! I tried to explain to her a little about my condition. All she wants to know is, am I looking for a job?

I told her that if I could work, I'd go back to my old job! Sometimes she understands, and sometimes she doesn't. She was in a nursing home when I went in, the hospital. So I, gave her, a pamphlet. To, read some, about it. It lists all the symptoms, associated with bipolar.

Then I told her, that I, am writing, a book. And that, I'm almost, finished.

She said, "Oh, yeah! Well, do you think, you can get some money, from it? I mean, sell it?"

I said, Yeah, Grandma! Do you think I'm going to, give it to people, for free? Yeah, right! I plan to, be rich, from this.

She said, "Oh. Well, I didn't know. That sounds nice. I hope you do get rich. I hope you make a million dollars!"

Thank you, Grandma.

But I wanted to say. Yeah, Grandma, I'm writing it for my health ... But, I am, writing it, for my, health! My health, and my wealth. I'm writing to tell my story. I'm writing to touch, heal, and deliver my readers."

Then she asked me, "Who told you to write the book?"

I said, God. I told her that I had written on the walls while I was crazy so I could see it when I was sane. I wrote, "Bipolar writer," before

I was diagnosed by a real doctor! I wanted to tell her the whole truth, answering her question by saying, "God and my mama." But I didn't want to scare her. I didn't want to see her cry. That's just too much information. It wasn't too much longer before she forgot what we were talking about. Good, because I don't want to cry either.

She told me again about the eye surgery that she has, coming up, in a few more days. Surgery that I scheduled for her. Then she remembered what we were talking about. She said, "So, why do you think that you had a nervous breakdown? Do you think it was just from stress?"

That's another question that I really don't want to go into a whole lot of detail about. But I said yes. Stress. A whole lot of stress. Plus, people say bipolar is hereditary. Maybe I got it from my dad's side of the family. Because, you remember, my other grandma had a nervous breakdown. It changed her for the rest of her life. I said, you never had a nervous breakdown, did you, Grandma?

She said, "No, not that I know of." But she has had a couple of heart attacks. She currently has a pacemaker. That was what it felt like I was having when I was sick. I felt that all the symptoms from panic, nervous breakdowns, bipolar attacks, heart attacks, and spiritual attacks , take over. All at, the same, time. All, rolled into, one!

Grandma had already told me that she hopes she lives, long enough, to read, my book. I said, I know, Grandma. That would, be nice! But, I really don't want her to read it in some ways. Because, this is real-life stuff! I didn't candy coat anything! She doesn't even know that I smoke cigarettes. I don't want her to see me like that. We'll have to highlight or blacken out the stuff that I don't want her to read. I left her house that day, hoping to have shared a little piece of myself, with her. Even if, she doesn't make it to, THE END.

I went home and looked over, the pictures, that I, just got, developed. Pictures, from A.J.'s, graduation. It was about, seven months ago. Next to the birth of my children, it was one of the proudest days of my life. He did it! I did it! I helped him to be able to walk across that stage. He could be in jail right now for murder or in a juvenile delinquent home. He was going to kill her! I don't *think* it. I *know* it. But no matter how hard she tried, she still couldn't break his spirit! All of us have our breaking points. But he was close to his! On that day, I snapped picture after picture. I hollered, when they said, "Don't holler!" I yelled! That's, my brother! Class of, '05. Congratulations!

Anthony Warren Jr. on Graduation Day.

However, I was disgusted to see, the fat pig. That didn't grace her presence, at my graduation! Why did you decide, to come to his, in a wheel chair fit for two. You managed to cram in three. But if that didn't take the cake. It also rained, the day of the graduation. It should have snowed! The thing about the rain was, we were having a big cookout for A.J. over at Ann's house. But the rain stopped. The sun came back out! But more was expected. Ann called to postpone the cookout, a cookout that was planned for over three months. No! I don't think so. We already bought all the stuff. His friends had been invited, and I was ready to party! My brother just defied all the odds for a young black male. When so many around me didn't do it, I wanted to shout it from the rooftops!

I begged for that cookout not to be canceled! I said I would cook even in the rain for my brother, if I had to! The fact was that the others hadn't even been to the grocery store for the cookout yet. I guess they felt like by time they went shopping for everything, the rain would be back. Well, they should have been more prepared! It's been three months in planning for this. Everyone had three months to go grocery shopping just like us. That's how my Aunt Ann is, though. She's always late! She always waits until the last minute, bless her heart! After she declined my proposition, we decided to venture out on our own. We almost had everything already! We collected some stuff from everybody's house, and then we went to the store and grabbed last-minute stuff. After that, we had a nice size cookout at the park. It was a ball!

It drizzled a little through the sunshine, but then it started raining harder, later. However, we had finished our cookout by then. I wanted to show A.J. how proud I was of him, not just tell him. You should always do what you say you are going to do! I think a few of the family members were jealous of our soiree. I didn't mind. You should have been there ...

On that same roll of film was a picture of Zay Zay and Maurice. She had graduated from kindergarten. I took pictures of her in her cap with her diploma! That was the last picture that she ever took with Maurice. I blew it up and gave it to her for Christmas. I also blew up that last picture that Maurice had with Tayon. Priceless memories!

Recently I saw a movie called, *The Gospel*. The first person that I thought about was A.J. I feel like, God is, telling or showing me that A.J. should be a preacher. He is a nineteen-year-old virgin. I don't think he's holding out because he doesn't want to have sex with girls, implying that he's gay. It's most likely because God is making him hold out until marriage. Either way, I'm behind him 100 percent. God has a bigger calling for my brother. I phoned to tell him of my vision now that he has graduated from high school. He was at a crossroads. He was choosing between becoming a chef or a preacher. He has been ministering to his friends, praying, and laying hands on them. I told him that I would support him with whatever he chose to do. Just listen to God. He'll tell you what to do.

I asked him, Don't you, go to church, every Sunday? He said, "Yeah. Every Sunday! In fact, every time the church doors, are open. Somebody's, church."

I said, well, that should, tell you, something. So, if you, want to start, your own, church. Shaun and I will be your faithful members! We'll be there every Sunday. And we will get you a bigger congregation, too. So just keep that, in mind. But whatever you do! Watch out, for the, <u>devil!</u>. He's hiding in plainclothes and will send people to steal and kill, your dreams.

Speaking of the devil, let me tell you about another time that he tried to tempt me, but God had other plans! I'd been ready to confront Tiffany at so many times and in so many places. Yet I wasn't prepared for this at all. I'd thought out all scenarios, then I ran into her at the Salvation Army toy pickup, a happy time of the year. I just wanted to see what I could get my kids and add that with what I already got them, and they were going to have a great Christmas! That's all I was thinking about as I walked towards the entrance, with my Aunt Eva.

Suddenly, I saw the face of a gorilla with a blonde wig on. I stuck up my middle finger and said to Eva, "Hold on just one minute. I have to confront her."

When she saw me coming, she put her head down as if to say, "Oh, my gosh! She's coming!"

I walked up to her. She was putting gifts in the back of her minivan, a fat person mobile. I said, Hey, you fat, nasty bitch! Hey, bitch, I been looking for you!

She peeked up and said, "I know you have," acknowledging that she was all of those things. Her sister and her sister's monkey husband were with her. Her sister said, "I know you are not going to walk up on my sister like that."

They were standing between us. I told her she didn't have shit to do with it! I also said a couple of other choice words to Tiffany. Then the sister's husband stepped up. I went to middle school with that dude. He was the ugliest dude in the whole school. He still belongs on *Planet of the Apes*!

He said, "You need to just back off." Then he grabbed my wrist! I looked at my wrist. Then I looked at him like he was absolutely crazy. I jerked my arm away. I think he just lost his mind! He better keep his fucking hands off of me! All the while, I was waiting for Tiffany to say something smart so I could pounce on her. "Say one thing smart and I'm going to fuck you up!" I said. Yeah, you been hiding, bitch!

She said, "You haven't been looking too hard."

I said, What? You talking shit, bitch? I closed in on her real fast! The other two hurried to get between us.

The sister said, "Yeah, she's talking shit!" I really wasn't.

The last thing Tiffany said was, "Don't mess up your kids' Christmas."

I thought about it and decided to retreat. If I got in a fight, I might be in trouble before Christmas. It was not worth the risk. I thought to myself, *Bitch, you don't care about my, kids! You just made one last attempt to save your ass!*

As I walked away, the sister started talking more shit, saying, "He's with her now. Your man is with her!"

I looked at her and said, I don't have a man!

There was silence. They all had this really stupid look on their face, like, "Dang, now we don't have anything else to say." I sure shut them up. Maybe they were expecting me to argue, to say, No, he's mine, and you can't have him! Yeah, right. I don't *want* him! If I wanted him, I'd have him. We just walked away. Little did we know the entrance was really down at the other end, so we made the long walk and the further we got, the more shit they wanted to talk! Just the sister and her husband, though, never Tiffany. I got so tired of hollering, and the wind was taking my breath away. It was that cold! Finally I couldn't holler any more.

My aunt and I got in line, trying to quiet it down enough to still get gifts. We heard them hollering, "Come back! Come back!" Come back for what? I was just right there in your face, and you did nothing! That would be a total waste of my time! Anything the sister, has to say. Is because, she is trying to, protect her, sister. That just got punked! I blocked her out.

We walked in a line through the door, then an old white man came out. He stood right beside me, but stared the other way, to the other end of the parking lot. He said, "I hope nobody's fighting out here!"

I said, they're not. See, they are leaving.

He said, "Good! We already had one big fight out there earlier."

All the while, I pretended like it wasn't me. Like I didn't have, nothing to do with it. I went on about my business, then we sat and waited for our number to be called. Eva said, "I thought you were just playing when you called that girl a bitch! You know how people do. You'll call each other a bitch sometimes. I was just standing there, smiling. Then I saw the expression on your face. I knew that I better take that smile off my face."

I said, naw, I wasn't playing.

Just then, a fair-skinned black lady that had witnessed what happened approached me.

She grabbed, my face, and said, "You are way, too pretty. To be using, that kind of, language! I mean, it! You are, too pretty, for all that. Don't be, fighting! It will, mess your, face up.

" I said, thank you! Her words, moved, me! So much, that I, wanted to, cry. Instead, I held it in. Where did she come from?

She said, "Whatever man you'll are fighting over is not worth it!"

I said, I know. I'm not with him anymore. That's just the first time I've seen her since! But it's over with. I said what I had to say! She said, "So, how many kids do you have?"

I told her two. But none by him!

She said, "Good! Because I was wondering what Christmas is like around there." We all laughed. Then she said, "Just consider it a blessing."

I said, yeah, I know. It's a blessing that we didn't get in this building, at the same time! Then the lady's number was called. She left, saying, "Always thank God! I saw a girl that was really pretty! Pretty, like you. And she got in a fight and got cut up really bad! So, it's not worth it."

This stranger just came from nowhere, and touched my life! As fast as she came, she was gone. I know for a fact that God puts certain people in certain places at certain times. I just want those people to know that I acknowledge who they are. Reverend J. E. Young is just one that I'll mention by name. He has died, but he was the pastor of my church for years. Ever since I was a little girl, I looked up to him. I had a puppy love crush on him as a child. I think he favors, my dad, in some ways. Ever since he died, my church hasn't been the same. We have guest preachers every Sunday. I don't want to go to another church. This church feels too much like home. I hate change! The church members feel like extended family members. I wanted to acknowledge them as that.

I would agree that our church was in a state of despair. We had to choose a new preacher. Would he be the right one for me? I've heard some good ones. And I've heard some bad ones. I'm praying that God will help us and weed out the bad!

I wanted to be on record saying that my preacher's funeral was the biggest that I'd ever attended! I've had my fair share. This funeral was so big, it had two overflow rooms with TVs to watch. The pastor was laid out in a coffin, one that lets you see the whole body, head to foot. He was decked out, like always. He always was a fancy dresser, from the cradle to the grave. My family said that was the first coffin that they've ever seen like that! We got there two hours early Just to get a good seat. There wasn't, a dry eye, in the house. I paid, my last, respects. I'll, see you, in heaven.

In my life, I have been blessed with a couple of unusual abilities. One ability is that I am able to see all my friends and loved ones one last time before they pass away. I'll go weeks, even months, without seeing the person. But I will see them one last time in an unusual circumstance, and then they die. That's happened too many times with loved ones to count! And the rain ... It always rains every time a loved one dies! I love the rain ... It's so cleansing! Something like tears. People say tears cleanse the soul!

I'm cleansing my soul by writing this book. To further this experience, I want to play a song dedicated to Rodney, called, "I Don't Ever Want to See You Again!" by Uncle Sam. Ditto! Listen to the words ... I don't want you because, instead of aiming to please, you aim to deceive. I want to tell you something while feeling this much at peace. I wanted to write to you and mail it, but was too scared of the outcome.

Here it goes: CARMA! I told you, what comes around, goes around! I told you that one day, a woman is going to break your heart! You are going to be head over heels in love with her. But no matter how hard you try, you'll never get her!

That's when I realized ... that girl is me. You always want what you can't have. I know you always get what you want. But, not this time. You can't have me! You don't deserve me. I won't be the only one .... Instead of deleting your name and number out of my phone, I kept it for the same reasons I listed earlier. And so, I wouldn't have to look at your name while scrolling through my rolodex. I changed your name to Has Been! That's not my husband! That's my Has Been.

My quest to void evil people from my life doesn't stop with Rodney. Kam kept trying to contact me after Maurice's funeral. I avoided all of her calls. I have so much disgust for her that I don't even want to hear her breathe! That's why I want to dedicate this song to her. What? Yeah, that's right! I'm going to dedicate a song to you. You'll probably never have another person to dedicate one to you. I've "Made Up My Mind," by Lyfe Jennings.

If any obese person has the right to take a breath on this earth, it would be Maurice! I don't want you to take up any more space in my book! You are taking up enough space in the world, so wipe your own shitty ass! Wash it while you're back there. You won't bamboozle me into that again! Why are you still alive? Why are you still here? Then I realized you are serving your life sentence, right here on earth. You'll be fat, funky, and miserable for the rest of your life ... Then when you die, I hope you go to hell! But if God has decided to forgive you, I won't hold it against Him. That's His decision. But when you do die - I won't come to your funeral. When I die, I'd appreciate it if you did the same. Why should I be the only one there laughing at your funeral? Plus, I'd probably spit on you anyway! So I'll just stay home.

When you do buy your copy of my book, it will be because you are nosy, not because you want to support me. I won't get that confused. But I have forgiven you, even though you never asked for forgiveness! And until you do, I don't think you'll ever get into heaven. But you won't stop me from going! The night that I went crazy, I forgave everyone who ever did me wrong! I felt like I was going to die. I didn't want to be held up on any technicalities! It's a shame when people can't even give the free things! An apology, is free! I won't, hold my breath. But, who am I? To try, to teach, you, something. You were the teacher, right? Yet through, all those, years. You only, managed to teach me, one thing! That's, how to see the devil, in people. Hey, Kam. They say, the greatest revenge, is success ... You lose! I win! So don't, waddle over to give me a kiss in vain, anymore! I'm through with you! My kids don't need, your fake love, either.

When my mom saw what you did, she turned over in her grave! But she got up for me. Someone once said, "If you panic, you are going to die." I died, that night. And she, brought me back to life! She made sure that I got to the hospital. To get the medicine that I needed. Who knew a mother could love so much?

Instead of evil spirits entering my body, a holy spirit entered it! Demons thrive on fear. But I'm not scared anymore! That's why at this time, I would like to dedicate a song to my mama! From me and the kids. But I'm sure Shaun, Smelly, and A.J. don't want me to leave them out. In saying....You are, "Once, Twice, Three, times, a Lady!" And I, love you, by Lionel Richie.

That's exactly why, I make sure to mother my kids in the same way! They'll never forget it! I don't believe in coincidences. There is a reason why, Ethel Darlene Cunningham, is not here, today. My uncle, Wilbert, said, "It was just her time. Her work here was done." But, why? Why, her? They didn't have the same medicines back then, that they have now! With all the medicines that they have today, doctors have been able to prolong life, even with diseases like AIDS. Certain medicines work better than others. The richer you are, the more medicines you get to try. Look at Magic Johnson. It wasn't magic, that cured him.

I'll give you another situation. I'm unaware of this particular man's finances, of which, I speak. The man who allegedly gave my father, AIDS. Is still, walking around today! Driving around, as a matter of fact. I saw him one day, while out driving. I saw him so clearly and vividly! It's like, his car slowed down just enough, for me to get a good look. I could have hit the car in front of me. I could have turned around. Chased him down, and shot, him! Killing, him. Watching his infected blood drip onto the, pavement............Take that, you murderer! That's for my mama! But, I didn't. Even though, I probably could have beat the charge ... God has a bigger and brighter plan for me!

While writing this book, I cried everyday, most of the day. My vision was blurred. But I continued to type. I typed so fast that sometimes I would look down at my fingers and wonder how they were moving so fast. I looked up at how much I had done and wondered, who could have possibly, typed all that! I relived each moment vividly, hearing the conversations and watching the movie. It took a lot out of me! But at the end, it will put a lot in me. I'll have more time for my kids, more time to do all the things that I want to do! Nothing but time, space, and opportunity. That's why, I'm dedicating a song, to myself. For encouragement, to go on! No one else is here to do it. To say, good job! Well done! This is what I think of myself. "At Your Best, You Are Love" by Aaliyah.

Love. Love is free. It's a shame when people can't even give the free things! So far, my life has been too bad, to be true. Now, it's time for, too good to be true! God made sure that I had everything I needed. Now, it's time for everything I want! It would be different if my life, started out bad, then got worse. But it didn't. I feel like Job from the Bible, who had all his family and belongings, stripped away. As a test, from God! I think I passed the test. And now I'm ready to reap my reward.

I don't remember where I was, but I do remember that I heard a voice recently. It could have come from a radio. It could have come from a TV. But that voice said, "It's gonna get worse, before it gets better!" I heard it, but I didn't think that it was relating to my life. How could my life possibly get worse?

After that, instead of making it from check to check, I found myself running out of money before the end of the month. Everything but the necessities got turned off! I had to humble myself enough to ask to borrow money. I haven't asked to borrow money from anyone, in years. They came to me for the loans.

You'd be amazed how people treat you, when you have nothing! The only one, I can, depend on, is my sister. She remembers, all those times. All those loans. And I appreciate that. But even she, has her days!

Another example, I remember asking one of my family members, to do me a favor. Nothing strenuous. He told me, I have to pay him, for anything that he does, for me ... And he's *family*! I was paying all those other times, but now that I don't have it to give. You still can't do it for me? With all the free stuff I do for you? But, that's okay. Now I know, how it is! Oh. You forgot, I'm about to be, rich. I hope you won't want anything free from me.

I am so proud of myself! I would have never dreamed that I would be an author, a writer - whichever one sounds more prestigious. But God has a purpose for all of our lives. It's up to you to find out what it is. Look for the reasons behind why things happen.

Nowadays, my main source of happiness comes from my children. They are always making me laugh. We have my mini me. She looks and acts, just like me.

DEVASTATING CONSEQUENCES

My mini me, Zay Zay

That means, since I'm the queen. She is the princess. And if she doesn't want to do anything else for the rest of her life, she can just be that - a princess. She always tries her best. She always succeeds and makes me very proud. She's my little helper. But she got her daddy's bushy eyebrows and his dancing skills. She can do every dance that he could do, especially the h-town stomp. It's so cute, it makes me laugh.

People say that the same things that make you laugh can make you cry! I know. Especially when you're bipolar. Before long, I had to leave the room. I don't want my daughter to see me cry because then, she starts crying. Since bipolar is genetic, she most likely has it, too. But as long as I keep her life as happy as I can, she'll be fine. I have to keep her mom healthy so she can live long enough to complete this task. I realize that's me. And that's exactly what I'm going to do.

My children look after me almost as much as I look after them, reminding me to check the food, reminding me to double-check the lock, on the front door. Zay Zay feels every emotion that I feel. She's not happy unless I'm happy. When I'm happy, she's jumping around with me. That's the way I like it. She's in elementary school now. And she's facing the mean comments that come along with it. She said that a little girl keeps calling her fat just because the little girl looks anorexic. I said, So what! Tell her she is ugly! Don't let those kids hurt your feelings." Now I have to teach her all the tricks, to being respected, as a, big girl. I won't tolerate nobody, hurting my babies' feelings.

It got to the point where I had to stop myself, from approaching this little girl! She don't want that because whatever I have to say is not going to be nice! Then I remember that she's just a little girl, so I found other methods of getting the problem resolved. But I don't play! Whatever I have to do from here on out is what I'll do! I don't want my children to hurt - ever!

Then there's, Lil' Maurice. I never thought, I could love a little baby boy, as much as I do! He is a joy to have around! He looks just like his daddy. Eyebrows and all. And stubborn like him, too. But he's built like his uncle. He has a smaller frame.

Tayon Maurice Hunter at five years old

And ever since he's been born, he's been all boy, meaning, really into sports. He loves basketball! He's been playing ever since he's been able to walk. He used to cry if his clothes did not have a basketball on them, or at least some type of sports ball. That's all I started buying for him. He grew out of that eventually. But not his love for basketball. Nowadays, he cries if he doesn't look cool enough. His clothes have to look cool. He has to have his bling, bling necklace! He even has diamonds in both his ears, courtesy of his dad. He likes to be, a pretty boy! He definitely takes after his uncle.

Every Christmas, all he ever asks for is a basketball goal and ball. I get him a bigger and better one every year! Now that he's four years old, he has his own basketball court in his room since we have carpet in all of the other rooms. I bought him a really thick piece of plywood. I looked at pictures of what a basketball court looks like, then drew it in black permanent marker. Now he can bounce his ball and dunk and whatever else he wants to do! That's how much I love my kids! I encourage, their dreams .... So, look out for the next big name, in basketball - Tayon Hunter! But no matter how famous he gets and how hard he tries to act, even at four, he has a tendency to pull on my heartstrings! First of all, just looking at his face feels likes I'm talking to Maurice. Which, tears me up all the time. But just the little things ... like one day while fixing one of his favorite sandwiches, anything with cheese on it! He looked up at me and said, "You are a good mom!" Who knew one little sentence, could mean so much??? I think, my mom knew.

25

Lately I came to the realization that not all men were bad. Not all of them cheat. It's based on the man. It's based on the situation. And it's based on the woman. Most likely, you are not doing anything wrong! I wasn't. It's just greed! Most men are greedy, like my father! I never thought about having a gay father. I never sympathized with girls on talks shows who had transsexual fathers. Dad didn't live his life like that! He was a masculine, nice-looking man. But looking back, I remember a couple of signs, though. Like, hanging out with a gay man, wearing flip-flops, and he did teach me how to cook. Remember, he was head chef at his restaurant. His decisions came with a lot of consequences! Consequences that rocked my whole world! Our world. My sister's, my brother's, my children's. Generations, that will be forever traumatized!

There is one last person, that I want to write (right!). As they say, last, but not least! This is what I want to say to you. Words to a killer ……. James Edward Cunningham.

What can I say, to you? What can, I say? To even start, to describe. How much, you cheated me? I'm mad at you, Daddy! Pissed, off! For what, you did, to my, mama. You killed, her! You killed her with something lighter than a feather! You ripped my encouragement away! She was always there, to tell me that I could do it! How dare you?! You promised to honor and obey. Yet you disrespected her, with your actions!!!! Even though, it has not been proven how you got the disease…..You've had your fair share of rumors!

I've heard some say you got it from another man. But, I don't know for sure. But if you are married with kids, you should have definitely, worn a condom! You changed my life. I won't say for the worse because some good did come out of it .Like my two beautiful children! That I know I would not have if both of you were still living today…….I only sought love and attention from a man. To replace the love that I was lacking at home once Kam moved in.

I don't hear from you, as much as I do, mom..... I take that as a sign to say that, you don't have anything to say. Or, you just can't talk, because your mouth is dry! It's too hot.

Now, this is it. It's over!!!!!! I received signs that said, I would meet, my husband, after I finished writing, this book! Boy, am I ready! And since, I'm psychic, I'll make these, my last words........ I have FAITH! That all that I've been through, will pay off! I'm putting it all out there. I have little encouragement. But, I'll take a chance ... I'll be rich! I'll be married! And I'll be happy! All at the same time.

THE END

Made in the USA
Columbia, SC
16 June 2025